SWEET TEMPTATION

Desire burned in White Bear's blue eyes. "Han-na," he whispered achingly. "Do not tempt me. I cannot stop if you do." She was surprised—and pleased—when his hand shook as he stroked her cheek.

"I don't want you to stop." And she didn't. She realized that she'd been longing for this from their first meeting.

"Look at me," he said. "I look like a *Yen'gees,* but I am White Bear—a savage!"

She blinked up at him. "You are no savage, White Bear. You are a man." Holding his gaze, she caressed his jaw. "You are you," she murmured.

"Kiss me, White Bear," she begged.

He lost the last vestiges of control. With a growl of pleasure, he caught her shoulders roughly and, devouring her lips with his mouth, pressed her down. He forgot his late wife, his son, his people—everything but his desire to have her . . .

Other Zebra Books by Candace McCarthy

IRISH LINEN

HEAVEN'S FIRE

SEA MISTRESS

RAPTURE'S BETRAYAL

WARRIOR'S CARESS

SMUGGLER'S WOMAN

WHITE BEAR'S WOMAN

Candace McCarthy

Zebra Books
Kensington Publishing Corp.

http://www.zebrabooks.com

ZEBRA BOOKS are published by

Kensington Publishing Corp.
850 Third Avenue
New York, NY 10022

First Printing: January, 1998
10 9 8 7 6 5 4 3 2 1

Printed in the United States of America

For Bob—This one's for you, "little" brother.

Prologue

England, 1747

The wind howled outside the Bird and Barrel Inn, buffeting the side of the building and rattling the windowpanes. Rain fell in torrents against the glass, obscuring the outside, adding to the cacophony of wind and thunder. The entrance door opened, and a strong, wet gust blew into the common room. Hannah Gibbons paused in sweeping the floor to watch as a slight feminine figure struggled to close the door. Just as Hannah was about to put down her broom to help, the dust she had just gathered into a pile swirled about, then settled as the young woman effectively closed out the storm.

The woman turned, and Hannah saw that it was Meg, her mother's servant girl. Her heart thumped hard. She knew that Meg would come only if Hannah's ill mother, Dorothy Walpole, had taken a turn for the worse.

No! Hannah thought. *Don't let her be dead!*

She felt the blood drain from her face as Meg saw her

and hurried forward. The maid's anxious expression made Hannah's hands clench the broom handle until her fingers hurt.

"Hannah!" Meg's cry drew Hannah's attention. "Your mum—"

Hannah felt a rush of alarm. "How bad?" she rasped, her throat closing up with fear. "Is she . . . d-dead?" Her eyes stung with the instant pinprick of tears.

Meg shook her head, and relief made Hannah exhale loudly. "She's in a terrible way, though, miss," the girl said. "You'd best come. She's been asking fer you."

Suddenly, the back of Hannah's neck prickled with the sensation of being watched, and she glanced toward the kitchen work area of the inn. Her stepfather stood in the doorway, his eyes narrowed, his expression without remorse. She experienced a feeling so vile that she gasped at its intensity.

Bastard! If she's dead, 'tis your fault! You worked her until she lost all strength . . . all will to live.

Swallowing convulsively, Hannah turned back to Meg. "Run back. I'll be along right away."

The girl nodded. She hesitated, and her eyes flickered with uncertainty as she glanced toward Hannah's stepfather. "Hannah—"

Hannah followed the direction of Meg's gaze. "Go along now," she told the girl softly. Her gaze turned hard as it fastened on Samuel Walpole. The man must have known—must have guessed—that his wife's condition had taken a turn for the worse, yet he stood as if he hadn't a care but to run the inn.

She scowled as she turned to set her broom against the stone hearth, ignoring the windswept pile of dirt left in the middle of the wooden floor. A heavy hand grabbed hold of her upper arm when she was nearly out the door.

"Where do you think you're going, daughter?"

Hannah tensed. Her mother's husband was certainly no

father to her, she thought. The man had promised to love and care for his wife, yet he'd shown only indifference to the pain and suffering of Hannah's mother.

She met his gaze and wondered whether or not she'd actually seen a brief flicker of emotion in the man's eyes. *Fear?* she wondered as she fought the urge to pull from his grasp. *Concern?* She couldn't tell, because the look vanished as quickly as it'd come.

"Mum is bad off," she said stiffly. "I'm going to her." Her tone dared him to stop her.

Samuel nodded and released her. "I'll come up soon," he told her gruffly, and Hannah wanted to protest, but didn't. Her mother was his wife after all. "Did the girl say how bad?" he asked after a moment's hesitation.

The girl's name is Meg, Hannah thought bitterly, but she only shook her head. His attitude had surprised her, perhaps because she felt vulnerable in her inability to make her mother well. Her only parent was dying—had been for nearly two months—and there wasn't a bloody thing she could do about it.

"Where is Dr. Brickel?"

"At her bedside, I'm sure," Hannah said. "Meg's a smart young woman. She would have sent for 'im as soon as she'd sensed a change in Mum."

"You'd better hurry then." Samuel's voice was unusually soft for a man who hollered more often than not.

Hannah nodded and opened the door. The wind burst in through the opening, hitting her face and tearing at her golden brown hair and thin homespun gown. She hadn't bothered to grab a shawl, but the chill in her bones came from fear for her mother's health rather than from the cold of the late-winter storm.

Was it possible that Samuel Walpole loved his wife? Hannah wondered as she raced around the building toward the door to her mother's quarters. *Dear God, why then hasn't he shown her?*

The inside stairwell to the loft rooms above the inn was warmer than the outside, but not much. Hannah felt her heart thundering loudly within her breast with each step closer to her mother's room. She was conscious that each stair riser brought her nearer to the dying woman who had borne and raised her, who sacrificed so much so that they would have food, clothing, and a dry roof over their heads.

If only her father had lived past his twenty-fourth birthday, Hannah thought. If James Gibbons had lived long enough to love and care for his family, then his wife would not have married Samuel Walpole. Dorothy Gibbons would be healthy, happy, and full of life. Instead, she lay in bed, her spirit broken, her health in a rapid state of decline.

Hannah couldn't help feeling that she was partly to blame for her mother's condition. If Dorothy hadn't had young Hannah at the time of her husband's death, then she wouldn't have worried how they were going to survive. She wouldn't have married the first man to show an interest in her.

Samuel Walpole. Hannah felt her anger burn with memories of the man who had wooed and then manipulated her mother. She had been five years old the first time she'd heard Samuel's abusive language toward his wife, followed by the sound of a heavy-handed slap and her mother's whimpers. When her daughter had questioned her the next morning, Dorothy had denied that her husband had hurt her, but little Hannah had known better. She'd seen on her mother's cheek the red imprint that could have only been made by a man's hand.

As she reached the top landing, Hannah thought of their years with Samuel Walpole. At times, they'd been almost pleasant, until a change occurred in Samuel's behavior and subsequently their lives. Samuel Walpole had mentally and physically abused his wife, and young Hannah could do nothing to stop him. She'd tried to persuade her mother to leave her husband, to start a new life in a different place, far away from the man who beat her, but Dorothy Walpole had refused to go. For better or worse, Dorothy had told her daughter, she would stay with the man she'd married.

"There is no one for us, but Samuel," her mother had said after she and Hannah had argued about leaving when Hannah was twelve. "He's a good man. He doesn't intend to be mean. 'Tis only the drink that stirs up the devil in him."

"How can you defend him?" she'd cried.

"He's my husband," her mother had said, "and I'm staying with him."

Hannah, too, had stayed, to protect her mother from Samuel's anger, often taking it upon herself. If she'd known, Hannah's mother hadn't let on, and Hannah wouldn't tell her. She had tried to shield her mother, but there had been little she had been able to do. Samuel was abusive only when he drank; and to his credit, he'd remained sober since the first day that Dorothy had become ill. He hadn't laid a hand on Dorothy or her daughter for well over a year now.

Hannah remembered, though, and she couldn't forgive him—ever.

Her mother's words defending Samuel rang hollowly in her mind as she entered Dorothy's bedchamber. The room was dark, lit with only a single candle on the bed table. Hannah's gaze went straight to the bed. She stood for a moment in the door opening, her chest tightening as she studied the pale, fragile figure on the bed.

Dorothy Walpole's closed eyelids looked sunken in a face that was gaunt and shadowed from suffering. Her mother's hollowed cheeks, as she neared death, were painful to see in features that had once been beautiful and full of life. Her skin was so white that it was translucent. Hannah could see the blue veins of her mother's hands where they rested above the bedcovers.

Meg sat at her mistress's bedside, her expression filled with sadness. Tears blinded Hannah as she moved closer to her mother's bed.

The girl turned, saw Hannah, and rose from her chair, offering it to her. "Did he give you any trouble?" she asked.

Hannah waved the young woman to resume her seat. "No," she said. "Not that I'd have let him." She went to the opposite side of the bed. A tightening catch in her chest made it difficult for her to breathe as she stood at her mother's bedside and studied the parent she so desperately loved. After a time, she looked up to search the room for the doctor. "Where is the doctor?"

"Dr. Brickel's gone," Meg said. "He said there was nothing he could do." The servant girl skirted the bed to touch Hannah's arm in sympathy. "She wants to die, Hannah. The doctor says there's no reason for her decline, but that she's given up the will."

"No," Hannah whispered achingly. She inhaled sharply. "No, Mum," she cried as she pulled from Meg's grasp to kneel beside the bed. "Don't leave me."

The thought of a life without her mother was unbearable. She captured her parent's hand and felt startled by its chill. Already, life was starting to leave her. "Oh, Mum . . ." she sobbed. "I love you. Please don't die."

There was the barest flutter of Dorothy's dark lashes, as if she struggled to open her eyes. Hannah saw another flicker of her mother's eyelashes against white skin, before Dorothy opened dull blue eyes to focus on her daughter.

"Hannah . . ." Her mother's voice was weak.

Hannah bent closer to hear. "Mum?"

"Love you . . ."

Hannah swallowed past a lump. "I love you, too."

"Samuel," Dorothy said.

Hannah stroked her mother's arm. "He's coming," she said, thinking that was what her mother wanted to hear. "Samuel will be here." She felt her mother tense beneath her touch.

"No! M-must tell you—" Dorothy paused to cough. Her chest rattled as she fought to breathe. Finally, she settled down, but her expression was anxious.

"Mum, what is it?"

"Yours . . . careful. Wants all. You."

Hannah frowned. "I don't understand." What was her mother trying to say? "Mum, tell me."

"You. Never me," she gasped. "You. James. This—Sam—" Dorothy began to cough and choke. Hannah cried out and tried to lift her mother up from the bed, hoping to help her, but still Dorothy noisily struggled for life. Then, with a loud rasping sound, Dorothy was silent . . . as life left her . . . finally at peace.

When her mother quieted, Hannah laid her back down and saw that her mother was no longer breathing. A long moment passed as she stood in shock, with her heart pounding, unable to believe that her mother had died.

"Hannah." Her mother's spouse stood in the doorway.

Hannah turned to gaze at Samuel with eyes blinded by tears. "She's dead." She swallowed against the painful lump in her throat.

Samuel Walpole stared at his dead wife for several seconds, then abruptly turned away, leaving as silently as he had come.

"Devil!" Meg muttered harshly, drawing Hannah's gaze. The young woman's face crumpled with grief. "Your mum—," she said. "She was kind to me."

Hannah nodded. Dorothy Gibbons Walpole had been a woman who was loved, generous to all who'd known her.

"I'll not stay to work for Samuel Walpole." The depth of anxiety in Meg's tone pierced Hannah's pain.

"I understand," Hannah said. And she did. Samuel Walpole was a hard man and a cruel taskmaster. Meg had stayed only for Hannah's mother. With Dorothy gone, Meg would rather brave the world and certain hunger than stay in the house of a man she despised.

A numbness settled over Hannah. She felt the loss of her mother, but it didn't seem real. She shed silent tears as she said a prayer for her mother's happiness, then leaned to kiss her still warm cheek.

"I love you, Mum." Hannah whispered. "I hope you're happy now." Was her father waiting in heaven to welcome her mother with open arms? Or would he be angry that she'd married Samuel Walpole? She looked up, toward the heavens. *She did it for me, Father. Please love and care for her.*

Free. The thought entered her head, startling her with its impact.

She was free to leave the Bird and Barrel, free to escape from Samuel Walpole. After her mother's funeral, there would be no reason to stay in Samuel's house, to sweep his floors or worry about her mother's protection.

A sob escaped from deep in Hannah's throat, and her tears fell freely. In the end, she'd done little to keep her mother from an early grave. *I'm sorry, Mum . . . I'm so, so sorry. . . .*

Downstairs, Samuel Walpole leaned against a table in the kitchen work area, opened up a bottle of whiskey, and poured himself a tumbler full. Finally, he was rid of his wearisome wife. Oh, he'd cared enough for her at first, he realized, but she'd lacked the strength a man needed in an innkeeper's woman . . . the strength that was evident in Dorothy's daughter.

Hannah . . . He took a swallow of liquor and felt the fire of it burn his throat on its way to his belly. Raising his glass for another swig, he recalled the heat he'd felt in his loins the time he'd caught sight of Hannah bathing one late afternoon in the kitchen, only a few feet from where he now stood. Hannah and Dorothy had thought he had gone to get supplies, but he'd met old man Bates on the road. Bates had offered to pick up what he needed, leaving Samuel free to return to his duties at the inn. It'd been early spring with the afternoons still cool. Hannah and her mother had warmed water to wash with, and both women were half-naked over a bowl of steaming wash water . . . slight Dorothy with her scrawny breasts and thin hips and Hannah with her sturdy, fine form. The sight of her white fleshy mounds crowned by dark pink nipples had made Samuel's mouth water.

He'd compared mother and daughter and found the daughter much more suited to his tastes. He'd had the mother, and she'd done little to nothing for him. But Hannah . . . Now there was a woman with the strength and looks to warm a man's bed and care for his needs. With Dorothy gone, Samuel thought, he could pursue her daughter.

He took a drink and then another, enjoying the way the spirits burned and warmed the cold, empty spot inside of him, the one that had come when he'd seen his wife lying pale and lifeless in her bed. He allowed himself to feel a brief moment's regret for losing the woman who had been his wife. He'd never meant to hit her all those times, but she'd done something stupid and he'd been unable to control himself—or his fists.

"Oh, Dorothy, I didn't mean to harm ya. Ya know it, don't ya? I'll take care of little Hannah, if she'll allow me." Samuel knew that Hannah didn't care for him as well as he would have liked, but he would show her that he could be good to her . . . if only she would be *nice* to him.

Bloody hell! He knew it wouldn't be easy to persuade Hannah that marrying him would be in her best interests. *And mine.*

Grabbing up the bottle, he went to sit in the common room and drank until not a drop was left and he was well and truly drunk.

When he was done, Walpole staggered outside and up the stairs to gaze upon his dead wife. Then, he went to find Hannah to show her how nice he could be.

Chapter 1

Pennsylvania Colony, 1748

"She is not going to take the news well," Caroline Abbott said to her husband.

"No," John agreed, eyeing their bondservant with concern as the young woman hugged the eldest of his two sons. "She's taken with our children. She seemed so sad and alone when she came here. 'Tis only been these last two months that the sadness has gone from her eyes."

He knew little about Hannah Gibbons but that she was an Englishwoman who'd not been a stranger to hard work—and she was alone in the world.

"Hannah looks much better than when she came to us," his wife said.

John agreed. The young woman was pale, but healthy when he'd purchased her indenture thirteen months past. There'd been a look in her eyes that told him Hannah had suffered a tragedy recently. It had been only the other day that he'd learned that she'd come to them a short time after her mother's death.

John knew about loss and painful hard times. In the first six months, life had been tough in the New World for all of them. His family had had difficulty making the adjustment in this harsh, primitive land, yet Hannah hadn't complained. She had worked as hard as the rest of them as they'd labored to build the house; and then later, as they planted and raised their first farm crops. Things had improved, but it was not the life they'd had in England. His wife's miscarriage a month past and the recent news of his father's death had made John realize that he should never have taken the family from home. A fortnight past, Caroline and he had discussed the matter and made the decision to go back to Rosefield, his late father's estate, his inheritance.

'Twill be easy enough be get rid of Windgate, John thought. Thomas Whitely, his neighbor to the west, had been wanting the property since the day John had moved his family into the house.

The money made from the sale would buy passage home for him, his wife, and his children . . . but not Hannah, for Hannah, he knew, wouldn't want to go. John didn't know what had driven the young woman from her homeland, but she had left, and he was sure that no amount of coaxing would convince her to return with them.

Which left him with only one option, and that was to sell her indenture. Hannah had three years of service left on her contract. He had hoped that Whitely would offer for her along with the land. It would make things easier for all concerned. Unfortunately, neither Whitely nor any other family in these parts had need of another mouth to feed.

"If Hannah were a man," Thomas Whitely had said, "then I might have considered the expense. A man's worth the coin in his ability to do back-breaking labor, but a woman . . ."

According to Whitely and a few of the other landowners as well, a woman was a liability more than an asset, especially a plain-faced woman such as Hannah Gibbons.

John didn't agree. Hannah had worked long, hard hours without a bitter word. She had cared for Caroline when she'd been with child and afterward when his wife had lost the babe. He'd considered Hannah well worth the money he'd spent for her voyage. The least he could do for the young woman was to see her kindly settled with a new owner.

John had nearly given up hope of finding a buyer for Hannah's service contract, until yesterday in Philadelphia, where he'd encountered Jules Boucher in the marketplace. The Frenchman had overheard his conversation with Robert Conn and had spoken of his interest in purchasing Hannah's indenture. The man said that he had need of a good woman to cook and clean house for him, and had promised that Hannah would have a good home.

Although Boucher's rough appearance would not have reassured John under normal circumstances, John accepted the man's offer. His desire to go home within the week had convinced him to believe the man's word.

"When are you going to tell her, husband?" Caroline asked.

John regarded his wife with affection. Caroline stood by his side near the garden gate, her appearance pristine despite the soiled spade she held in her right hand. "Now. I'll tell her as soon as I send the children to help you in the vegetable garden."

Caroline gazed at the woman, who had been a godsend to her in the days when disappointment and poor health had nearly overwhelmed her. Hannah had been the rock that Caroline leaned on when her days seemed as dark as

the nights. "I shall miss her. Isn't there a chance she'll
return with us?"

"I think not, dear. Whatever she once had in England
is gone, and I suspect her memories of home are too
painful for her."

John watched Hannah with his children. Her attention
was now with his youngest offspring. The young woman
knelt on the grass, her coarse homespun bunched about
her knees, as she played a game with his four-year-old
daughter Anne. While she sang a song, Hannah reached
out and tickled the child in the ribs whenever she came
to the lyrics about a little bird. Anne laughed with delight
each time Hannah ended a line with a teasing tickle.

John headed in their direction. Both females, caught
up in their playacting, remained oblivious to his approach.

"Fly high, fly wide! Little bird, little bird!" the woman sang.

"Hannah."

"Papa!" the child cried, seeing him first.

"Hello, little bird," her father replied, and Anne giggled.

Hannah had paused in the game to flash him a smile.
"Good day to you, Mr. Abbott. Annie and I were just
singing." She grinned at the little girl. "Weren't we, little
bird?"

John had caught his breath as the smile lit Hannah's
face, lending her features a beauty that startled him. He
tensed, for he hated to be the one to destroy that look.
But he could no longer delay telling her of his decision
to go home.

Hannah must have sensed his uneasiness, for her smile
vanished. He saw her glance beyond him to where his wife
stood, looking pensive, near the garden gate.

She whispered into Anne's ear and then straightened,
watching as Anne ran toward her mother. When the little
girl was gone, Hannah faced John.

"Master Abbott?" she said. "Is something wrong?"

He noted, not for the first time, the differences between his bondservant and his wife. Hannah was tall and sturdy, while Caroline was feminine and fragile. He studied the young woman a long while before answering. Would she be strong enough to accept what he had to tell her?

"Mr. Abbott?" she asked again, alarm darkening her gray eyes.

John glanced at his two sons, who played happily on the lawn only a few yards away. "Boys, your mother needs help in the garden."

"Aw, father," James said. His brother wasn't any happier.

"James, Michael. I want you to go—*now!*"

Grumbling beneath their breath, young James and Michael obeyed their father and left.

John pointed toward a bench near the house. "Let's sit down, Hannah. There is something I must tell you."

Hannah sat, feeling stiff and unnatural and filled with fear.

John Abbott, she saw, tried to reassure her with a smile, but failed miserably.

"Have I done something wrong?" she asked, feeling chilled.

He shook his head. "No, no, Hannah. You are a hard worker, and Mrs. Abbott and I are grateful for your help."

He looked away from the relief he must surely have seen in her gray eyes. "The thing is—" he said, then hesitated before continuing, "Caroline—Mrs. Abbott—and I have decided to return to England to live."

Hannah stared at him with horror. Dear God, she wouldn't return to England! Not unless she wanted to face prison. "Please," she gasped. "I cannot go back."

John nodded. "I realize that, Hannah. 'Tis why we must talk. My wife and I don't want to lose you, but we understand that something drove you from your home." An intensity entered his expression as he held her gaze. "I don't know why you indentured yourself—"

He had issued an invitation to tell him what forced her from her homeland, but she ignored it. She couldn't tell him—she just couldn't! But what was to become of her?

She swallowed hard. "Master Abbott," she began. Afraid to ask, Hannah looked down and pretended an interest in her shoes. He continued to wait patiently for her to continue. How could she explain that she couldn't go back to England because the authorities would arrest her for murder? She had killed her mother's husband. The memory of her crime made her physically ill. She respected John Abbott more than any man she'd known. She couldn't bear to see his look of disbelief, then disgust, and finally his expression of fear when he learned that the woman who had cared for his wife and children was a murderess who had fled England to escape the consequences of her crime.

"I can't go back—*ever,*" she whispered. "Please don't ask me to explain."

"I won't force you to tell me, Hannah," he said, much to her relief. "You've been a good servant. Caroline and I are grateful for your help when she—we've—needed you. I'll not ask you to come back with us, because I can sense that whatever drove you from your home must be painful for you."

Hannah closed her eyes, fighting the mental image of her mother lying pale and lifeless. Then, there was the nightmare of Samuel Walpole's hands on her, violating her, touching her where no man had a right to touch. She could feel again the smooth wooden back of the chair against her fingers as she grabbed the chair and swung it, not just once but twice as the first blow glanced off Samuel's shoulder. The jarring thud of her second hit made direct contact with the man's flesh and bone as she hit him against the head and the side of his neck. Samuel had fallen to the floor, deadweight, a severe gash where the chair had clipped him.

She shuddered in the bright morning sun and hugged herself with her arms. It was a warm spring morning in the New World, but Hannah had become lost in the memory of England and that winter again.

Would she ever forget the sight of Samuel Walpole lying bleeding and dead on her bedchamber floor?

"Hannah." John Abbott pulled her from the past. "It's all right. We'll not make you come with us." He raised his voice as if he were trying to make her understand. "You don't have to go."

She blinked and tried to focus on her owner. Then what was to become of her? she wondered anew. Dare she hope that he would free her? Perhaps forgive the balance of her years of indenture?

She frowned. After he'd paid dearly for her passage and keep? Not likely. "What shall become of me?" There, she thought, she had said it. Now she waited for the bad news.

"I've found you a new master, Hannah," he said with an encouraging smile. "A Mr. Jules Boucher. The man has assured me you'll have a good home for the remainder of your service."

Jules Boucher, she thought. "A Frenchman?" she gasped. The prospect did not set well with her. "Where does the man live?" Maybe the man was a kind gentleman like John Abbott with a wife and family. "Will I be working for Mrs. Boucher?" The questions came to her, one after the other. She wanted to learn everything there was to know about the man who would own her for the next three years. "What does he do?"

John seemed unable to meet her gaze. "He is a fur trader, I think. His home, I'm told, is to the north."

"And a wife?" she asked, her voice weak. "Does he have a wife?"

"I don't know," he admitted. John must have sensed her unease. He looked at her directly. " 'Tis the only way for you to stay here, Hannah."

Hannah inhaled sharply. "I see." She read more into what he didn't say. No one in the area wanted another servant. Well, then she had little choice, but to go wherever this Mr. Boucher took her, she thought. Wife or no wife. It would be hard enough to leave the Abbott family, for whom she'd come to care about a great deal. Now she had to learn to deal with her fear of venturing into unknown territory with a stranger.

Did the man have a real home? she wondered. Or would he drag her from one place to the next as if she were a servant hired to pander to the man's every wish? Would he treat her kindly as John Abbott said, or would she be sorely used as her mother had been by Samuel Walpole?

Hannah shuddered and then stiffened her spine. Frenchman or not, she would accept her lot. She couldn't return to her homeland.

"I shall go with Mr. Boucher," she said, as if she had a choice, which, of course, she didn't.

John Abbott nodded, but did not smile. "Thank you, Hannah."

A Seneca Indian Village, near Lake Ontario. One month later.

The smoke from the Indians' cookfires drifted into the air and swirled upward to escape through a hole in the longhouse roof. The morning was young. All that lingered from the early-morning rain was a dampness about the earth and the sweet scent of spring. Droplets of water clung to the leaves of the forest trees surrounding the compound, and bare feet got wet when one walked through the grass. The center of the village was muddy where only yesterday it had been hard-packed dirt where the Iroquois children had run and played their games.

Inside a longhouse, a woman sorted through a basket of wild berries while her daughter sat by her side before their cubicle, stirring the simmering contents of a cooking pot. In the housing compartment next to theirs, a child slept on his platform bed while his mother sat on the dirt floor, embroidering a doeskin tunic. In the cubicle across the way, a warrior dug beneath a sleeping platform and withdrew a small bow and quiver of arrows. A young boy stood behind him, waiting, his face a mixed picture of fear and excitement.

"White Bear prepares his son for the hunt," Singing Rain murmured as she stirred the contents of her pot one more time.

Her mother snorted. "White Bear acts from duty to his son, not love. Eagle Soaring wants not to hunt, but to please his father." The old heavyset woman sighed, and her expression softened. "He grieves for her still."

Singing Rain tensed. Her mother had spoken of the one who had been White Bear's wife. "That cannot be," she said. "It has been eight summers since her death." It was wrong to speak of the dead by name, even if the deceased was a friend as Wind Singer had been. Wind Singer had reached the end of the Great White Path and now shared a place with their deceased grandfathers.

"Then why does he not live in the longhouse with his clan? He lives alone now but for his son. He comes only to gather supplies. White Bear still mourns the mother of Eagle Soaring. He has looked at no one since her death. He barely looks at his son, because it pains him to see the child's mother in him."

"He should marry. It is not right that he buries himself in the past."

Rising Moon's gaze narrowed upon her daughter. "And you would wish to share his sleeping mat?" she asked perceptively. "Have a care, Singing Rain. It will take much to lure White Bear from his memories. The woman who tries will not walk an easy path. The trail will be a hard and rough one."

Her attention returned to the brave who was like no other. He'd come to the Seneca as an Englishman boy, but he'd grown into a true Seneca warrior, more highly skilled with Iroquois weapons than one who had been born from a village matron. He was more unyielding and fierce than the other braves, but there had been no denying his loving devotion to his wife, Wind Singer, daughter to Man with Eyes of Hawk. It was tragic that Wind Singer had died giving birth to White Bear's son. White Bear hadn't been the same since his wife's death.

"White Bear is a warrior to fight for," Singing Rain murmured.

"The battle will not be easily won," her mother replied. "But you are right, the woman who wins White Bear's love will find the direction of her earth's journey a happy one."

"Father? Will we see a bear while we hunt?" Eagle Soaring asked.

White Bear adjusted a quiver of arrows on his son's back. "There are bears in the forest," he said. A quick tug on the strap and he was satisfied that the quiver was secure. Only then did he meet his son's gaze. He felt a tightening in his chest as he looked into dark eyes and skin so much like the woman he'd loved . . . and lost. "Are you afraid to meet a bear?" he asked sharply.

The boy lifted his chin. "You are a mighty warrior. I am not afraid."

"Good." White Bear handed his son a small version of the bow he himself carried and turned to gather his own weapons. "It is good to be brave. A warrior must be able to think with a mind clear of fear to be the best hunter . . . whether it is our meat or our enemy that we encounter."

His son regarded him with adoration. "Singing Rain said that you are the best warrior in all the village."

White Bear raised one eyebrow. "Singing Rain knows

little of such things." He glanced across the longhouse to find the same woman's dark eyes following his every movement. There was a look of hunger in her expression that he had seen before, a look that made him uncomfortable, for he had no interest in Singing Rain or any other village maiden. He had married and loved the only woman for him, and she was dead. Taken cruelly so that his son could have life. For that, he'd never forgive himself. If he hadn't planted his seed in her, Wind Singer would be alive still . . . and loving him.

Since his wife's death, White Bear had felt like only half a man. During those first months, he had ceased to care about anything—certainly not whether he lived or died.

"Father, is Running Brook coming with us?"

White Bear nodded. Running Brook was the son of He-Who-Comes-In-The Night. The hunting party would consist of the two warriors, their sons, and two other braves—Sky Raven and Black Thunder. They would be venturing to the south, where the young boys would learn about hunting skills and the most plentiful areas in which to find game. Eagle Soaring would be the youngest member of the hunt. Running Brook was born four summers before Eagle . . . at a time when White Bear didn't know what it was to love someone above all else.

He thought about his sister, Sun Daughter, who like him had not been born to the Iroquois, but had come to them as Abbey Rawlins, a young Englishwoman, past the age of eighteen. Abbey had been searching for him when she'd been captured by the Onondaga. Like him, his sister had found the secret of love when she married the leader of the Onondaga people who tended the Iroquois council fire. White Bear had respect and a fondness for Kwan Kahaiska, his sister's husband. Kwan, too, had been born to white parents until he'd been kidnapped at the age of nine and adopted into the tribe. Kwan had come to the Iroquois a child only a year older than Eagle Soaring now.

But Kwan had proven himself to have the courage of a mighty warrior, a man who was as wise as he was kind. His name meant Great Arrow because of his skills with the bow.

Kwan had promised to meet up with them near the great trail, where he and his son, Strong Oak, would join their hunting party. Strong Oak was eight summers, born two months before Eagle Soaring.

They had spent so little time together, White Bear thought, he and his son. Until two summers past, Eagle Soaring had lived in the house of his grandmother, Woman with Dark Skin, Wind Singer's mother. Grief had so stricken White Bear after his wife's death that he had gone off by himself, returning months later, a stranger to his people—and his son. Previously he'd plucked his scalp but for the warlock on his crown as was the practice of the Seneca warriors to keep his enemy from grabbing hold of his hair during battle. While away, White Bear had allowed his blond hair to grow. For weeks, he didn't care if he encountered his enemy. Life had ceased to have meaning for him. Until one day after two months of living alone, he'd come to the village of Kwan Kahaiska, where he'd seen and been scolded by his sister. Sun Daughter had screamed at him, reminding him of the son he'd left behind—Wind Singer's son.

"Did you love her so little that you would neglect her child?" Sun Daughter had exclaimed.

White Bear, who was unkempt, bearded, and with hair that did not quite touch the back of his neck, had been hurt and angry, and then he realized, he'd been full of self-pity. He stayed a week with the Onondaga, while he sought guidance from the gods—the Christian God he'd learned about as a little boy and the Indian gods, whom he'd come to revere and respect as a Seneca. He cleaned himself up, shaved his beard, but left his hair to grow, realizing that he preferred it that way. He wasn't afraid of the enemy, so he didn't see a need to pluck his scalp again. Then, with a heart that was heavy from the loss of his beloved wife, he headed back to his people . . . and the tiny son he'd left behind.

The return to the village hadn't been easy. His people had looked at him, not seeing the man they'd known in the man he'd become. As time passed and they saw the pain in White Bear, they understood and accepted him.

Because his son looked like his mother, White Bear had difficulty looking at him without hurting. He allowed the babe to stay with his grandmother until one day when the child was six years old, and White Bear had dreamed of Wind Singer. In the dream, Wind Singer was unhappy that White Bear did not know his son, and she begged him to change that.

Disturbed by the dream message upon awakening, White Bear had gone to Woman with Dark Skin and asked for his son. The woman looked into White Bear's eyes, as if reading his soul, and agreed that Eagle Soaring should live with his father.

Two years later, Eagle Soaring was eight, but White Bear still felt as if he and his son were strangers.

White Bear studied his son, as the boy tested the string on his bow, and felt a shaft of pain that Eagle's mother couldn't be here to see the boy off to his first hunt.

"You will be kind to Strong Oak," he said to his son.

Eagle Soaring's expression flickered with surprise and then hurt as his father's words registered. "I like Strong Oak, Father. He and I are brothers."

White Bear did not smile. "It is true that you are like two bear cubs on a honey prowl when you are together. You must watch that you don't anger the bees and get stung."

"I do not like honey, father," the boy said seriously.

"I talk not of honey and bees, Eagle Soaring," White

Bear said, surprised by this serious side of his son, "but of the dangers of a man hunting for food."

"Ah," the child said. "I will be careful, and so will Strong Oak. We will not run from our fathers when we see a bear, nor will we rush forward to pierce the bear with our arrows. We will shoot when we can kill with only one draw of our bows. And in the hours before we set out into the woods, we will practice our hunting skills by hitting leaves from Father Tree."

"Will not Father Tree get angry?" his father asked, curious as to the boy's response.

Eagle Soaring drew himself to stand straight to all of his four-foot frame. "I will beg forgiveness of Father Tree for his pain, and He will understand, because new leaves He will grow, but a man may get only one chance at bringing down a deer."

White Bear grunted, pleased. "You will remember the deer's spirit?" he asked.

"Oh, yes, father. I will ask the spirit of the deer to allow me to take its life, and I will seek his forgiveness as I make him understand that by taking his life I save my own and that of my people."

"You will make a good warrior, my son," White Bear said. He looked away, missing the look of gladness that lit the boy's expression.

But another brave saw and didn't like it. "It is time." He-Who-Comes-In-The-Night stood at the door of the long-house, within a few feet of White Bear's cubicle.

White Bear nodded. "Let us go then. Eagle, you must tell your grandmother that we leave now."

"He is not ready," Night said after the boy had left.

"He is ready," Eagle's father insisted. He narrowed his gaze as he studied the brave. Night was a fierce-looking warrior. His face had been painted with streaks of red, and his only hair was a small tuft of black that formed a warlock on the crown of his head. White Bear knew that Night resented him. Unlike his elders and his people, He-Who-Comes-In-The-Night did not accept the adopted white English as one of the People. That the boy, Jamie Rawlins, had been accepted and given such a mighty name had never sat well with the Iroquois brave.

White Bear wondered whether it was wise to take Eagle Soaring on his first hunting trip with He-Who-Comes-In-The-Night and his son. As the father disliked White Bear, the man's son, Running Brook, bore resentment toward Eagle Soaring. It was Kwan's decision to join them that had White Bear agreeing to the hunt. He felt sure of Eagle Soaring's safety with Kwan and Strong Oak by his side.

"Come," Night said. "The sun rises high in the morning sky. We must go now."

White Bear nodded and followed the man from the longhouse.

Chapter 2

He was worse than she had expected. Hannah watched Jules Boucher's approach and felt a shiver of revulsion. Coarse and crude, he was a frightening spectacle for any lone woman, especially one who was essentially at the man's mercy.

The Frenchman was unkempt, with shaggy brown hair that fell past his shoulders and a thick red beard that was always filthy with bits of food from his last meal. He was large, with a barrel chest and thick limbs. His buckskins were stained; his fur cloak was matted. The man hadn't bathed in all the weeks Hannah had been with him; he reeked of whiskey, sweat, and damp animal fur. Monsieur Boucher was a vile specimen of humanity, and, disgusted by the man more than his bathing habits, Hannah couldn't wait to be free of him.

For the past three weeks, they'd been traveling through the wilderness, sleeping and eating out in the open, where the insects left red welts on her exposed flesh and sleeping on the hard ground made Hannah's muscles and joints

ache. She had long given up the hope that the fur trader
had a wife and a house. It hadn't been long after their
departure from Windgate that she realized that Boucher
had lied to John Abbott. The Frenchman had never had
any intention of providing a comfortable home for her.
He'd purchased her indenture from the Abbott family with
the sole purpose of selling her for a profit.

Unfortunately for him—and for her as well, he'd been
unable to find a buyer willing to pay his price. His lack of
success was a continued source of his anger, and Hannah
feared that if circumstances didn't change his anger soon,
her situation would only worsen.

"Woman!" Boucher threw the carcasses of two rabbits
on the ground before Hannah, who was sorting through
a basket of wild berries. "Skin 'em now," he growled. "And
don't damage the fur."

Hannah's stomach lurched as she gazed at the dead
animals. She'd never met a man with such a disregard for
life. She could accept that animals needed to be killed for
food and clothing, but did the man have to find so much
pleasure in the killing?

She wondered if he'd taken up the fur trade so that he
could satisfy his lust for killing at will and without punishment.

"What are you waiting for?" his voice boomed at her
when she hadn't moved.

Hannah didn't flinch; she wouldn't give him the satisfaction of seeing her fear.

In answer, Hannah grabbed the rabbits and stood.
Would it ever end? Hadn't the man killed enough yet? He
had enough skins and pelts to cloak an entire regiment
of the British army!

As she stared down at the rabbits, she shuddered
inwardly. God's teeth, but she hated the prospect of skinning another dead animal. Ignoring Boucher's angrily
muttered curses, she headed toward the stream. A quick

glance back in his direction as she set down the rabbits told her that Boucher was busy building a fire.

She crouched by the stream, exhaling with relief to know that he no longer watched her. Swallowing hard, Hannah picked up the knife that she'd left on a rock at the water's edge.

As she began the grisly task of skinning the first dead rabbit, Hannah thought again of the man who owned her indenture. To his credit, Boucher hadn't once gazed at her with lust, nor had he touched her indecently, which was another reason that she'd not attempted to escape. The other reason was that the Frenchman wanted to get rid of her as much as she wanted to be free of him, so her situation with him was only temporary.

"He's annoyed that I'm not fair of face," she said beneath her breath, grateful that she wasn't much to look at. Hannah recalled the man's expression when he'd first set eyes on her. She thought he looked startled, then disappointed. She'd gotten the distinct impression that Boucher felt cheated in his dealings with the Abbotts. After a brief, cold glance in her direction, Boucher had ignored her until it was time to leave, when he'd acted as if he'd purchased an albatross. Hannah had been glad. Better for the man to be indifferent than to feel lust, she thought.

Except for her stepfather's interest, she never thought she was the kind of woman to attract male attention. But Samuel Walpole's behavior that last night had changed that. She realized now that her form if not her face could incite a man's lust. One unobtrusive look at her new master had spurred her into taking an action that was cautious, but uncomfortable.

On the night of Samuel's murder, she had been shocked and mortified to learn that her late mother's husband was aroused by the size of her breasts. Determined not to incite her new owner's lust, Hannah had taken to binding her breasts beneath the bodice of her homespun gown. The constriction, although not overly severe, was painful. She knew she couldn't hide her curves; she had just wanted to minimize them.

She did other things to detract from her appearance as well. Her silky brown tresses were pinned back into a severe bun. Her gown was loose, disguising the womanly shape of her waist and hips. She traded her serviceable shoes for a man's pair. She'd left her soap behind, wanting no feminine scent lingering about her to entice a man's senses—or his interest.

Hannah had no way of knowing whether it was her efforts to appear less womanly that kept the gleam of lust from Boucher's eyes or that the man simply wasn't interested in women in general. The reason didn't matter. She didn't intend to find out.

Hannah worked quickly, trying to ignore the blood, feeling queasy and light headed as she started on the second rabbit. Dear God, how could such a small creature have so much blood?

She shuddered as she fought the urge to abandon the task and scrub her hands with sand and water. The bit of blood on her fingers took on nightmarish proportions to her; her hands looked as if they were permanently stained while her brain told her it wasn't possible. In the back of her mind, she understood why she felt that way, yet she couldn't control her thoughts . . . the mental images.

Red. Blood. *No!* she thought. *Red—why were her hands so red?*

Every time she saw blood, even the blood of an animal, she became engulfed by the memory of crimson pooling beside Samuel's head on the floor of her bedchamber.

Hannah wondered if the experience was her punishment for the crime of murder. To be a servant to a fur trapper, who killed animals with joyful regularity, before he handed them to her to dress. To be forced regularly to endure the sight and feel of blood on her hands.

"Now that you're done skinning them, you can cook dinner," Boucher growled from behind, startling her. "And don't burn the meat."

Hannah rose and stared at him. "I've not burned it before."

His hand shot out and slapped her. "Did I say you could speak? I hate mouthy women." His look hardened. "Just do what you're told, and we'll get along fine."

Cheek and jaw stinging from the blow, Hannah stifled the urge to hit back. It wasn't the first time the man had hit her, but it would be the last. She would kill him, she swore, if he ever so much as laid a hand on her again. Shocked at her own thoughts, Hannah bent to pick up the rabbits. She had murdered one man, how could she think of murdering another?

I have to escape, she thought, *before I do something I'll regret. I don't need the stain of another man's blood on my hands.*

Poison. She could poison Boucher's food, and he'd be none the wiser until it was too late and the deed was done. *With poison, there'd be no blood.*

The fire that Boucher had built crackled and popped as Hannah set about preparing a rabbit. While she worked, she allowed her imagination to run wild, inventing different methods of taking Boucher's life.

Peeking at the Frenchman out of the corner of her eye as she worked, Hannah realized that she couldn't kill him. An animal he might seem, Jules Boucher was, in fact, a man . . . one of God's human beings. And she would not take another man's life.

Her only options to be free of him were if she were sold, as Boucher wanted, or if she somehow managed to escape. Whatever happened, she wouldn't allow the man to mistreat her again, she vowed. She would be docile, biding her time, until the right moment. And then, one way or another, she would leave.

Hannah awoke well before Boucher the next morning.

It was still dark, but there was a promise of the new day, the barest hint of a soft glow in the distant horizon. After a quick check to ensure that the Frenchman was sleeping, she rose from her rough pallet on the ground and moved silently toward the stream. Following the pathway of the water for some distance, Hannah stripped, sighing with relief when the cloth binding her breasts was freed. After tearing a strip from her underskirt, she waded into the stream. She floated for a moment, allowing the water to caress and soothe her aching flesh. Then, as she'd done twice before since her departure with Boucher, Hannah washed, using the sand and silt from the stream bed to scrub her body clean.

The water was chilly, but Hannah luxuriated in the freedom of movement and the gentle lap of the water against her skin as she sat on a rock in the stream's current. She eyed the water dubiously for a long moment, longing to wash her hair, but wondering if she dared to. It wouldn't be long before Boucher woke up and came looking for her. The last thing she needed was to be caught naked . . . in so vulnerable a position, with her gown several yards away and without a weapon to protect her.

Still, her desire for clean hair was strong, so she took out her hairpins, then leaned forward, shaking her head, until her long brown tresses brushed her face and fell into the water. She bent farther and with her hands wetted her hair thoroughly, rubbing the strands until they squeaked and she felt they were clean. She straightened and flung back her head, sending water in all directions. She wanted to laugh from the pure sensual enjoyment of the moment but didn't, for the sound would attract Boucher, whose arrival would steal her brief second of happiness as a snap of his trap surely stole some poor animal's life.

The glow in the sky had brightened, a visible reminder that she'd best get dressed. As she rose from the water, she looked down at herself critically and saw a woman with full rose-tipped breasts, her skin white where the sun hadn't kissed it. Her nipples puckered in the early-morning air. She hugged her middle as she waded through the water toward her clothing on the shore. Reaching for her gown, she had the strongest sensation of being watched. Hannah froze and glanced around, but saw no one.

Afraid to be discovered, she hurriedly stepped into her petticoat and tugged hard to pull the fabric over her damp skin. The material got stuck at her hips. She cursed silently and yanked harder, covering her hips, her waist, before struggling to maneuver her arms into the sleeves.

"I thought you had run away," a male voice with a French accent said.

She gasped and tried to pull the bodice up in place, before she turned to face her owner. "Why? I've never tried to run before," she replied. Her back was to the man, but she was afraid that he had guessed that she'd been binding her breasts. She was afraid to move, to turn, lest he should see that she possessed, in actuality, more curves beneath her homespun gown than previously displayed.

She had to find a way to get rid of him so that she could finish dressing, she thought.

"Please, monsieur," she said, hoping that she could convince him. "If you will allow me a moment of privacy, then I will tend to your breakfast."

A long moment of silence was her answer. Alarmed, Hannah glanced over her shoulder to see that he stood, unmoving, within ten feet away.

"Monsieur, please."

"You have taken down your hair," he said softly. As she'd feared, a strange gleam had entered his eyes.

She scowled at him. "One must take down one's hair in order to wash it."

"I have not seen it this way before."

Hannah shivered, not caring for his tone . . . as though

his voice belonged to a man who had discovered a fine treasure in something that he'd once deemed worthless.

"Monsieur Boucher—"

"You are cold," he said. "I will help you with your gown."

"No!" she exclaimed. "I do not need your help. I only need a few minutes alone."

"I think it is unsafe for me to leave you," he said thickly. "I did not realize that you had charms beneath that ugly dress of yours. If I had—"

With a final yank, Hannah managed to pull her shift bodice into place. She was clad in only a thin layer of muslin as she daringly confronted the man who, she realized, had seen too much of her skin and now looked at her with much more than indifference.

Hannah swallowed hard. She had seen that look before . . . on Samuel Walpole's face . . . just moments before she'd been forced to kill him.

"Am I not permitted a few moments of privacy?" she dared to adopt a scolding tone. "Must you stand and gawk away the morning when there is a fire to be built and miles to travel?" She spun back to slip the gown over her underskirt. "Surely, you have something that must be done—"

Boucher's hand descended on her shoulder, startling her. She jerked back and faced him, her gaze warily searching his expression, as she expected to be struck.

"You have forgotten something," he said quietly, and she saw that he referred to the piece of white fabric lying on the ground. He bent to pick up the strip of cloth that she'd used to bind her breasts. "What is this?"

Holding the material aloft, he alternately eyed the fabric and her. A long thin strip of fabric. A feminine form with a larger bust. As comprehension dawned, his face changed in a way that frightened her.

"You seek to play games with Jules?" he said through

tight lips. With a sudden eeriness, his mouth curved upward, and his eyes gleamed. "I could enjoy playing games with so delightful a lady."

His features darkened with fierce anger. "Only I do not like to be tricked, woman, and you have succeeded this past few weeks in a way that no one has before—and no one shall again."

She flinched as he touched her neck, stroking the damp skin above the scoop neckline of her shift, his caress chilling her more than any winter night.

"You are hungry?" she asked, hoping to change the subject and the direction of his hunger. "I shall cook for you now—" She started to brush by him, only to have him grab her arm. With a quick jerk, he pulled her against him.

"I am not anxious for breakfast. There is a need in me that only the warm flesh of a woman's parted thighs can satisfy."

Hannah glared at him, refusing to cower. "I'll see you in hell first."

He laughed. "Later, perhaps, but I shall enjoy the journey riding my fair lady until she screams with each thrust of my man root."

He grabbed hold of her hair as she struggled, yanking back her head to study her mouth . . . her eyes . . . the long slender white column of her throat.

"God's teeth, how could I have missed this?" he said thickly. "You are a comely wench with your hair down and your lush form damp from a bath and straining against your bodice." His grasp on her hair was relentless. With his other hand, he caressed her from cheek to chin and down her throat, to where her pulse throbbed wildly in a hollow at the base.

"I shall use what I have bought. If I had only known it before, our journey would have been all the sweeter for our joining."

"I will not lie with you."

Boucher laughed. "You, mademoiselle, do not have a choice in the matter. I have bought and paid for you with legal tender. You are at my beck and call for as long as I see fit—"

"Or until you can sell me!" she challenged.

He shrugged, unconcerned. "Perhaps." His hot gaze seemed to devour her breasts, which strained against the damp bodice of her shift. "Unless I choose to keep you, now that I've found a use for you."

"Touch me, and I will kill you," she vowed. She had done it before; she could do it again, she thought, quickly revising her early decision.

"You?" His chuckle lacked amusement. "I think not. You are a healthy wench, but you haven't the strength of Jules Boucher."

Hannah thought wildly. *Keep calm. Only with a rational head can you outsmart him.* And what would she do once she did? *Escape.* It was the only way now. The choice had been taken from her. She would flee from the Frenchman and brave the Pennsylvania wilderness alone.

"You are right, of course," she said, thinking quickly. She needed to buy time. She allowed her voice to drop suggestively. "You are a big man . . . a man no doubt skilled in pleasing a woman . . ."

Jules Boucher smiled slightly. "I am glad that you have realized it."

"No doubt, I shall need all of my strength to keep up with a man of your . . . charms."

The man's smile became a grin. "No doubt."

"You would not want me to faint from hunger and lack of strength then," she said, managing to keep her tone weak and subservient.

"You may fix our meal first," he said, his gaze narrowing. Hannah's burst of excitement was dampened as he continued. She realized that the Frenchman would not be so easy to fool after all. "Do not try anything stupid, mademoiselle. Now that I have found this treasure, I will not allow it to slip away without having sampled it myself."

Hannah forced a smile. "You are an intelligent man. How could I think otherwise?" She bent to pick up her gown, intending to dress.

"I'll take that." Before Hannah had a chance to react, Jules Boucher had snatched the garment from her hands.

"But it is cold, monsieur." She could have bitten her tongue when she saw that her comment only drew attention to her body's reaction to the dampness and the air.

"I will warm you after breakfast," he said in a strangled voice, before he walked away, taking the extra fabric layer of protection with him.

I'd sooner be gored by an angry boar, Hannah thought. She closed her eyes and silently prayed for a way out of her present predicament.

An apt comparison, she realized as she reluctantly headed back to their camp. An angry boar, Boucher would no doubt be if she—and he—lived to see the end of the day and their "relationship."

"Father? Do you see him?" Eagle Soaring's eyes sparkled with excitement as he studied the large buck several hundred feet away.

"Shhh, Eagle," White Bear said. "A good hunter makes no sound, no movement but for the silent drawing of his bow string."

The man and boy watched as the deer bent his head to graze on a clump of grass not far from the base of a tree. White Bear tapped his son's shoulder and motioned him toward a copse, which offered cover from the animal's sight.

"Now, father? Can I shoot him now?"

White Bear glanced down to see the anticipation in his

son's expression. His enthusiasm for the hunt was enough to make any father proud. He would make a good brave someday. *If only his mother could see him.* "You must wait until the buck is closer, Eagle." His voice was gruff with renewed grief as thoughts of the child's mother resurrected the pain." You cannot send an arrow straight and expect it to circle the trees to take your quarry."

Eagle Soaring's face fell at his father's scolding. "I am sorry, father."

His features unrelenting, the warrior nodded. "You will learn, my son." Unable to bear gazing into eyes so like his beloved Wind Singer's, he turned his attention to the buck. "He moves into range. Make your bow ready. Remember to hold steady, or you will lose the advantage of surprise." A glance in Eagle's direction told him that his son had paid attention to his instructions well. The boy stood, his feet braced apart, his bow raised with notched arrow on a taut string.

White Bear watched, fascinated, the boy's concentration as Eagle waited for the right moment to let the arrow fly. He heard the child say something under his breath, saw the spring pulled tighter. *That's it, Eagle Soaring. Wait for the right moment. Shoot in haste, and you lose what you so desperately seek. Wait in patience, and the prize will be yours.*

A sharp cry rent the air, startling the deer and the boy. The deer went crashing through the brush before father or son could get an accurate mark on him. Eagle let loose the arrow, which went sailing through the air to land in the dirt where the buck had stood.

Eagle looked up at his father with fear. "I did not mean to shoot—"

"It is all right, son. Did you hear that cry?"

"It was not the deer?"

White Bear shook his head. "It sounded like . . . a child." *Or a woman,* he thought, but didn't voice his suspicions. Just then, another wild cry of fright filled the quiet, chilling White Bear to the bone. Whoever had cried out was in trouble and needed help. Suddenly, White Bear experienced an overwhelming feeling of urgency.

The sound came again. They couldn't ignore it. Someone was in trouble.

White Bear met his son's gaze and nodded. Then, the two of them ran in the direction of the frightened cries. The scene they came upon made White Bear draw up quickly and put out his arm to halt his son.

"Father," the boy whispered.

White Bear bent low to talk quietly to his son. "We must listen and wait, Eagle Soaring." He straightened and, through a narrowed gaze, studied the gathering in the small clearing by a stream. He-Who-Comes-In-The-Night and the two Seneca braves stood talking with a big, bearded white man. A white woman was crouched defensively near the water's edge. She looked ready to bolt at the least little provocation. White Bear wondered if she'd been sorely used by the white man, for when she looked at him, it was with hatred, not with the affection of a woman for her lover.

The Indian stared at the woman, and realized that it had been a long time since he'd seen such smooth, white skin. His wife's skin had been dark, like the color of smoothed walnut. While Wind Singer's hair was dark like the other women of the Seneca village, this English-woman's hair was light brown, unbound and tangled, with tiny bits of leaves and twigs clinging to the silky strands.

From this distance, White Bear couldn't see the color of the English's gaze, but he guessed it was light—like his own, perhaps green or gray rather than the blue shared by him and his sister, Sun Daughter.

The white man and He-Who-Comes-In-The-Night seemed to be arguing now, but there was no real heat, and it puzzled White Bear. Then, he saw the bearded man point toward the woman, and the woman cried out and scrambled to her feet and stepped back. Her arms crossed protectively over her breasts, she eyed the Senecas as if they had threatened to kill her.

"No!" she exclaimed as He-Who-Comes-In-The-Night approached. She thrust out her hands as if to ward off the warrior's blows. "Stay away. Don't touch me."

It had been a long time since White Bear had spoken English, but he hadn't forgotten the language of his birth.

"Father." A tug on his arm drew the man's attention back to his son. "What is he doing?" Eagle whispered. "Why is that woman crying?"

White Bear felt a jolt as he turned back to gaze at the enfolding drama. Eagle Soaring was right; the woman was crying. Her sobs intermingled with her orders for the brave to stay away. He couldn't watch from a distance any longer. He didn't know why, but he needed to know why the Englishwoman cried. His heart kicked hard within his chest as the Seneca brave reached out to touch her hair. She jerked back, but he grabbed a handful of light golden brown strands and yanked, making her yelp with pain. Strangely, Night's rough treatment halted the woman's tears. She glared at the fierce warrior, startling not only Night, but White Bear, who felt a sudden admiration for her.

"Come, Eagle, and we will learn more," he said with a frown. "But be silent, for this is the business of grown men."

Chapter 3

"Get . . . off . . . me!" Hannah cried as she shoved against the weight of the Frenchman. She had been sitting near the stream, mending a tear in her gown. Satisfied with the breakfast she'd made, Boucher had gone to check his traps—or so Hannah had thought. Since he'd caught her bathing, the Frenchman had been persistent in his "seduction" of her, and it'd taken a lot from Hannah not to jerk away whenever he'd touched her hair or brushed against her. He would have forced himself before now, if not for the trip for supplies.

Boucher had dragged her with him to trade furs for food staples at an isolated farm several miles from their last camp. The Frenchman had seemed distant, preoccupied, but a lustful gleam would enter his gaze whenever he looked her way. Hannah had known it was only a matter of time before Boucher tried to rape her, but she thought she'd be prepared for him.

Moments ago, when he'd come up behind her, suddenly pushing her to the ground, Hannah realized that Boucher hadn't left to check his traps, but to sample from the stash of whiskey he'd acquired in trade for three fine beaver pelts when they'd stopped for the night at the farm.

The whiskey had renewed and intensified his lustful urges.

His hot, alcohol-laced breath hit her full in the face, making her gag. "I said to get off me!" she spat. She struggled beneath him, hitting him in the shoulder with her fist.

The Frenchman grunted and got mad. "You are mine to do with what I choose," he hissed.

"No!"

"Do not make me hurt you. Be still, and you will like what Jules has to offer."

She gave a snort of derision. "I'll kill you first!" she vowed, but Boucher only laughed.

Grabbing her hands, he pinned them above her head. "You are ineffective against Jules's strength."

Hannah feared he was right. She couldn't move. The weight of his heavy form bore down on her, frightening her as nothing had before. She couldn't breathe. She could barely think. Vulnerable and alone, she wondered if Boucher would be successful where Samuel Walpole had not been.

No! I will not let him rape me! She was light headed and dizzy. It took everything in her to think, to remain rational, to fight the panic that was rapidly building as Boucher pressed down on her, making her fully cognizant of his arousal.

She forced herself to relax, realizing that by pretending to accept her fate she would lower the man's guard. Closing her eyes, she released a breath. "All right," she said in a weak voice. "Just don't hurt me."

Boucher studied her thoughtfully. She avoided his glance, until it dawned on her that he preferred a willing partner, not a meek one. She fluttered her eyelashes and met his gaze. "Jules," she whispered, "I didn't realize how strong you are. How . . . *big* . . ." And then she flashed him a smile—an extremely feminine smile designed to charm.

He seemed taken aback only for a moment, then his eyes lit up with excitement. "You will enjoy Jules, you will see. Many ladies have enjoyed my touch, just as you will."

Not in this life, she thought, and prayed that he would ease up on his grip soon. Hannah realized that Boucher was too befuddled by alcohol or too vain to question the fact that only seconds before she'd been fighting him.

He shifted, as she'd hoped, rising just slightly above her, but he didn't let go of her hands. "You should not have hidden your charms from me, *ma chérie.* You have made Jules unhappy with your deceit."

"I didn't mean to upset you," she said, injecting a breathy quality to her voice, "but with all the traveling we've done, a woman must protect herself. Surely, you understand? Not everyone is as—" She struggled to finish the lie. "—gentlemanly as you."

He blinked with confusion and scowled. "You are playing with me. I do not like it."

"No," she cried. "I wouldn't do that. You have treated me kindly since you've owned my indenture. Why would I do such a thing?"

Boucher relaxed. *"Oui,"* he said. "It would be foolish of you, now wouldn't it." He released one hand to stroke her hair. It took everything inside Hannah not to flinch from his touch and lose what little trust she had gained.

"I promise you it will be good."

"I know," she whispered, struggling not to show revulsion.

"You will cry out with joy as I show you what it is to experience Jules Boucher."

"No!" she exclaimed suddenly, losing the battle of pretending. Gathering strength, she faced him defiantly. *"Never!"*

"You will," Boucher insisted angrily, shaking her against the ground, making her teeth rattle. He dropped and pinned, his breath rasping in his throat.

A sudden movement in the forest caught Hannah's attention as an Indian appeared in the parted brush.

"No," she gasped. Hannah froze with fear as she saw that she and the Frenchman were no longer alone. Her mind raced as she tried to gauge how the Indian's arrival would affect the situation.

Boucher was furious. "You dare say 'no'? You tease Jules?"

Hannah swallowed and shook her head. Her eyes mirrored her discovery as she glanced up at the Frenchman and pointed toward the woods. "Savages—there!"

The man stiffened, then vaulted to his feet to face his visitors, leaving Hannah sprawled on the ground with her skirts hiked up to reveal her calves and her shift bodice off one shoulder. She shifted and crawled to the water's edge where she could go no farther. Tugging her bodice into place, she viewed the exchange between men with curiosity and a great deal of fear.

He-Who-Comes-In-The-Night was puzzled. The man of furs seemed anxious to get rid of the white female. The woman was too pale, it was true; but she had a shape that was pleasing to this brave, and she looked healthy enough to do much work in the fields.

The Seneca brave stared at her hard. The Frenchman had been enjoying her when they'd arrived, but it was apparent that the woman did not find the same enjoyment. Still, she was spirited, Night thought, and a man had to respect such spirit. It would be amusing for him to tame that spirit. He would buy her and make her a slave for Slow Dancer, his wife. Slow Dancer was always complaining that she could use the help of a slave.

"You would sell her?" He-Who-Comes-In-The-Night asked the white man.

Jules Boucher nodded. "She will make a good slave in your lodge house," he said. "She works hard. She is not much to look at, but she is not ugly either. I will give her to you for ten beaver skins."

Night glared at Boucher with unconcealed anger. "No white woman is worth the lives of ten beaver. You may keep your pale-skinned woman."

"Eight skins," Boucher said. He sensed that the Iroquois's interest in Hannah was keen, at odds with his last statement. For whatever reason, He-Who-Comes-In-The-Night wanted the woman, and Jules had decided that this might be his only chance to get rid of her. Despite what he'd told Hannah, his lust for the woman wouldn't keep her in his care indefinitely. She had proven to be more trouble than she was worth.

Besides, he thought, *if I please this savage, then I will have a source for trade.* He could trade trinkets for the valuable skins and earn more with a minimum of effort.

"Six beaver," the Indian said.

"You drive a hard bargain, monsieur," Boucher said, inwardly pleased. If the truth had been made known, he would have taken three beaver pelts in exchange for the girl. Still, he would hold out a little longer. After all, he did pay Abbott for her. She was a bargain, or so he thought. Abbott had been so anxious to see her settled, that Boucher was sure that he'd sold Hannah for much less than he'd originally paid for her. "Seven skins," he told the Indian.

Night hesitated a long moment, his gaze studying the white woman who stood near the edge of the stream, her arms hugging her middle. "Five beaver skins, one skin of buck, and one muskrat."

"Done!" The Frenchman was pleased, but hid it well. He didn't want the savage to think that he hadn't gotten his worth in trade. "She is worth much more, but you seem like a good man, so I will accept your offer."

The Indian said something to his friends, who stepped forward with two buck skins. "We will bring you more skins before the sun sets in the night sky."

After a brief hesitation, Boucher nodded.

"Come," He-Who-Comes-In-The-Night ordered the woman with a wave of his arm.

Although the men had conversed in the strange Indian tongue, Hannah guessed what had occurred from their faces and their actions. She shot the Frenchman an anxious glance.

"You have sold my contract to a savage?" she cried.

"Be careful whom you call a savage, *ma chérie,*" the man said. "Night here is a good man, but he takes unkindly to insults. You would be wise to hold your tongue while in his company."

"Bastard," she exclaimed. Had he so little concern for her—one of his race—that he would hand her over to bloodthirsty beasts? Her heart beat rapidly with fear. She had heard horrible tales about the Indians, some that had made her stomach clench as she'd pictured their poor helpless victims. "Have you no decency? What did you trade me for . . . two animal skins?"

"Seven actually. These two are a deposit." Boucher smiled, clearly pleased with himself and her reaction to her new status. "You will be happy with the Indians, I think." His eyes gleamed. "As long as you do what you are told. Unlike me who is generous to a fault, the Senecas expect their slaves to obey them. And your master, He-Who-Comes-In-The-Night, is no different than others."

Slave, she thought with a convulsive shudder. From a beloved servant to a savage's slave. Would she be forever punished for her crime? For surely, this must be her reward for killing her mother's husband.

She had thought that her life with Samuel Walpole had

been bad, and for a while it seemed that she was being forgiven for defending herself against the man—when John Abbott had bought her indenture and given her a reason to smile again.

Then, she'd been sold to Boucher, and while her days weren't as good with him as with the Abbott family, she'd been able to look forward with hope to a better future. The Frenchman had wanted to sell her, and she had prayed daily that the person who took possession of her indenture would be as kind as John Abbott.

But an Indian! These beasts would have no notion of indentures and how they worked. Four years! She'd had four years to serve, and she had survived with the knowledge that someday she would be free . . . to work for pay . . . perhaps own her own home. These Seneca would not free her at any time. She was doomed to remain a slave until her last breath here on earth.

The savage was waving her to follow him. Hannah studied him . . . his fierce expression enhanced by the paint streaked across his brow and cheekbones. The small, stiff tuft of hair—his only hair—that stuck straight up from the crown of his head. His bare chest tattooed with strange markings. She noted the strength in his wiry body, which had been salved in bear's grease, shivered to think of that strength used against her whenever the man deemed it necessary . . . or for sport.

His cohorts looked as dangerous. There were two other Iroquois adult man with Night, and one other who looked like a child of eleven or twelve. They gazed at her as one who was beneath them. Their stoic expressions gave her gooseflesh, and instinctively she took a step back, right into the stream. She stumbled, fell, but recovered herself quickly. She was soaked, though, and the water made the muslin shift cling to her with shocking disregard for propriety. She clasped her arms across her breasts, aware that her nipples showed clearly through the thin, wet fabric.

I won't go! she thought. How could she? Better to die now than to endure the Seneca's cruel, evil tortures.

"Hannah." Jules Boucher drew her attention. "Get out of the water." His tone was grating, angry.

She glared at him, but obeyed. With all these men eyeing her so intently, she had very little choice.

The one Boucher called Night spoke rapidly to the Frenchman. Boucher answered back, his reply in Iroquoian. Frustrated, Hannah wanted to know what they were saying.

Boucher's tone rose as it filled with annoyance, and Hannah's body jerked with alarm when she saw the Indian reach for the knife tucked into his string of his breechclout.

A loud discussion ensued between the savage and the Frenchman. Boucher's demeanor become placating as he reasoned with the Indian with the knife. Hannah viewed the other Indians with trepidation, until she saw with relief that they seemed willing enough to allow the one Indian to handle the matter alone.

The Indian gestured toward Hannah, and she wondered what he was saying when Boucher finally nodded, albeit reluctantly.

Boucher approached her. "Get your things together. You're going with the Indians."

Hannah felt paralyzed with fear. "What happened? Why were you arguing?"

He scowled. It was the first time he'd dealt with the Iroquois. He'd had dealings with the Onondaga, the Mohawk, and the Cayuga. He'd even dealt with a different tribe of Seneca, and each time he'd felt he'd made out better than anticipated. Boucher had been so sure that this experience would be as profitable as the others, but now he wondered. The Seneca expected him to hand over Hannah for only two skins. The Indian promised to return with the other pelts, but Boucher didn't believe him. When Boucher had tried to reason with the savage, telling him that he would hand over Hannah as soon as the Seneca brought the rest of the promised skins, the Seneca had become angry, threatening to kill Boucher and take the woman without payment. The Frenchman had known when to back off during an argument. He was no match for three Indians and a boy. For a brief moment, he had entertained the idea of grabbing the boy as hostage, but then he realized if he did so, he'd be pronouncing his own death sentence.

He glanced toward Hannah and wondered if she would suffer at the Indian's hands. He felt a second's regret that he hadn't noticed her charms sooner. It would be a shame to waste such a woman on the Iroquois, but it couldn't be helped. A bargain was a bargain, and he doubted that he could get out of the deal if he wanted to. In order to eliminate the tension, Boucher studied the hides and pretended that he was extremely impressed with the quality.

"You are a wise man, He-Who-Comes-In-The-Night," he said. "You bring me good skins. I will accept your conditions."

"Good, white man. I will let you live." He waved for Hannah to come to him. When she didn't move, his gaze turned hostile. "Make the woman come to me, Boucher, or I will hurt you both."

"Hannah!" the man exclaimed. "Come over here ... *now!*"

Something in Boucher's tone got her moving.

Impatient with her progress, the Frenchman hurried to grab her arm to jerk her forward. "Do you want to get us both killed?" he muttered beneath his breath.

Hannah's stomach contracted. "What does he want?"

"You're going with him now."

"No!" she said, stopping to dig in her heels.

"Damnation, woman. These people mean business! If you do what they say when they say, you may live to see another sunrise. If you don't . . ."

"God will punish you for doing this, Boucher."

Boucher's smile was grim. "He already has, mademoiselle. He already has."

Hannah stood before the fierce-looking Indian, her skin clammy and her nerves on edge. Should she try to escape through those trees?

"Don't even think it, Hannah," Boucher warned, as if reading her mind. "You'll not get outside of two yards alive."

She closed her eyes and prayed. She didn't know which was a worse fate: to die while imprisoned in Newgate or to suffer being a slave at the hands of this savage. *Dear Lord, forgive me for my sins. I didn't mean to kill Samuel. But I couldn't allow him to steal my virtue.* She laughed silently as she debated whether or not a murderer could still be considered a virtuous woman. In the end, Samuel Walpole had won anyway; Hannah continued to suffer because of that man and what she'd done to him.

The Seneca muttered something harsh and pointed toward a forest trail. Hannah took that to mean that he wanted her to precede him down the path. She glanced toward where she left her gown and her small pile of meager belongings. She started to retrieve them only to have her hair caught up in the Indian's grip and earn a severe lashing from the man's tongue.

A male voice hailed the group from the forest thicket. She looked over to see an Indian man with a boy enter the clearing. The warrior spoke directly to Hannah's new master. His eyes never once settled on her, but she could feel his presence as if he studied her keenly. She felt a tingling as she observed him. He was an impressive figure, standing far above the rest. His hair, unlike the others, was long and hung well past his shoulders. As he moved from the shade of the trees into the light, she was startled to see that golden strands intermingled with a dark shade of blond.

A white man? she thought. No, there was nothing remotely civilized about the half-naked Indian who conversed with He-Who-Comes-In-The-Night. She shivered as she continued to stare. He wore a loincloth like the other savages. His chest was bare, smeared with grease, and tattooed across his upper breast. He was muscular without being bulky. His glistening corded arms looked to have the strength of steel. His legs were bare, his calves and thighs displaying the same force of power and energy as his other limbs.

Perhaps his mother had been an English captive, she thought.

Hannah's gaze returned to He-Who-Comes-In-The-Night. She recognized tension in her new master, and sensed that she was the topic of discussion, the source of friction between him and the blond Indian.

"What is your business here, Night?" White Bear asked the brave as he entered the clearing. He and Eagle Soaring had stood, for a time, some distance away to gauge the unfolding drama. He'd been unable to remain still for long after he saw the woman stumble in the creek.

"I have dealings with this bearded white man." He-Who-Comes-In-The-Night was clearly annoyed with White Bear's arrival. "But it is no concern of White Bear."

"I only seek to help."

Night narrowed his gaze. "Where is Great Arrow?"

"He will be along."

"Does he have beaver skin?"

White bear nodded. "One beaver, maybe two."

"Will he trade with He-Who-Comes-In-The-Night?"

"If you have something he wants," White Bear replied. "Why do you need so many skins?"

Without answering, the warrior turned away to speak with the bearded man.

White knew why Night wanted the beaver pelts; he didn't need the brave to tell him that he'd traded for the woman. Bear's gaze settled on the woman, and he was taken aback by her spirit. If she had cried like a helpless female before, there was no sign of it now. She looked back at him, her eyes unwavering, as she stood with arms crossed, waiting for Night and the bearded man to decide her fate.

He frowned, wondering why a white woman would be traveling alone with this bearded white man.

"Is the woman this man's wife?" he asked Night.

"She is my slave," the Seneca replied. "He has sold her to me."

White Bear's gaze again gauged the white female. For an Englishwoman, she was not unattractive, but neither was she a raving beauty. Her hair, a light shade of brown was clean, shiny, and hung well past her shoulders. Her eyes were light-colored—probably blue like his, he surmised, but he couldn't be sure because she was too far away. Large and widely spaced, her eyes were fringed with thick, dark lashes. Her skin was miraculously smooth and unmarked; apparently, she'd never been in contact with the English's disease that had killed many of the Indian brothers and sisters. Her nose was small. Her mouth was full, the lips nicely shaped and pink. Her form was lush, and the garment she wore did little to conceal her breasts, waist, and hips.

Why would the white man sell her? he wondered. He didn't realize he'd spoken his thoughts aloud, until the bearded man answered him.

"She is a servant, nothing more. I purchased her from a family many weeks ago, but she is slowing me down. She is a hard worker, but I do not have fields to clear and plant, nor do I have a family. What need do I have of her then?"

"I have beaver skin," he said, and He-Who-Comes-In-The-Night glared at him.

"I do not need your help, White Bear."

A sharp, birdlike call heralded the arrival of the Onondaga brave, Kwan Kahaiska, and his son, Strong Oak.

"Greeting, brother," White Bear said. He smiled as he noted the boy's newly acquired prize of the hunt. "I see your hunt has been successful."

The Onondaga laughed as he ruffled the hair on the young boy's head. "Strong Oak felled the buck with one arrow." His tone held pride for the accomplishment of his son.

The child standing with White Bear broke from his father's side to examine and exclaim over Strong Oak's deer.

"Where is your deer, Great Arrow?" He-Who-Comes-In-The-Night asked carefully.

"We need only one deer to feed my lodge house," Kwan said. His gaze went to the woman and bearded man. "What is this? You have taken captives when there is no battle?"

"Night takes no captives. He buys slave from bearded white man."

"Great Arrow," Boucher said with unconcealed surprise. "You are Great Arrow of the Onondaga?"

"Who inquires of me?" Kwan said.

"I am Jules Boucher, French fur trader. I have heard much of you from your brothers, the Cayuga."

Kwan Kahaiska frowned. "All men do not speak the truth."

"Long Nose says you are a mighty hunter. He says you led the people with fairness and strength."

"Ah, so it was Long Nose," Kwan said, his brow clearing, much to his brother-in-law White Bear's amusement. "Long Nose speaks the truth as with certainty the sun rises with each new day."

Night wasn't happy. He could not ask for the boy's first kill, and he wouldn't take any skins from White Bear.

"A brother of such a fine warrior as Great Arrow will pay only two skins for the white woman," Boucher said magnanimously.

"You would take only two skins?" Night asked in disbelief, having forgotten that only minutes before he'd threatened to kill both the Frenchman and the woman because the man had wanted to keep the woman until Night returned with the rest of the hides.

"That is kind of you," Kwan said with a frown. He regarded Night thoughtfully. "You would buy this woman?"

The Seneca warrior nodded. "She will help my woman in the lodge house."

Kwan inclined his head. "Your woman is ill then."

Night grew flustered, a demeanor that was foreign to him. "She is healthy enough. She has been asking for a slave to help her, and I, her husband, would provide her with one."

"Ah . . ."

"You will take my offer then," the Frenchman said.

"Aye," He-Who-Comes-In-The-Night said. Unlike the hostile feelings he harbored for White Bear, he respected Great Arrow, for he'd seen the power of the Onondaga sachem, and preferred to overlook the origin of the Indian leader.

"That is it then." Jules Boucher picked up the two beaver skins and nodded toward Hannah. "She is yours. Take her."

Something kicked in White Bear's gut as he watched Night grab her chin and inspect her as a white man would view a prized beast.

"Get your grubby paws off me, you filthy beast!" the woman exclaimed. She struggled to pull away and was cuffed by Night for her actions. White Bear averted his glance, unable to watch, unwilling to interfere where he knew he had no right.

"You must forget that she is English," his brother-in-law told him in an aside while He-Who-Comes-In-The-Night tied up his slave's hands and ankles and put a gag across her mouth.

"She is not woman, but a slave," Kwan said. "And she belongs to He-Who-Comes-In-The-Night."

"Have I said differently?" White Bear asked, as he inspected an arrow before inserting it into the quiver on his back.

"One does not need words to convey a message, brother," the Onondaga replied, leaning close so that only White bear could hear. "Be advised that your eyes tell what is in your heart. Do not let Night see, else you will have a new enemy among your brothers."

White Bear's gaze met the eyes of his brother-in-law, who was also his friend. "You see much in my eyes, for you have seen much in my sister's."

Kwan didn't smile. "You are my Sun Daughter's brother, but you are also my brother. I see what is there to see. Have a care, White Bear."

"I will do well to avert my gaze then?"

This time the Onondaga's lips curved with amusement.

"You are no coward that you will not gaze into the eyes of another—even your enemy."

The Seneca sighed. "I will stay out of Night's business. I will look the other way while he *cares* for the white woman."

Hannah had barely taken in the fact that there were two Indians who could have been white, when her new master seized her cruelly by the hair and chin, proceeding to shout at her in his strong, garbled language.

She yelled back, furious at such treatment, until she realized that her only chance of escape was to pretend submission until the opportunity presented itself.

She forced herself to relax, to look away from the dark

piercing gaze that cut her down like a finely sharpened blade.

"Sahd-yenh'," the Indian called Night barked at her. He pointed to the ground. The Indians released her.

He wanted her to sit. Assuming her new passive role, Hannah glanced about fearfully and nodded.

Then, the Seneca crouched to tie her wrists at her back with a piece of sinew. She had to stifle a protest when he moved to the front to bind her feet. He left a length between her ankles of about a foot or just slightly over, enough for her to walk, but not run. Hannah could see herself tripping and stumbling the whole way to whatever their destination was.

Her gaze settled on the blond Indian, only to feel her heart beat rapidly when she saw that he studied her with what might be construed as sympathy. The look was gone so quickly that Hannah was sure she had imagined it as the man's eyes hardened before he looked away. As he spoke briefly with another Indian, Hannah saw that the second warrior had a look similar to the first one, savage, but not as dark or as angular featured as the others. She blinked as her mind raced with unanswered questions.

Her new master hauled her to her feet and gave her a shove that nearly sent her tumbling to the ground. She grabbed hold of something to steady herself and realized that it was the Frenchman.

"May God rot your sorry soul, Boucher!" she hissed in an undertone, jerking away as if stung.

The man was unrepentant. "You should worry about your soul and not mine, mademoiselle. For I have yet to meet the devil. One cannot say that about you, is this not true?" He grinned. *"Au revoir,* Hannah."

Soon, the Seneca party left the bearded man's camp, said farewell to their Onondaga brothers, and headed home to the village with the woman who had become He-Who-Comes-In-The-Night's new slave.

Each time she stumbled and nearly fell, White Bear would look away, determined not to see, not to care, for the woman was a slave, and he had no business interfering with one who belonged to a Seneca brother.

Chapter 4

The trail was long and full of obstacles, not really a path at all, but some unworn cut through brush and bramble toward some unknown destination. Hannah, tired and sore from stumbling over hidden branches and rocks, wondered how much longer she'd be able to keep up with the Seneca's grueling pace.

Two braves and a child walked before her; while He-Who-Comes-In-The-Night, the blond Indian, and the boy, who seemed to hang on the fair-haired Indian's every word, followed behind.

As she tried to step over a large rock, she tripped and fell headlong into a pile of dried leaves and twigs. She scratched her face and breathed dirt as she tried to scramble upright. Her ankle bonds kept her from getting any leverage, and she struggled valiantly to get up, only to fall back down. The gag cut her mouth, making it impossible to complain or ask for help. Not that she expected the savages to assist her, but she wasn't even able to vent her frustration.

A firm hand about her right arm hoisted her upright—not ungently. Her skin burned from the warmth of his fingers. She turned, startled by the act of kindness, and found herself drowning in the depths of the blond Indian's deep blue eyes. She stared, as if mesmerized, her blood rushing to her face and neck, as he slid his hand down her arm to where the leather tie bound her wrists. Her breath quickened at his expression. He stared at her wrist bonds and then at her mouth gag, his gaze darkening with anger. She blinked, feeling the ridiculous need to allay his concern. His features softened as if he'd read her thoughts, and his fingers soothed the rubbed area of her wrist. She wondered what he was thinking, if he could feel her rapidly beating pulse beneath his fingertips. The shock of their exchange held her immobile, until a harsh growl disrupted the contact, making her jerk from his gentle hold. Hannah blinked and stepped back, reeling from a dizziness brought on by his unexpected nearness.

Sharp, angry words cleared her head, defiling the forest quiet, and she was dismayed to witness her master He-Who-Come-In-The-Night's argument with the man who'd helped her. She tensed, her first thought to help the blond Indian, until the stark fact hit her that she was a bound slave and powerless to speak or do anything, least of all, interfere in a heated discussion between two savages.

Hannah stood, slightly out of reach, wondering if she'd be the next to suffer Night's fury—and wondering what the Indian had done so wrong in helping her.

The brave listened calmly while He-Who-Comes-In-The-Night ranted and raved and carried on, waving his arms in his anger. When Night had ended his tirade, the blond Indian nodded as if in agreement, and the discussion between the two men continued. Hannah felt a burst of admiration for the blond man, who remained at ease, despite the dark Indian's lash of fury.

Disturbed by her feelings, Hannah tore her gaze from

the man who'd helped her, only to inadvertently center it
on the young boy, who listened to the adults' conversation
with wide eyes. The child, whose skin seemed darker than
the others, suddenly looked her way. Her stomach tightened. There was something intriguing about the little boy,
something painful in his dark eyes that tugged at her
insides, and made her want to take him into her arms for
a motherly hug. He had a look about him that was familiar—yet not. She gazed at him with affection with the hope
of gaining his sympathy and his trust, but he frowned and
averted his glance. Stung, Hannah continued to study him,
wishing she knew the direction of his thoughts, wondering
why it mattered.

A prickling along her spine had her glancing toward
the two Indian men. Night had disappeared. The golden-
haired Seneca stared at her, something dark and disturbing
warring within his expression. She inhaled sharply, releasing the breath shakily only after he broke eye contact. Her
thoughts churned riotously within her until he walked
away, disappearing into the forest brush.

Alone and feeling lost, she became aware of physical
discomfort. Her nose throbbed from bumping it when she
fell, and her jaw hurt from the pull of the cloth gag. But
although her ankles stung and were rubbed raw from the
sinew ties that bound them together, she was more conscious of tingling along her arm and at her wrist, where
the blond Indian had held it. There could be no denying
the strength of his grip, but she felt unnerved by his gentleness. Perhaps it was because up until then she'd experienced only rough treatment by the Seneca. Clearly, the
Indian's behavior had displeased her new master as much
as it had made an impact on her. It was amazing, she
thought, how one small act of kindness could take on extra
meaning when the world around one seemed so alien,
hateful . . . and inhuman.

Black Thunder and Sky Raven stood nearby, silent

guards, who would catch her if she tried to run. And her urge to flee increased with each moment that lingered with the memory of the blond Indian's kindness and her perplexing reaction to it.

He-Who-Comes-In-The-Night seemed to materialize from the forest, and the blond Indian appeared minutes later. The two men began a discussion with Black Thunder and Sky Raven, while the two boys in the hunting party stood off to one side, as if waiting for the adults' dictates.

Hannah silently wished the golden Indian to look at her directly, so she could convey her gratitude, her thanks. But the man didn't bother to meet her gaze, and he didn't help her later when they set off on the trail and her master cuffed her before shoving her into line.

Any good feelings she'd had toward any of the Indians—even the blond one—vanished as they continued the trek, without thought to her well-being or creature comforts. Soon, her bodily pains didn't bother her as much as the discomfort she felt in having to relieve herself.

By the time Night called a halt to make camp, Hannah's abdomen hurt so badly that she was sure that she was going to explode if she wasn't allowed to piss within the next few seconds.

Night said something to one of the other two adult males, and the brave approached Hannah and undid her mouth gag.

Hannah closed her eyes and flexed her jaw as the Indian untied her wrists and then her feet. "Please—the bushes," she said, pointing to an area only a few yards away, the closest thing she could discern that would offer her a measure of privacy. "I need to relieve myself."

The Indian looked at her without comprehension.

Night glanced over and spoke sharply to the man, who replied rapidly and in an equally sharp tone.

Hannah turned to search for someone who might understand. Without meaning to, her gaze settled on the one who'd helped her earlier—the Indian with the light hair.

"Please," she said. "I must go to the bushes. I . . ." How could she explain what her problem was? And to an Indian, for goodness sake?

The man called out to He-Who-Comes-In-The-Night, and when Night answered with a tone of irritation, the Indian's reply held annoyance.

"The slave is a woman. She needs to relieve herself," White Bear angrily told Night. "Look at her, Seneca. See how she stands? It is not hard to know that she is suffering."

"So she suffers," Night said with apparent unconcern. In fact, he was furious that he himself had not thought to see that the woman needed to attend to her personal needs.

"Father," Night's son came to the brave's side. "The woman is trying to tell you something."

The man sighed. "Take her to the bushes. It has been hours. I suspect she needs to make water."

"Yes, father."

White Bear watched Night's son approach his father's slave with caution. A glance at the woman's red face made him realize that it was too late. The puddle on the ground beneath her feet confirmed it.

He saw the boy note the woman's state, watched as the child returned to his father to report what had happened.

Night glanced toward the slave over the top of his son's head, his dark eyes angry, a scowl across his brow making him appear more fierce.

Bear studied the woman's reaction to her master's anger. She was clearly embarrassed but not afraid as Night went to her.

"Stupid woman, could you not wait? Now you will stink like the filthy *Yen'gees!*"

"There is water beyond that hill," Black Thunder said.

Night nodded. "Good. Take her to wash. See that she does it quickly."

The Indian turned to take the woman's arm. She shrank back as if expecting to be struck, and he tried to explain where he was taking her.

"She doesn't understand," Eagle Soaring said to the man.

"I know this."

The boy drew himself up as if what he had to say was important. "My father knows some of the English. He can tell her what she needs to know."

An interested gleam entered the Indian's eyes. "Ask your father to come here."

The boy left to do the man's bidding, and White Bear came to help the brave seconds later. "You have a need?" Bear asked.

"You speak white man's English?"

"I did at one time. But it's been many moons . . . many summers ago."

"The woman is to come with me to the water to wash. She does not want to go. I need her to understand this."

The last thing that White Bear wanted to do was to gaze into the woman's eyes . . . to talk with her in the language of his birth. Her presence on the trail had caused him enough concern, because he'd been unable to remember that she was just a slave . . . Night's slave.

"I will try to make her understand," White Bear said. His gaze went to He-Who-Comes-In-The-Night, who was preoccupied with teaching his son how to set a rabbit trap. "Night will not like it, but I will try."

Black Thunder smiled. "If you are quick, Night need never know."

"White woman," Bear said, the English words feeling strange on his tongue. "You will go with Black Thunder. He take you to water so that you can bathe."

Hannah was startled to be addressed by the Indian in

English. "You speak my language!" Her next shock was to gaze into eyes so blue that the sky on a clear, sunny day paled in comparison.

"I speak some. Once I spoke more, but not now."

Of course, he speaks English. Up close there is no denying that he is a white man. How did he come to live with the Indians—and at what age? Young, she thought. He must have been young, because he was most definitely one of them—an accepted warrior of the Iroquois.

"Who are you?" she said. Her face warmed as she recalled her previous reaction to him. Gesturing toward the others, she asked, "Who are they?"

"I am White Bear of the *Nun-da-wä'-o-no*," he replied, his voice deep and smooth. "The English call us Seneca. They are my people. That one there is He-Who-Comes-In-The-Night. You belong to him."

"So I gathered," she said with unexpected humor.

"This warrior here," he said of the man beside her, "he is Black Thunder. He sees you need bath; he will take you to water."

Hannah colored a bright red as the Indian spoke, bringing attention to her most embarrassing predicament. "I . . ." What could she say that wouldn't make her feel worse? She hadn't made the bushes; a body could wait only so long. "A bath? I would like to wash. You will take me?" she asked hopefully. As she waited for his response, she felt her body and mind betray her yet again. She flashed the other Indian a glance to see if he'd noticed.

His brow furrowed as the blond Indian shook his head. "It is not my place to do so. Night has asked Black Thunder to take you. The warrior will not hurt you. I know him well. He will wait until you are done and then bring you back unharmed."

His words made her curious about the other brave. "I take it that he does not speak English," she said.

"This is so," White Bear said.

"Does my master? Ah, He-Who-Comes-In-The-Night?" When the Indian confirmed her suspicion that Night did not, she asked, "Are there others among your people who speak English?"

"Some do. Most do not."

Hannah grew thoughtful. To befriend those who do might prove to be valuable in any future plan of escape.

"No one will help you leave us, white woman." His tone had become sharp.

Her heart tripping, she shot him a surprised glance. "What makes you think I want to escape?"

The blond man firmed his lips "Your face tells White Bear all. You are a woman who wants to be servant to no man. Least of all He-Who-Comes-In-The-Night."

"What is she waiting for?" Black Thunder said, getting impatient with their talk in English. "If she is to bathe, it should be now before the sun sets in the night sky."

White Bear nodded before turning again to Hannah. "Black Thunder will take you to bathe now." His gaze raked her from head to feet, making her flush again with embarrassment. "Have you no other clothes?" His gaze slid down her length as if undressing her with his eyes, making her shiver. She glared at him, determined to ignore his effect on her.

"I did, but your friend was in too much of a hurry to let me take them," she said. And then she remembered an Indian had taken her gown. "That man—over there," she said, pointing to the man. "He has my gown."

The blond Seneca nodded. "Sky Raven. I will speak to him." He said something to Black Thunder, then left to talk with Sky Raven.

He was back within moments, a scowl upon his brow, holding her only other garment. She'd been forced to abandoned her belongings back at Boucher's camp when Night had stripped her satchel from her arms just before he'd tied her wrists and ankles.

"You will return this garment to Sky Raven when the other is dry," White Bear said.

"But these are my underclothes. I need both!"

His gaze hardened to a dark shade of blue. "You will return the gown to Sky Raven. Night has given the gown to him. As Night's slave, you must honor his wishes."

"Fine," she snapped. Why should she worry about her gown when it was her very life she should be concerned about?

She addressed Black Thunder. "All right, Indian, lead me to water."

"You must not try to escape," White Bear called after her as the other warrior escorted her away.

Hannah flashed him an annoyed look. "Do I look like a fool to you?"

He peered at her from beneath lowered eyelids. "You are a desperate woman, who wants only to get away. Is that not the same thing?"

Black Thunder was quiet as he took her through the woods until they reached a small pond. She'd expected only a brook, much like the one she and Boucher had camped by. The sight of water deeper than her calves delighted her, especially given the nature of her problem—having to bathe while a savage stood guard.

"Please," she told the Seneca, "turn around. It isn't decent for you to watch me." As she spoke, she made a twirling motion with her right arm, but the Indian appeared puzzled.

"Turn around," she said. "Turn around!" She spun in a circle to show him what she meant. When that didn't work, she covered her eyes and then daringly reached out as if to cover his. The brave grabbed her hand to stop her, his expression fierce as if he thought she was attempting to trick him.

She was uncomfortable with her wet clothes, and wanted only to undress and step into that clear, calm water. She debated for a moment how to make the man understand, and then threw her hands up in the air and gave up. Hannah set her gown near the water's edge and then flashed Black Thunder an angry glance.

"All right, you want to see a white woman bathe, then see her you shall!" she muttered as she unbuttoned the tiny buttons and ribbons that fastened the bodice of her shift. Without ceremony, she waded into the pond and then submerged herself, shift and all. After a few moments, she slipped off the garment. The air was cool, but the water was warm, so she stayed crouched beneath the surface of the water. To her dismay, the brave continued to watch her.

"Fine," she mumbled. "You want to watch, then I'll give you something to watch." She balled up her shift and tossed it onto the bank. Then, she dipped below the surface and swam toward the middle of the pond, skimming through the water like an otter at play.

She heard the Indian call out from the shore. Hannah popped out of the water, flicked back her wet hair, and regarded the man warily. The brave was frantically waving his arms ordering her to come closer. She stared at the Indian, debating whether or not he'd come in after her if she didn't obey him and remained where she was. The water felt wonderfully refreshing. She felt cleansed and alive, and she wanted to enjoy the moment without thought for the savages or her captivity.

The brave looked angry. Hannah decided that the brave would enter the pond if she didn't move soon. Sighing with disappointment, she swam until she was a few yards from where Black Thunder stood. The Seneca calmed when he saw that she had listened and understood.

She saw the Indian pick up her wet shift. The gown still lay where she'd left it, and the man retrieved it. Holding it up, he babbled something in his native language. He shook it, sounding as if he were scolding her.

Hannah stared at him, wondering what he was saying, unwilling to move from the protection of the water. Did he want her to get out? And with him standing so near, holding her only garments?

"I don't know what you're saying, but if you're telling me to get out, you can think again. I've changed my mind," she said to him. "If you don't move, then I won't. I am not going to come out of this water while you stand between me and my clothes."

It seemed a battle of wits as the Indian continued to scold and Hannah refused to budge. When the brave threw down her garments and started toward the water, Hannah shrieked and ducked under the water to swim as fast as she could in the opposite direction.

When she surfaced some distance away, she glanced back to see that the Indian had halted and that the blond Indian had joined him near the edge of the pond. She tried to ignore the sudden leap of her senses when she'd first caught sight of White Bear. The two Seneca were deep in a discussion about her. She witnessed Black Thunder point wildly in her direction while he continued speaking rapidly to the other brave. Their discussion ended abruptly with Black Thunder striding back to camp, leaving White Bear alone by the pond to guard her.

"White woman—" Bear called out to her.

"What did your friend want?" she asked after she had swum closer. "Why was he so angry?"

"You were not trying to escape?"

Hannah was incredulous. "How could I escape? I told you I'm no fool! The bloody savage had my clothes!"

"He said that you would not listen to him."

"I couldn't understand him!" she exclaimed. "When I realized he wanted me to swim closer, I did! What more did the man want?"

White Bear sat down on a boulder near the edge of the

pond, his actions bringing her attention to the flex of his leg and thigh muscles. "He did not understand—"

"Naturally," she said sarcastically, angry with the havoc this man dealt to her peace of mind.

To her surprise, the man smiled—actually smiled, as if he knew his effect on her and was pleased by it. The impact of his amusement, compounded by the startling blue of his eyes, made Hannah's pulse race. She couldn't deny that for an Indian—hell, even for an Englishman, he was an attractive man. Too attractive, she thought, because looking at him tended to make her want to forget that he was a savage—and not a civilized gentleman. She frowned. If civilized gentlemen, she mused, indeed existed.

White Bear looked away, releasing her from the lure of his beautiful eyes. For a long moment, she stared at him freely, studying his hair, his face, his muscular form. He had picked up a handful of pebbles and was tossing them into the water, away from Hannah, watching the pattern of ripples made by the splash impact of the tiny stones.

As he shifted to throw another rock, Hannah saw a glint of silver at his left ear as the sunlight caught the surface of his pierced earring. He moved and she saw one at his right ear also. The sight of his earrings startled her, but she found the jewelry oddly masculine and attractive worn on such a man.

He looked up, his gaze fastening on hers. "Do you enjoy your bath?" he asked, his deep voice sending a shiver down her spine despite the warm temperature of the water.

To hear him talk about her bathing as if it were a natural thing to discuss between a man and woman who were strangers had an unsettling effect on her.

"The water is warm," she said cautiously.

He stood abruptly. "Perhaps I should wash, too."

"No!" Hannah panicked at the thought of him entering the water while she stood only yards away, naked and vulnerable and much too aware of him as a man.

He frowned. "I do not mean now, white woman."

"Hannah," she said. "My name is Hannah."

An odd look flickered briefly in his expression. "You are done with your bath now?" he asked, holding her gaze captive with the sudden dark intensity of his blue regard.

"My clothes are over there," she said, hoping he'd take her meaning and move away.

He picked up the dry garment and draped it over the boulder where only a moment ago he'd sat. The wet shift he shook out and examined it, before rinsing the fabric in the pond.

His actions made Hannah feel curiously light-headed. The simple act of his handling her undergarment should have enflamed her anger, but instead she was moved by his thoughtfulness is washing off the dirt and dry leaves that clung to the material.

And her skin tingled and burned for reasons she refused to examine too closely.

He set the newly washed shift over a branch of a tree and then returned to the lake. At the shoreline, he began to untie his loincloth.

"*What—*" she gasped, "*—are you doing?*"

The loincloth fell to the ground as he looked up. "I will take a bath, too," he pronounced as if it were the most natural thing in the world.

"No!" she cried, but it was too late. White Bear was wading into the water, a fine, bronzed specimen of man. A fine bronzed specimen of a *naked* man.

Staring, Hannah tensed. Her heart slammed against the back of her throat as the water rose up over his calf muscles ... his knees ... to inch slowly, tantalizingly, up his thighs. Her eyes widened at the sight of his manhood. Her body jerked, and she hurriedly looked away.

Dear Lord, she was in the pond with a naked savage! Her head spun as panic seized hold of her. She wheeled and started to swim toward the center of the pond, struggling to get as far away from him as she could. She couldn't seem to move; the water seemed solid. Her limbs felt leaden, while her mind whirled with danger, a dizzy desire, and fear.

A splashing behind her alerted her, before she felt a wet masculine hand enfold itself about her ankle, drawing her toward him.

"No," she cried. "Please don't touch me! Let me go!"

She thrashed in earnest, the past twisting with the present despite White Bear's grip, which was firm but not cruel, not at all like Samuel Walpole's.

"Te-ah, ex-aa!" His breath rasped in her ear as he dragged her against him. She kicked and clawed at him, catching his shoulder with her nails. He hissed out in pain and caught her arms in an iron grip. He managed to capture her flailing legs between his solid, muscular calves, and then he shifted them both until her nude body was pressed fully against his naked form.

She was sobbing now. Unable to move, she cried at feeling helpless, to realize that what she'd fought so hard to protect would soon be violated, ruined.

Having subdued the white woman's wild struggles, White Bear stared at her, stricken by her anguished cries, shaken by her irrational fear of him. He continued to hold her without moving; he didn't want to frighten her further. She was soft, smooth, wet curves pressed against his hardness. He stifled a groan at the sudden, startling burst of heat that enveloped him as she brushed against him in the water.

Her sobs lessened, but then the tears that trailed her cheeks tore at his gut, making him bleed. *"E-ghe-a, ex-aa-gä-uh',"* he whispered soothingly. "Do not fight. I will not harm you."

She stilled as she finally understood that he meant her no harm. Encouraged, he released her slightly, transferring his firm hold to her waist, but allowing her to float with more than a foot between them. He held her gaze, but was very much aware of the white breasts that bobbed gently in the water only a few inches away.

Blinking up at him, Hannah slowly raised her hand and rubbed away her tears. She suddenly realized that the Indian wan't forcing her he was just holding her. The hands at her waist were large but gentle. There was an odd tenderness about White Bear's eyes that softened the blue . . . along his mouth that made her wonder about his lips.

"You are fine now?" he asked softly.

She nodded, her fear gone, but her pulse thrumming with uncertainty . . . and a physical awareness that had her averting her gaze from his compassionate study of her.

"I would not hurt you," he said, his husky voice shimmering along her naked skin. "Why did you run?"

"I thought—I thought—" What did she think? That he was her mother's husband, Samuel Walpole, resurrected from the dead to finish what he'd begun? How could that be? White Bear was nothing like Samuel Walpole. *He's a man, isn't he?* a voice reminded her. She closed her eyes. *But he hasn't hurt me. He's shown me nothing but kindness. Why did I panic? Why did I struggle to get away?*

"Ex-aa-gä-uh'," he murmured. "You must not leave. You will only hurt yourself."

"White Bear," she breathed, all fear gone. How could she continue to fear this kind and gentle man? *Like a bear cub,* she thought. "White Bear—" Her breath hissed with sympathy as she spied the scratch on his shoulder. "Did I do that?" she asked with horror.

"It is nothing. This bear is too strong to be injured by a small white woman."

She raised her eyebrows. "I am not small, sir," she said without thinking.

A wicked gleam entered his gaze as he looked down at her breasts. "No," he said thickly. "You are a woman, fully formed."

Hannah shivered, wanting only to break the strange spell this savage continually wove around her. "Please—can't we go back?"

He stared at her a long moment, his attention on her mouth, until her lips tingled and burned. "I would have my bath first," he said, and then he released her.

She took the advantage to turn and put some more distance between them. "I'll wait for you on the shore—"

"Te-ah, ex-aa-gä-uh'." He grabbed hold of her once again, but this time she didn't panic, for she was certain this man always kept his word . . . and he'd promised not to hurt her. "You will stay in the pond while I bathe."

"But—"

His eyes twinkled with amusement. "Shy, *ex-aa-gä-uh'*?" She swallowed hard as she shook her head.

"O-yan-ri—good." White Bear smiled, and the grin transformed his face, making him younger, making him boyishly appealing to Hannah.

He released her, and she dipped her head below the surface, coming up with closed eyes. She hoped he would hurry with his bath. Being together with him in this way was dangerous to her peace of mind.

She was naked, and so was he. She tried not to think of it, knowing all the while that she'd be unable to forget this moment—or how White Bear looked when he'd entered the water.

She kept her eyes closed, but could hear White Bear splashing around. She was afraid to look, frightened of what she might feel if she saw him rubbing himself with his hands as he sluiced water over his strong, muscled body. His chest was sleek and smooth, that much she remembered. His legs had a fine smattering of golden hair . . . and his shaft was cradled within a nest of darker, but still golden, curls.

Heat curled in her lower abdomen. She felt the air about her thicken and warm; she had difficulty breathing.

"I am done, *ex-aa-gä-uh'*." His amused voice was near her ear, startling her with his sudden nearness. She gasped with surprise and went under. She was sputtering when White Bear pulled her up. He grinned at her. "You swim like a robin."

"Robins don't swim," she said. "Oh, you think I can't swim either."

His chuckle sent her heart hammering. "Come, Night will be looking for you."

The mention of her master dampened the lighthearted mood. She was a slave, a prisoner. How could she have, for one moment, forgotten that?

Hannah lingered in the water as White Bear stepped dripping from the lake. Her eyes widened as she drank in the beauty of his male form. She looked away, wondering how she was going to find the courage to get out and get dressed.

To her surprise, White Bear didn't scold her for not following.

"I will wait for you by that tree," he said, drawing her glance. To her relief, his loincloth was back in place and he was tying the strings. The sheen of water was still on his skin.

Then, she realized what he'd just said, and she felt the warmth of gratitude that he'd allow her to dress in privacy. But his next words annoyed her. "Do not try to run, Hanna. I will come after you if you do. If you run, then we will have to keep you tied up. Isn't it more pleasant to be able to move freely?"

He was right, darn him, but she was furious anyway. If she ran, would he be able to catch her? One glance down at his glistening thigh and calf muscles and Hannah had her answer. The man looked as if he could run for miles without tiring ... while she would get barely a half mile before her legs cramped up with the exertion of trying to escape.

True to his word, White Bear left her to stand beneath the tree, turning his back to give her a moment's privacy. Not one to look a gift horse in the mouth, Hannah quickly got out of the water and hurried to dress, the tremors along her skin reminding her who it was that stood only a few yards away. She stepped into the gown, feeling the fabric tug as it brushed against her. Putting on the garment proved as difficult as when she'd tried to pull up her shift while Boucher was watching. She had nothing with which to dry herself, and the fabric refused to glide over her wet skin.

With a few mumbled words of frustration, Hannah tugged and yanked until the gown was finally over her waist, then her breasts. She glanced toward the tree and was relieved to see White Bear still in place with his back toward her. Her damp shift looked odd and very white against the sun-bronzed skin of the man's arm.

Fortunately, her gown fastened up the front, so once she had the garment in place, it was simply a matter of fixing the buttons.

"Han-na, are you ready to return?"

She had done up two buttons and felt strangely vulnerable as she hurried to fasten the rest. "Not yet!"

"Can this brave help you?"

"No!" she cried, remembering how she'd felt in the lake.

He spun at her impassioned cry, his narrowed gaze pinning her where she stood. "You need help," he said, starting to approach.

She gasped. "No! I mean—thank you, but I can manage alone." She bit her lip as he continued to come closer. "Please stay where you are! I'll be right there!"

He froze, his face a picture of puzzlement. "I would not hurt you."

Her eyes shot to his. After a second, she nodded. "I'm sorry," she said. "I know I should thank you. I know that your friend would have stood and watched while I dressed, but I . . . well . . . I haven't had the best experience with men."

White Bear looked as if he didn't understand. "I have seen you without clothes. I did not hurt you."

Gathering her composure, Hannah grabbed up her shoes and walked gingerly through brush and grass to get to the man's side. She was breathing hard when she reached him. "I know," she said without meeting his gaze. "I'm sorry."

"You should put on your shoes," he told her.

She nodded, saw a fallen log, and walked over to sit down so she could don her shoes.

The first knowledge that she had of White Bear's approach was his voice directly above her, his words of concern shivering down her spine. "The white man— he hurt you?" White's Bear's question took Hannah by surprise.

She glanced up to find him leaning against a tree only two feet away. He had moved so silently that she hadn't sensed his actions. That the Indian possessed the ability to move silently without her detection was disconcerting to say the least.

"No," she said after a moment of recovery. "He did not hurt me."

He frowned. "I heard you cry out."

Her smile was twisted. "Oh, Boucher wanted to—tried to, but he didn't get the chance. Your friend . . . Night?" White Bear nodded. "He came before Boucher could finish what he had in mind."

"You shared his sleeping mat?"

"No!" Hannah exclaimed. She forced herself to calm down. "No, he wanted it, but . . ." Her voice dropped in the hope that her meaning was clear. She really didn't want to talk about it . . . or remember. The encounter had been too much like Samuel Walpole's assault, only Jules Boucher had come out of the experience alive.

"This Boucher—he is not your husband then," White Bear said with a tone that might or might not be satisfaction. "He is the one who has made you frightened of White Bear."

"Do Indian men sell their wives?" she asked, her mind catching on something he'd said, something he'd implied.

He seemed shocked by her question. "We do not!" A spark of humor entered his blue eyes. "But the *Nun-da-wä'-o-no* are not Frenchmen."

Hannah couldn't fight the smile that tugged at her lips and warmed her insides. "You do not care for the French."

He nodded. "I do not care for white men. They treat our people like we are animals, and they are mean to their own kind."

"The Iroquois do not hurt one another?" she asked, her interest piqued.

"The *Nun-da-wä'-o-no* are brother to the Mohawk, just as the Mohawk are brother to the Onondaga and my people. We have learned to fight only when it is necessary. The white men—the *Yen'gees*— their need to possess more drives them to attack and kill each other. They will take a woman's life or a child's. It matters not to them. We see all children as a gift from the spirits. Each child belongs to each matron, each warrior. We do not cast aside our young because we do not know the father or his mother does not have a husband."

Having put on her shoes, Hannah stood. "That sounds beautiful, but you must have people who fight or argue."

"This is so," he said with a nod. Another smile lit up his intriguing face. "We are only human after all."

They started back toward camp, only to have Night suddenly appear before them, a scowl on his face.

Hannah heard him speak sharply to White Bear and wondered what it was that bothered Night about the blond

Indian. Was he angry because White Bear had been nice to her back on the trail? Was he afraid that the man would help her escape?

The Indian's behavior toward one of his own seemed strange to Hannah.

White Bear suddenly continued ahead without looking her way, and Hannah was left to return with her fierce master.

They didn't stay to camp as Hannah had thought, but continued on the trail long into the night until apparently He-Who-Comes-In-The-Night decided that it was time to rest. Hannah was exhausted. Fortunately, she had remained free from her bonds, but the going wasn't much easier than before. Night had been angry with her since coming to get her at the pond. He hollered and shoved at her at the least little provocation, his rough handling making her trip and fall several times during the journey.

The Indian seemed to dog her footsteps as they traveled for what seemed like days. When they finally stopped for the night, Night made sure that she slept near him, as if he was afraid she'd run if he didn't watch her. While it had occurred to her to escape, Hannah realized that to make an attempt at night after a long, wearying day would be not only reckless but suicidal. The Seneca knew these woods as an Englishman knew his backyard, and they didn't appear to be tired.

Watching Night give orders to one of the other braves, Hannah decided that any escape attempts she made would be after making careful plans to ensure her survival. She'd need to be rested, to have plenty of supplies to sustain her, and to have some idea about the direction she should take.

Since their time by the pond, White Bear had kept his distance, and Hannah was disappointed when he continued to keep it again the next morning on the trail. She thought it odd that after the intimacy of the two of them naked, sharing the pond yesterday, he refused to meet her gaze today. She wondered if it was because he wanted to avoid Night's displeasure—or if he had his own reasons for pretending she wasn't there.

Had he felt it, too? She recalled the way he'd gazed at her breasts, and thought, *He felt it . . . and it disturbs him as much as it does me.*

Despite her feelings of uncertainty when she was with him, Hannah missed talking with White Bear. His English was stilted and awkward as if he hadn't used it in a long time, which he'd admitted to being the case, but still it was her language, a language she'd be able to understand. She knew nothing of the language of the Seneca. Their words sounded harsh, guttural, and their rapid delivery made it impossible for her even to guess what they were saying.

As she ate the venison they had given her, she glanced over and saw Sky Raven eyeing her strangely. A frisson of fear trailed up her spine, and she looked away, hoping the man would lose interest. Her nape prickled as she sensed when the Indian started to approach. She scrambled to her feet, ready to retreat if it were necessary. Someone called to the brave—White Bear, she realized, and the Indian changed direction toward the Seneca warrior.

White Bear and Sky Raven spoke briefly, before Raven headed into the forest. Bear turned and caught her glance. She stared, mesmerized by his look, her heart hammering until he nodded abruptly and turned away.

"You are the slave of Night, not White Bear," someone said, startling her.

She spun and found herself gazing down into the eyes of a child. A dark-skinned child. "Who are you?"

The youth raised his chin. "I am Eagle Soaring. Warrior of the Seneca. Son to White Bear."

Hannah's belly flip-flopped. "You are White Bear's son?" *White Bear was married,* she thought as the boy nodded. Her chest burned. She felt disillusioned and betrayed, and wondered why.

"You speak English."

He nodded, but looked cautiously about. "I am learn from my grandfather, Man with Eyes of Hawk. He is sachem, great leader. He says I must know what the white man says so that he cannot harm us."

Hannah wondered why it was his grandfather and not his father who was teaching the boy English, but she kept her thoughts to herself. Another empty piece to the puzzle that was White Bear. "Your grandfather sounds like a wise man."

Her reply obviously surprised the child. "This is so."

She smiled, but he didn't respond in kind. Eagle Soaring looked like a proud Indian warrior in miniature. That this dark-skinned child belonged to White Bear, an Englishman by birth, shocked her.

What was the child's mother like? A pain centered in her breast and radiated outward. *White Bear has a wife.* Was she a beautiful Indian maiden who had captured White Bear's attention and his heart?

Hannah couldn't help staring at the boy as she tried to see something about him that was White Bear. But she couldn't see any resemblance . . . other than the erect way both man and child stood.

Suddenly, Eagle Soaring stiffened, as the other boy in the Seneca hunting party approached them.

"What are you doing with my slave, Eagle Soaring?" Running Brook asked in Iroquoian.

"I do nothing with your *father's* slave, Running Brook."

Running Brook scowled. "Then why do you stand here? It is not your place to guard the woman. If anyone should do so, it is I, for she is to belong to my mother."

"I was merely studying the creature," Eagle Soaring said. "It is not often that I see one such as she."

Running Brook turned his attention to Hannah. "She

is a big woman. She can do much work. My mother will like it.''

"Who is he? What is he saying?" Hannah asked.

Eagle Soaring pretended he didn't hear her. "Her skin is light. Her eyes are light," he said. "Why is it that these white people have no color?"

The other boy looked at Hannah as she spoke again. Suddenly, he grinned. "Hear how she babbles? It is because they are stupid!"

Eagle Soaring chuckled in an attempt to humor Running Brook. "But you are not stupid, Running Brook."

Running Brook's expression sobered as he nodded. "This is so. I am Seneca. We cannot be stupid. It is not in us."

"Do you know what she is saying?" Eagle asked.

"No. Do you?"

"I do not," the boy lied.

Running Brook shook his head ."Stupid white woman," he said.

"Even stupid whites will try to escape, Running Brook," Eagle warned.

"This one will not escape us. My father watches her like a hawk."

"Your father is wise then."

Running Brook nodded, and the two boys walked away, leaving Hannah to wonder about their conversation.

Chapter 5

Late afternoon the following day, Hannah detected the scent of roasting meat. The smell, along with the reaction of the Seneca braves, told her that they were near the Indian village. While fearful of what awaited her there, she was almost grateful to be at their destination. They'd traveled long, arduous hours through a forest region that was mountainous and vast. She was tired, sore, and her leg muscles screamed with each step she took.

Suddenly, a shrill bird call pierced the quiet, startling Hannah, but not the Indians. After the sound came again, Black Thunder responded in kind by whistling through his cupped hands. Shortly after the warrior's reply, a single Indian brave came out of the forest ahead, his face wreathed in smiles as he greeted the party of hunters. The brave seemed less fearsome than the other men, and, staring, Hannah realized why—his features lacked the brightly colored face paint that added to the hunters' fierce appearance.

It was the blond Indian who did most of the talking

to the newcomer as the group continued along the trail through the forest. Hannah stared at White Bear, fascinated by his pronunciation of the Seneca language. Neither Night's words nor those of the other braves had invoked such a curiosity in her, beyond what they were saying. White Bear's tone sounded musical instead of harsh, making her wonder about the man. While He-Who-Comes-In-The-Night's responses had been clipped, abrupt, and angry, White Bear's sentences flowed like the lyrics of a song.

He glanced her way as he talked, his blue eyes darkening as his gaze reached across the distance as if to stroke her softly. She flushed, averting her gaze, recalling their time together in the pond.

A burning sensation at the back of her neck caused her to glance behind her. Hannah felt the blood drain from her face. He-Who-Comes-In-The-Night was glaring at her, cutting her with his sharp, angry gaze.

Surely, he can't sense my interest in White Bear? Hannah thought. *Despite what happened by the pond—what is my interest—except that I'm curious about a man who was born English and now lives as a savage among savages?*

A wooden fence loomed ahead, making Hannah shudder at the first sight of her prison walls. At least seven feet high if not taller, the wooden stockade was a fortress made of posts as far as she could see; sharp points crested the tops of the posts, a deadly deterrent to enemy entry. *Or a slave's escape,* Hannah thought with a shiver.

She would never escape with those fence walls to keep her a prisoner. How many Indians lived inside? And what heinous tortures did they practice on their poor helpless victims?

A hard fist thumped into the small of her back sent Hannah pitching forward as He-Who-Comes-In-The-Night shoved her to hurry on. She bit back the yelp of pain before it left her throat and continued forward. The gate to the stockade was guarded by Seneca sentinels, who nodded a solemn greeting to the hunters as they passed.

Hannah hugged herself with her arms as she followed the others in line through the gate opening and got her first glimpse of an Indian village. Large rectangular houses with domed roofs had been erected in a semicircle, facing a large dirt yard or common area. A huge structure that Hannah could only assume was some kind of gathering house closed the circle. Naked Indian children played a game near one end of the village square, while two bare-breasted Indian women tended a large cooking pot suspended over an open fire. Face flaming, Hannah looked away from the unclothed Indians, her gaze focusing on a fully dressed old man, who sat smoking a pipe outside a small hut unlike the other village buildings. The Indian's facial expression was stoic as he puffed rhythmically on his pipe while watching the children play.

As the returning hunters entered the yard, several of the children noted their presence and stopped playing to run over and greet them. The commotion in the yard drew the village women from their longhouses. Their smiling expressions changed as each one caught sight of Hannah.

Suddenly, Hannah found herself surrounded by naked women and children, talking excitedly. They shoved her and pulled her hair. The Indians babbled as they fingered the fabric of her gown and tugged on the sleeves. The Senecas pushed closer, crowding her, stealing her breath, making her panic.

"Get away!" she gasped. "Please!"

The volume of the Indians' voice increased as they pressed yet closer. Hannah fought for air as she struggled to remain standing. *White Bear!* her mind cried. Where was he? Couldn't he see that his people were crushing her, hurting her? And what about her new master—He-Who-Comes-In-The-Night? Had he abandoned her to the Seneca's games of torture?

Help, someone! I can't breathe! Dear God, what are they doing?
A woman cuffed her on the head, and Hannah's head
reeled from the blow.

Suddenly, she heard a commanding voice and felt a
burst of fresh air as the Indians stepped away. Hannah
blinked, then saw the crowd part to allow an old woman
to pass through. The Indian was obviously a matron of
some authority. Her dark eyes were bright and intense as
she examined Hannah as she approached.

"You are big for white woman," the Indian said in
English. "Strong. You will work hard within the village."

"You speak English!" Hannah exclaimed.

She nodded, a slight dip of the head that maintained
her regal bearing. "Some." She turned and went to the
hunters. The woman spoke briefly with the men, before
she returned to Hannah's side. "Come." She gestured to
Hannah to follow her.

Hannah obeyed, wondering what would happen to her
if she refused, not willing to take the risk to find out. She
felt uncomfortable with the way the Indians stared at her
as she passed. A hush had come over the crowd at the
woman's appearance, and the murmur of voices rose as
the matron left, taking Hannah with her.

The matron stopped at the door of a small building,
lifted the animal skin that draped the doorway, and waved
her inside. "This is the house of my brother," she said,
allowing Hannah to precede her into the structure.

The house was dome-shaped, built of sticks, mud, and
grass, unlike the longhouses, which had been formed from
tree bark secured to wooden posts. The inside of the hut
was dark but for the light from the glowing embers in a
pit in the center of the room and the small beam of light
that filtered through the smoke hole in the roof.

Hannah entered a few feet and stopped, unsure what
to do. As her eyes adjusted to the dark interior, she saw

that there was nowhere to go, for the house had only one room and she now stood in the middle of it.

The matron who'd brought her sat down on a mat beside the fire pit and added fuel to rouse up the fire. "Woman with Dark Skin is wife to our sachem," she said. "This is her house. She is not here, gone on a journey. You will stand until her husband says to sit."

Hannah nodded, although her tired, aching body wanted nothing more than for her to sit down. "Why am I here?"

"He-Who-Comes-In-The-Night tells me you are slave for Slow Dancer."

"Slow Dancer?"

"The brave warrior's woman."

"And you?" Hannah dared to ask. "Who are you?"

To the Englishwoman's surprise, the woman smiled. "I am called Moon Woman. Man with Eyes of Hawk is my brother."

"And he is?"

"Sachem of our people—the *Nun-da-wä'-o-no*, the great hill people."

Hannah acknowledged that she understood, and silence reigned for a time as she thought about what she'd learned, how the knowledge might help her to escape someday. Moon Woman seemed content with the quiet as she, apparently, waited for someone to appear. Suddenly, there was a flurry of motion as a woman threw up the deerskin flap and burst in from outside.

She spoke fast and furiously at the matron, who sat patiently, seemingly unfazed by the woman's angry outburst. Moon Woman merely answered the newcomer with soft tones, but the woman continued to be angry.

The flap was lifted again as a brave stepped in to join them, and the angry woman turned the direction of her ire on him. It took Hannah only a second to recognize the warrior as her new owner, He-Who-Comes-In-The-Night.

Night spoke sharply to the woman, who, after returning an equally sharp reply, spun on her heels and left the building.

Hannah was surprised to see Night offer Moon Woman what seemed to be an apology of sorts, before he left the hut with only a brief glance in Hannah's direction.

"That woman—"

Moon Woman smiled. "Slow Dancer."

Night's wife, Hannah thought. "Why is she angry?" Moon Woman's patient understanding had given Hannah the courage to ask questions.

"She has just learned she has a slave. She did not like that her slave was brought to the house of the sachem without entering the house of Slow Dancer first."

"She is afraid that I will be taken away?"

"No."

"I don't understand—"

"It is not your right to understand the ways of the *Nun-da-wä'-o-no,* white woman." An old man had entered the structure, his dark eyes glittering in the firelight, his long white hair flowing past his shoulders. He swept past Hannah and took a seat on a mat on the floor beside Moon Woman, greeting the woman in their language before he sat down. *Moon Woman's brother,* Hannah thought. *The leader of these Seneca—Man with Eyes of Hawk.*

The Indian matron spoke softly, almost affectionately, Hannah noticed, and then the man focused his piercing dark gaze upon Hannah.

"So, you are slave to He-Who-Comes-In-The-Night," he said.

"Not by choice, I can assure you," Hannah replied without thinking.

The Indian narrowed his gaze. "You speak too freely. You will suffer if you do not change your ways."

Was that a threat? Hannah wondered. There was nothing menacing about the man's tone. A warning then. She straightened her back, unwilling to show fear to this man, the sachem. That he knew English didn't surprise her. She had learned that he did from the boy, Eagle Soaring, the man's grandson.

Four of the savages spoke English. That meant that she would have no trouble communicating with at least four people in the village. How many more knew the English language? That there was even one had amazed her, that four could speak English well enough to be understood was astonishing to her.

"You don't want to hear my thoughts," Hannah said.

He sat back without answering, nodding his thanks when Moon Woman handed him a wooden ladle. He drank from the vessel, taking his time to quench his thirst, leaving Hannah to wonder whether he was annoyed or angry. As he lowered the ladle, he made a sound of appreciation that suggested that he was only grateful for the drink he'd been given. Handing the dipper back to Moon Woman, he turned back to stare at Hannah with appraising eyes.

"Sit," he commanded, and Hannah did. "You may speak freely while in this house," he said, his comment surprising her. "But others will not take to hearing from a slave, so you would be wise to be silent once you leave here. Do only what you are told."

She nodded, but the reminder of her new position within the village stung. Would she never be free to live the life that she wanted?

Moon Woman refilled the ladle with water from a leather pouch and handed it back to her brother.

"You have thirst?" Man with Eyes of Hawk took the ladle and offered it to Hannah.

Hannah eyed the vessel as if it had sprouted wings.

The man frowned. "You refuse to drink from the same bowl as your sachem?"

"No! I—I am thirsty." She reached out to take the dipper of water. Her gaze met his as she lifted the ladle to her lips but had yet to drink. "Thank you," she said softly.

He inclined his head and waited while Hannah drank. The water was cool and delicious, sliding down her parched throat, soothing her as she sipped. She continued to drink until there wasn't a drop left in the bottom of the vessel. When she was done, she realized that unlike the Indian she'd been noisy while she drank, slurping the water greedily in her enjoyment. Embarrassed, she was red-faced as she returned the ladle to Moon Woman, who held out her hand for it.

"I'm sorry." she said. *Why am I apologizing to a savage?* Because the *savage* had exhibited some manners, while she had slurped the water like a dog lapping thirstily from a rain puddle.

He didn't acknowledge her apology, but picked up a piece of a bread that looked to be fashioned from corn. He nibbled at the corn cake as he continued to stare silently at her.

Finally he spoke. "You are here to learn what is expected of you. You are here because He-Who-Comes-In-The-Night traded furs for you. You belong to Slow Dancer, wife to He-Who-Comes-In-The-Night. You will listen to what she says and obey. If you do not, you will be punished. No one will help you. It is the way of our people to tend our own slaves."

"But how will I know what to do when I can't understand your people's language?"

"Slow Dancer will show you what she wants done. You have been brought here to take the place of Slow Dancer's sister, who was killed by a white man. Do not try to run. He-Who-Comes-In-The-Night will hunt until you are found. When he finds you, you will not live to see the next sun."

Hannah shuddered.

"Do you understand this?" the sachem said.

She wanted to tell the old man about her indenture,

how the Indian had only bought her for the remaining four years of service, but she realized that even if she could make him understand the concept, the terms of her service contract had changed from the moment the two deerskins had traded hands.

"What are you called?" he asked her.

"Hannah."

The man nodded. "Han-na." He looked thoughtful. "What does this mean? Han-na."

She blinked. "I—ah—I'm not sure." It seemed a strange question for the sachem to ask her. What did her name mean? She searched her memory. Did her mother ever tell her? "Graceful," she exclaimed, remembering. "My name means 'graceful.'" She scowled and shook her head. Her mother had chosen the wrong name for her.

The old man frowned. "What is this graceful?"

Hannah wondered how she could explain it. "It means to move with beauty." She bit her lip. "Without falling." Unsure how to make him understand, she rose slowly, carefully so as not to alarm him. "To move with grace." She walked with a glide a few feet and then returned.

The sachem nodded vigorously. "Like a bird moves in flight." He spoke to his sister in Iroquoian, and Hannah wished she could understand. When Moon Woman answered, it was the first time she'd said a word since her brother had entered.

Moon Woman rose and with a nod instructed Hannah to follow her. The matron waited until Hannah was out in the sunlight. "I will take you to Slow Dancer," she said.

"Thank you," Hannah replied. She hesitated a moment and then said, "Thank you for the water." She wondered if, like the sachem, Moon Woman had taken offense when Hannah had been slow in accepting the dipper. She hoped not; she didn't want to offend Moon Woman, as the matron had shown only kindness to her.

Moon Woman didn't answer as she started across the

yard, apparently expecting Hannah to follow her. The children had resumed their game, and their laughter sounded childlike and carefree, reminding Hannah of the Abbott youngsters at play. The women were nowhere in sight, having gone back to their homes, but for the few who watched over the community cooking pot. There was no sign of the hunters or any other of the Seneca men. Hannah sighed. No sign of White Bear.

Still, Hannah felt as if curious eyes watched her as she trailed Moon Woman across the compound. She glanced around and saw that no one was gazing at her directly.

I must be imagining it.

Then she felt a tingling along her spine and saw that someone was indeed studying her. It was her new master, Slow Dancer, who stood waiting near the door of the largest longhouse.

As they reached the woman's side, Moon Woman spoke to Slow Dancer, who nodded and narrowed her gaze upon her new slave. The sachem's sister addressed Hannah. "This is Slow Dancer. You will do what she says. You will live by her goodwill and hers alone. Do not anger her. She is a good woman. Obey her and you will not die."

Die? Hannah thought with horror. That prospect of being killed because she'd displeased her master hadn't occurred to her.

She and Slow Dancer stared at one another a long time, gauging each other's measure. The Indian woman was about five and thirty, Hannah decided, and pleasant-looking. Slow Dancer wore her dark hair pulled back and secured at her nape with a strip of leather. Her face had a fine dusting of powder with a reddish tinge, and her lips looked as if they'd been stained with berry juice. She wore a doeskin skirt, fringed at the bottom and decorated with dyed porcupine quills. A beautiful colorful medallion of silver, beads, and porcupine quills hung from around Slow Dancer's neck to nestle in the valley between her bare breasts. Hannah glanced at the necklace and looked away, embarrassed by the Indian woman's naked display. On her feet, Slow Dancer wore highly decorated moccasins, which looked much more comfortable than Hannah's old pair of men's shoes.

Master and slave took stock of each other. Hannah saw herself as the matron must see her . . . brown hair unbound and tangled . . . her face pale and streaked with dirt. She still wore the gown that she'd "borrowed" back from the warrior. Made of coarse homespun fabric, the gown was plain, ankle-length, and a drab shade of gray. The stitching on one sleeve had been torn by an Indian child.

Hannah waited for the woman to speak, to give her a direction, but Slow Dancer seemed in no hurry to move. The Englishwoman had no choice but to stand patiently.

The animal skin that curtained the doorway behind Slow Dancer lifted. He-Who-Comes-In-The-Night stood in the opening, his expression grim as he noted the two women.

"What is it?" he asked his wife in Seneca. "Do you not like your new slave?"

Slow Dancer faced her husband. "She is pale, but sturdy. She will work well, I think."

Night beamed. "I thought you would like her."

His wife's face took on a look of suspicion. "Why?"

The brave seemed taken aback. "Because she looks strong."

The woman nodded.

"You said you wanted help," her husband said. "I saw the woman with the Frenchman and knew that he wanted to sell her."

"You do not find her white skin attractive? Her brown hair the color of ripened corn husks?"

He smiled. "I want only a woman with hair the color of the night sky, with eyes that dance in the firelight, and whose lips are red like the wild berries in the field . . . and just as sweet."

Slow Dancer's lips curved into an affectionate grin. "You know the right words, my brave warrior. I hope that you mean them." She turned abruptly and motioned to her slave.

Hannah watched the exchange between man and wife with growing curiosity. When Slow Dancer gestured for her to enter the longhouse, Hannah did so, conscious of Night's gaze on her as she passed him to go inside.

The inside of the structure was enormous. Running along its length, on each side, were rooms or cubicles, each constructed to house a family. In the corridor down the center there were fire pits for each family's cooking fires. Some pits, it appeared, were shared by two families.

As she followed Slow Dancer down the corridor, Hannah saw that some pits held only glowing embers while someone kept a fire kindled within others. She looked up. Dried pumpkin, squash, and corn with braided husks hung from the center roof ridge pole above.

There were no windows in the large structure, only an opening at each end that allowed entry and exit through a communal storage room beyond each door. The only light was that which filtered in through the smoke holes above and the glow created by the Seneca's cooking fires.

Slow Dancer's family living space was to the left and toward the center of the longhouse. The woman paused near the opening while Hannah entered hesitantly. The tidy appearance of the cubicle took Hannah by surprise. There was a sleeping platform built about a foot and a half off the dirt floor, with another platform used for storage built a few feet above. It looked like cooking items that were stored below the sleeping platforms and stacked neatly in one corner. The living space was clean and uncluttered, making Hannah wonder why Slow Dancer wanted a slave.

The Indian woman watched her intently. Feeling uncertain, Hannah gazed back. Slow Dancer muttered something as her hand shot out to grab hold of Hannah's gown sleeve. When Hannah didn't respond, the Seneca woman became angry and barked another order.

"I don't understand," Hannah said, feeling helpless.

When she realized that Slow Dancer wanted her to take off her gown, Hannah retreated. Horrified, she shook her head.

Slow Dancer tugged on the fabric, ripping it, and released it, furious when it tore. Free, Hannah held on to the torn sleeve and started to inch back out of the cubicle.

Livid, the Indian woman came after her, while she babbled angrily in Iroquoian.

Suddenly, Hannah came up against a solid wall. She gasped and spun, gaping with horror at the Indian warrior who stood blocking her escape.

Slow Dancer caught Hannah's arm and jerked her back into the cubicle, angrily barking out orders. Hannah couldn't fail to get the message, and she gave in as Slow Dancer thrust her against a platform, righting herself when she stumbled.

The brute of a savage stood in wait, as if to see that the woman's slave gave no more trouble. Alternately studying the two Indians, Hannah swallowed hard. Her gaze darted about wildly in its search for an escape route. But there was no place to go, no place to run.

She didn't want to go half-naked like the savages! But what other choice did she have?

She took another long look at the frightening warrior behind her before glancing again at her new master.

"Dus'hah-wah!" Slow Dancer commanded. *"Oh-neh'."*

"All right. All right," Hannah muttered beneath her breath. "You want the bloody gown, you can have it! Just give me time!"

Afraid of suffering the consequences of disobedience, she closed her eyes, took a calming breath, and then began to undress with hands that shook.

Dear Lord, she thought, *am I to be stripped of my clothes—and my dignity?*

She suddenly wished for White Bear. She had no reason to fear him. In the end, he had behaved honorably by the pond. White Bear would help her with Slow Dancer.

Chapter 6

She felt humiliated. Hannah stood with her back toward the cubicle opening, one arm across her naked breasts, her other hand shielding her pubic region, while Slow Dancer studied and pawed her gown as if fascinated with the garment.

The warrior hadn't moved. Hannah could feel his piercing gaze assessing her physical attributes. She was mortified; it didn't matter that he could only see her back. She wanted to run and hide, but there was nowhere to turn. She was trapped, a prisoner of the Iroquois Seneca.

As she studied Slow Dancer, she wondered what the woman planned to do with her. Would she be forced to suffer the continued indignity of being without clothes? She blushed, envisioning the Indian men watching her, following her about the village with their eyes, while the women bullied and pushed her, and finding her lacking, called her names.

White Bear. He was an ally among the savages. She had a mental image of the golden-haired warrior, how he looked when his bright blue eyes had stared through the water at her bare breasts. She shivered, but not with fear. Why couldn't she put him out of her mind? He kept appearing in her thoughts . . . cropping up in her dreams.

It was because he was white like her, she thought. That was the reason she felt a kinship of sorts, felt safe with him.

He's not an Englishman, an inner voice taunted her. *He's pure savage, just like the rest of them.*

Her heart wanted to deny that. She wanted to believe that there was someone within the village to whom she could turn for help, whom she could trust. She was drawn to him, she told herself firmly, simply because he was the first of the savages to speak English to her.

Memories of home intruded in her thoughts . . . of all she'd lost . . . first, her mother, whom she'd adored, and then the Abbott family. She missed her mother desperately . . . and she missed working for Mr. and Mrs. Abbott, caring for their children, cleaning their house. For one brief year, she'd learned to be happy again.

She was a murderess. There was no getting around that, but she hadn't meant to kill Samuel. It'd been self-defense. An accident. Must she suffer for her sins for the rest of her life?

Tears stung her eyes, and she had to swallow past a painful lump. She wished things had been different. She wouldn't have hit Samuel so hard; she would have tried not to kill him, just knock him senseless so that she could get away. And then she would still be in England, and not here with the savages in these godforsaken colonies.

Hannah glanced past her shoulder, saw the brave had left, and released a relieved breath. Now if only she could get some clothes!

"Please," she beseeched Slow Dancer. "My gown—may I have it back?" She reached to get it and got her hand slapped for her efforts.

"Te-ah!" the woman screeched. *"Te-ah!"*

Hannah knew she could forget the gown. He-Who-Comes-In-The-Night had promised the garment to another, but Slow Dancer wasn't about to give it up. Hannah wondered what was going to happen when the brave, Sky Raven, came to reclaim it.

Hannah searched wildly about the cubicle for something to wear and saw the animal pelt draped over one end of the sleeping platform. After gaining Slow Dancer's attention, she pointed toward the fur. "Please," she said, "may I have this? I'm cold." She pretended a shiver to make the woman understand. "If I can't have my gown back, please may I use your fur?"

A prickling at the back of her neck made Hannah turn. White Bear stood behind her, his expression stoic but for the fire in his crystal blue eyes. She felt the blood drain from her face and then the quick burst of heat enveloped her when she saw the way his gaze slid down her naked length, settling for a long moment on her backside. She nearly choked in indignation. What had happened to the honorable man?

Savage, you mean, an inner voice taunted.

White Bear's eyes rose slowly as if he were interested in her reaction, and for a long moment they stared at one another. Gone was the gentle Indian who'd held her so gently; his expression belonged to a different man. Her face burned with embarrassment. Hannah glared at him over her left shoulder, trying valiantly to cover herself with her arms. Unconcerned, White Bear stood solid and formidable, his arms at his sides, his smooth bare chest stealing Hannah's breath as it drew her attention.

He moved, raising a muscled arm to scratch himself, his gaze never wavering from her face. Drawn by the movement, Hannah followed it to his right nipple. Her heart fluttered, and her mouth went dry.

White Bear's blue eyes burned as he dropped his hand.

Every exposed inch of Hannah tingled and flushed with awareness, frightening her with her reaction to him.

Hannah wanted to cover herself and hide, and uncaring of the danger, she had thought to flee from longhouse. White Bear's eyes narrowed, and she saw him tense as if he were privy to her thoughts. Desperate, she jerked from the captivity of his gaze with a gasp and pleaded with Slow Dancer, silently begging God to make the woman understand. "Please," she said, "I need something to wear. Anything! Please!" She heard her voice rise on a growing note of hysteria.

Slow Dancer continued to ignore Hannah and admired the gown as she held the garment up against herself. Suddenly, she saw White Bear and frowned. The matron made a quick check about the longhouse as if searching for someone. After a moment, she relaxed, and a smile curved her lips as she excitedly showed White Bear the gown.

He murmured something to her in Seneca.

Looking pleased, Slow Dancer nodded and glanced at her slave with a chuckle after White Bear had made another comment.

They're making fun of me! Hannah thought. Her fear became a burning anger. She glared at White Bear. Did the man have no feelings? No shame, that he would mock an Englishwoman, when he had to have known damn well how humiliating this all was to her?

"What did you say to her?" she snapped.

The brave raised an eyebrow at her tone, the slight movement clearly mocking her now if he hadn't been before. She flushed and looked away.

Slow Dancer whispered something to White Bear, who withdraw his gaze from Hannah to smile at the matron. They spoke in soft tones. Hannah glanced back and forth between them while they conversed. Her fingers balled into fists while she longed desperately to understand them.

She was the fool, standing there without clothes while

White Bear and Slow Dancer talked as if she existed only for their amusement, uncaring of her feelings.

Hannah shivered with cold as she struggled to hold back tears. She faced her tormentor. "White Bear, please," she cried. "I need clothes!"

The warrior didn't answer her as he gazed back. Something darkened in his blue eyes as he continued to stare, until Slow Dancer spoke and he seemed impelled to answer.

"White Bear!" she whispered pleadingly. *"Please."* Her anguished entreaty made him frown and glance her way.

"Please," she begged huskily. "Help me."

He didn't say a word. How could he not say a word? After holding her gaze captive, he broke the connection, said something jeering to Hannah's master, and left without turning, as if totally deaf to her wild cries.

The tears of anger and pain, that she'd been holding in check, fell freely, slipping silently down her cheek until Hannah raised a hand to dash them away before Slow Dancer could see them.

Devil! she thought. *Savage. Bastard!* She wanted to lash out physically at White Bear for being so heartless, for pretending that he hadn't understood. Something inside her of died and was reborn. She stiffened her spine as she discovered a new strength, a new will to get through this . . . to survive.

Her tears dried as she dropped her hands. Naked or not, she had nothing to be ashamed of; she wouldn't allow them to defeat her. She would bide her time, escape, and then she would find a way to live!

The image of White Bear's handsome, rugged face came back to haunt her. What more could she have expected? He was an Indian, for godsake. It didn't matter that he'd been born with some white blood. Maybe he did have some Seneca blood flowing in his veins. *No, he wouldn't have such fair hair if he did. He'd be darker . . . like Eagle Soaring.* And while his skin was bronzed, almost copper-colored, it was a coloring made by the sun—and not a trait allotted to him at birth.

She recalled how kind he'd been along the trail, explaining things to her, making the journey for her in some respects less fearsome. *A pox on the savage!* she thought. She'd harbored a false hope that the Indian would help her. She'd awarded him a gentle humanness that just plain didn't exist. But she knew better now. Despite his lineage and the obvious difference in hair and skin color from her other captors, White Bear was as much a Seneca as the rest . . . a savage among savages.

With a new resolve to protect her own interests, Hannah reached toward the fur on the platform with the intention of drawing the blanket around her naked form. The movement drew Slow Dancer's attention. When the matron glared at her with a sudden viciousness that took her by surprise, Hannah dropped the end as if stung. Her arms instinctively resumed their protective position as she stepped back from the angry woman's reach.

Her courage returned, buoyed by her newfound strength, and Hannah calmly decided that the only way to communicate was to try some hand motions.

She pointed to the garment in Slow Dancer's arms. "Gown," she said carefully, quietly. She managed to smile to show the matron that she was pleased that Slow Dancer liked the gown. "Keep it." She then shivered and hugged herself with her arms. "Cold," Hannah said. "Brrrrr. Need clothing." She gestured to the fur. "Warm. Blanket. Need blanket." She made a motion that showed that she wanted to wrap something around herself. "Need something!" she all but squeaked, feeling frustrated. "Blanket," she said, pointing again to the fur pelt. "May I have this?" She closed her eyes briefly before opening them again. *"Please."*

Slow Dancer looked at Hannah with a new fascination as Hannah, using a combination of words and improvised sign language, continued to plead and make her understand.

The Indian matron stared at Hannah and then glanced toward the sleeping platform when Hannah pointed to it for what must have been the tenth time. Suddenly, Slow Dancer's dark eyes brightened, and Hannah felt a resurgence of hope.

"Yes," the Englishwoman said softly. "Yes, beaver skin. Warm. I want to use it."

But Slow Dancer shook her head, then reached up, instead, toward the storage shelf above the bed, where she pulled something from beneath some other belongings toward the back.

With a look of satisfaction, the woman stepped back and held up a doeskin skirt, which she then suddenly thrust against Hannah's chest. Startled, Hannah lowered her arm just in time to catch the garment before it fell to the dirt floor.

For a long moment, the Indian captive studied the skirt, which was beautifully made but which, she soon realized with dismay, was inadequate modest attire for someone her size. She need a shirt! Determined not to forgo a bodice covering, Hannah started to hand back the skirt but then promptly thought better of it. Recalling her and the matron's recent difficult exchange, she knew she had to take what she could get—or she'd end up with nothing.

She donned the skirt quickly and returned her arms to cover her breasts.

Did all Indian women wear nothing above the waist? She swallowed. Even in the wintertime? And what if they did? It didn't matter, because she—Hannah Gibbons—was no savage. Whether it was common practice or not, she would still feel uncomfortable without adequate, modest clothing.

"Han-na, you do not like the *gä-kä-ah*."

Recognizing the soft voice, Hannah turned with relief to face Moon Woman's familiar face.

The Seneca matron stroked her own skirt. *"Gä-kä-ah.* Is what you call skirt?"

"Oh, Moon Woman!" Hannah exclaimed. "The skirt— it is lovely, but I need my gown! I can't wear this without a shirt or covering!"

Moon Woman smiled. "Why are you unhappy? Why are you ashamed? You, white woman, are no different than Seneca woman."

"I'm sorry," she said, not wanting to offend. Moon Woman was the closest thing to a friend or ally. She thought of the naked children. "I know it's your way to go about without clothes, but I can't—" she whispered, her voice trailing off with horror. She shifted her arms higher to hide her lush breasts. Her ineffective attempt made Moon Woman's dark eyes flash with amusement and the gentle smile on her lips widen into almost a grin.

The Indian woman's face suddenly turned serious as she addressed Slow Dancer. "Sister, do you have tunic for slave?" Moon Woman asked.

"Why do you ask? What is wrong with *gä-kä-ah?* Doesn't the white woman like it?" she said, her tone turning sarcastic as she mentioned the slave.

"The *gaä-kä-ah* is too good for her." Moon Woman clicked her tongue as if scolding the woman for her failure to see that. "The white woman needs a tunic to cover her pale skin. She is different, and so draws attention. Do you want the men of the village to stare at the *Yen'gees?*"

"She is ugly. Why should they look at her?"

"This is true. She is not attractive by our standards. Perhaps I am mistaken when I saw more than one brave staring as your slave walked by." She pretended to assess critically Hannah's features. "You are right. She is ugly. Do not give it to her. Allow her to keep the *gä-kä-ah.* No

Seneca warrior will see something in the white woman that isn't there."

Her dark eyes on Hannah, Slow Dancer looked uncertain. "No, I will get slave tunic," she said. "Moon Woman is wise. It will not hurt to keep the white woman covered. I do not need to tend to *Yen'gees* skin turned red by the sun's fire. I do not need that—it is old and not so good as the *gä-kä-ah*."

"Han-na," Moon Woman said. "Her name is Han-na." She smiled at Hannah. "Han-na, Slow Dancer will give you *ah-de-a-dä-we-sä* for skirt. This will be bet-ter?"

Ah-de-a-dä-we-sä? Hannah thought, wondering what the word meant.

"From here to here," the matron said, showing her the area the garment would cover.

The garment was a shift of some sort. Hannah nodded, grateful for the woman's continued kindness. "Thank you."

The woman inclined her head. "Do not let Slow Dancer know you like *ah-de-a-dä-we-sä*. She will take it back if you do."

"I see." Hannah blinked. She did see. Slow Dancer wasn't being kind; she'd been convinced by Moon Woman to make the change. The Englishwoman wondered what the matron had said to get Slow Dancer to exchange the garments.

Slow Dancer forced Hannah to undress and return the skirt before she gave the Englishwoman the *ah-de-a-dä-we-sä*, which was a deerskin tunic. The tanned skin of the garment wasn't as soft and smooth as that of the skirt, but the length was enough to cover Hannah from neck to knee. She was satisfied.

Moon Woman stood by during the exchange, and then with a nod at Hannah and a few words for Slow Dancer, she moved on to an area of living space at the far end of the longhouse.

Moon Woman lives here in the longhouse, Hannah thought, glad of the knowledge. If she had trouble understanding Slow Dancer, then she could turn to Moon Woman for help.

Hannah felt much better. The garment wasn't modest by English standards, but compared to the other Indians, she felt fully clothed in the *ah-de-a-dä-we-sä.* The tension brought on by the experience left her. She began to feel hopeful that her time with the Indians would be tolerable and brief . . . that it was only a matter of time until she'd find a way to escape and be free again.

There was no area within the compound that was large enough to grow the dried corn, pumpkins, and squash that hung from above. Nor could there be a field herein from which the Indians had picked the basket of berries she'd seen as she'd passed. *Which means that they don't spend all of their time inside this stockade-fence.* Which meant that she would have to bide her time until she was allowed outside . . . before she could begin to formulate an escape plan.

Escape. Where would she go? she wondered as she fought back doubts. To whom would she flee?

A matter of no concern for the present, she decided. She would only take each day as it came . . . and she would know what her options were and which one to choose when the time was right.

He shouldn't have watched, but he couldn't help himself. The white woman was no concern of his, being slave to another, but something about her drew his attention.

White Bear stood in the common yard and studied the woman Hannah as she followed Slow Dancer to the village gate. The women were going to the fields; there was much work to be done there. Hannah would work the rows that belonged to Slow Dancer.

As his gaze followed her across the village square, he recalled with a clenching gut the way she appeared during the journey when she'd been bathing naked in the pond along the trail. The ache intensified as he fought the memory of her standing in Slow Dancer's lodging quarters, trying to hide all that was woman ... her white skin ... her generous, soft curves. The look in her eyes when she'd spied him studying her ... and the answering heat within him that seared him so suddenly that he'd been shocked into staring.

He closed his eyes as pain washed over him. His body's reaction to the white woman left him feeling as if he'd betrayed his marriage ... his late wife.

Han-na. Had he ever seen a woman so pale ... so soft? Her back was smooth where her hair fell in silken golden brown waves to well below her shoulders. There was a small indentation at the base of her spine, just before the rounded full curve of her backside. Spying it, he'd felt the most incredible, shocking urge to place his lips there ... and nuzzle her skin.

But what most astonished him was that his desire didn't end there. He had admired the form of her thigh, the gliding slope to the back of her knee, and he'd envisioned her lying on her stomach, while he'd gently held her calf so that he could run his mouth along the entire back of her leg from thigh to knee to ankle.

White Bear clenched his jaw as he grappled with his emotions. He wanted to touch Hannah everywhere, caress and run his fingers along the honey-dark lines made by the sun. The ultimate sense of betrayal came when he wondered how it would be to lie with her, to plant himself between her warm womanly thighs and thrust hard and deeply.

The shaft of pain that followed nearly destroyed him. How could he dishonor Wind Singer with a slave? Han-na was nothing. A slave that belonged to another. And she was a *Yen'gees*. Unbidden came reflections of a time when he had enjoyed the attention of English females, a time when he was young and foolish. He'd been seven and ten when he was captured by the Seneca. Newly come to the colonies, he'd been a silversmith's apprentice with his friend Walt to Walt's uncle in Philadelphia. Their capture had occurred when the two friends had been on a journey to deliver a silver tea service to the wife of a wealthy landowner whose property was deep in the thick of the Pennsylvania wilds.

In the year that preceded their capture, he and Walt had been old enough to have drawn the attention of women while young, foolish, and inexperienced enough to have enjoyed the silly flirtations. And then life for them had changed with the Indian raid. One moment they'd been two boys laughing over a shared jest and the next they'd been Indian prisoners, fearing for their lives as their hands and ankles were bound with strips of leather.

Walt had eventually been released, while he—James Rawlins—had become White Bear, an adopted Seneca son who later took a Seneca wife. He was no longer an Englishman, and the change within him had been complete.

White Bear had found contentment with his wife among the Seneca. He'd felt a sense of belonging, of understanding a people who'd been long misunderstood. After over ten years as an Indian, he had forgotten his English. When he'd discovered that Sun Daughter, his only living family of English blood, adored her Onondaga husband and taken to the Iroquois way of life, there'd been no need to recall anything at all from his old life . . . including the Englishwomen.

But then He-Who-Comes-In-The Night had traded for the white woman, and suddenly White Bear was having strange feelings . . . strange desires. Han-na was unlike any

Yen'gees he'd known in his life. She'd been a servant—not a lady of leisure.

She wasn't small or dainty, nor did she wear frilly gowns. She was tall, near enough to his own size. She looked sturdy, strong and ripe enough to bear healthy children.

But that wasn't to say that she wasn't all woman. She had curves in all the right places—tempting curves that lured a man's gaze and made him think things he had no right to be thinking . . . and make him experience feelings that made him betray his wife.

Slow Dancer had paused to speak with Walks-In-Circles, while Hannah stood patiently by her side. White Bear tried to but could not keep his eyes off the slave.

His gaze narrowed as the women moved on. He continued to observe Hannah as she went ahead, then stopped near the gate and waited for Slow Dancer to precede her.

She is angry with me. Because he didn't help her with Slow Dancer that first day.

Good! he thought. She could be angry. It didn't matter. It wasn't his place to help her. Slow Dancer would have been furious if he had—and with good reason.

Hannah glanced over and saw him standing near the gathering house. She stiffened. He felt the change in her— the sudden tension—before she abruptly looked away.

White Bear inhaled sharply and slowly released the breath. So she was angry! Good, he told himself. She was nothing . . . a slave.

Why couldn't he stop thinking of her?

Han-na wasn't happy being a slave. But then why should an Iroquois worry about a prisoner? A Seneca did not care if a slave was happy—as long as she did her work. And Han-na did her work.

He—White Bear—had been a Seneca slave once. The cruelty he'd suffered at the hands of Red Dog, father to He-Who-Comes-In-The-Night's father, had made him a true Seneca warrior.

Han-na must learn to accept her place. It was possible that she, too, might learn to be happy within the village. If so inclined, Slow Dancer could make Han-na her adopted daughter instead of her slave.

White Bear didn't know why he should allow her to concern him.

She doesn't. He decided that the feeling would fade with the memory of his English past.

And then Han-na gave him another look before she hurried through the gate toward the fields. Her expression held no anger, but a blankness that bothered him more than her fury did. She looked . . . as if she'd given up and no longer cared about her life one way or another.

Everything within White Bear stilled. He'd seen the same look on a slave, and he'd not lived long afterward.

He didn't care; he couldn't care. White Bear tried to close his mind to the woman as he headed toward his longhouse, but the image of her last look continued to disturb him long after she'd left the village.

Chapter 7

He stepped off the ship in Philadelphia and searched the quay for a familiar face. The man didn't expect to see her, but he had hoped. He cursed as someone jostled him from behind.

"Move out of the way, you fool!" the offender exclaimed as the man stumbled and righted himself, putting himself in another's path.

"If your brains be in your head instead of your arse, you'd have given me a moment to get out of the blasted way!" he shouted back.

The man raised a hand to the left side of his face, rubbing the red, raised scar that cut across his cheek and ran into his hairline. The area was rough, a constant reminder of the pain he'd suffered because of Hannah. His eyes burned with hatred as he tried to soothe away the painful memory, but was unsuccessful. The worst of the injury was not the pain so much as the unsightly red puckered skin, the result of stitching up the jagged cut the bitch had given him.

"I'll find ya, my dear," he vowed. "You'll wish you'd

been nice to Samuel. You'll wish you hadn't done this."
He fingered his scar, his face turning red with the memory.
"I woulda been good to you. Now you've left me no choice
but to kill ya . . ."

Someone hit him in the back, and he dropped his satchel
and spun, his features contorted with rage, his fists raised
to strike.

"Sorry, mate!" the young sailor said. He looked to be
a young lad of fifteen. He didn't wait for the man's
response, but continued on his way, struggling to carry a
wooden trunk by himself.

The man growled, but managed to get his fury under
control. "Watch the bloody hell where yer going!" he
bellowed at the boy's back. Now his face *and his back* hurt.
He picked up his satchel and eyed the line of buildings
along the road ahead. He saw a shipping office and decided
he would start to look there.

A wagon lumbered along the cobblestone street, cutting
off his path, making him jump back to avoid being hit.
With a muttered oath at the driver and the American
colonies in general, Samuel Walpole left the dock area to
begin his search for his stepdaughter.

She hated the village. The air was dry and dusty with
the dirt from the common yard, and the bugs were terrible,
much worse than when she and Boucher had been on the
trail. Inside the longhouse, it was dark, smoky, and too
hot. But what Hannah detested most was the Indian who
had traded for her, He-Who-Comes-In-The-Night, her master's husband. He was forever ordering her to fetch and
carry for him, and Slow Dancer wasn't happy with Hannah's continued attention to him. Slow Dancer was a tough
taskmaster; and while she was patient with teaching Hannah some new chore, she seemed to resent Hannah doing
things for her husband.

I don't like it either, Hannah thought with a scowl. *He orders me around, because it pleases him to see me grovel. Slow Dancer doesn't like it, and I can understand why. I've seen the way her husband watches me. I want to cover my legs beneath my tunic, but he'd probably just laugh if I tried, and Slow Dancer would only become more angry with me.*

Inside the longhouse, Hannah grabbed the small basket of green corn and sat down on a woven mat to husk it. The season's corn crop would not be harvested for weeks yet. The few pieces they'd picked were for honoring the spirits during the Festival. There was plenty of stored dried corn from last year: Hannah was to grind the dried corn next.

She studied her fingers as she tugged open the first green ear. Though clean, her nails were jagged and torn below the fingertips. She had a sore on the pad of her index finger from learning to use a fine animal-bone awl to make the holes for stitching deerskin and a cut across the back of her right hand from when she'd slipped and fallen on a slime-covered rock in the shallows of the lake.

The Seneca bathed every day, and Hannah had to admit that she liked the daily ritual, although she was sure in the first weeks she'd sicken and die from the frequent exposure to water and air. When Slow Dancer had first taken her to the lake, Hannah had undressed with the village women and gone into the water, naked, without arguing. Once she'd overcome her initial attack of modesty, she had actually enjoyed herself. The water had soothed and stroked her work-worn, aching body, and the careful laughter of the gathered women had made her smile and forget for a little while that she was an Indian prisoner and a slave. Because she'd been taught at a young age that it was dangerous to bathe too often, Hannah had been hesitant when Slow Dancer had taken her to bathe the following day. But she'd gone into the water, spurred on by a sharp word from her master along with strong, disapproving looks cast her way from the women. She'd scurried into the lake, despite her fears. The water had been warm, but she'd shivered as she ducked below the surface, so convinced was she that she'd be ill come the next morning after washing twice within twenty-four hours.

When she'd suffered no ill effects the next day, Hannah had gone willingly—and quite happily—when the time came for the women to congregate at the lake. She'd bathed daily with the women ever since, but their time there seemed hurried now, not leisurely—and she wished that they would linger longer.

The lake wasn't cold, but it would be when the seasons changed and the chill of the winter set in. She wondered what the Indians did then, just as she was curious about the men's bathing habits. Did they bathe individually and meet at the lake as a group, like the women?

With her thoughts of the men came a sharp mental image of White Bear naked, the water lapping against his thighs, and Hannah's mouth went dry. She tried to banish the vision, but it lingered to taunt her, reminding her that she was a woman with a woman's feelings, a woman's desire . . . and she had seen a beautifully formed man without clothes.

She bit her lip and tried to force him from her mind, concentrating instead on the job before her. She tried not to think of White Bear's expression as he soothed her fears . . . his glowing eyes as their naked bodies brushed in the water. Her breasts tingled with the memory. She'd been unable to forget how he'd held and comforted her, unable to forget her startling physical reaction to him once she knew that his intentions were not to hurt or to force her.

Hannah heard a man's voice, and her gaze searched the longhouse for its source. Her breath caught until she saw the brave. He was speaking to a young boy from the family that shared its cooking fire with Moon Woman. The warrior's hair was dark; he was built differently than White Bear. She breathed easier.

Shaken by her thoughts of the blond brave, Hannah forced her attention back to the corn. She peeled back the husks of several very young ears, exposing the rich, full kernels, leaving the greens attached, then braiding the ends as Slow Dancer had taught her. When she was finished, she stacked the ears in a neat pile and rose to get a mortar and pestle made of stone. There was a pile of dried corn waiting to be cracked for corn cakes and hominy. Using a sliver of sharp flint, she scraped the corn from the cob into a basket. She then dumped some kernels into the small stone bowl and set about grinding them into a fine flour.

She was alone in the cubicle. Slow Dancer was visiting with a matron at the far end of the longhouse. He-Who-Comes-In-The-Night had left that morning on a hunt, and Running Brook, the couple's son, was out in the yard with the other young boys in the village. Slow Dancer had only one child of her body, but the women regarded all children as their own.

Hearing Moon Woman's voice, Hannah saw the matron across the way, talking with another clan member. In the two weeks that she'd been with the Indians, she'd learned a great deal from Moon Woman about their ways. Moon Woman was head matron of the longhouse, which housed the women of the clan of the Deer and their families. A clan member could not marry another, because they were family. There were eight clans among the Seneca, all named after animals—Bear, Beaver, Hawk, Snipe, Turtle, Deer, Wolf, and Heron. Of the eight, there were four sets of two clans who were too closely related for marriage. A Wolf clansman could not marry a member of the Deer, and while a Wolf could marry a Bear, a Bear couldn't marry a Snipe, because the Bear and Snipe were of the same division and kin to each other.

Moon Woman, Slow Dancer, and the other women in the longhouse were of the clan of the Deer. He-Who-Comes-In-The-Night, Slow Dancer's husband, was of the Snipe clan. After marriage, a brave moved into in the longhouse of his wife's clan. Above the door of each longhouse, which housed up to twenty families depending on its size, hung a symbol of the clan. A carving of a deer hung above the door of the longhouse where Hannah lived, proclaiming that the house belonged to the women of the *Na-o-geh,* the Deer clan.

Hannah had been amazed to discover that the house, fields, and household equipment belonged to the village women. After marriage, a man came to his wife's longhouse with only the clothes on his back, weapons fashioned by his own hands, and a few meager personal items. As long as the marriage existed, he lived in the longhouse and his wife took care of him.

Despite the fact that she tended to her husband and children's daily needs, and worked, planted, and harvested the fields, a Seneca woman's life was no more difficult than an Englishwoman's, Hannah decided. A matron had much influence over the men. Although she didn't actually govern, she could sway the governing men's opinion with a look or a private word ... and in some cases, Hannah learned, by withholding food from their men when their inability to see reason made them difficult.

She was dismayed when her thoughts turned again, as they had way too often of late, to White Bear and the woman who'd been his wife. Her curiosity had made her bold with Moon Woman, asking questions when she probably shouldn't have. White Bear's wife, Hannah learned, had been the daughter of the sachem, Man with Eyes of Hawk, thus making her Moon Woman's niece, although Hannah doubted that the Indians actually regarded relationships in that way. She didn't know the name of White Bear's late wife; even Moon Woman had refused to tell

her. The matron did explain that because the woman was
dead, her name would not be spoken by her people out
of respect for her and the tender feelings of her family
and friends, who, after the period of mourning, although
joyful that she was happy in the house of the Great Spirit,
continued secretly to harbor a feeling of loss. What was
she like, this woman who had captured White Bear's heart?
Was she beautiful and kind? Did she love him with a passion
equal to a man who, in his grief, had looked at no other?

She closed her eyes to see White Bear's face . . . his
muscled body, which made her flush with heat and sent
her heart racing whenever she happened to see him.

What would it be like to have a man like that hold her?
Love her above all else? There was a look about White
Bear that bespoke the pain he'd suffered because of his
wife's death. Hannah knew that after his wife's death White
Bear had disappeared from the village for a time, returning
to his people after several long months a changed man.
In leaving, he'd left behind an infant son, Eagle Soaring.
She recalled the young boy who'd spoken English to her
on the trail. Hannah understood now why the child hung
on to White Bear's every word, following the brave like a
puppy trailing after its adored master.

Hannah understood how Eagle Soaring felt. There was
something about White Bear that drew one's attention.
Something in his eyes that made her want to know his
thoughts. She had to stop thinking about him! He didn't
speak with her, barely looked at her, yet he was fast becoming an obsession with her.

And he had a child, although it seemed to her that
White Bear and son were not at ease as other braves were
with their sons . . . like He-Who-Comes-In-The-Night and
his son, Running Brook. If nothing else, she'd been able
to observe Indian relationships. As a people, the Seneca
were generous to the villagers, and she decided that as a
people they were generous to their own, especially their

young. Parents never punished their children by hitting. Hannah thought that at times they were too lenient with them. When she'd mentioned her observation to Moon Woman, the matron had confirmed that none of the Seneca—or any of the other six Iroquois nations—believed in striking their children—or hurting them physically. They shamed them instead, using embarrassment to humiliate them in front of their friends and other family members, in the hopes that the ridicule would discipline the child in a way that would prevent a repeat of their crime. This method of child-rearing continued to amaze Hannah, who had heard, but not yet seen, the cruel tortures that the Indians inflicted on their captives. It seemed a direct contradiction in a people's behavior to tear out the fingernails of a prisoner yet see the horror of spanking a recalcitrant child.

When she expressed her feelings to the matron, Moon Woman had explained to her that an Indian's greatest shame was to be humiliated in front of others. She told Hannah of a young girl who'd been so shamed by her mother for sneaking out of the longhouse at night to meet up with a young Indian brave, who was forbidden to her. Moon Woman described how she was verbally berated in front of her fellow villagers and had been so despondent afterward that she'd taken her own life by drinking hemlock water.

Hannah had been appalled by the story. But she understood then how some punishments might be more effective than others. From the wild behavior of some of the young Seneca boys, she decided that there was very little that Indian parents didn't tolerate in their children. . . .

Remembering the way Moon Woman had tried to reassure her that the Iroquois way was best, Hannah smiled as she continued to shuck corn. Moon Woman was a kind matron; she'd been unfailingly patient in answering a slave's questions. From the astonished look on some of the women's faces, Hannah realized that it wasn't common practice to explain their ways to a slave.

As she continued her conversation with Walks-In-Circles, Moon Woman glanced over, caught Hannah's gaze, and gave a barely perceptible nod in greeting.

"Why do you bother with the white woman?" Walks-In-Circles said to the matron after she'd followed the direction of Moon Woman's gaze.

"Bother?" Moon Woman asked, searching the woman's eyes. "It is no bother to answer a few questions."

"But she is slave."

"Because Slow Dancer has not yet decided whether or not to take her as daughter."

Walks-In-Circles snorted. "The *Yen'gees* will remain a slave. Slow Dancer does not like the way He-Who-Comes-In-The-Night follows her with his eyes."

"Night is not the only one who watches Han-na," Moon Woman said. She knew she could speak freely to this woman, who was not only her kin but her friend.

The other woman's gaze sharpened. "Who?" she said tightly, perhaps thinking of her own spouse, Marked Arm.

"The one who once was once among the *Yen'gees.*"

"White Bear?"

Moon Woman, understanding the woman's astonishment, only smiled.

"This cannot be true. White Bear has not—"

"Looked at another since," the head matron finished for her. She flashed the white woman a glance. "She is not displeasing for a white woman. White Bear has been alone for a long time now. It is only natural that he will want a woman to warm his sleeping platform."

"But she is a slave!" Walks-in-Circles exclaimed.

Moon Woman nodded. "And he will not touch her while she is slave."

Walks-In-Circles made a sound of satisfaction. "As is

right." She studied the white female and found her lacking. "You believe that Bear finds this woman attractive?"

Moon Woman shrugged. "I did not say that . . . only that he watches her, but it may be that he is remembering another place, another time, when he lived another life."

"Ah-h-h." Walks-In-Circles could understand that. She remembered a time when she was young when the winter snow had fallen so high that she and her family had been confined to the longhouse. It had been a time for stories as they had sat around the cooking fire. It had been a good time until the days had become many and the food supply had dwindled. The men of the village could not hunt for meat. The storm had raged on, and the cold had seeped past the bark walls of the longhouse, and her family had huddled together wrapped in several layers of furs. They had been forced to conserve wood so that it lasted until the snow had stopped. Walks-In-Circles considered it to have been the best and the worst time in her life. She imagined White Bear saw his memory of the *Yen'gees* as a time much like that terrible winter.

As if their conversation had conjured up the man, White Bear entered their longhouse. His gaze swept the interior in his search for someone, and having spied Moon Woman, he immediately approached her.

"White Bear," Moon Woman greeted, having sensed a strange tension within the warrior after he'd seen the white woman in Slow Dancer's cubicle across the corridor. "You have need of me?"

The brave nodded, but seemed distracted, and Moon Woman saw him glance briefly across the way.

Moon Woman recognized that White Bear seemed disturbed about something. "What is it, Bear?" she asked gently.

"I wish to seek your advice and assistance."

Walks-In-Circles made a sound of surprise, drawing the brave's attention.

The head matron flashed the woman a look and motioned to White Bear to follow her to her living area. "I will speak with you where we may sit." When they were inside her cubicle alone, Moon Woman offered him a smile of encouragement. "Is something troubling you?" she asked.

White Bear flinched, as if startled to find himself here in Moon Woman's longhouse, asking for help. "I am worried about Eagle Soaring," he said.

The matron tensed. "Is he ill?" Her tone was sharp with concern.

He was quick to assure her that his son was physically fine. "But I feel as if I should not have taken him from the house of his grandmother."

Moon Woman frowned. "You wish to send him back?"

"No," he said, recalling a certain dream in which his wife had come to him and demanded to know why he ignored their son.

"White Bear, I do not understand then. What is it that concerns you? What do you want?"

"I want to trade for the slave Han-na." There, he had said it. Until he'd actually done so, he'd had no idea how determined he was to bring her into his lodge. He tried to gauge Moon Woman's reaction, but whatever the matron was feeling after his pronouncement, she wasn't letting on. He quickly went on to explain. "I have had a wife, and I will take no other, for I will not love another in this life. I have taken Eagle Soaring from a house of women. I need someone in my lodge who can prepare my deer and cook our corn. I need one who knows the way of our women, but who will not makes the demands of a wife."

Moon Woman's raised eyebrow, the first sign of a reaction since he'd made his desire known, made his face heat. "And what are these demands?" she asked somewhat crisply.

"I cannot love where there is only emptiness. I cannot give that which is not in me to give."

The matron's expression softened. "You are lonely."

His whole body seemed to jerk. "No," he denied, wondering if it were true. "I have Eagle Soaring. I am not lonely. I am simply in need of a slave."

"And you want Han-na," she said with a thoughtful look.

His heart tripped at the woman's choice of words. "I have seen how hard the white woman works, while Slow Dancer works little." He stared for a moment at the dirt floor. "I have more need of the slave than Slow Dancer."

Moon Woman frowned. "And what is it you want of me?"

White Bear shifted uncomfortably. "I would have you approach Slow Dancer with my offer. Night will not want me to trade for the slave. Slow Dancer will agree if you speak with her."

He waited with stilled breath for Moon Woman's response. He wanted the slave. She would be good for Eagle Soaring. He needed a woman within the lodge. White Bear knew it was wrong to live apart in a small house of his own, but until he'd taken Eagle Soaring, he had wanted to mourn his loss alone, away from the others within the longhouse. Although it was unusual for a Seneca other than a sachem or shaman to live alone, he had been allowed to live in a small bark hut of a size much like the sachem's. He'd known that he should have moved into the house of his clan after Eagle Soaring had come to live with him, but he still hadn't been ready . . . and he wasn't so yet.

"You want the slave Han-na," Moon Woman murmured, as if trying to absorb what he'd said.

He nodded. "Will you help me?"

*   *   *

Dear God, he's in the longhouse, Hannah thought. Her senses grew alert to his presence. White Bear hadn't visited since her first day, and the memory of that time alternately gave her pleasure and made her angry.

She'd seen him about the village; it would have been hard not to notice White Bear's golden color against the darker complexions of the other Seneca. He lived with his son in a small structure hidden behind the longhouse of the Bear clan. Hannah had discovered his residence quite by accident when she'd gone to the longhouse for Slow Dancer. As she'd exited the house of the Bear, she'd happened to catch a glimpse of White Bear's golden hair. Curious, she followed him, reaching the back of the building in time to see him disappear inside a small hut. Hannah had wanted to approach, to talk with him, but she'd resisted the urge and returned to her master.

What is White Bear doing here? she wondered. Then she saw that he went with Moon Woman. What did he want with the matron?

Should she walk down for a distance and see?

Drawn by curiosity, Hannah set down an ear of corn, rose, and moved on trembling legs into the central corridor for a better view. Anticipation made her heart beat faster. Her gaze searched the direction White Bear and Moon Woman had gone, but she didn't see them. A quick look in the opposite direction assured Hannah that Slow Dancer was still visiting. She searched for an excuse to leave the cubicle and found it in a piece of deerskin, partially embroidered and cut for a moccasin. *I can ask Moon Woman for advice on the quillwork,* she thought. She could say that she needed help, because she'd had difficulty interpreting Slow Dancer's directions.

She experienced a tingling along her spine as she headed slowly down the corridor toward Moon Woman's living area, her thoughts on White Bear and how he would receive her. White Bear was leaving just as she neared the cubicle. A jolt of sensation shot through her as she spied him. When he caught sight of her, Hannah froze, and then her heart started to pump harder.

He stared at her as if unable to look away. Hannah returned his gaze, caught, her nerve endings humming with life, as she wondered what to do, to say.

"White Bear," she murmured in greeting.

He nodded abruptly. His glistening blue eyes continued to hold her captive. Then, he broke the contact, and something within Hannah objected when he turned to leave. It took Hannah a moment to react. She hurried after him. White Bear was in the storage area of the longhouse before she caught up to him.

"White Bear!"

The brave stilled, then spun slowly to meet her gaze. She approached the remaining few feet, clutching the deerskin to her breast, aware of the thundering within her chest. "You are well?" she dared to ask. As a slave she had no right to talk with him, but she didn't care.

A strange look passed over his features. "I am well," he said softly. After a moment's hesitation, he asked, "Slow Dancer—she is treating you fairly?"

Hannah nodded, unable to speak, startled by this sudden new awareness of him.

He frowned. "And Night? How does he treat you?"

At the mention of her master's husband, Hannah looked away. "He is Slow Dancer's husband. He is ... not ... unkind," she said after some hesitation.

His hand shot out to grab her arm. "Has he hurt you?" he asked curtly.

She gasped. "No! No, I am unharmed." She glanced up, saw the scowl on his face, and her pulse raced while her mind struggled to assimilate the reason for his outburst. Hannah recognized that the emotion simmering in his blue eyes was concern. For her. Her heart leapt with joy that he cared enough to be angry. "I am all right," she said softly, assuring him with a smile.

His grip was warm and firm, creating a thrumming within her, a heat that made her long to burrow against him and feel the strength of his arms. She was shocked by how much she wanted to be held by him, to experience the tender passion of his kiss. "No," she whispered in denial. She shivered at the strange, wild, pleasurable sensations within her body created by the thought of being in his arms. She fought to break free from the illusion.

"Han-na?" He was frowning. He transferred his hold to her shoulders.

"I-I'm fine."

He looked disbelieving.

"Night forces me to work . . ." she admitted to him, "but he hasn't hit me since we came to the village."

His hands squeezed her lightly before he released her. Hannah sensed a lessening of the tension within him.

"And Running Brook?" he asked, his voice soft.

Hannah's lips firmed at the mention of Night's son. He was much like his father—who reminded her of a strutting cock displaying his plumage. While Night was arrogant and sly, Running Brook was downright cruel—not only to Hannah but to his own mother. When his father was near, the boy was subtle in his behavior to his mother, not openly hostile. But when Night was gone, Running Brook did things to cause his mother concern, things that often resulted in more work for his mother and the slave. Hannah had not given the child the satisfaction of knowing that his behavior bothered her.

"You do not need to answer," White Bear said. "I can tell by your eyes that Running Brook is being Running Brook." He shook his head. "It is not this Seneca's place to correct him, but I would if it were. I fear that the boy is one who will never understand what is right."

Hannah smiled. "Then I'm not the only one who thinks he's impossible?"

White Bear raised both eyebrows. "Impossible." He grinned. "Yes, Running Brook is impossible, and you're not the only one who knows this. Even Slow Dancer sees this, but she is reluctant to change him."

A question had been niggling at the back of her mind for some time. Hannah decided to ask it. "Night doesn't like you, does he?" She bit her lip, wondering if she'd gone too far.

"No."

"Yet Slow Dancer likes you."

"This is so."

She inhaled sharply. "I don't understand."

White Bear looked away, as if unwilling to explain. "When I came to the Seneca, I was a slave. Now I am a warrior son. Night doesn't like it."

Hannah sensed that there was more that he wasn't saying. "White Bear—"

He met her gaze again with unwavering blue eyes. "To him, I am still a *Yen'gees* who married the sachem's daughter. Night wanted my wife since they were very young, but she would not look at him." With that revelation, he spun and exited the longhouse. Hannah wanted to go to him, to ask more, but she heard Slow Dancer calling her.

Hannah experienced a dart of jealousy for White Bear's wife, and then was angry for being envious of someone who was dead. What right did she have to be jealous? There was nothing between her and White Bear. Nothing at all!

But she wondered if that was true as she went back to the cubicle, where she found Slow Dancer waiting for her with a great deal of impatience.

Hannah held up the buckskin. "I would learn more about making moccasins," she said in halting Seneca. "I finished cracking the corn."

Slow Dancer snorted. "You knew where I was. Why didn't you come for me?"

"I was in the storage room, looking for porcupine quills for the moccasins," Hannah said slowly, carefully, hoping that the matron wouldn't guess that she lied. The Indians dyed porcupine quills and stitched them on their moccasins to form various beautiful designs.

"Did you find them?" Slow Dancer asked.

Hannah shook her head. "No," she admitted.

"Then it is good that I have some red quills for you to use." She eyed the pile of young corn with satisfaction, before her glance lit on the half-filled bowl of corn flour. "You have not ground all the corn."

"Oh, I didn't!" Hannah pretended to be surprised. "I thought I had. I'll finish it now."

Slow Dancer's face softened. "You may crack the corn for flour later. I will get the quills for you, and then you will learn how to sew them onto moccasins."

Relief that her story had been accepted made Hannah weak . . . until she happened to glance toward the lodge of Walks-In-Circles to find the Indian woman studying her through narrowed eyes filled with suspicion.

"Well, what did the brave want?" Walks-In-Circles asked when Moon Woman had returned.

"He wants a slave." The matron hesitated. "Han-na."

Walks-In-Circles made a disapproving sound. "This isn't good. She belongs to Slow Dancer. It's not right that White Bear claims her as his own—even if he was with Night when the Frenchman gave her away."

"No," Moon Woman said. "He wants to trade for her."

The younger matron was surprised. "He wants to buy the slave? Not claim her?"

Moon Woman nodded.

"Why?"

"To have someone to cook and work for him and Eagle Soaring, he says."

Walks-In-Circles sniffed. "Eagle Soaring belongs in the house of his mother's people—the Beaver clan."

"Woman with Dark Skin has allowed White Bear to take his son into his own lodge. It is her choice, and we are not to question it."

The sharpness of Moon Woman's reply took the young woman aback. It was rare that the head matron scolded her sisters and daughters. Walks-In-Circles felt the sting severely.

"You are right," she whispered.

Moon Woman placed a gentle hand on the other matron's shoulder. "I understand your concern, but it is a matter for my brother and his wife . . . and White Bear and his son."

In answer, the Indian woman inclined her head. But then her gaze flickered with curiosity. "Why did White Bear come to you?"

"He wants me to help him."

Walks-In-Circles gasped. "To win the slave?" Her tone reflected her astonishment.

"Yes."

"And will you help him?"

Moon Woman understood Walks-In-Circles' confusion, for she was feeling it herself. She took a breath and released it slowly, while she glanced briefly into the cubicle across the way. Hannah was there with Slow Dancer, but it was only moments before that Moon Woman had seen White Bear with the slave. Earlier, while speaking with White Bear, she'd thought she'd learned the reason for his continued interest in the slave. But after seeing them together, deep in conversation, their bodies telling more than their words, Moon Woman had begun to wonder if her own previous suspicion about White Bear's desire for the woman was well founded.

"I have told him I will," she said. The matron worried whether she'd made the right decision. For a brave to want a slave for his sleeping mat was a foolish one. *And a slave who longs for a warrior husband will know only the pain of being a slave. There can be no love between them.*

While Moon Woman wanted nothing more than to see White Bear with a new wife, she didn't want it to be the white woman.

"I have had a wife and I will take no other," White Bear had said.

Moon Woman frowned with concern. She could only hope that there was truth in White Bear's words. If not, there could only be heartache ahead for them.

Chapter 8

Something was occurring within the longhouse. Hannah didn't know what, but she felt the tension simmering among the members of the Deer clan. Slow Dancer had been quiet. Her husband glared at Hannah from time to time and seemed unusually subdued, while their son Running Brook acted as perplexed as Hannah felt. But when the other Indians began to cast her frequent, speculative looks, Hannah became afraid.

What's happening? she thought. Hannah had been a captive of the Seneca for weeks now. Since her captivity among the Seneca, she'd settled in, forgetting the English-told tales of horror and Iroquois torture with her adjustment to daily life. She'd seen the people celebrate the Berry Festival, in which they gave thanks to their god for nature's gift of wild berries. It was a different side to the Iroquois, a side that English soldiers and fur traders had not seen. The Indians had danced, made speeches, and enjoyed a feast of sweetened berries in celebration of their thanks. Despite her work in the preparation of the feast, Hannah had enjoyed being an observer. She'd come to accept and respect that the Indians had their own special order of life. She felt she knew enough about the Indians to recognize a change in their mood.

She was uneasy as she went about her daily chores. Her position these last weeks had given her a certain sense of freedom; she could move about the compound freely on one errand or another without a Seneca warrior or matron following her every footstep. She'd been in the village long enough for the Indians to have accepted her presence. They'd no longer eyed her with curiosity or unconcealed contempt. She belonged to Slow Dancer, and because she obeyed her master, she was acknowledged a slave—and thus mainly ignored.

And then yesterday everything had changed. Whether she walked across the yard to bring a basket of beans to the sachem's house or followed Slow Dancer to the lake for their daily bath, Hannah was conscious that wherever she went, she was the object of intense study that had forced her to assume she was at the root of this strange, new tension.

But why? What had she done?

Even the children paused in their game-playing to eye the white slave.

"Han-na." Moon Woman's voice interrupted her musings.

The Englishwoman glanced up from the mat she was weaving and, seeing the matron, set the work aside, and scrambled to her feet. "Moon Woman!" she exclaimed.

The matron's solemn expression did not allay Hannah's fears. "Come, Han-na." She turned abruptly, as if expecting her command to be obeyed, and Hannah's uneasiness became real fear.

Hannah wanted to ask Moon Woman where she was going, but the obvious change in the woman's manner discouraged any questions.

When she saw that they were headed to the lodge of the sachem, she was unable to keep silent. "Moon Woman, where are we going?" she asked. "Have I done something wrong?" Fear made her voice tremble.

The matron paused and looked back, her expression softening when she saw Hannah's concern. "You have done nothing wrong," she said, and continued on without waiting for Hannah's response.

But then why have I been summoned by the sachem? Has Slow Dancer decided that she doesn't want her slave? She felt a constriction in her throat. She recalled something Moon Woman had once told her. That it was up to the new master to choose the captive's fate. Slow Dancer had been quiet, uncommunicative; she'd been unhappy with her husband's attention to Hannah.

Dear God, has she decided to have me killed?

It was dark within the sachem's lodge; Hannah blinked to adjust her eyesight. Man with Eyes of Hawk sat on his mat, puffing on his pipe, while White Bear sat to his left. The blond Indian wore a silver armband about his corded right arm, drawing her gaze for a brief moment to the muscle beneath the circlet. She swallowed and raised her gaze.

Hannah experienced a flutter in her stomach when she encountered the blond Indian's blue eyes. He stared at her, seeming to read her soul, and she felt the quickening of her pulse.

What is he doing here? Why have I been brought before them? She searched White Bear's expression before turning her attention to the sachem. Man with Eyes of Hawk's eyes narrowed as he studied her. He said something in Seneca too rapidly for Hannah to understand. White Bear nodded, his reply too soft for Hannah's ears.

Moon Woman exited the hut, then returned moments later with a waterskin. As the matron began to pour out cupfuls for the two men, the sachem waved Hannah to sit down.

"You have been slave to Slow Dancer," the man said. Hannah nodded. "Now you will belong to another."

Hannah felt a jolt. "Another?" she whispered.

Man with Eyes of Hawk inclined his head.

The knot in her belly tightened. "Who?"

"I have traded with Slow Dancer."

Surprise made her speechless. "You, White Bear?"

"White Bear has need of a slave to cook and work for him and his son."

Disappointment made her tense up. "I see."

"You will go and get your things," Hannah vaguely heard Man with Eyes of Hawk say. "Then you will go to White Bear. You will work and live in his lodge. You will help his son."

"I have no things to get," she said. She felt numb, uncertain. A strange tingling of pleasure started at her nape and radiated lower. She would be living with White Bear. The realization that she'd be sleeping under White Bear's roof, eating his food, and caring for his belongings made her giddy with nervous excitement.

White Bear rose lithely to his feet, drawing Hannah's attention to his chest and stomach . . . and finally his leg muscles beneath his loincloth.

Sensing Moon Woman's regard, Hannah looked away from her new master. *Master.* Just the thought of the term with White Bear and all that it implied made Hannah's breath quicken with anticipation.

Her gaze settled on the head matron of the Deer clan, then skittered away from Moon Woman's intent look. She could tell in that quick second that Moon Woman was concerned with the new arrangement. And Hannah sensed that there was something else bothering Moon Woman. The Englishwoman wasn't sure she really wanted to know.

"Come." White Bear moved toward the door, passing

her as he went. He was close, too close, and Hannah wondered if her awareness of him would lessen with time together under one roof.

Hannah started to follow him.

"Han-na."

She paused and looked at the sachem. "White Bear has paid highly for you. Obey him."

Her head swam as she nodded.

Sensing the disapproval hidden beneath Moon Woman's shuttered expression, Hannah showed her bewilderment as she held on to the woman's gaze.

The matron looked at her a long moment and then her lips formed a smile that erased the disapproval and offered her encouragement.

Hannah returned the smile hesitantly, then responded to White Bear's unemotional command to follow.

Outside the bright summer sun seemed to mock Hannah's misgivings while mirroring the joy of having an English-speaking master. Or was it the joy in knowing that it was White Bear and no one else who had wanted her enough to pay a high price.

He was silent as they crossed the compound, skirted the longhouse, and approached the man's lodge. The tension within Hannah mounted as she waited for him to speak.

White Bear held up the deerskin flap and motioned for her to enter. Hannah's skin tingled as she brushed by him and moved inside. The hut was like a miniature square longhouse, but the size of one cubicle. A sleeping shelf had been built on three walls, each with a separate platform for storage above, much like in the larger longhouses, except that in the multifamily dwellings the sleeping platforms were on the back wall only. A pile of thick fur pelts lay upon each sleeping shelf. The storage area held cooking supplies, spare clothing, and tools. In the middle of the structure was the fire pit, where the fire had been banked to preserve the hot embers. On the bed built into the right wall lay a bow and a small quiver of arrows. Under the platform, there was a child's pair of moccasins.

As White Bear dropped the door flap, the house fell into a semidarkness, which created an immediate sense of intimacy inside. Hannah had moved to the other side of the fire and was taking note of the supplies stored above. She felt the brave's approach in the sudden prickle of awareness at her nape and behind her knees.

"I will not treat you unkindly." The deep vibration of White Bear's masculine tones caused a riot within her senses. His blue eyes seemed to glisten in the darkness when she turned to meet his gaze.

"I know," she said softly.

"Eagle Soaring, my son . . . He does not know you are here yet." He seemed to hesitate, as if unwilling to continue. "He is a good boy."

Hannah smiled. "I know. I've seen him about the village. He's not mean like Running Brook, and he doesn't try to act tough like Small Mouth." Her lips quirked, although she tried to hide her amusement. She still couldn't get used to some of the Seneca names. Her gaze intensified as she studied her new master. White Bear. She wondered how it was that he'd gotten his Indian name.

White Bear reached past her toward the storage shelf, tugging down a folded garment made of soft deerskin. "You may have this. Soon, when the leaves fall from the trees, the air will become cold until you can see the mist of one's breath. These leggings will keep you warm when the snow blankets the forest." He held the offering out to her.

Hannah accepted the deerskin and saw that there were indeed two legging pieces that would cover her from thigh to ankle. By his behavior she realized that the brave felt as awkward about their new relationship as she did, as it was still too early to be thinking of the winter months.

The door flap was lifted with a sudden flurry of motion

as White Bear's son barreled into the lodge. He stopped short at the sight of Hannah.

"Father," he said, "what is *she* doing here?"

"She is here to help us," White Bear said.

"Then it is true? You have bought the slave?"

White Bear flashed Hannah a look. "It is so."

Eagle Soaring studied the white woman from beneath lowered eyelids. "I don't want her here."

Hannah had had trouble following their conversation, but she did understand when the boy objected to her presence. She tensed, wondering if White Bear would send her back to Slow Dancer. "White Bear, if you'd like me to leave."

He held up his hand to her. "Eagle Soaring," he said, "Han-na is a good slave. She will work hard for us. She will grind our corn and cook our food."

The boy firmed his lips and crossed his arms over his chest. "We do not need a slave to cook for us. We eat in my mother's longhouse."

White Bear no longer flinched when Eagle Soaring mentioned his mother, because the young called all of the sisters and matrons of his clan mother or grandmother.

"We can still eat in the house of the Beaver clan, but this is our house, and there are times I wish to take food in my own lodge." White Bear's tone was sharp with irritation.

"But, father—"

"Eagle Soaring," White Bear interrupted, "Han-na is here because I wish it. You will accept her presence."

The child hung his head in the shame of being scolded. "Yes, father."

The brave addressed Hannah in English. "You may look about our lodge to learn where we keep things." He gestured toward the area below the sleeping platform on the left side. "There is ground corn there and beans newly picked. In the barrels, under there, you will find venison and dried corn." He eyed the interior of the house critically. "You will sleep there," he said, pointing toward the sleeping platform on the left. That place is Eagle Soaring's," he said of the opposite bed. "I will sleep there." He would sleep on the center platform. "Come," he said to his son, "get your bow. We will practice for the next hunt."

Eagle Soaring's face brightened as he looked up. At his father's nod, he scurried toward the sleeping platform for his bow and quiver. Hannah, seeing his intent, grabbed them from the bed to pass it to the boy.

"Do not touch them!" he spat in Iroquois. The child scowled at her as he jerked them from her hands.

Hannah was wounded by Eagle Soaring's animosity toward her. She didn't understand it, for the youth had been friendly on the trail. "I'm sorry. I only meant to—"

"Do not touch my things!" the boy hissed in Seneca, and Hannah had trouble following his words.

If he wants me to understand, why doesn't he use English? I know he can speak it. Hannah felt a burning within her breast. *He doesn't want me to feel welcome. For some reason, he resents me, and I don't know why. I'm only a slave.*

Eagle Soaring glared at her and left, his abrupt departure leaving the deerskin swinging behind him.

Alone, Hannah stood in the middle of her new home and eyed her surroundings. *Now what?* She didn't know what White Bear expected from her. He'd said something about corn and venison, she vaguely remembered. *He wants me to cook, but what else? It will be hours before he wants to eat. What am I to do in the meantime?*

She sat down on the sleeping platform that White Bear said would be hers and stared ahead without seeing. If she had thought for a second that her time here would be easier than with Slow Dancer, then she'd been mistaken. Eagle Soaring's behavior told her otherwise.

Hannah sighed and focused her gaze, noting the sleeping arrangements, noting the distance between her bed and those belonging to White Bear and his son. The coming weeks would seem like forever unless she found out a way to get along with the child.

Her thoughts spun as they centered on the father. She still reeled from the realization that a man—White Bear—was her new master . . . and her new master would be sleeping only inches away from her. In the lodge of Slow Dancer, she had slept in the cubicle on the ground by the fire. The sleeping platforms had been used only by family members, not by a slave.

One thing has improved, Hannah thought. She'd not be sleeping on the ground this night. The platform was about eighteen inches off the dirt floor. Cushioned by a soft beaver pelt, her bed would help her to rest comfortably.

I can't just sit here all day. I'd better take stock of White Bear's supplies. Perhaps there is a garment that needs work, although I doubt it. These clothes made of deerskin were well made and durable. Her tunic had worn well with little care.

Memories of when Slow Dancer gave her the garment had her wondering if the woman would ask for the return of the tunic and her moccasins . . . and then what would she wear? She'd have to ask White Bear.

Spying the leggings where they lay on the bed, Hannah felt a wave of warmth that the brave had given them to her. She wouldn't need them until the cooler months, but she appreciated that he'd harbored enough concern for her comfort.

She pushed herself off the bed and began to search through the supplies on the storage shelf. There'd be venison or dried corn in the small barrels stored below her sleeping platform, she knew. She would see what the brave had in the way of cooking implements and what food he needed. Then she would plan her work accordingly.

*   *   *

It was dusk, that time when the sun had vanished, but its glow continued to illuminate the sky. Hannah knelt near the fire pit, stirring the contents of the cooking pot with a paddle. She had made hominy, a mush made of ground corn, sweetened with a dab of maple sugar. The porridge bubbled as it simmered, emitting an aroma that made Hannah's mouth water. It had been early morning since she'd eaten last, and hunger had been gnawing at her belly for some time. The Indians took only two meals, finding sustenance in the communal cooking pot those times in between when they felt hungry. Earlier, Hannah had decided, after getting a glimpse of the unappetizing-appearing stew, that she wasn't so hungry she couldn't wait until the evening meal. She'd had no idea what kind of stew it was, but it had chunks of something she couldn't identify, and she wasn't willing to taste them to find out what they were.

White Bear and Eagle Soaring would be in soon to eat, Hannah thought. Fearing that the hominy would burn, she searched for something to remove the pot from the fire.

She was startled to find a piece of linen rolled into a tight little ball and stashed behind the barrel of stored venison. Hannah tugged the fabric out and saw that it was a man's shirt—an Englishman's shirt. It wasn't large enough to fit White Bear nor was it the small size worn by an eight-year-old boy. Then, she noticed that the fabric was older. When was it that White Bear had come to the Seneca?

Sixteen, she thought. He'd been sixteen or seventeen. Her hands shook as she stared at the shirt. The shirt had belonged to the young White Bear. She tried to imagine him as an English youth with fairer skin and darker hair, before age and the constant exposure to the sun had changed his appearance. She couldn't see the softening of his features, for his appearance now was so rugged, so riveting to the eye that the image of the man filled her mind's eye as soon as she tried to picture the child.

For a long moment, she stood there, holding the shirt, fighting a tangle of emotions that entwined the past of a young English boy with her own. She closed her eyes, seeing disjointed pictures of her past . . . her mixed feelings when her mother had married Samuel Walpole . . . her horror the first time she'd heard her mother cry after her husband's angry abuse . . . her rage when it occurred again and again . . . and her frustration when she couldn't get her mother to listen . . . and leave.

Hannah shuddered and, with her right hand still clutching the linen shirt, hugged herself with her arms as she tried to ward off the chill brought by that last moment within the inn when she'd stared at all the blood surrounding Samuel's head . . . and run.

"Han-na."

She fought to breathe as she struggled to banish the memories . . . and at the same time, she saw glimpses of a young man with blond hair and eyes of the clearest blue . . . eyes that focused upon her and found her wanting. *No!*

"Han-na!" White Bear's deep voice penetrated the fog of horror.

She blinked and came out of the nightmare to stare at the brave as if entranced. "White Bear?"

He nodded as he approached. "What is wrong? Have you hurt yourself?"

Hannah shook her head. Oh, she had hurt herself, but it was injury not to the body but to the soul, and she could find no cure for it. "I was looking for someone to take the pot from the fire." Tightening her fingers about the shirt, she was suddenly very much aware of the garment within her hands.

White Bear glanced down, and the blue of his eyes intensified as he saw what it was she held.

A fine trembling seized her. "I found it behind the barrel," she whispered, pointing toward the area. "I was looking for something—a bit of cloth—anything, and I discovered this." She lifted it up.

The brave snatched it out of her hands. "You should not have touched this."

A burning seared her stomach lining. "I'm sorry. I had no idea what it was . . . I didn't know."

With a grunt, White Bear abruptly gathered the shirt back into a ball and stuffed it back where Hannah had found it. His behavior was odd, and it fed Hannah's curiosity and her desire to know more about this Englishman turned white savage. But his expression wasn't encouraging, so Hannah kept silent, vowing to try to learn more from Moon Woman.

She'd been with White Bear for just under a week now, and while Moon Woman seemed distant during the first couple of days that Hannah had gone to the brave's house, the matron had returned to being more open and friendly toward the slave. Other than the times Hannah gave him food, Eagle Soaring simply ignored her, and his behavior hurt her, because she liked children and wished to befriend the young boy.

Eagle Soaring entered the house, his gaze barely acknowledging Hannah's presence as he took a seat on a mat near the fire where the slave would serve him his meal. His father, apparently recalling Hannah's words, had removed the cooking pot from the fire, setting its cone-shaped bottom into a hole in the dirt floor he must have dug for that purpose. Then he sat on the mat to his son's right. Tension hung in the air within the house, making Hannah feel awkward and a bit shaky as she gathered the bowls for the hominy.

She knelt near the pot and began to ladle out the first

bowlful. The smell of sweetened roasted corn wafted up to her nose as she filled the first bowl and set it before White Bear. His son glared at her as if angry that she didn't serve him first. Ignoring him, she doled out another portion, conscious of the heat of the bowl as it set it in the dirt before Eagle Soaring. When she was done, she rose to get two drinking cups fashioned from a gourd that had been scraped clean and dried, and poured out two cupfuls of clear, fresh water that she'd collected from the lake that afternoon and carried in a bag of tanned deerskin. It was only after she'd served father and son their water that Hannah returned to the pot to dish out her own meal.

Hannah had dipped the ladle into the porridge when Eagle Soaring choked, then suddenly spat out his food. Startled, she dropped the utensil into the pot.

"You are all right?" White Bear asked his son.

"Yes, father," the child said politely, but then he shot Hannah a look of anger that accused the slave of having done something to the hominy to make it stick in his throat.

Hannah's eyes burned as she looked away. It wasn't the first time she'd been treated this way by the boy, but never after having suffered the anger of White Bear. A full week and it seemed that things were never going to change. Hannah had cooked and kept the lodge in good order, but the boy hadn't softened in his attitude, and now White Bear was angry, because she'd discovered something he'd wanted to keep hidden.

Then why didn't you just get rid of the shirt if it brings you pain? she thought defiantly.

She reached in to retrieve the ladle and inadvertently bumped her hand on the side of the hot clay pot, burning her wrist as she did so. With a gasp, she withdrew her hand and rose, studying the tender area to see how bad the burn was.

Suddenly, White Bear was standing beside her, taking

hold of her arm so that he could see the damage. His touch was gentle. Her skin tingled. Studying his bent head, she forgot her injury in enjoyment of his concern for her.

White Bear's breath hissed out as he examined her tender flesh. His blue eyes were warm as he met her gaze. Hannah trembled.

"You have much pain?" he asked huskily, all traces of his anger toward her gone. Instead, he regarded her with a caring that triggered a thundering within her breast and made her face flush with heat.

"I'm—a little," she amended, looking away from his beautiful blue eyes.

"Sit," he told her, gently pressing her to obey.

Hannah sat, conscious of Eagle Soaring's discontent. She glanced at the boy to see him staring toward her hand, and she held it up for his inspection. The child narrowed his gaze, firmed his mouth as if the wound was of no consequence, and diverted his attention back to his food.

White Bear was fumbling on the shelf behind her, but she didn't look back. A few seconds later, having found what he'd been searching for, he sat down beside her and picked up her arm, turning it before placing it in his lap with the burned area of her skin upward. Heat suffused Hannah from head to toe as she sensed White Bear's regard, but she refused to meet his gaze, afraid of what she'd see—or of what he'd see in her expression.

"The skin will heal," he said to her in English. "I have some medicine for the burn. It will hurt as I administer it, but will feel better soon afterward."

She nodded, then said, "Thank you."

He opened a small pouch and dipped his finger inside, withdrawing some unknown substance, which he then spread on the burn with the lightest touch. She could feel his breath against her skin as he worked, the gentleness of his finger as he smoothed the paste over the entire area of the burn and a bit of the surrounding skin. The back of her arm warmed where it lay across his thigh. She could feel the smoothness of his skin and envision the power of the taut leg muscle. She suddenly had trouble breathing. The constriction within her chest eased when White Bear released her arm and rose to put away the medicine.

Hannah felt a tingling where only moments before his fingers had held her.

Throughout White Bear's ministrations, Eagle Soaring had continued to eat as if nothing had happened. He was done well before Hannah had a chance to dish out her own bowlful. The boy thrust his bowl in her direction as if demanding a second helping, and Hannah looked at it a moment before taking it with her left hand—the one that she hadn't injured. She started to rise to serve the child another helping, knowing that her refusal wouldn't help to endear her to the boy, but White Bear was behind her, forcing her to remain seated.

"You will wait until Han-na has eaten before you ask for another," White Bear scolded his son in Iroquoian, but the child knew that Hannah had understood, which didn't help matters any. "Han-na has hurt herself. It isn't right that you continue to eat like her pain means nothing."

Which, of course, it didn't to Eagle Soaring, Hannah knew.

When, seconds later, he placed a filled bowl before her, Hannah realized that White Bear had been getting her meal for her as he spoke. His caring made her eyes water at the same time Eagle Soaring's barely concealed fury made her heart bleed.

"You must eat, Han-na," White Bear addressed her again in English, which was odd because he rarely did, using only Seneca since she'd become his slave . . . unless it was to briefly explain the meaning of a Seneca word or phrase. "If it pains you to use your hand, I will feed you."

Hannah's face warmed with the thought. "That's not necessary. I can still use the hand."

He nodded, then took his son's bowl and filled it. "Here, Eagle Soaring, a warrior needs food to grow strong."

But the child waved it away. "I am not hungry."

White Bear stared at him a long moment, saying nothing, and then, with a shrug, he set the boy's bowl next to his own and resumed his seat—and his meal.

Holding the wooden spoon was difficult, but Hannah managed, her hunger suddenly taking hold again. Eagle Soaring sat silently, while the two adults finished their meal. Once, he'd tried to leave, only to be told by his father to remain seated until everyone was done. The boy did, but he wasn't pleased, and his frequent, hostile looks toward Hannah said that he blamed her for his present unhappy state.

On the trail, Hannah had thought the relationship between father and son was a good one, Eagle Soaring's obvious adoration of his father like a beacon of light in the young man's eyes. But since then she'd seen differently. While it was true, the boy adored his father, there was a distance between them that bothered her . . . a distance that Hannah suspected came from within the father—and not the son. It would explain why Eagle Soaring saw her presence within the lodge as a threat. The child would regard anyone as an intruder if he was unsure of his father's love.

Somehow, some way, Hannah decided she would learn more about the two and find a way to help them.

Hannah set down her bowl and, moments later, White Bear had finished both his bowl and his son's discarded second helping.

"You may go if you wish," White Bear told his son.

Eagle Soaring got up and ran out of the house with a brief pained look toward his father, one that White Bear missed but which firmed Hannah's resolve to do something.

Chapter 9

Night had fallen, and the Indian village was quiet. White Bear lay within the cocoon of his sleeping platform, listening to the late-evening sounds. Crickets chirped in rhythmic chorus. In the distance, frogs croaked out their songs from the lakeside. But it was the sounds from the sleeping Hannah that affected him the most. Her soft inhalations of breath shivered across his skin like the caress of a woman's touch. Each time she rolled over, he could hear the rustle of her movements. She slept within inches of him. If he shifted himself farther up on the bed, he would be able to see the top of her head, where their two platforms met.

He stared at the wooden storage shelf above him, unable to sleep, disturbed by his thoughts about the slave. He didn't want to notice the little differences in the house since she'd come. The wildflowers she'd picked and stuck in a spare pot. The way she'd carefully spread out the fur pelt across his sleeping pallet each morning after he'd gotten up. He rolled onto his side, aware of how she'd fashioned a mattress for each bed by stuffing dried corn husks between the wood of the platform and tanned deerskins. It was a common practice of his people, but he hadn't slept on a mattress since he'd lived with Wind Singer. It had seemed fitting to be uncomfortable when his wife was dead.

Thoughts of Wind Singer brought a fresh wave of pain. He was dishonoring her memory by his thoughts of Hannah, but he couldn't seem to control his mind.

I am sorry, dear one. He caught back a sob. *Forgive me. If not for me, you would still be alive.*

He had killed her. He had planted his seed in her, and she'd died giving him the son he'd always wanted.

And then I failed you by leaving him alone.

A subtle shifting, a soft sigh . . . White Bear grew alert to Hannah's movement in bed. The image of his wife left him, and he saw her instead . . . her eyes wide when he'd decided to bathe with her . . . her expression of fear as he'd grabbed hold of her in the pond to keep her from harm. What was it that frightened her? He'd done nothing to inspire such terror. Hannah had spirits of her own she was fighting, he thought. Just like him.

A shaft of heat burned his loins as he recalled how soft, how warm she'd felt against him as they'd bobbed in the water together, naked. Once her fear of him had left, she'd gazed at him with gray eyes glistening with desire. She felt it, too. This strange pull between them.

She slept naked. The image hardened his manhood. He knew exactly where she'd laid her tunic each night after she took it off. She'd worn it to sleep the first few days, until she became comfortable with the privacy of the sleeping platform and the deerskin curtain that hung from the storage shelf above.

And with us.

Not that Eagle Soaring had given Hannah any reason

for trust. He treated her like a slave, nothing more. *Why does this bother me when I know it is his right to do this?*

Because he himself was having trouble seeing Hannah as a slave. She was a woman with woman's feelings. And something about her reached out to him, grabbing his attention . . . and his desire.

No! He had no right to think of her. She was not Wind Singer. She was not his wife.

A sudden restlessness seized hold of him, and he threw up the flap and got out of bed. He had to fight back a moan of anguish as he stared at the closed flap of Hannah's platform. Fire burned along his skin while he fought the urge to lift the deerskin. He curled his hands into fists as he struggled to control his feelings . . . his longing for the impossible.

She's a slave.

He didn't care. She was kind and warm, and he wanted her.

No! Stop it. You had a wife, and now you have a son. Don't even think of lying with the woman!

His jaw tightened as he spun from her bed and left the hut. He needed to be alone.

The guard, River Mud, nodded to him as he escaped the village for the lake. Darkness closed in around him as he followed the trail. An owl hooted from a treetop. The crickets sang louder. The sound of a splash in the lake ahead had him hurrying toward the water. The air was clean and fresh . . . and woodsy.

The lake loomed ahead, a dark expanse of liquid relief. The only light came from a moon partially concealed by clouds, but White Bear didn't care. He ran toward the water, tugging off his loincloth as he went. He tossed the garment on the shore before he plunged into the water.

The water was cold as it surrounded him, the chill of the night having long since cooled the lake. White Bear waded out a few feet, then dived under and began to swim with hard, fast strokes. He tried not to think while he cut through the water, heading away from land, uncaring of the distance. He wanted only to forget . . .

Hannah heard White Bear leave his bed, and she climbed off the platform. Her gaze focused on his bed and the signs of a troubled sleep, and she began to dress hurriedly. She sneaked out of the house and crept across the yard, searching for White Bear . . . and then she saw that the gate was open.

Her heart raced as she neared the exit. She wondered how she'd get past the guards. She didn't know why, but she was sure that White Bear had left the village. And she was determined to follow him.

If I don't get killed while trying to leave.

She was shocked to find that the guard was not at his post. Hannah hung back from the gate and listened, just to make sure. Then, she saw the Indian. The guard was relieving himself in the woods. Face flaming, she turned away, searched the opposite side, and seeing no one, sped on silent bare feet into the night.

She didn't know if White Bear had gone that way, but she headed toward the lake, lured by the sounds of the night. She'd found a calmness about the lake that was comforting to her. She stumbled on a root and was angry with herself for not taking the time to put on her moccasins before she left. She'd been too anxious to see White Bear.

Hannah had a mental image of the brave, the pain she'd glimpsed in his blue eyes at times when he didn't know he was being watched. She'd seen a longing in his expression whenever he gazed at his son, but he never looked at Eagle Soaring long . . . as if doing so hurt him.

The noises of the night pressed in on her along the trail, making her wonder if she'd been wise to venture out alone. Insects buzzed and chirped and hummed. A twig snapped, drawing her attention. She peered into the darkness, but didn't see anything. She hurried on.

The shore along the lake looked deserted, and Hannah was disappointed that White Bear wasn't there. She hadn't realized, until that moment, just how much she wanted to see him, talk with him, find out what was wrong.

As if he'll talk with you, she scolded herself. *You're a slave. Why would he talk with a slave?*

For the same reason, she thought, that she wanted to comfort an Indian. Because they were people ... with feelings and needs. And there was something between them; Hannah didn't know exactly what it was, but there was a pull that drew them together.

She sighed and wondered how long she'd be able to remain, before White Bear returned to the hut—or someone else within the village discovered her gone.

It was strange, but she hadn't thought of escaping for some time. *Since I moved into White Bear's lodge.* Why should she be in a hurry to leave when White Bear treated her kindly? She had no place to go. No family. No home. Nothing.

"Oh, Mum," she whispered, memories of her mother suddenly strong. "I do miss you." There were times while in the Indian encampment that she felt so alone, even when she was surrounded by the women, times when the events of the past overwhelmed with painful thoughts. It was at these times that she longed for her mother the most, when she wished their life had been different.

Her mother would have enjoyed the women's gathering at the lake, Hannah thought. The laughter, the conversation ... if only Dorothy had known such ease, such happiness, even if for just a little while. But, no, Dorothy had had Samuel Walpole instead. Hannah shuddered, recalling the vile man who'd ruined her mother's happiness and whose death haunted her own daily life. Would she ever forget? Feel vindicated? He was an evil man, but it was hard to reconcile that she'd committed murder to protect herself.

Hannah stared at the lake, lost in the nightmare . . . and then suddenly she saw *him,* and she felt free of the dream.

He was far out in the lake, a mere speck in the water, but she knew instinctively that it was White Bear. She found a seat on the shore to wait for him. Her eyes followed his progress as he swam toward shore. It could have been an hour, but it seemed like only minutes before she could make out his features. His head bobbed in and out of the water as his arms maneuvered him closer to where she sat.

She felt the change in her body from her first sight of him . . . the sudden infusion that pooled in her stomach and radiated along her skin . . . the increase in her heart rate . . . the curling sensation of pleasure brought on by watching him.

He didn't see her as he came out of the water, his naked male form dripping. The moon peeked out from behind a cloud just as he stepped onto shore, highlighting his magnificent body, making his wet skin glisten.

He flicked back his hair with his hands. Hannah caught her breath as she watched the play of his arm and chest muscles. Desire burned low in her abdomen, frightening her, for she'd never felt it before . . . and after Walpole and Boucher, she hadn't thought herself capable of feeling anything but contempt for a man.

Passion. Was that what she was feeling? She could think of no other word to describe the feeling that gripped her hard whenever she was near him.

Suddenly, she wished she'd never come, for she didn't trust herself . . . her longing for the Indian.

He's a savage.

No, he's not. He's treated you kindly.

She'd seen a look of longing in his eyes when he'd gazed at her, but yet he'd remained distant . . . respectful. He'd done nothing to make her fear him. Was that the behavior of a savage?

"No," she mouthed silently.

He turned to stare at the lake, still oblivious to her presence, which surprised her, for she would have thought he'd have sensed that she was near. She gazed at his back, enjoying the way his broad shoulders tapered to his narrow waist . . . the slight flare of his hips. Hannah felt a fluttering in her chest as she stared at the tight muscles of his buttocks. Startled by the overwhelming urge to touch him, she closed her eyes and was shocked by the sudden mental image of her lying beneath him, her hands caressing those hard muscles. The force of the desire that tore through her stole her breath even while it made her burn.

Her gaze dropped to his calves and feet. She had seen them before, but never in such a light . . . It was strange how even a man's legs and feet can evoke physical sensations . . . especially White Bear's legs and feet . . .

She should be embarrassed, watching him this way, but she wasn't. She was too fascinated, too drawn to the man.

A cloud passed before the moon, throwing the lake area into darkness. White Bear didn't move for a long moment, and when he did, it was only to lift his head as if he was battling to find courage within himself.

Hannah swallowed hard, moved by the aura of pain that settled about him. He looked lost and alone, and her eyes burned while she fought the urge to go to him . . . to take him in her arms to comfort him. A shudder went through him as she watched. His pain was hers as she rose from the log, wanting, needing, to help him.

A twig snapped as she took a step. In a flurry of movement, White Bear crouched to the ground and spun on his feet, his weapon raised, his naked body poised to fight. He glared into the darkness; the blade of his knife gleamed in the pale light.

He stared, and she witnessed his surprise . . . pleasure . . . anger . . . and finally his carefully guarded expression.

"Han-na?" he asked huskily.

"Yes, White Bear," she replied softly. He was naked, but

she didn't care, felt no shame. Her appreciation of his form drew her out. Hannah stepped from beneath the shadows of the trees and into the clearing that led down to the lake.

For a brief moment his features revealed a vulnerability that tugged hard on her heartstrings. "What are you doing here?" he said.

Her heart raced as she approached. She knew she shouldn't look at him, a man without clothes, but she couldn't help it. He was beautiful. Magnificent. If he was self-conscious about his state of undress, it didn't show. "I heard you leave," she said. She paused within several feet of him.

He raised his eyebrows. "You followed me." His face darkened with the tone of his voice.

She nodded. Her whole body hummed with life as she held his gaze. Her spine tingled. Her pulse rate went wild. Heat warmed her both inside and out. "I wondered if there was something wrong."

She caught his scowl before he turned back to the lake without answering her. She could feel his tension surround her, drawing her closer, binding her to him as one would slowly fasten an object by tightening a rope.

"How did you get past River Mud?" he asked mildly, almost conversationally.

Her last memory of the Indian made her face warm. "He was otherwise engaged."

Something in her tone must have alerted him, because he spun to face her. She blushed under his scrutiny. "And if he'd been there?" Emotion flared in his blue eyes. "What do you think he would have done if he'd caught you?"

Hannah shivered as she moved closer. "I don't know," she whispered, but she had a good idea—and none of it pleasant.

White Bear's arm snaked out and he grabbed her, jerking her to him, tightening his hold. He was furious. Han-

nah saw it in the angry blue gaze that glared at her, felt it
in the tautness of his body, the crushing grip of his strong
arms.

"Are you not afraid?" he asked.

She didn't speak, for she was too overcome.

"River Mud has little regard for any slave. If he found
you, you would have suffered. It would have been me who
would punish you," he rasped. "Do you understand?"

She nodded. Her heart pounding wildly. His grip on
her arm was tight, but not cruel . . . but he was oh, so angry
with her. "I'm sorry," she said sincerely.

He sighed and released her. "You must not leave the
village alone." He moved away from her, toward the lake.
The water lapped at his ankles.

"If I had asked, would you have let me come?" she
dared, needing to know. She joined him in the lake. A
sudden tension hung in the air between them, yet Hannah
wasn't afraid . . . never afraid. Not even when he was angry
with her. She knew deep in her heart that he would never,
could never, hurt her. *Which is why the thought of his punish-
ing me hurts him,* Hannah realized.

"Te-ah," he said.

Hannah's chest tightened. "No?" she whispered.
"Why?" She saw his jaw tighten. "White Bear?"

Desire swirled in White Bear's gut along with pain and
guilt . . . and a longing so intense it took all of his strength
not to cry out with it. He felt his control start to slip. "You
do not know!" he burst out. "How can you not? Must I
show you why it's wrong?"

She stared at him, confused. "White—"

With a deep groan, he caught her to him and covered
her mouth with his own. She stiffened, and then, to his
astonishment, her lips softened and parted slightly beneath
his. Spurred on, he pressed for further intimacy. He sought
entry into her mouth, spearing inside with his tongue.
Hannah whimpered as he tasted her sweetness, gloried in

her warm softness, in her scent. It had been so long since he'd held a woman that he was shocked by the sensation, the rightness of holding her. She moaned, and he thought she felt it, too.

He raised his head to see, and was stunned to glimpse her tears. He released her immediately and stepped back, awash with shame for allowing his more base instincts to take over. He gave her his back; he didn't want to see the condemnation in her eyes . . . the condemnation that accused him of using a slave. He was horrified by his behavior, even while he admitted that he couldn't regret having experienced that burst of joy of having her in his arms. "Do you see why I would say no?" he said hoarsely.

Pain cut through his heart, making him bleed. He had never meant to touch her, to dishonor Wind Singer's memory. But he was alive—alive! He had always been a man of deep passions. He'd both loved and hated his father for not saving his dying mother. If not for his sister Abbey, he would have destroyed himself with his guilt. Then he'd hated the Indians who'd stolen his freedom. His hate, his fury at them, had given him the courage and strength to past their tests until he was looked upon as one of them . . . and elevated from slave to warrior. When he'd met Wind Singer, he'd been wary of everyone. It hadn't mattered that the Seneca had made him a son. He didn't trust them, feared their cruelty, until he came to understand that there was a gentleness about the people, too. Wind Singer, daughter to the sachem, had taught him that when she'd bathed his wounds and stroked his injured pride. She had given him affection and asked nothing in return, thus earning all he had to give, which was his heart. She had inspired a passion of a different kind . . . feeling so strong, so pure that he'd been overwhelmed. He had married her with the blessings of the village matrons. He had loved her and been happy for the first time in his life. Then, Wind Singer had died, and his passion had been in his pain, a self-destructive force that had nearly cost him not only his life, but his son . . .

He had thought he'd had his passions—himself—under control . . . until he'd met Hannah. She initiated feelings he was unable to control. Passion. Lust. Tenderness. Confusion. All of these things he felt, and more. And it was his inability to rein in his emotions that frightened him more than anything. Hannah disturbed him more than anything—or anyone—in his entire life.

She hadn't said a word, but he could feel her accusing gaze, felt sure that she was deeply wounded by his lack of control.

Then, he felt her touch on his shoulder. The simple, light contact created a chain of reactions within him.

"White Bear—" Her voice sounded thick with tears.

He forced himself to face her. She dropped her hand. Her eyes were downcast, and he couldn't read her expression. He raised her chin with his finger and his breath caught as he studied her face. There was a sheen of moisture in her eyes, but they weren't tears of anger or hate. Her expression held concern . . . for him . . . for his pain. Overcome with emotion, he cupped her chin, stroking her satin skin with fingers that trembled. "Han-na . . ."

She blinked and lowered her eyes, so that her lashes formed dark, feathery crescents on her cheeks. He brought up a hand to touch her throat, where he could feel her throbbing pulse.

He stared at her mouth. "Han-na—"

Hannah burned beneath his gentle touch. She wanted nothing more than for him to kiss her again, but would it help . . . or simply complicate matters? "Tell me what's wrong." She held his gaze until his thumb traced her lower lip. Her mouth softened, and she closed her eyes. "Is it your son?" she asked.

"Eagle Soaring?" he asked in disbelief. He removed his

touch and stepped away. Hannah wanted to cry out at the loss.

He scowled. "There is nothing wrong with my son—"

"But I thought—"

He studied her through narrowed eyes. "You thought what?"

He's angry, Hannah thought. She felt chilled. "I . . . nothing," she murmured, turning away.

He caught her arm. Startled, she stared at him, her throat tightening as she noted his tense expression, the tic along his jaw. "You seem distant from one another," she said.

"Distant?" He looked furious now. "There is nothing wrong between me and my son!" he insisted, released her arm.

She shrank back from his fury. "I didn't mean to anger you," she said, her voice shaky as she inched away.

As quickly as his anger came, it went. "Han-na," he said softly. "I am sorry. I did not want to frighten you." His expression softened as he followed her.

"I shouldn't have come," she whispered, her heart beating rapidly at the look in his blue eyes.

"But you did," he said.

"I should go back." She spun to make her escape.

"No!" He caught her easily, grasping her shoulders and turning her to face him.

Her breath stilled in her throat as she gazed up at him. He felt so strong, so . . . male. He should have frightened her, but the truth was that he didn't. She wasn't afraid of what he'd do, but of what he *wouldn't* do. She wanted so badly to kiss him that she leaned into his hands.

"Han-na!" With a deep-throated groan, he bent his head and captured her mouth. He kissed her with longing, his mouth tenderly worshiping her lips, her cheek, before sipping from her lips again.

Tears filled Hannah's eyes at the wonder, the beauty, of

his kiss. She sensed that he held himself in check, and the knowledge thrilled her, spurring on her own response. She caught his shoulders, sighing against his mouth at the male power of him, the warmth of his skin.

He lifted his head, his eyes heavy-lidded and dark with desire. "Han-na . . ."

"White Bear," she whispered. Closing her eyes, she pressed into him. "Kiss me," she begged. She'd never felt this way about any man . . . and suspected that she never would for any other. The realization stunned her.

And then he was kissing her as he hadn't before . . . more deeply . . . more intimately, and she gloried in his passionate demand. He devoured her with his mouth, tracing her lips with his tongue, brushing nibbles across her nose, cheek, and chin.

"Open for me, Han-na," he instructed huskily.

She complied, then whimpered with pleasure while he held her tightly and their mouths mated in imitation of what their bodies longed to do. He released her mouth to trail a burning moist path down her throat, lingering for a moment at the base where her pulse beat rapidly. Her nipples tingled as if longing for his touch. Her stomach quivered as her mind flew ahead, wanting . . . longing . . . envisioning how it would be when he finally took her.

She felt her knees weaken when he nuzzled beneath the scooped neckline of her tunic. When he cupped the area where deerskin covered her breast, she gasped and arched her back, pushing the soft mound into his hand.

"Please," she whispered, grabbing his hand to press against her lips.

A flame flared in his eyes as she kissed his palm and rubbed it against her cheek. *"Ha-yo-go-sote'-o-gä-uh,"* he murmured.

Moved by his loving tone, she took his hand and gently placed it at his side. "Don't move," she told him. Holding his gaze with her own, she placed her hands on his chest and explored his sleek, damp, hard flesh. He closed his eyes and released a shuddering breath while she touched him . . . his shoulders, his arms . . . back to stroke his chest muscles . . . to worry the tiny nub of his nipple. She rubbed a finger back and forth over the tip, enjoying the way his nipple beaded under her touch. She placed her hands at his waist, slid her hands to his hips and back up to his waist and chest.

He stared at her, his expression mirroring his joy at her touch. Encouraged, Hannah dared to move her hands down the front of his, to his stomach, loving the way his belly went into spasms beneath her fingertips, relishing his male groan of pleasure. Her gaze dropped to the area that proclaimed him a man.

"Oh, my!" she exclaimed breathlessly at the evidence of his desire. His shaft rose stiff and ready from a curly nest of dark golden hair. Hannah felt an answering liquid warmth between her thighs. Her fingers trembled in her desire to touch him.

He caught her hand when it started to move lower. *"Te-ah,* Han-na," he said huskily. "It is happening too fast."

His gaze burned as he held her wrist gently before placing her hand on his chest. White Bear's cool, damp skin had warmed from their embrace. The pounding of his heart beneath her hand mirrored her own. She closed her eyes as he stroked her back, conscious of his clean scent, the water droplets on his shoulders . . . the soft body hair that covered his arms and legs. She raised her hands to his shoulders and ran her fingers through the long strands of water-darkened blond hair that lay against his neck and back. Her blood caught fire as she pressed against him, her nipples straining against the deerskin of her tunic. She wanted nothing more than to feel him pressed against her naked flesh.

The water lapped at their ankles. A fish jumped in the lake behind them, making a tiny splash. The air caressed their bodies, sensitized by their contact. Hannah shifted so that she could further explore his chest. She circled his nipple with her fingertips, watching the way the water glistened on his skin. Then she bent close and pressed her lips to his chest, licking the nipple with a tiny sweep of her tongue.

White Bear groaned and wove his fingers into her hair, clutching her head to him a moment, before he set her back. He captured her face between his palms. While he devoured her with his hot gaze, he murmured to her in Seneca, then kissed her closed eyelids . . . her cheeks . . . her nose . . . and finally her lips.

At his gentleness, Hannah felt her knees weaken, and she started to stumble. White Bear caught her. After he'd steadied her, he released her and held out his hand. "Come."

The invitation was full of promise. Hannah's heart raced with anticipation. Her mouth tingled from the memory of his kiss. Her breasts throbbed with desire.

She swallowed as she placed her fingers trustingly into his hand. His gaze held her fast as she felt the warmth of his fingers as their hands entwined. He smiled, and the smile reached his eyes. His expression was tender, inspiring trust. "Come, *ex-aa-gä-uh'*," he said as he led her from the lake.

Hannah went with him willingly, her pulse racing with anticipation. He took her along the edge of the lake and into the forest, in the opposite direction of the village. And she wasn't afraid. This was what she'd been longing for . . . since the day he'd first come to her in the pond . . . and she'd known that he was different than any other man.

Chapter 10

Neither man nor woman spoke as they entered a secluded clearing along the edge of the lake. The crickets' chirping seemed to echo the throbbing of Hannah's heart as White Bear stopped, turned her to face him, and, with a muffled groan, pulled her into his arms. But he didn't kiss her. He cradled her head against his chest; his tenderness moved Hannah the way no words ever could.

She stood with her cheek pressed against the area of his beating heart, content to stay there forever, for she felt cherished.

His hand moved down her hair over her shoulder to stroke her back gently. She turned her head to press her mouth against his skin. His sharp inhalation of breath told her that he had felt the caress ... but she couldn't tell whether or not he liked it. Hannah pulled back to gaze up at him. The flame in his blue eyes told her he had.

"White Bear," she murmured.

He cradled her face between his palms, holding her gently. "Han-na ... *O-gä-uh.*" He dipped his head and kissed her. As their mouths met, fire shot through Hannah's limbs. Her knees felt weak as he continued to kiss her, rubbing his mouth across her lips. She put her hands at his waist and moved them to clutch his hips, feeling the increase in her body heat as her fingers encountered the curve of his naked flesh.

Hannah felt dizzy as she met him kiss for kiss. He lowered her to the ground while he continued to worship her mouth. She didn't realize that he had done so until he broke away to gaze down at her, and she became conscious of the pine needles cushioning the earth where she lay and the turgid male heat of him pressing against her thigh. He was at her side. He bend his head to nibble along her neck and burrow his face in her hair. Then, he trailed his mouth lower, to the collar edge of her tunic. He tugged the deerskin to bare the upper swell of one breast. She gasped when he nuzzled the area with his mouth while he palmed the other breast. She cried out and arched up, wanting to know more, feel more, for she trusted this man . . . was drawn to him both in body and heart.

White Bear shifted to his knees, and she felt his hands at her thighs as he grabbed the tunic hem to tug the garment upward. The brush of his knuckles against her skin made her burn. She sat up, and he pulled off her tunic. The night air caressed her naked flesh. "White Bear," she murmured.

He stared at her, and her stomach fluttered at his look. Her nipples pebbled under the flaming heat of White Bear's gaze. She fought the urge to cover herself, but he took her arms and spread them wide before he pushed her back gently, so that she lay vulnerable and naked before him, her hands at her sides.

She is perfect. White Bear felt a jolt of desire so intense that he had to control the urge to mount her, to thrust into her so completely that her wild cries would drown out all other night sounds. But he couldn't forget how she'd struggled in the pond, and he didn't want to frighten her. There was something about this woman that touched him. He didn't want to think of what he was doing, of the past; he wanted only to feel. It had been so long since he felt a woman's skin, felt her breath sigh across his cheek. He wanted to give her pleasure. There was a look of innocence in her gray eyes that gave him pause. He shouldn't, but how could he not when she was so lovely? So giving and warm?

Her skin was smooth and white, her breasts full with tempting dark pink nipples. Her belly was flat and silky, and he gave into the temptation to cover it with his hand. She gasped, and her eyes grew black with passion, making his own body throb and burn. As he allowed his fingers to drift lower to her hip, she moaned, closing her eyes. She was so sweet, so warm . . . so alive.

He gazed at her dark nest of curling hair, and realized that he wanted her as he'd wanted no other. He raised his head to gauge her reaction as he slid his hand toward the apex of her thighs. She jerked in reaction but didn't try to stop him, and, with a thick moan of need, he touched her, delving into the soft hair with his fingers, rubbing the tiny feminine nub, before inserting a finger deep inside her.

"No!" she exclaimed, trying to close her legs.

He understood her fear. "Sh-sh, Han-na," he soothed, withdrawing his hand to the top of her thigh. "I will not hurt you."

She shuddered, briefly closing her eyes. "I know."

"I want only to give you pleasure," he assured her.

She nodded.

He dared to touch her belly again, and while she looked scared, she didn't protest. White Bear then parted her legs, and she cried out and tried to press her knees together. He released her and sat back on his haunches.

"I will not force you," he said. It had been so long since

he bedded a woman, but he was sure that he'd never felt this hard. It wasn't right for him to take her, but he couldn't seem to stop his desire for her.

Hannah gazed up at the golden man above her, stunned, that he had backed off when she'd objected. How could this man be a savage? A savage cared little for one's feelings, but this man cared . . . and she was grateful . . . and over-whelmed. He'd been so gentle . . . treating her with near reverence. How could she not trust him? Want to feel him deep inside? He was nothing like Walpole or Boucher. He wouldn't hurt her, wouldn't force her.

With a growl of frustration, he started to rise. Hannah sat up and grabbed his arm. "No," she said. "Please. Don't go."

His muscles tensed beneath her fingers. *"Haht-deh-gah-yeh'-ee!"* he exclaimed. He glared at her. "You don't know what you do to me!"

He ached as she did! She felt heady. Her expression was as soft as her smile. "I think I do," she said. She trailed her fingers down his arm to capture his hand. "I do," she murmured thickly, eyeing him through heavy-lidded eyes. Daringly, she placed his hand on her breast and gasped at the contact of his strong masculine fingers on her skin. She arched into his warmth, rejoicing when he began to knead the soft curve gently with his fingers.

He shifted to get closer. Desire burned brightly in his blue eyes. "Han-na," he whispered achingly. "Do not do this. I cannot stop if you do." She was surprised—and pleased—when his hand shook as he stroked it against her cheek.

Hannah trembled as he cupped the side of her neck with his other hand. "I don't want you to stop." And she didn't. She realized that she'd been longing for this from their first meeting. She'd responded to his kindness; she'd been hurt by his indifference, because she wanted more from him, much more.

"Look at me," he said. "I look like a *Yen'gees,* but I am White Bear of the *Nun-da-wä'-o-no*—a savage!"

She blinked up at him. "You are no savage, White Bear of the *Nun-da-wä'-o-no.* You are a man."

"Han-na . . ." he rasped, his eyes a mirror of his pleasure.

She felt a surge of tenderness for him. She rose up on her knees. Holding his gaze, she caressed his jaw. "You are you," she murmured.

White Bear gazed at her, entranced. His manhood was so thick and full, it hurt him. Her touch seared his skin and drove him nearly wild as she slid her hand down his throat, over his shoulder, to his chest and a hardened nipple. But he kept still, in control, because he didn't want to hurt her, frighten her. Perhaps there was some English gentleman left in him after all, he thought. But as she continued to stroke and caress him, the savage in him began to rise to the surface. He struggled to keep himself in check. It wasn't easy as she bent her head and touched her mouth to his nipple. He groaned and clutched her head. *"Han-na, no—"*

"Kiss me, White Bear," she begged him prettily.

He lost the last vestiges of control. With a growl of pleasure, he caught her shoulders roughly and, devouring her lips with his mouth, pressed her down. He was like a man frenzied with need as soon as he fell on her. He kissed her lips, nipped her ear, nibbled her throat, and bit lightly on her shoulder, his breath quickening as he did so. He forgot his late wife, his son, his people—everything but his desire to have her.

She gasped and whimpered as he touched her and loved her with his mouth. He could hear her breathing change, knew that she felt the increasing pressure between her legs, and felt a warm rush of affection for her. She was a woman, made for him—a man. He had to have her! But he wanted her to feel the same. White Bear was careful as he wedged his leg between her thighs to prepare her for his entry. He brushed her opening with the tip of his staff, glorying in her passionate cry.

"Han-na, *Ah-gä-weh*,'" he muttered thickly. *Mine.* And then, with a gasp, he pressed himself home, pushing himself in slowly, deeply, until he was buried partially inside her. Her liquid warmth welcomed him. The sensation was so wonderful that he couldn't hold back a moan. Her muscles inside were tight, slick, and his haven.

He eased himself in deeper, felt the barrier of her maidenhead, and hesitated. Breathing hard, he tried to regain some control. Hannah put her hands on his buttocks and squeezed. "Han-na!" he gasped. Passion took over and he thrust deeply, forcing himself inside. She stiffened beneath him, and he gritted his teeth as he again fought for control.

He raised himself up slightly. A weight settled in his chest. "Han-na, I am sorry."

Her eyes glistened with tears as she looked up at him. He closed his eyes against the sight of her tears, and fought for control. He felt a wrenching of his gut that he'd brought her pain, and wondered how he was going to stop when everything inside of him urged him to finish.

With a heartfelt moan, he started to withdraw, but Hannah clutched his hips, stopping him. His eyes flew open.

"Don't stop," she said. "You haven't hurt me." He felt her tremble beneath him as he speared her deeply again. "You . . . I never knew it could be like this."

He was shocked to see that her tears were not of pain, but of joy. Cocooned in the pleasurable warmth of her admission, White Bear grinned. "We are not done—"

He joined with her more fully and began to thrust, easing his penis in and out gently, setting a rhythm that made her gasp and whimper. As if demanding more of him, she lifted to meet his thrusts.

Heat spiraled in Hannah's abdomen, and pleasure radiated from between her legs as White Bear teased her with his gentle thrusts. When he cupped her breast to bring it to his mouth, she cried out in ecstasy. She became frantic to touch him, to taste the dark nipple in the midst of golden skin.

White Bear plunged harder, faster, and Hannah's gasp held a little fear, for gone was the gentleness, the tenderness that had so inspired trust.

She shoved at his shoulders with both hands, but then felt a rush of tingling sensation that had her grabbing at him to pull him closer instead. She gasped for air as the pleasure heightened, until her mind couldn't function . . . all that existed was the man above her and the glorious ecstasy of their being joined. She reached her passionate peak only seconds before he did. Hannah whimpered, then cried out his name as her body tensed in the throes of her climax. She shuddered, gasping, until it was over, and a wondrous lassitude took its place.

Hannah was aware of the thundering of their mingled heartbeats. White Bear's breathing sounded as if he'd been running as it stirred the damp tendrils at her ear, making her tingle.

He felt heavy against her, but she had no desire to move. She liked having him on top of her. She should have felt soiled, ashamed, but she didn't. The experience had been wonderful. And if she'd had a doubt that White Bear had enjoyed it, she had only to remember his triumphant groan as he found satisfaction. And she smiled, pleased.

All too soon, he shifted off her to her side. He didn't look at her, and that fact made a lump of doubt form in her throat. But she didn't comment. She lay on her back, closed her eyes, and tried not to think of the consequences of what had just happened.

Then, White Bear reached out to pull her against him, and her heart nearly burst with happiness. She lay with her breast against his breast, while he stroked her head, her arm . . . her back. Content, Hannah sighed, closed her eyes, and slept.

"Mr. Boucher? Mr. Jules Boucher?"

Jules glanced up at the man who'd addressed him. He was an ugly fellow, with beady brown eyes, a sharp nose, and a bright red jagged scar across his left cheek. His powdered wig was slightly askew. And he was English, which made the Frenchman instantly wary. His gaze narrowed. *"Monsieur* Boucher," he corrected.

The man's eyes flashed. "Monsieur, then." He pulled up a chair and sat at the Frenchman's table in the common room without waiting for an invitation.

Jules's jaw tightened. "What do you want?" he asked rudely.

The man smiled evenly, and the drawing of his scar distorted his face, pulling up one side more than the other. "Some information."

The Frenchman frowned. "Information does not come cheaply, monsieur."

"Mister," the English man said mockingly. *"Mr.* Walpole. Samuel Walpole." He didn't offer his hand.

"Oui, Mr. Walpole." Jules took a gulp of his whiskey, then plunked his glass down hard on the tabletop. "Pete!" he called. "I'll have another!" While he waited for another drink, he rubbed the rim of the empty glass slowly with his middle finger. His gaze returned to the Englishman. "If you have nothing to say, Walpole, then I suggest you find another table." He hated Englishmen, and he sensed that this one was as greedy and arrogant as the rest of them.

"Hannah Gibbons," the man said, watching him closely.

Jules froze. "What about her?"

"I'm looking for her. I understand that you purchased her indenture."

Take advantage of this offer to enjoy Zebra's newest line of historical romance novels....Splendor Romances (formerly Lovegrams Historical Romances)- Take our introductory shipment of 4 romance novels -Absolutely Free! (a $19.96 value)

Now you'll be able to savor today's best romance novels without even leaving your home with our convenient and inexpensive home subscription service. Here's what you get for joining:

- 4 BRAND NEW bestselling Splendor Romances delivered to your doorstep every month
- 20% off every title (or almost $4.00 off) with your home subscription
- Shipping and handling is just $1.50.
- A FREE monthly newsletter, *Zebra/Pinnacle Romance News* filled with author interviews, member benefits, book previews and more!
- No risks or obligations...you're free to cancel whenever you wish...no questions asked

To get started with your own home subscription, simply complete and return the card provided. You'll receive your FREE introductory shipment of 4 Splendor Romances and then you'll begin to receive monthly shipments of new Zebra Splendor titles. Each shipment will be yours to examine for 10 days and then if you decide to keep the books, you'll pay the preferred home subscriber's price of just $4.00 per title. That's $16 for all 4 books with $1.50 added for shipping and handling. And if you want us to stop sending books, just say the word...it's that simple.

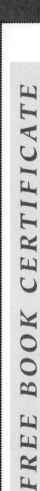

4 Free BOOKS are waiting for you!
Just mail in the certificate below!

If the certificate is missing below, write to: Splendor Romances, Zebra Home Subscription Service, Inc., P.O. Box 5214, Clifton, New Jersey 07015-5214

FREE BOOK CERTIFICATE

Yes! Please send me 4 Splendor Romances (formerly Zebra Lovegram Historical Romances), ABSOLUTELY FREE! After my introductory shipment, I will be able to preview 4 new Splendor Romances each month FREE for 10 days. Then if I decide to keep them, I will pay the money-saving preferred publisher's price of just $4.00 each... a total of $16.00. That's 20% off the regular publisher's price and I pay just $1.50 for shipping and handling. I may return any shipment within 10 days and owe nothing, and I may cancel my subscription at any time. The 4 FREE books will be mine to keep in any case.

Name _____

Address _____ Apt. _____

City _____ State _____ Zip _____

Telephone ( ) _____

Signature _____ SP0198
(If under 18, parent or guardian must sign.)

Terms and prices subject to change. Orders subject to acceptance by Zebra Home Subscription Service, Inc. . Zebra Home Subscription Service, Inc. reserves the right to reject or cancel any subscription.

The Frenchman became uneasy. "And if I had?"

"I want to see her."

"I'm afraid that's not possible."

Walpole's face became even uglier in his anger. "I have a right to see her, Boucher. She's my stepdaughter." Samuel smiled at the Frenchman's stunned expression.

"Your stepdaughter?"

Samuel nodded. "I've been searching for her. She ran away after her mother's passing. She was extremely distraught. She has a family who want to see her, who care for her," he lied. "They're willing to pay a great deal to have her back home."

Boucher scowled. "Although it pains me to admit this— I can't help you. Hannah is no longer in my employ."

Walpole eyed the unkempt Frenchman with contempt. The man was huge, dirty, and looked as if he hadn't washed in over a year. He smelled like it, too. He's been startled when the innkeeper had pointed Boucher out to him. His mouth twisted. He wondered how Hannah had dealt with him. "But you know where she is—"

"Not exactly, monsieur."

Anger formed a knot in Samuel's stomach. Damn it all, but he'd thought he had her! She was all that kept him from returning to England to claim his prize, from living the remainder of his life in comfort. And now to be thwarted once again!

"What the bloody hell do you mean by 'not exactly'?" he hissed. His head pounded. His scar burned. He wanted to hit something—someone, and if Boucher didn't give him the right answer—and soon, it was likely to be the Frenchman.

Jules Boucher placed his hand on the handle of the knife strapped to his belt and drew himself straighter in his chair. "It means, monsieur, that I know to whom I sold her indenture, but not where the man is."

"And he is?" Walpole's voice was soft. He had seen the

Frenchman's hand shift to his side, and realized that he had best keep control or lose what little help the man had to offer.

The Frenchman looked uncomfortable all of a sudden. "I sold her to a Seneca." His hand tightened about his weapon. "He-Who-Comes-In-The-Night."

"Seneca!" Walpole bellowed, drawing the attention of the other patrons of the inn. *"Do you mean you sold my stepdaughter to a bloody savage?"*

Boucher's hand moved, and the knife appeared above the table, the blade forward ready to strike. "The Indian paid for her. I certainly had no use for the woman. She's too headstrong."

In a flash of movement, Walpole jumped up and pulled out a pistol. "Monsieur Boucher," he said through clenched teeth, "you had best tell me what you know about this Indian, before I get it into my head to pull this trigger! She's an innocent female, for God's sake! Don't you know what the savages do to women!"

Jules threw back his chair and stood. "Don't!" he cried as Walpole raised his pistol. "Listen to me! There were four of them, Walpole! I had no choice but to sell her to them. If I hadn't, we'd have both ended up dead!"

"So instead, my stepdaughter may well be dead," Samuel said, lowering the weapon. "Or worse."

The Frenchman's face turned a bright shade of red beneath his bushy beard. "There was nothing I could do."

"There is now."

Jules was wary as he reclaimed his seat. "What? You expect me to steal her from the Seneca? Monsieur, if you think I would be so foolish as to enter an Iroquois village with the sole intention of kidnapping Hannah from under their very noses, then you are more stupid than I would have given you credit for."

Walpole slammed his fist on the table. "She's my step-daughter, you sonavabitch! Family! Just find out whether or not she's alive. If I have to, I'll hire someone else to steal her from the savages."

"You just want me to locate her?" Jules said, sounding fairly hopeful.

Samuel nodded. "There's coin in it for you if you do." He named a price that made the Frenchman's eyes gleam with greed.

"Why don't you look for her yourself?" Boucher said.

"I've been looking for her, but now you're the only one who has some idea where she is." He rubbed his fingers over his scar. "I'm not well. I've been recovering from an injury. I must leave it up to you to find Hannah." He drew a deep shuddering breath, suddenly the picture of the anguished father of a missing child. "Boucher, I implore you. Find Hannah. If you can get her safely away from the savages, then do so. I'll make it worth your while."

"It could take some time," Boucher said.

Samuel nodded.

"I'll need to send word to you from time to time. Where can I reach you?"

Walpole told him that he would be staying here at the inn, where he would expect to hear news. "You will send word each week. If I do not hear from you, I will assume that you have given up the quest."

"Fair enough."

Walpole stood just as a wench brought Boucher a tumbler of whiskey. "You had best hope that she is alive, Monsieur Boucher." His use of the French title was intended to mock the man.

Jules's mouth tightened. "I cannot control what the Indians did to her."

"You sold her to them!" he shouted, sounding distraught.

"And I will find her for you," the Frenchman said in a quiet voice.

At the man's tone, Walpole's anger dissipated. "Yes, you

will find her," he said. He appeared like a man who'd
suddenly been defeated. "Once a week, Boucher."

"You had best make that once a fortnight, Mr. Walpole.
It will not be so easy to get word through from the wilderness."

"Very well," Walpole said, raising his narrow chin.
"Once a fortnight." He started to leave and paused to
add, "Do not let Hannah know that her family has hired
you, Boucher. We do not wish her to worry over our concern for her." His brown eyes turned hard. "Do you understand?"

Jules nodded. He understood that there was more to
the man's search for his stepdaughter than Walpole was
telling. But he didn't care. The money would be reward
enough and incentive enough to follow the man's direction. "I understand perfectly, Monsieur—Mr. Walpole,"
he said.

And Walpole smiled, a taut slash of his lips which puckered his scar so that it looked as if he had a hideous growth
on his cheek.

She woke up, feeling warm and pleasantly achy. Hannah
opened her eyes and was startled to find herself on her
bed platform in White Bear's lodge. She vaguely recalled
being picked up and cradled in a strong pair of arms. She
smiled. White Bear must have carried her back to the lodge.
She remembered feeling safe and warm and cherished as
he'd placed her on her bed and covered her with a beaver
pelt. She sighed with the memory of lying with him . . . It
had been wonderful, beautiful . . . Her body warmed where
she'd felt the imprint of his mouth and hands.

Smiling with satisfaction, Hannah closed her eyes and
stretched . . . and suddenly realized that she was naked
beneath the fur. Her eyes flew open with horror. She shot
upright in bed.

River Mud! She groaned. Had White Bear strode into the village naked while carrying her, a woman with no clothes? Had the Indian guard seen them together? She felt her face warm with embarrassment. Where was her tunic? What a sight it would have been—a handsome, muscled, blond Indian carrying the naked, white Englishwoman!

She brushed back a lock of her hair with a shaking hand. No, she thought. White Bear would be more discreet. He wouldn't want his people to know that he'd been out late at night, sleeping with a slave.

A slave . . . She hugged herself with her arms. Did he really see her in only that way? Or did he think more of her?

She thought back to his tender lovemaking and decided that he had to care for her a little.

Hannah heard movement from the other side of the deerskin curtain. Someone was awake. White Bear? Her heart throbbed. Or his son? She blushed to think that his son might have guessed what had happened between her and White Bear. *He's only eight years old. If he did hear or see anything last night, he wouldn't have known. He's too young to know!*

She knew she should get up, but she felt self-conscious. If it was White Bear, how would he react when he saw her? With embarrassment? Or would he gaze at her with pleasure, with the memory of the night in his beautiful blue eyes?

She pushed aside the curtain and peered out. Whoever had been inside had left the lodge. She shoved the deerskin out of her way and climbed out of bed, noting as she did so that the curtains of the other two sleeping platforms had been tucked back onto the storage shelf. Both beds were empty.

Her skin tingling, she looked for her tunic, and was

relieved to find it where she usually left it. *So White Bear noticed,* she thought, pleased.

Her body, perhaps changed by her experience last night, seemed more sensitive to the soft brush of her tunic as she pulled the garment on. It was late, she could tell by the way the light slanted in through the smoke hole in the roof. Did anyone know why she'd overslept? She closed her eyes. Dear Lord, she hoped not!

She hurriedly searched for her moccasins and found them where she'd left them the previous night, on the dirt floor under her bed, beside the storage barrels. Then she tended the fire, adding dried corncobs for fuel, staring mesmerized, but really deep in thought, wondering how last night would change things.

Hannah knew she should be ashamed of what she'd done, but she wasn't. She'd not known that lying with a man could be so mind-shattering. *Not just any man,* she thought. *Only White Bear.*

Because of her experiences with her mother's husband and with Jules Boucher, she should have been afraid to be with the Indian, should have fought him away instead of welcoming him with open arms. But she hadn't wanted to fight him. She had wanted to join with him, was glad she had. *If only I knew how White Bear felt about it.*

The fire popped, jerking her from her thoughts, reminding that she had morning chores. She was hungry. She found some of the corn flour she'd ground only yesterday and went about making corn cakes. Eagle Soaring came in as the first of the cakes were done. She nodded in greeting and placed two corn cakes on a plate for him. She handed him his meal. He didn't say a word, but took the plate and began to eat. Hannah stood silently, watching the boy, wishing she could befriend him, wishing he would let her.

Activity at the door made Hannah glance up as the flap fell behind White Bear. She blushed and averted her gaze, feeling awkward. Her mind was filled with his image; her body throbbed with life. He murmured something to his son, then sat beside him on a woven mat. Hannah hurried to give him food and then hung back, unsure how to act, feeling embarrassed by the memory of their lovemaking.

"Are you not going to eat?" White Bear asked.

His voice startled her. She met his gaze, but saw nothing in his blue eyes that told her the previous night was special. It was as if their time together hadn't occurred. Her stomach burned with her disappointment. Hadn't it meant anything to him?

Use your head, Hannah, she told herself. *Did you really expect him to mention it in front of the boy?*

She realized that he was staring at her. "Yes," she murmured as she quickly went to get her meal. The corn cakes could have been dust for all she knew. Her mouth was dry, and she couldn't taste a thing. Her stomach quivered with the tension she was feeling.

Soon, the meal was over. Eagle Soaring rose first, spoke softly to his father, and left the lodge. White Bear hung behind, and Hannah's pulse tripped as she waited for him to mention the previous night. But he didn't. After a few moments of silence, during which he ate the second helping of food she'd given him, White Bear rose to his feet. Hannah swallowed hard, hurt by his behavior.

"Han-na," he said, and she looked at him hopefully, "I am teaching Eagle Soaring to fish."

She nodded, even while she felt the pain in her chest that he could seem so detached.

"Can you cook fish?" he asked as he dug among his belongings on the storage shelf.

"Yes."

He turned, apparently having found what he wanted. "Good." He didn't smile at her or meet her gaze. She had surrendered herself to him, but he wouldn't even look at her!

"Moon Woman will come for you. This day we begin preparations for the *Ah-dake'-wä-o*. It is our Green Corn Festival. She will show you what to do for this lodge." He paused. "Woman with Dark Skin returns to the village this night." His voice sounded odd.

Hannah looked at him. There was a tightness about his jaw that said that he was greatly disturbed by something.

"This night I will present her to you. You will make yourself ready," he said.

She felt a weight in her chest as she inclined her head. Woman with Dark Skin was Eagle Soaring's grandmother. How was she to get ready? She had nothing to wear but this tunic. She touched her tangled hair and realized she must look a fright. Was that his subtle way of saying that he was ashamed of the way she looked?

White Bear met her gaze and seemed about to say something more when Eagle Soaring appeared at the door. "Father?" the child said. "I am ready."

The blond brave swung his attention to his son. "You have your *Kagh-sig-wa?*" he asked, holding up a spear.

The boy nodded. "We must hurry, Father. *Ik-no-ha* will be home today."

"You are so anxious to see your grandmother?" the child's father said. He grinned, and the transformation was startling to Hannah. She could envision him the way he must have looked as a youth—a charming, young Englishman, who drew the attention of women.

He can smile like that at his son, but he barely looks at me, and when he does, he keeps his thoughts hidden. Yet, I see that he is upset, and I can only assume it's because of what happened last night. He regretted their time together. Pain slammed into her, making it difficult to breathe.

Dear God, how could I have given myself to him!

The memory of her response brought a hot knot to her stomach. She wanted to cry, but didn't, for she couldn't let him see. She realized now that she'd been hoping for more from him; she'd been foolish enough to have thought their relationship would change. *What relationship?* she thought with self-reproach. *You're his slave, not his wife!*

White Bear said something to her, and she must have replied, but she wasn't sure. Steeped in a misery of her own making, she couldn't remember what either of them had said. Her eyes burned as she watched them leave. A painful lump had risen to her throat, and it took all of her control not to cry.

When they were gone, Hannah still didn't cry. The hurt seemed too great for tears. What had been a wonderful experience for her had been nothing more than a physical outlet for White Bear. The lump in her throat remained for most of the morning. Going to Moon Woman's and behaving as if nothing bothered her was the one of the hardest things she'd ever had to do.

Later that afternoon, Hannah prepared a new dish that Moon Woman had taught her. She still hurt, and for the first time in a long while, Hannah thought of escaping. How could she live with White Bear's indifference after she'd given all to him?

She felt the blood drain from her face. All? She shuddered as she closed her eyes. She had not only given her body to the man, but she'd given her heart as well.

How was she going to go on as if nothing had happened? As if she didn't care?

Chapter 11

She was in the lodge, preparing the first of a number of dishes for the Green Corn Festival, which would begin the next day, when she heard the children out in the village center shout out with glee. Hannah froze, knowing that the woman had returned. Woman with Dark Skin. The woman who was White Bear's mother-in-law. The matron had been helping a seriously injured clanswoman in another village for over two months. From the delighted sounds of the children, it was evident that the Seneca were glad to have Woman with Dark Skin back.

Hannah carefully set down the bowl of shelled lima beans and scrambled to her feet, curious to see the woman who had borne White Bear's wife.

Her heart pumped wildly as she raised the door flap and went outside. She glided along the length of the long-house for a glimpse of the village yard. At first, all she saw were the children, laughing and singing and jumping up and down. Some of the youngsters moved, and Hannah saw the sachem's wife. Her face drained of color. She gaped in shock. Woman with Dark Skin was small, but it wasn't her stature that had startled Hannah. It was the fact that Man with Eyes of Hawk's wife was a woman of color. She was a Negro. Her skin was coal black; her hair was white. Woman with Dark Skin was hugging a child against her side, and Hannah saw that the boy was Eagle Soaring, her grandson.

Seeing the woman and boy together caused a myriad of conflicting thoughts chasing one after another in Hannah's mind. She was appalled. She was charmed by the woman and child's obvious affection for each other. *White Bear had married a Negro!*

Hannah couldn't believe it, didn't know how she felt about it. She had assumed the woman's skin was darker than the others, because of her name, but she knew that Indian names were often deceiving. Their naming practices orchestrated by several within the village, their titles changing for various reasons at different stages of their life.

White Bear had married a Negro, she thought. Not a full-blooded Negro, as Man with Eyes of Hawk had been the woman's father. White Bear's wife would have had skin the color of warmed milk with chocolate.

Jealousy clawed at Hannah's breast as she envisioned her golden warrior with his creamy-skinned wife. She stared at Eagle Soaring, seeing in him features that might be his mother's. The almond-shaped dark eyes. The nose that came from his grandfather—Man with Eyes of Hawk.

Watching the loving way the child held on to his grandmother's waist, Hannah experienced a wave of pain so intense that she reeled on her feet from its impact. What had recently occurred to her was confirmed. She could never be anything more to White Bear and his son than a slave. How could she have thought differently? And if White Bear had held her tenderly for one night, it was not love that had driven him.

Pity? Dear God, she hoped not. She didn't want his pity; she wanted his love.

Her breath caught in her throat as she suddenly spied White Bear on the edge of the clearing, in the opening of the longhouse of the Hawk clan. He was smiling as if pleased to see Woman with Dark Skin, obviously waiting with patience for his time to greet her.

His gaze shifted her way suddenly, and Hannah tensed. He stared at her a long time, and it seemed as if his demeanor changed upon seeing her. He wasn't happy. She didn't know the basis of his anger, but she felt it radiate from him across the distance, enveloping her in painful, tight waves.

Tears filled her eyes, and she had to look away. She didn't leave, but studied the woman and child. It hurt her to see them, but she hoped to understand her own feelings, to put her jumbled thoughts into some kind of order.

She blinked to dispel the moisture gathering to distort her gaze. Hannah turned her attention to the village gateway, fought the strongest urge to run and escape the truth of her position.

You gave yourself to a man who loves only a dead woman.

"No!" she whispered, and turned away. She walked blindly along the length of the longhouse toward the solitude of the small lodge. She stumbled inside, crying softly now.

"So now you know," a soft feminine voice said.

Hannah gasped and halted just inside the door. Moon Woman was in the hut, seated on Hannah's sleeping platform as if she'd been waiting for her return for some time.

The slave trembled as she looked away. "I don't know what you mean."

The matron slid off the platform, rising to move within a few feet of Hannah. "You thought that because White Bear was once an Englishman that he would chose you for his next wife. You thought that he would forget the mother of Eagle Soaring, in his preference for one of his own kind.''

"No," Hannah whispered. "That's not true."

"But now you have seen Eagle Soaring's grandmother, and you know that White Bear cares not about the color of skin. Now you know that the woman he loved was someone most white men would consider unworthy. Because of this, you have realized that White Bear is unlike all other white men. He is a complex man with deep passions. He saw the woman he wanted, and he wooed her before he made her his own. And she was a woman with color. Daughter to a woman with dark skin. And this upsets you. You have seen the warrior's affection for his woman's mother. You are hurt, because you know now that to him you are only a slave."

Pain lanced through Hannah's chest with each of Moon Woman's words. "No," she cried. "You are wrong! I am not upset! I know I'm but a slave. I know that I can be nothing more. Why should I care if he has love for his wife's mother?"

"Or his wife?" Moon Woman said softly, almost unkindly.

"Why have you come here?" Hannah gasped. "Have I done something wrong? This morning was I not an avid pupil?"

Moon Woman's expression softened. "I have not come to cause you pain, young one." She touched Hannah's cheek and her fingers came away wet with Hannah's tears. "I come to make you understand, to save you pain, before it becomes a terrible agony. You have been a good slave. But you are a slave, and thus are not eligible to become a warrior's wife, unless your status changes."

Hannah's lip quivered as she held the woman's gaze. "I know my place," she said softly, weakly.

The matron frowned. "I heard the words and your sincerity, but it is true? Does your heart believe this?"

"Yes," Hannah replied, looking away.

"Did White Bear do something to give you hope?"

The Englishwoman heard the censure, the disapproval in her voice, and thought only to protect the man she loved. "He has done nothing." *Except make me soar,* she thought. She lowered her head to hide her blushing face.

Moon Woman studied her a long moment in silence. Hannah regained control of her emotions and met her gaze without expression, in the hope that she'd be able to convince the woman.

"Good," the older woman finally said. "Now, did you shell the beans for the succotash?" she asked. "There is much to do before the sun rises in the morning sky. You must wear this garment for the festival." She turned toward the bed, and it was at the moment that Hannah noticed a garment made of soft white doeskin of the finest quality. Moon Woman handed her the kilt.

"You want me to wear this," Hannah murmured, her cheeks flushing as she thought of all who would look upon her bare breasts. *White Bear.*

Moon Woman nodded. "There will be much feasting. *Ah-dake'-wä-o* is our Festival of the Green Corn. It will continue for four days. It is an important celebration of thanks, much like our Berry Festival, only bigger. There will be guests from other villages. Our men will dance and my brother, the sachem, will have many words for the Great Spirit. Later, we will enjoy dishes made from last year's corn and food that we have taken early in the season. It is a time for rejoicing." She paused, and her eyes seemed to darken. "It is a time for families, for renewing their close ties."

For a moment, Hannah forgot her concern over wearing the kilt as she listened to Moon Woman, fascinated with her explanation of the Green Corn Festival. But she detected some hidden meaning in her last words. Had she been warning Hannah against intruding in the family of

White Bear? Was she telling her that the slave should be there to watch and serve, but not to interfere?

"Tomorrow, we will go to the lake as women as we usually do, but this day we will practice the cleansing ceremony that our women have performed for many generations. You will come to the lake to wash and be readied as a slave. You must prepare your body and your thoughts for the Green Corn Festival."

Hannah nodded. She would do this, she thought. She hoped she could get through the first day without dying from embarrassment. Her breasts tingled as if someone was already staring at them.

"Come," Moon Woman said. If she saw Hannah's discomfort, she gave no clue. "There is one newly come who has yet to see the slave who helps to care for her grandson."

"No!" Hannah protested. She didn't want to meet Woman with Dark Skin yet; she wasn't ready for this meeting. "I . . . can't we wait until the morning at the lake?"

The Indian woman eyed her thoughtfully, and Hannah's breath stilled as she waited for a reply. "She would not judge you," she said.

Hannah's heart jumped. "Please," she said.

Moon Woman's dark lashes flickered against her cheeks as she continued to eye the slave. "There is much to be done," she said after a moment. "You will be presented to Woman with Dark Skin when the sun rises in the sky and glistens on our great lake."

The matron gave Hannah some further directions for the next day, and then left Hannah alone in the lodge, slumped over with relief at the brief period of respite she'd been given.

Her relief was short-lived when a figure filled the doorway, and she looked up and saw the object of her chaotic thoughts. White Bear stood in the opening, making her senses leap. She experienced a chill as he stared at her through eyes darkened by anger. He looked away as he entered, filling up the room—and Hannah's heart—with his raw, powerful presence.

His anger hurt, demanding an explanation. Had she done something wrong? Or was it some other thing on his mind? "White Bear? Is something—"

The brave stared at her a long, uncomfortable moment. He spun and left the hut abruptly, leaving Hannah gasping with pain at his dismissal of her.

"White Bear!" she called. "White Bear!"

But he didn't answer her or come back.

As she fought the pain, Hannah recalled Moon Woman's words. She realized that the woman was right. She had harbored the hope that White Bear would forget his late wife and turn to her for love, because she was an Englishwoman and most certainly he would have chosen a white woman over an Indian one. He had loved his wife, but now there was someone better—she.

Stupid woman. How could she have been such a fool?

Hannah closed her eyes, and her mind filled with images of the previous night . . . when White Bear had held her and kissed her . . . and trailed a fiery path across the swollen, taut peaks of her breasts with his mouth. To her dismay, she felt desire moisten the area between her thighs. She cried silent tears, feeling like a fool, angry with herself . . . and him.

She hated him!

Liar, her mind screamed.

"I will not break down because I made a mistake in giving myself to a man in a moment of weakness," she whispered.

Hannah straightened her spine. It wouldn't happen again . . . not, never, again, she vowed. Not with White Bear or with any man.

With that thought firmly implanted, Hannah went back to work preparing for the upcoming Festival of the Green Corn.

* * *

He waited for the woman to greet her people. White Bear didn't approach her until she'd been reunited with her husband, giving them ample time in the privacy of their hut. Later, when he saw Woman with Dark Skin crossing the compound, he was drawn to her side.

She smiled when she saw him coming. His own lips curved with affection as she met him halfway. She was the mother of his late wife, and she was a kind woman who smiled with her eyes. She gave of herself to all of those around her. She had been White Bear's ally when he'd fallen in love with her daughter. Woman with Dark Skin had been a staunch supporter in the marriage of Wind Singer to White Bear, a new warrior. And the brave loved her.

"Grandmother," he murmured, awarding her a warm smile. "It is good to see you again. It has been too long that you have been away from your people."

She nodded. "I have missed this village. I have missed Man with Eyes of Hawk and our people, the *Nun-da-wä'-o-no*. Eagle Soaring has grown so! I see more of his father in him." She regarded her son-in-law with fondness. "You have done well with him, White Bear."

White Bear's smile fell. "I cannot take the place of his mothers," he said quietly, quietly alluding to the females of the child's clan. "He is a good boy." He felt a flash of pain. "I should have not left, ignored him. I know it is the way of our people that his mothers and his mothers' brothers take care of the children." He paused, overcome with emotion. "I thank you for allowing this father to care for his son."

It was the way of the English to take part in the rearing of a child, but not that of the Iroquois. Woman with Dark Skin knew this, and she'd been generous in her love for Eagle Soaring so she stood by his wish to raise the child.

White Bear held the woman's gaze, feeling great affection and respect for her. "I am sorry that I left the village after . . ." He couldn't say it. Wind Singer's death. Her name and her sweet face had stayed in his mind—a continuing litany to his love for her . . . his agonizing loss when she'd died. As he stared at Wind Singer's mother, he knew that she understood how he'd felt . . . and his reasons for going away. "Grandmother," he continued, "I thought only of myself, and it was wrong. You have been good to my son." His voice dropped to a husky whisper. "Thank you."

"There is no need to thank me, White Bear. Eagle Soaring is the seed of my seed. I had my time with him. It is only right that you have yours."

His gaze glistened. "You could have kept him, but you gave him to me, because I asked it."

"You had a dream, White Bear," the dark woman said. "Our dreams are not to be taken lightly. It was written that you should be the one to teach Eagle Soaring the ways of being a man."

White Bear nodded. He, too, believed this.

Her obsidian eyes were warm with caring for him. "You are a good warrior and a kind man. My daughter married well."

A burning guilt had White Bear averting his gaze. He had betrayed her daughter's memory. He had lain with the slave Hannah. How could he have done such a thing? And worse yet, he wanted to be with Hannah again. He closed his eyes and immediately saw her face. Just gazing into her beautiful gray eyes sent a jolt of longing through him. Her smile had the power to stop his breath. Her presence surrounded him with warmth . . . with caring. His belly fluttered as the memory of their time together in the woods played itself over and over in his mind. She had surrendered herself to him, trusting him implicitly, perhaps blindly. She had responded to his touch like a spark fanned into flame.

It was wrong for him to feel anything for the slave, but he couldn't stop thinking of her, wanting her. Hannah was hurt and confused; he knew this, but there was nothing he could do. He'd committed a terrible wrong, and now they were both paying for it. She paid in his withdrawal, his aloofness, he in pretending an indifference he was far from feeling . . . in the gut-wrenching longing that haunted his days and invaded his nights.

To his shame, Hannah's face had taken Wind Singer's place in his dreams. This new knowledge made it more difficult to face his late wife's mother. Woman with Dark Skin would be appalled to learn that the man who had married her daughter desired another. His feelings weren't just about lust, but something more, which made his sin all the more greater.

"I should go," he said without meeting her gaze. He sensed her puzzlement, and garnered the strength to look at her and smile. "You have much to do, and I am keeping you."

Woman with Dark Skin's eyes narrowed. "I have all the time that you need from me," she said softly, tugging hard on the strings of White Bear's heart—and intensifying his guilt.

"You are too generous with me, grandmother," he said, the smile reaching his eyes, even while his chest constricted with the pain of his betrayal to Wind Singer's memory. He turned to leave. "Welcome home," he whispered. He headed toward his lodge.

"It is easy to be generous to you, my son," the matron called to him as he left. "You are worthy of all I have to give—and more."

And the claws of guilt clamped down harder, for he knew he was not worthy at all.

* * *

The morning temperature was warm. The sun shone bright in a beautiful blue sky. Hannah had gathered her new Seneca costume and gone down to the lake with the women. Moon Woman was already there when Hannah arrived. Hannah hesitated when she saw who was with her. Woman with Dark Skin stood on the shore, conversing with Moon Woman and two other matrons. Hannah recognized Rising Moon and Walks-In-Circles. Rising Moon's daughter, Singing Rain, stood behind her mother, staring at Hannah as she came down the path.

Hannah felt a constriction within her breast as Moon Woman glanced in her direction as she continued toward the lake. The sachem's sister murmured something to Woman with Dark Skin. Hannah's steps faltered as the sachem's wife turned and fixed her gaze on Hannah.

Taking a cleansing breath, Hannah walked toward the group and nodded a respectful greeting.

"Han-na," Moon Woman said, "you have brought your *gä-kä-ah.*" She smiled at seeing the white garment draped over the slave's arm. "Good."

Hannah returned her smile weakly. She didn't know what to say, was uncomfortable in the group's presence because of the woman she had yet to meet.

"Woman with Dark Skin," Moon Woman said, "this is the slave Han-na. She belongs to White Bear." Hannah's heart tripped at the matron's choice of words. "She has been caring for your grandson."

Woman with Dark Skin looked at her a long moment. Her glistening dark eyes were not unkind, but curious. Hannah gazed back, unsure what to say. Her first glimpse of the matron's white hair from a distance had Hannah believing that the woman was quite old. On closer inspection, she was surprised by the woman's smooth skin and youthful face. Woman with Dark Skin was less than two-score.

"You are big and strong," the matron said in stilted English, her first comment startling Hannah.

"Ah, yes—"

The woman smiled. "That is good. Strong woman is good worker." Her gaze dropped as if to gauge Hannah's figure beneath her tunic. "Eagle Soaring—he has not troubled you?"

Hannah shook her head. The boy didn't like her, but he had done nothing to make her life difficult—not like Slow Dancer's son Running Brook had.

"He is a rascal, that one," she said with affection. Her obsidian eyes clouded with pain. "He is much like his mother."

"I'm sorry," Hannah said without thinking.

Woman with Dark Skin looked at her with surprise. *"Nee-yah-weh'-ha,"* she murmured, switching back to the Iroquoian language.

Hannah acknowledged the matron's thanks with a nod, then stood uncertainly, wondering what she should do next. Silence reigned as the women perhaps mourned a moment for Woman with Dark Skin's daughter.

"You have made ready for the Green Corn Festival, Hanna?" Moon Woman said, breaking the quiet sadness.

The Englishwoman inclined her head. "I have shelled all the beans and prepared the corn, and I have cut the squash just as you taught me."

All four women looked approvingly at the slave.

"It is time for us to prepare ourselves." Moon Woman glanced at Hannah's bare feet. "You have finished your moccasins?"

Hannah nodded, feeling pleased with herself for crafting the footwear herself. "I have them here." She held them up, displaying the artwork. She had spent a lot of hours making holes in the deerskin with a bone awl and then stitching on with sinew-dyed porcupine quills in a pattern she had created herself. The moccasins were a fine fit, and she was proud of them. Everyone nodded in approval.

The women began to undress then in preparation for their bath, only this time, Hannah noted, their mood was solemn, as if the bath itself was a sacred occasion.

Hannah hesitated a moment before taking off her tunic. Woman with Dark Skin's earlier comment about Hannah's strength made her feel self-conscious. But then she saw that she was no longer the focus of the matron's attention. The sachem's wife had removed her clothes and stood, naked, at the edge of the lake with several of the Seneca women, the water lapping at her dark bare feet. Reluctant to cause a delay of the ritual, the Englishwoman undressed quickly and joined the others.

The lake was warm. Hannah closed her eyes in appreciation of the morning sun and water. She dipped below the surface and started to scrub herself, taking extra care, because of the occasion. She washed her hair and rinsed it off by slipping under the surface. The women talked and some even giggled, and Hannah was relieved to see the somber mood lighten to a more festive one. This time, as usual, was for the Seneca females.

It wasn't long that Moon Woman called the attention of the others. "Let us waste no more time," she said. "We must prepare ourselves to show our respect for *Hä-wen-ne'-yu*. Today we will thank the Great Spirit for the gifts of our Three Sisters. We will thank him for all the things we have been given on this earth."

Hannah saw several of the women nod in agreement. They began to leave the lake to make ready for the festival. First they dressed in their finery. Hannah put on her new white doeskin tunic and carefully folded up the other one to be worn again after the festival.

Moon Woman wore a beautifully decorated kilt and over-dress, a tuniclike top which was much shorter than Hannah's. Several of the Indian maidens wore only kilts, leaving their breasts bare, as they normally did. All the women had their very own special garments, which they donned just for celebrations.

Once dressed, the women began to do their hair. First, they rubbed their locks with an oil made from sunflower seeds, after which they parted their hair in a straight line through the middle. The matrons plaited their locks in a long single braid at their nape, which they doubled back and secured with a delicately crafted hair band. The maidens wore their hair in two braids tied at the end with pieces of sinew, some of which had beads strung on the ends. Being unmarried, Hannah divided her hair for the two braids.

The women painted the parts in their hair with vermilion, a red pigment that added color to their appearance. Hannah did likewise. Then, following the others' example, she dusted her face with a powder made from grinding up an inside piece of a dry-rotted pine tree. Her powder puff was the soft head of a cattail plant. Next, she grabbed a wild berry from a basket that Moon Woman had brought down to the lake, and she mimicked the Seneca women's actions and used the red juice to add color to her pale cheeks.

When they were ready, the women headed back as a group to join their men in the village ceremonial house, the largest longhouse Hannah had noted her first day.

There were many gathered in the large rectangular structure already. The children, the men, and those of the tribe who rise before the people to offer thanks to *Hä-wen-ne'-yu,*—the Great Spirit—on the people's behalf. Hannah saw Eagle Soaring with several young boys about his own age. He wore his breechclout, and today he sported a string of animal teeth with silver and pretty shell beads around his neck. His chest was bare as usual, and the moccasins he wore were the ones Hannah had seen beneath his sleeping platform that first day she'd belonged to White Bear. He didn't look her way, but she didn't expect him to. He didn't like the slave very much and would not acknowledge her among the gathering of his people.

There was no sign of White Bear, and Hannah told herself she was relieved. But despite their present relationship—or lack of—Hannah longed to see him. He'd rejected her, but she was drawn to him against her will. He owned her, but he didn't love her. He had initiated her into the joys of womanhood with a gentleness that she suspected most Englishwomen never experienced with their husbands. He had brought her pleasure. She wanted more from him . . . something he couldn't give, but she couldn't help hoping . . . even when she knew it was hopeless.

"Han-na." Slow Dancer had come up silently from behind her, having recently entered the building.

Hannah's eyes flickered with surprise. "Slow Dancer," she greeted. Her former master wore Hannah's English gown with its repaired sleeve. The garment was too large for the matron, but it was obvious that Slow Dancer loved it. Hannah stifled a smile.

"You are content in the house of White Bear?" the woman asked, startling Hannah further.

What could she say? *"E-ghe-a."* Yes.

The matron grunted, pleased. "That is good." She seemed genuinely happy that Hannah had been well placed.

Hannah decided that Slow Dancer was happy that the slave was no longer bound to care for the woman's husband, He-Who-Comes-In-The-Night.

She frowned. For the most part, Night had not bothered her, except for the occasional dark, angry look he gave her when their paths happened to cross in the village center.

Moon Woman had confided that White Bear had paid

dearly for her indenture. What did he have to give to purchase her from Slow Dancer and He-Who-Comes-In-The-Night? She wanted to ask the matron, but knew it wasn't her place to do so. Someday she would ask White Bear . . . when he was no longer angry with her . . . for whatever reason.

Moon Woman and Walks-In-Circles joined Hannah and Slow Dancer. The Indians were taking seats around the perimeter of the room. Moon Woman gestured to the area where Hannah was to sit. The matron then took a seat on Hannah's right side, while the Indian maiden, Singing Rain, sat at her left. Hannah glanced at Singing Rain, but the girl's attention was focused on the warriors at the opposite side of the building.

A group of braves Hannah recognized as the village drummers entered the circle and sat in a row, each one with his *Gä-no-jo'-o* before him. They began to beat their instruments in a rhythm that filled the building like the echoing cadence of Hannah's heart. Man with Eyes of Hawk appeared before his people, dressed in his ceremonial finery. He wore his breechclout, but was barefoot. His long gray hair hung below his ceremonial skullcap. The cap was a band of silver with an eagle feather; sinew straps formed a net of sorts that cradled his crown. He stood straighter and taller than Hannah had ever seen him. The sachem was obviously proud of his role in the sacred festivities.

The drummers picked up the beat as Man with Eyes of Hawk and two other men came to the center of the room. Once the drummers had begun their playing, the villagers were silent, their expressions solemn.

Rum-tum-tum. Rum-tum-tum! The drumbeat reverberated throughout the gathering house. Her blood warmed; Hannah felt her anticipation rise as she responded to the primal rhythm that mirrored the body's life. Her heart kept time with the drummer. Her breathing changed as a strange excitement took over, until her physical being pulsed in time to the beat established by the *Nun-da-wä'-o-no* drummers.

Man with Eyes of Hawk held up his hand, and the drums fell silent. The quiet seemed louder than the noise, for Hannah's body continued to throb in rhythm. All eyes were on the sachem, who waited a respectful minute as his gaze swept the room.

The drummers began to beat their instruments softly as the sachem extended his arms and turned his gaze toward the heavens.

"We have come together once again to give thanks to the Great Spirit for the bounty we have been given. Let us begin!"

The drummers ceased. The ceremonial longhouse fell quiet. Four Indian braves entered the building, wearing adorned kilts and clutching turtle-shell rattles. They came to the center of the room and began to sing and shake their rattles. They chanted to the rhythmic jerk of their Indian instruments. Their voices rose and lowered as they praised the Great Spirit and the other spirits of life in song. Hannah thought how the English would regard the occasion and the music as heathen. She thought they were beautiful.

The singers continued their song, and a group of warriors dressed in kilts and moccasins, their bare chests gleaming with bear's grease, began to dance in along the perimeter of the room. Some wore decorative wristbands. Some had armbands of copper, silver, or animal hide decorated with beads and dyed quills. The brave in the lead wore a knee rattle, a band of deer hooves that clacked as he danced. Hannah knew that there were at least fifteen dancers. They moved slowly, gracefully, their feet rising and falling to the shake of the turtle-shell rattles that accompanied the song of praise and thanksgiving.

As the dancers moved past, shifting into her line of

vision, Hannah's attention fell on a dancer farther down the row. Her heart gave a lurch as she saw his long hair. His locks looked darker, as they'd been oiled like hers with a tonic made from the seed of the sunflower. There were two other dancers who wore not the scalplock of a warrior, but long hair, but there was no doubt in Hannah's mind that this one was White Bear. She had caressed that body, felt the hardness of his muscles with her fingertips. She lived with him, cooked for him, and had observed him when he was not looking, because doing so gave her so much pleasure.

Her pulse raced as she studied him with longing. He looked extremely masculine in his kilt. He wore a highly decorative fringed belt. A wide copper band encircled one massive forearm, while a silver band gleamed from about his opposite arm.

Hannah stared at him as he danced, his movements graceful as they were meant to be in the Great Feather Dance. He lifted his foot about five inches off the ground and stomped it to the ground with each beat of the singers' rattles. The stomp wasn't fierce, so much as a fluid step which accompanied the slow-moving sweep of his arm. Step right. Pause. Step left. Pause. White Bear raised a hand, gestured with an arm. He moved his body in various positions unique to the other dancers in the line.

She gazed with fascination at the play of his muscles as he danced. He held himself erect, using only his arms and his feet to display the emotion of the Great Feather Dance. How could such a masculine man be so graceful—and how was it that his grace did not detract from but added to his manliness?

The song stopped, but not the instruments. White Bear had a short distance to go before he would be directly before her. The dancers kept moving, stepping in time with the rhythmic shakes of the turtle-shell rattles. Hannah watched his approach with the burning heat of desire.

She wondered what he was thinking as he moved. Did he think of the Great Spirit, for whom the dance was being performed? Or did he think of his dead wife? She stared at him hard, wishing she could read his mind. Was he thinking of her? A painful knot formed beneath her breast. Did he ever think of her . . . and the glorious time they'd spent in each other's arms?

If he does, it is only with regret, she thought. For if he felt other than regret, then he would look at her, smile at her. He would treat her more than the slave she'd been before they'd become intimate with each other.

The two singers began their next song; the pace was faster. The dancers moved faster to keep in time. White Bear danced by, taking Hannah's heart with him as he continued with the line that circled the room. This dance was longer than the last, and a fine sheen of perspiration had formed on the participants' skin as they stomped past Hannah a second time . . . and then a third.

Hannah could see some of the dancers tiring. White Bear looked warm, but his movements continued to be graceful even at the increased pace. He didn't look tired; he didn't even appear to be slightly winded.

Movement to Hannah's left drew the young woman's attention to Singing Rain, who had her gaze glued to the same man who had stolen Hannah's heart. Hannah felt a queer flicker of something in the pit of her stomach. Singing Rain was lovely, an Indian maiden to capture the heart of any Indian brave, Hannah thought. *And she wants White Bear.*

Hannah looked at the man she loved and then at the woman beside her. Singing Rain was more suitable for White Bear. She was Seneca; she was of the right clan for them to marry. And from the woman's expression as she watched White Bear, it was obvious that Singing Rain adored him.

The lump of constriction within Hannah's chest moved

to her throat as she gazed at the man she loved . . . and would never have. She fought off the jealousy, the pain . . . and she wondered how she could continue to be White Bear's slave.

Chapter 12

The second day of the Green Corn Festival was much like the first. It began for Hannah at the lake with the village women and continued in the ceremonial house where the Keepers of the Faith—villagers elected by the People to oversee such celebrations—gave speeches and officiated over the religious worship. Each morning was set aside for the Great Spirit. Thanks were given to *Hä-wen-ne'-yu* and the spirits governing all forms of life. Special homage was paid during this feasting to the Three Sisters—corn, beans, and squash, and also to the spirits who gave these gifts of sustenance to the People.

On the previous day, the Great Feather Dance had been the dance of worship. This day, after an oration given by Man with Eyes of Hawk, the *Nun-da-wä'-o-no* watched as several of their own performed the Thanksgiving Dance. This dance was much like the Feather Dance but with short breaks between songs, during which Black Thunder, one of the Faith Keepers, gave short speeches, giving thanks to the spirits. The male performers did not wear full cos-

tume as they did the previous day, but kept to their loin-
cloths.

Seated on the same bench as yesterday, Hannah watched
the proceedings with the interest of one who understands.
As the first song came to an end, she listened to Black
Thunder thank the lake for its water of life, the maple for
its sap, and the trees for their shade and timber. As he
spoke, he released a handful of tobacco over a flame that
was burning in a fire pit in the center of the longhouse.
As the leaves burned, sending smoke up to the roof hole
above, the Keeper of the Faith spoke eloquently of the
People's appreciation of nature's gifts. While he spoke in
the break between songs, the dancers continued to step
in time to the rhythmic shake of the turtle-shell rattles.
When Black Thunder was done, the Seneca singers started
a new song, and the dancers began to perform again as
they continued to circle the perimeter of the large room.

White Bear was not among the dancers that day. Disappointed, Hannah searched for him, and her whole being
reacted with gladness when she spied him among those on
the crowded benches on the opposite side of the building.
Eagle Soaring was with him. Hannah was pleased to see
father and son together, until she saw the boy was seated
between White Bear and the maiden, Singing Rain. When
the maiden hadn't sat down beside her earlier, Hannah
had wondered where the young woman had gone. And
now she knew—the maiden was with White Bear.

A knot formed in her stomach when Singing Rain said
something to White Bear over the top of Eagle Soaring's
head. They looked like lovers, the way the two leaned
toward one another, Singing Rain's obvious adoration for
the brave, White Bear's smile as he responded to the young
woman's charm.

Unable to bear the sight, Hannah looked away, centering
her attention on the dancers instead. But the image of

Singing Rain and White Bear remained imprinted on her memory, making it painful for her to breathe.

Nothing had changed in her relationship with White Bear. After yesterday's festivities, Hannah had helped with the community cooking pot, where the feast of succotash simmered. Earlier yesterday morning, she had contributed her lodge's share of the corn, squash, and beans, and had taken a turn at watching the mixture as it cooked, stirring it frequently so it wouldn't burn. The communal feast had ended the festivities for the day. Each woman had taken a large serving of the meal to share with her family in the privacy of her lodge. Being the only woman in the lodge of White Bear, Hannah had accepted and brought back the meal, even though she was a slave.

White Bear and Eagle Soaring had been waiting when she'd returned to the lodge, and Hannah's spirits had risen as she'd anticipated the shared meal after such a wonderful day of celebration.

But Eagle Soaring's mood was sour. White Bear was reticent, barely speaking as he ate from his plate. Both had disappeared shortly afterward, leaving Hannah alone with the empty dirty bowls and plates—and her riotous, painful thoughts.

Hannah stole another glance across the way and wondered where White Bear had gone last night. *Was he with her?* The thought of the two of them in the woods, making love as she and White Bear had done made her exhale sharply with pain. *No!* She couldn't bear the thought.

White Bear looked up; and suddenly, their gazes collided. Hannah felt herself stiffen, but she was unable to glance away. The brave stared across the room, his expression unreadable.

Why? she asked him silently. *Why are you acting this way? What did I do wrong?*

His features seemed to soften. Hannah blinked, unsure if she was imaging it or if he was actually smiling at her.

He was!

Her heart began to thump wildly. Heat warmed her cheeks when his gaze dropped to her bare breasts and then raised as if to study her reaction. She gasped and touched her fingers to her necklace that Moon Woman had given to her yesterday.

Singing Rain touched his arm, and White Bear turned his attention to the maiden. Hannah felt a prickle of jealousy, even while her skin tingled from the lingering heat left by his gaze.

For Hannah, the rest of the morning passed in a blur. She was conscious of the golden warrior across the room and felt the frequent heat of his blue gaze from time to time as the speeches continued and the *Ga-na-o-uh,* the Thanksgiving Dance, ended and a new set of dancers began the *Ga-so-wa-o-no,* the Fish Dance. The Fish dance was accompanied by singers, the playing of the drum, and rattles made from gourds. Two singers sat on woven mats, facing each other, in the center of the room. Using their instruments, they sang and played their music, increasing the volume as they marked time.

The women joined in this dance. Hannah was startled to see White Bear and Singing Rain among the dancers. The participants danced in a column of sets of two. White Bear and Singing Rain danced face-to-face, White Bear dancing backwards for a time before the two turned and Singing Rain danced backwards along with the group of partners who were facing the same way.

It hurt Hannah to watch them, but as if she were a masochist, she was unable to look away. Finally, the dance was over, and as White Bear left the maiden's side, the pain that Hannah had felt eased.

Finally, it was time to go out into the yard, where the dining feast would begin. As she had on the previous day, Hannah retrieved a large clay bowl from White Bear's hut and went back to the village square to fill it. But this evening

White Bear lingered over his meal. He stayed after Eagle Soaring had left to join in games with the other Seneca children, and she felt his gaze on her while she ate.

She was conscious that she wore only a kilt, of his eyes that fell for a time on her bare breasts. Yet, it wasn't an uncomfortable feeling. She pretended that his interest wasn't unusual. She pretended an indifference she didn't have and that she wasn't reliving in her mind the night they'd spent kissing and caressing . . . and had been intimate.

"Han-na." His soft voice startled her; she nearly upended her plate of food.

She met his gaze, instantly noting how blue his eyes appeared this night. "Yes?"

He opened his mouth, then closed it. "You have enjoyed the Green Corn Festival?" he asked. Hannah had the impression that that wasn't what he'd meant to say at all.

She nodded. "Especially the Feather Dance," she said teasingly. She was stunned that she could tease him after the hurt he'd caused her since that fateful night.

His sensual lips twitched before he gave her a full grin. As he continued to study her, his expression suddenly sobered. "Han-na, we must talk."

She didn't want to talk. She was afraid of what he had to say. "No." She stood and began to collect the dirty dishes to take down to the lake to scour with sand and then rinse.

Hannah could feel the ripples of his shock from her answer. Seconds later, she heard his resigned sigh.

"Han-na," he murmured, "I did not want to hurt you."

His voice, so soft and so apologetic, triggered the hurt and anger at his behavior this last few days.

"Well, you did hurt me, White Bear," she shot back heatedly. Tears stung her eyes as she looked up from the stack of bowls to meet his gaze. "You did hurt me," she repeatedly brokenly. "And you mustn't do so again." She grabbed up the bowls, rose, and swept past him to the door.

"Han-na!"

She heard him from outside, but kept walking, for her tears were gathering to fall, and her throat was a tight constriction over a painful lump.

"Han-na! Wait!"

She spun back quickly. "I can't!" she called back, shaking her head. "I can't."

There were a few people in the yard. A group of boys, which included White Bear's son, were playing a game. An old woman was at the communal cooking pot, stirring its contents, a small bowl in her other hand. A young brave, whom Hannah recognized as one from another Seneca village, puffed on a pipe as he watched the boys.

Hannah continued toward the village gate, knowing that no one would stop her from going to the lake. At the water's edge, she bent and grabbed up some silt from beneath the water. She dropped the dirt into the first bowl and used her fingers and the silt to loosen the food film left by the succotash. Her reluctance to return and face White Bear while her emotions were still too raw had her taking her time with the dishwashing. She scrubbed each bowl and each plate twice, and then she sat for a while on a rock by the lake, staring out over the water, looking for peace.

It bothered her that White Bear had such power over her thoughts and feelings. When he made love to her, she'd soared, despite the fact that she'd been a virgin before she'd lain with him. She thought she'd never felt such pain—other than when her father and then her mother died—as when White Bear ignored her, pretended she wasn't there . . . and after she'd surrendered all of herself in those magical moments in the forest clearing. Then, when he'd smiled at her across the gathering room, she'd felt such a burst of joy, she was ashamed to look back and realize that she was that vulnerable to the man.

She was tired of being treated that way. She didn't care if she was his slave. She was Hannah Gibbons. Circumstances might have temporarily put her in the man's lodge, but she was a human being with feelings ... She had given him no cause for complaint! How dare he act as if she had lured him into committing an act that he now regretted! She was the inexperienced one here! But no more! No more would she allow her heart to rule her head. It was time she planned for her escape. It was time to squirrel away food supplies and other items she might need on the trail. First, she needed to find a hiding place for the things she'd need to take with her.

She rose and began to search. Her gaze swept the forest in her search for a hidden storage space. She retraced her steps along the trail to the village, and, seeing nothing suitable, she returned to the lake.

Her gaze fell on the area where she knew the small hidden clearing lay beyond the thicket. She experienced a funny little quiver at the thought of that clearing. There, only a short time ago, she'd lost her virginity. It had been a wondrous place out of time. After several days of heartache, Hannah was surprised that she could still think of that time with joy.

Stop it! she scolded herself. *Stop it now! He doesn't care for you! Why can't you get it through your thick skull!*

She closed her eyes and saw his face smiling at her, the way it had only that very afternoon. He'd looked like he'd wanted to devour her. *He still desires me, although it pains him to know this!*

She picked up the dishes and set them behind the rock, out of sight of anyone who might wander to the lakefront. Then she headed toward the thicket and the tiny clearing beyond.

Despite White Bear's recent indifference toward her,

Hannah didn't believe that he made a habit of making love to any available female. No, she thought, if she was certain of one thing, it was that she was the first woman he'd touched in a long while . . . perhaps since he'd lost his wife.

Which meant? *Nothing.* Perhaps he hadn't thought himself capable of responding to another woman. *Until I came.* She scowled. *Lucky me.*

It was still light out. The days had shortened, but the hour was early yet as Hannah stepped carefully through the woods, searching for the spot where White Bear had taken her.

Suddenly, she was there. As she entered the clearing, she stepped on the pine needles, releasing their pungent scent. Memories exploded at the pleasant odor. Hannah closed her eyes, and it was that night again . . . and White Bear was lying beside her, kissing her, touching her . . . laving her with his mouth until she cried out—not once, but several times—in ecstasy.

She shuddered and hugged herself with her arms. When she lifted her lashes, her eyes were filled with tears, and she felt an aching void.

Oh, White Bear . . . Longing swept through her, making her reach out and grab hold of a low branch of the nearest tree. Why her? Why here? Why not some male bondservant on a prosperous English colonial farm?

Someone within her reach.

The snap of a twig alerted her to the possible presence of an intruder, but when she searched her surroundings, the only sign of life was a chipmunk scurrying through the brush and up a tree.

She released a ragged breath and pulled herself together. She was here for a purpose, and it wasn't to indulge in memories of her and White Bear. She needed to find someplace to hide food and a weapon, and perhaps a fur blanket with which to keep warm in the cooling temperatures of the coming autumn nights.

Just past the clearing, she found a hollow in a tree, the hole in the base hidden beneath a tangle of briar bushes. She wouldn't have found it, if she hadn't been looking for such a place. In fact, her first thought was simply to stash some things beneath the thornbushes themselves, until it seemed as if God was with her by gifting her with the hollowed-out tree.

Perfect, she decided. As she returned for the dishes at the lake, her quest successful, Hannah wondered why she wasn't thrilled with her discovery.

Jules Boucher and the two men he'd hired—one at the inn before he'd left and the other at the last trading post he'd visited—arrived at the Seneca village at dusk on the second day of the Green Corn Festival. The village yard was empty, but for a young woman carrying a basket of beans, a wizened old man stripping the bark off a long branch with a bone-handled knife, and a couple of dogs feeding on a chunk of raw venison. The compound was unprotected by stockade; the Frenchman wasn't surprised, for many of the Iroquois had abandoned the practice of walling in their villages. Some, who remained uneasy with the white men—both the English and the French—and their quest to acquire land, beaver pelts, and the favor of the Indians who could help them attain both, continued to live within their fences. Fortunately for the three white men, these Indians were of the trusting lot.

The longhouses were arranged haphazardly. There were a couple of small huts, and the only clearing was not a large one in the center of the village, but one oddly shaped yard, which was nothing more than the largest break between buildings.

Jules approached the old man. "Grandfather, I am a friend. I am seeking a warrior of the *Nun-da-wä'-o-no*. His name is He-Who-Comes-In-The-Night."

The old man stared at him without answering.

The Frenchman stifled his impatience. "Grandfather, is this the village of Man with Eyes of Hawk?"

"Te-ah," the man said, shaking his head. "This is the village of the sachem Mud-Slinger, but he is gone to celebrate the Festival of Green Corn with our brothers to the west."

"Then you do not know of the brave, He-Who-Comes-In-The-Night."

"I know of him," the old man admitted.

"Is he here?"

The elder shook his head.

"Then where is he?"

The man smiled. "To the west. In the village of Man with Eyes of Hawk."

"Can you show me the way?" Boucher felt excitement that he was finally getting close to the man who'd purchased Hannah Gibbons.

"What do you want with him?"

The Frenchman clamped his teeth behind his smile. "To speak with him. He has something of mine that he has been keeping safe for me."

The man's gaze narrowed with suspicion.

"A woman," Jules admitted, hoping to win the old man's trust. "A white woman."

The Indian studied him thoughtfully as if trying to decide whether or not to trust the white man.

"I have gifts for your people," Boucher said. "Steel knives. A jug of whiskey."

The old man's dark eyes brightened. "I will tell you how to get there."

* * *

She heard the sound as she headed back to the compound. It sounded like a wounded animal, Hannah thought. Or a woman. Or a child.

She moved in the direction of the muffled whimpering, picking her way carefully through the brush without making noise. Then she saw him. Hannah's insides turned to ice. Eagle Soaring sat on a boulder, his head bent, his face out of view, but she knew he was crying.

Has something happened to his father?

As quickly as that thought came, it vanished. If White Bear had been hurt or ill, the child would be at the village with his family, not hiding his tears in the woods.

She hung back, debating whether or not to approach, and then moved closer, unable to ignore the boy's pain. Hannah noted that he didn't hold his arm or leg or any part of himself that might have alerted her to a physical injury. Which meant that something else was hurting him.

Drawn to comfort the child, Hannah went to him. It was a moment before he realized someone was there. Once he did, he shot up from his seat and crouched defensively, grabbing up a stick from the ground. His gaze narrowed.

His expression hardened when he saw it was Hannah. "What do you want?" he demanded.

Hannah's heart melted, for she could see his eyes were red-rimmed, and his cheeks glistened with the remnants of his tears. "Are you all right?"

"Yes," he said, dropping the stick. "Why would I not be?" He scowled as she went to the rock and sat down. She looked up at him and patted the rock beside her in a silent command for him to sit. After a moment or two of staring at her, he sat.

Eagle Soaring was quiet. Hannah could tell that he was uncomfortable with her presence. But she was sure that she'd seen relief on his face when he'd first recognized her.

"Tell me," she encouraged softly.

"There is nothing wrong!"

She raised her eyebrows skeptically.

"There isn't!"

Hannah thought a moment, then scowled, recalling a scene she'd witnessed another day when Slow Dancer's son had bullied the boy. "It's Running Brook, isn't it?"

He shot her a stunned look, and she smiled. "You forget I lived with his family." She gazed straight ahead while giving the boy time to formulate a response. When he still didn't reply, she said, "I've seen the way he treats some of the children." She purposely didn't mention his name. "And he was mean to me when I was slave to Slow Dancer." Her lips twisted as she brushed back a stray lock of hair behind her ear. She still didn't look at him. "Running Brook is not a nice boy."

"He isn't," Eagle Soaring agreed.

She turned to face him and saw him blush. Hannah thought he was remembering the occasions in which he hadn't been pleasant to her. "You are nothing like him," she said gently.

"I'm not?" He looked vulnerable as he met her gaze.

She shook her head. "No, you're not. You are not a mean boy, Eagle Soaring. You don't want me in your lodge, but I think I understand."

"You are not angry with me?" He looked puzzled.

She grinned. "No."

"I do not understand you, white woman."

"Hannah," she said.

"Han-na," he murmured. "Why are you not angry with me?"

"You do not need my help. You and your father were managing fine without a slave. I understand that you feel that I am an intruder."

"Intruder?" he asked, apparently not sure of this English word.

"A person who comes in where she is not wanted. Someone who is in the way."

He shrugged. "Maybe my father and I were not managing so well, before you came," he mumbled, turning away. He picked up a rock from the ground and tossed into the forest thicket. The noise made as it hit the leaves sounded loud in the quiet of the woods.

Hannah felt a welling of tenderness for the boy, who was beginning to show signs of needing her friendship. Unwilling to destroy the moment, she remained silent in the hope that he would open up and talk.

"You cook good."

Her lips twitched. "Thank you," she said in Iroquoian. Their gazes met, and they smiled.

Her expression sobered. "It is all right to cry, Eagle Soaring."

Shame flickered across his face as he looked away. "Warriors of the *Nun-da-wä'-o-no* do not cry."

"I think they do."

He shot her a startled look, and she said, "I think your father cried when your mother died. Don't you?"

The boy frowned. "You think this?" He looked hopeful, vulnerable, and she saw the little child in him seeking reassurance.

His expression tugged on her heartstrings. "Yes, yes, I do. White Bear was hurting. He loved your mother, and it hurt him when she left you."

"I killed her," he said glumly.

It was Hannah's turn to be shocked. "No, Eagle Soaring! Don't ever think that!"

His eyes filled as he nodded his head. "It is true. My mother died because she gave me life." A tear escaped and ran down his cheek.

Without thought, Hannah reached out and wiped it away with her finger. "I don't believe your father thinks that."

A sob escaped from the child's throat. Hannah wanted to pull him into her arms for comfort, but was afraid to. Their budding friendship was just too new.

"I killed her," he said brokenly.

"Oh, Eagle Soaring!" She discarded the need for caution and wrapped her arms around him. She felt a lump rise to her throat when he wrapped his arms about her and burrowed his head against her side.

She hugged him and murmured soothingly, while she allowed him the comfort of her arms. Hannah had no notion of time as she held Eagle tightly. After the boy was quiet, he still didn't move away. Hannah wondered how often the child had needed comfort . . . and with no mother to offer it to him.

Eagle Soaring pushed himself from her arms. "I must go. My father will be looking for me," he said.

She stood as he did. He shifted uncomfortably and seemed afraid to meet her gaze. "Thank you," she said.

He looked at her then, his gaze questioning.

"For letting me be your friend for a little while. Sometimes I get lonely."

The boy's gaze sharpened as he stared at her. She couldn't be sure, but she thought he was pleased by her statement.

"But don't tell anyone," she said. "What is said between friends should always be kept a secret, unless they both agree that it is all right to share their secret with another."

Eagle Soaring's face brightened. "I will promise to keep our secret." He looked relieved.

"As I will keep all things between us a secret," she said. She couldn't keep the smile from her face as she watched him scurry back toward the village, the burden he'd carried made lighter by his father's slave.

But then her smile vanished as she thought about the

fact that she'd be leaving soon. Was it a mistake to befriend Eagle Soaring when she had no intention of staying?

An image of the child's father made her close her eyes and wish for something she couldn't have . . . the man and the child . . . a family.

The image changed to a man lying on a wooden floor, his head in a pool of blood. Hannah shuddered and hugged herself with her arms. Even if White Bear loved her, wanted her, he would turn from her once he learned the truth.

She, Hannah Gibbons, was a murderer. She had taken a life.

No man would love a murderer, she thought, her eyes misting.

And what man would want a murderer to care for his only child?

Chapter 13

"It's so beautiful," Hannah murmured to herself, studying the lake through a break in the trees.

She was alone, and it was late. She had come to stow away food in the tree hollow just beyond the clearing where she and White Bear had made love. The night was much as it had been when they had been together, only the moon was brighter and there wasn't a breeze.

The moonlit water seemed to beckon her to come closer. She started through the brush, carefully placing one moccasin-clad foot before the other.

The third day of the Green Corn Festival had been tiring for her. Morning had begun as it had the previous two days, but that afternoon, the Indians had feasted and played games, and the festivities had continued until dusk. Indian guests had arrived, and Hannah had been kept busy helping Moon Woman with the food and the sleeping arrangements for the additional people.

The day had been pleasant. Hannah had noticed that Eagle Soaring's curious gaze had sought her time and again throughout the day. She sensed a change in the child's attitude toward her, and she was pleased. Last night, she'd decided that she wouldn't push the child into friendship. She had made it known to Eagle Soaring that she was there for him, but she would wait for the boy to come to her.

Her arms were achy and she was hot. The temperature of the August night was cloying. The gentle lapping of the water against the shore invited her to swim.

She stared out over the water for a moment, debating whether or not she should give in to the urge or head back to the village before someone came looking for her.

No one will come looking. I haven't tried to escape, so they think that I've accepted my lot. And hadn't she? . . . Until she'd fallen in love with White Bear? She'd been away from English civilization for a long while. Someone could be seeking her for Samuel Walpole's murder. *No,* she thought, *no one would come to the colonies to search. Not a place where there are savages.*

She allowed her lips to form a smile. These people might seem like heathen savages to the English, but despite their primitive ways, she'd seen little of their savagery herself. They were people, just like her. They had some strange customs and ceremonies, but she found most of them beautiful, deeply religious, and emotionally moving. She knew there was a side to them that would shock her, but she'd yet to see it. She hadn't been tortured. She was a slave, but oddly, she was treated at times like one of the maidens and not like a slave at all. Hannah thought that it might be Moon Woman's influence, but she couldn't be sure.

Moon Woman had always treated Hannah fairly. Hannah knew the woman wouldn't mind if she lingered at the lake. She could stay for a while and return through the gate and no one would think anything of her absence. It seemed strange that a slave could have so much freedom.

It was true that Hannah had nowhere to go, no one worrying over her disappearance, but the Indians didn't know that. They weren't aware that she was murderess without a family.

A fish jumped in the lake ahead, its foray to the surface accompanied by a plopping sound. With her food safely stashed, Hannah decided that she could afford the luxury of a late-night swim.

She still wore the kilt, and it wasn't long before the skirt and her moccasins were discarded, so that she stood with her naked white curves bathed in the soft moonglow. *Ribbitt!* A frog called to its mate from some hidden nearby place. Behind her, the crickets and other insects that came alive each summer night sang in chorus, their combined voices filling the forest with music. Hannah closed her eyes for a long moment and allowed herself to forget her concerns, to absorb the peace that was nature's gift on this hot August night.

The water soothed her ankles as she stepped in. She sighed with pleasure as it swirled about her calves, then her knees, and her thighs. As the warm liquid caressed her higher . . . past her waist . . . past her breasts, she shivered with pleasure. Her lower limbs, most particularly, were sore. She lay back in the water, and her legs floated to the surface. The water stroked her head, fanning out her hair, so that when she moved about, the dark strands tickled her neck, back, and shoulders.

Hannah lay motionless for a time, gazing at the sky, studying the stars twinkling in the night sky. For a while, she was able to shut out all but the beauty of the night. She felt as though she understood the Indians, their respect for the land, their reverence and gratitude toward Mother Earth. Too often, she thought, the English were too wrapped up in their daily lives to appreciate the gifts God had given them.

She allowed the earth to soothe her and take away her

fears. Alone, undisturbed, Hannah closed her eyes and felt comforted by the night.

"It is time you take a wife, White Bear," Woman with Dark Skin said. "You have been alone too long. A man needs the companionship of a woman."

Startled, White Bear could only look at his late wife's mother. She had found him in the forest, among the trees, near his wife's resting place. He'd started guiltily when she'd spoken, for his mind had not been on Wind Singer, but on Hannah. His thoughts had been consumed with Hannah of late . . . her quiet presence within his lodge . . . the care she'd taken with preparing their meals . . . the way his heart leapt whenever he glanced at her.

Did Woman with Dark Skin know? As he turned and gazed into her warm, dark eyes, he decided that the matron didn't know, hadn't guessed that he had betrayed her daughter's memory with his lust for the slave. He silently hoped that he could continue to spare her the pain of knowing.

"Why do you say so?" he said, his gaze moving back to Wind Singer's grave.

"It has been eight summers, White Bear," she said. "It is not natural that a man not have a wife to hold him . . . to comfort him. The days can be long, but the nights longer still. While I was gone, I missed my sachem husband as he missed me. I think of our time apart, and my heart bleeds for my daughter's husband."

His throat felt constricted as he turned to face her. "You have said the way of it—I am your daughter's husband."

She shook her head. "Then, I have said it wrong, White Bear," she said softly. "You were my daughter's husband. My child is dead. You are alive. Her son is alive. As I understood your need to teach your son, I understand a man's desire for a woman." She regarded him with affection. "A man's need for a mate."

Pain contorted his features. "I had a mate," he said in a choked voice. "I need no other."

"That is not so. You have a long life ahead of you. It pains me to think that it will be empty of love . . . a woman's love."

His mouth softened with a smile. "You love me, grand-mother."

She snorted. "You have the knowledge of it, but it is not the love of a mother of which I speak. It is the love in which two people join . . . in which they love not only with heart and mind but with their bodies."

"I have no love to give," he said stiffly.

"You have more love than all the braves of this village. I know you, White Bear. I have seen you when you were but a boy. I have watched you grow. I have seen your love for my Wind Singer blossom."

She smiled at his astonished expression. "You and I were once other than of the *Ho-De'No-Sau-Nee,*" she said, referring to all the Indians that were Iroquois. "It is not a bad thing for the English to speak the name of our beloved deceased. It is a good thing—is it not? It is our way of remembering our love for them . . . of keeping their memory alive."

She touched his arm, felt his tense muscles relax beneath her fingertips. "It has been hard not to speak of her. Just as it must have been hard for you. I should have told you this before. I have seen you grieve for Wind Singer eight years—too many years. I have kept silent, because a part of me understands and has accepted the Indian ways. But it was wrong of me to do this. You better than anyone know the struggle one faces who is caught between two peoples—those we left behind and our new people, the families of our heart."

"I didn't know," he whispered as he faced her and

pulled her into his arms. He hugged her against him, taking comfort in her need as well as his. He held her frail body a moment, then released her.

Woman with Dark Skin looked troubled as she stepped back and regarded the man she loved like a son. "I was wrong," she said.

"You were not wrong," White Bear replied. "I was. I have dishonored your daughter with my continued grief. I have hurt our son with my refusal to go on."

The matron grinned, a flash of white teeth accompanied by a glimmer of warmth in her lovely dark eyes. "I hear a new hope in your voice, my son. Perhaps you are ready to go on?"

He caught his breath, aware in that second that she looked very much like her daughter, the way Wind Singer had appeared whenever she'd been pleased with him. "It might seem so," he said, surprised that the memory of his late wife no longer gave him so much pain. Wind Singer was gone. He was finally accepting it. And he had Woman with Dark Skin to thank for his acceptance.

"Good!" the matron said. She became thoughtful. "Let me think . . . which maiden might our matrons choose for you . . ."

White Bear's heart gave a lurch. He didn't want his new wife chosen for him, although it was the way of his people for the village matrons to do so.

"Singing Rain?" she wondered aloud. She shook her head. "No, not Singing Rain," she said, and he felt relieved until she said, *"O-non-kia O-kon-sa." Hair Face.* Hair Face was a widow, an older matron with a man's face and a female's body.

White Bear knew he'd been fortunate to have married his chosen woman the first time, but he feared that once he admitted he was ready to marry again, he would be forced to take someone he didn't want to love . . . or someone who was displeasing to him.

He scowled and then laughed as he caught the teasing twinkle in the matron's ebony eyes.

You can't expect to marry the one you love . . . not when the woman you want and love is a slave, an inner voice taunted him.

Shock made him tense up. He loved Hannah. It was true. He had denied it, because he had been fighting Wind Singer's memory, battling with guilt. He had regarded any feeling for Hannah as a betrayal to his dead wife.

Woman with Dark Skin had given him hope again. With his guilt gone, he realized that he wouldn't have made love to Hannah if he hadn't already given her his heart. He might have told himself that he'd been just satisfying a male physical need, but now he knew that it was his growing love for her that had driven him to take Hannah into his arms.

Woman with Dark Skin had continued to mention and discard several Indian women's names as prospects for his new wife. Finally, she looked at him, and said, "You know what you want in a wife, White Bear. You find your mate, then you confide in me. I will see that your choice is yours."

White Bear grinned at this woman, and understood—again—why he held her in such high esteem. "You are a kind woman with a loving heart, grandmother," he said.

She wrinkled her nose at him. "I am a wonderful woman, White Bear—you speak the truth." She touched his cheek. "When we are alone, will you be so kind as to call me mother instead of grandmother? There are certain *Ho-De'No-Sau-Nee* customs that I do not care for. I have no problem with Eagle calling me grandmother, for I am the same to him," she said. "But, I am not old enough to be grandmother to both the son and his fine *older* warrior father."

His rich laughter made her grin; it had been so long since she'd heard it. Their past lives had given them a secret bond.

"Yes, mother," he said fondly.

"Thank you, White Bear."

The night was magic. Hannah lay on her back, floating, enjoying the simple pleasure of just being alive. All her worries seemed trivial the more she allowed the lake to soothe her, envelop her in its warmth. For a while, she drifted . . . like a lily blossom on the water. She was safe here, several hundred yards past the Seneca bathing area. No one could see her here. No one would look for her here.

Except White Bear.

Strangely enough, even the thought of him didn't disturb her calm. The lake and her surroundings had done such a good job of freeing her from her cares. She passed over thoughts of their strained relationship and concentrated on Eagle Soaring instead.

A smile curved her lips. *He's becoming my friend. He knows he can trust me.* The knowledge brought her such pleasure that it only added to the magic of the night.

The feelings she'd had when she'd found him crying should have surprised her, but instead the need to comfort him, to hold him, had seemed natural and somehow right.

She scowled as she thought of Running Brook. She didn't know exactly what He-Who-Comes-In-The-Night's son had done, but she could guess. The boys had been playing a game with the other children; Running Brook would have found some way to humiliate Eagle Soaring, perhaps even accusing Eagle of cheating at the game.

Running Brook needed to be taught a lesson or two, Hannah thought. He needed to be made to realize that everyone had feelings and their feelings should be treated with respect—not cruelty.

Hannah frowned, her thoughts of Running Brook nearly ruining her peaceful evening. She forced him from her mind and thought of Eagle Soaring's grandmother, Woman with Dark Skin. In the days since her return, Hannah had had occasion to study the matron and her relationship with those around her. She was quite an extraordinary woman; her generosity of spirit seemed so complete. She gave of herself to the villagers without asking in return, and she was rewarded with the love of her family and her people.

Thinking back to her initial reaction to the color of the woman's skin, Hannah felt shame. She had judged her—and unfairly. Moon Woman had been right; she—Hannah—had silently proclaimed herself better than the matron because she had lighter skin. She had been uncomfortable with Woman with Dark Skin's relationship to Eagle and White Bear. It didn't make her proud to have reacted that way, and knowing that she felt differently right now didn't change her guilt over it.

Woman with Dark Skin was the kind of person who forgave—and loved—and put others at ease. Hannah didn't think she was worthy enough to be forgiven, although there was no doubt in her mind that the matron would forgive her if Hannah confessed her grievous sin.

The tension had crept back, tightening Hannah's muscles. She forced herself to relax by telling herself that Woman with Dark Skin would be upset to know that she had ruined Hannah's peace.

The Englishwoman smiled, and her muscles began to uncoil as she concentrated once again on the beauty of the star-studded sky. She could hear herself breathing; each inhalation and exhalation of air into her lungs was magnified beneath the water. She closed her eyes and cleared her mind of all thought.

Han-na!

She smiled. It seemed like someone was calling her, but, of course, no one was looking for her. If someone had been, she wouldn't have come here. No one knew of this place, no one but . . . *White Bear.*

Her breath stilled as she listened, sure she had imagined the sound, but wanting to be certain.

She heard the movement of the water about her body, but nothing else. She exhaled slowly and smiled. There was no cause for alarm. Eagle Soaring was with his mother's clan, the clan of the Beaver. White Bear had been with several Seneca and Onondaga warriors, playing the games that the Indians enjoyed during festival time and that had followed the feasting of dishes made from the Three Sisters as well as other available meat, fruits, and vegetables.

"Han-na!"

Hannah blinked and listened again.

"Han-na!"

Certain she'd heard her name, she jerked upright in the water, and felt the violent seize of a cramp in her left leg. She gasped as she jackknifed and went under, her hands clutching the painful limb. Hannah sank below the surface, then came up sputtering, trying to catch her breath, while battling not to cry.

"Han-na!" His voice was closer. "Han-na!" White Bear was suddenly there beside her, reaching for her arm.

She cried out as he grasped her arm and caused her pain as he pulled her closer.

"Hanna, what is it?"

Beyond the realm of pain, she could sense his concern. "My leg!" she said with another gasp. The cramp intensified, making her cry out and filling her eyes with tears.

"Han-na, I'm going to bring you in," he said soothingly. "Try not to fight it. Let me take you along through the water." His sapphire gaze begged her to listen to him, to trust him. "You will do this?" he asked, his voice soft.

She nodded, then drew in a sharp breath as the pain renewed itself. After a few seconds, it started to ease, and Hannah was shocked to see her pain mirrored in the face of the man who held her gently and who had been waiting for her agony to ease before he maneuvered himself so that her could slip his arms around her from behind. Her leg throbbed as her muscles threatened to tighten again. She lay back against White Bear, conscious of his warm strength as he threaded his arms beneath her own. He held her with his hands locked just under her breasts. She should have been embarrassed, but she felt only relief . . . relief and gratitude that he was there to pull her from the lake.

"Relax, Han-na," he said, his voice at her ear. "Relax, and I'll help you. I know it hurts, but I'll make it better."

. . . *better,* she thought. *Yes, White Bear will make it better.* His tender concern for her made her want to cry again.

"Han-na?" he said huskily. "Are you all right?"

She nodded, and felt the wet heat of him radiating from his chest to her back. "I'm all right," she said weakly, unconvincingly, for her cramp was intensifying again. She closed her eyes and willed herself to listen to the silent words in her mind—the words previously spoken by White Bear. *Relax, and I'll help you.* And then *I know it hurts. I'll make it better.*

"White Bear," she whispered, as he began to swim with her toward the shore. She didn't think he heard her. "White Bear?"

His hold about her tightened. "Han-na, don't talk. Just close your eyes and let me pull you from the water. You can tell me later."

She nodded, but she knew he wouldn't see it. He was too busy concentrating on swimming toward the shore. Somehow she had managed to float quite a distance from land, and now White Bear had to take her in all that way.

He didn't speak; she didn't expect him to. She lay concentrating on everything but the throbbing muscles of her leg . . . the strong arms of the man who held her . . . the intimate position of his hands near her breasts . . . the brush and bump of their naked bodies as he swam using just his feet. He shifted his hold on her. Grasping her with only one arm, he stroked through the water with the other one. Their new position felt more intimate to Hannah. He swam with her cradled in one arm, pressed against his length, while he swept his other hand through the water in an arc beneath the surface. Her uninjured leg tangled with his. The contact of sleek limbs touching sent a sharp stab of desire thorough Hannah. She quickly tried to move it away, and her movements caused her left leg to seize up with pain again.

And then White Bear was lifting her into his arms and striding through the forest toward the secluded clearing. His breath caressed her face. He carried her effortlessly. She sighed and rested her cheek against his chest until he gently set her down on a bed of pine needles.

"I'll return," he said, rising to his feet. Through pain-glazed eyes, she saw his compassionate blue gaze waver . . . She blinked and watched his magnificent naked body as he disappeared through the break in the trees on his way back to the water.

True to his word, he was back within seconds, clutching her white doeskin kilt and the slip of deerskin that could only be his breechclout. He set them on the ground beside her as he knelt by her side.

She tried to mask her pain as she looked at him. She saw from his expression that he knew she was hurting. He seemed unaware of his own nakedness. Her own leg hurt too much for her to care that she herself was unclothed.

"Lie back, *O-gä-uh,*" he instructed gently.

Her eyes continued to study him while she did what she was told. White Bear grabbed hold of her leg gently and tried to straighten it. She cried out, and, contrite, he murmured soothingly to her.

"I know this will hurt, Han-na. Your leg is like iron."
He smiled gently at her startled expression. "No, *O-gä-uh*,
your muscles—they are hard. I must work to soften them."

He looked at her as if asking permission. It seemed
strange that he would ask when she was lying there, helpless
and without clothes, a slave at her master's mercy. *Mercy*,
she thought, her gaze caressing the face of the man she
loved. White Bear had an ample supply of mercy.

"Han-na?" He still waited for her answer.

Her nod gave him her permission.

She drew in a sharp breath as he began to rub her sore
leg. His touch was firm. He kneaded her taut calf and
rubbed down to her ankle. His whole attention was on
softening her leg muscle, while she began to concentrate
on his bent head and the warmth of his masculine fingers
as he brushed and pressed against her skin.

The leg had begun to feel better. The throbbing wasn't
as extreme. Hannah closed her eyes and allowed a sigh
of relief to slip past her lips—and then a soft moan of
pleasure.

Did he hesitate for just a moment? she wondered without
opening her eyes to check. She couldn't decide, for he
continued to work on the leg, touching her, caressing her,
filling her senses with the pleasure of his hands.

She wasn't aware that there was a change in his touch
until she felt his fingertips flutter against her belly. Even
then she was too wrapped in the pleasure, the relief, that
she didn't notice that White Bear had moved from near
her feet to her side where he had more access to the whole
of her.

She felt his breath against the tip of breast just a bare
second before her nipple was warmed by his mouth.

Her eyes shot open. She shuddered as she saw his head
bend to her breast once again, felt the gentle wet tugging
of lips, teeth, and tongue.

She knew she should stop him. The last time had been glorious, but he had hurt her afterward when he'd ignored her, when he'd pretended this magic between them had never existed.

Stop him, reason argued.

I love him, her heart cried out in response.

He'll hurt you again! logic interfered.

No, I won't let him. I love him. Please, please let me enjoy these moments of happiness with him.

But to her shock, White Bear suddenly stopped kissing her breasts, touching her . . . loving her, as if he'd read her mind and regretted his loss of self-control.

"White Bear?" she whispered, his withdrawal already giving her pain.

His eyes were shut tightly. He seemed to be fighting some inner battle—perhaps the battle of lust against conscience.

Hannah felt an infusion of warm tenderness for this man. *He doesn't want to hurt me.* He hadn't lied earlier when he'd tried to tell her. She hadn't believed him, but now she did. His private struggle convinced her as nothing else that he cared . . . more than he would have liked to.

He lifted his dark golden lashes, revealing brilliant blue eyes that revealed both his torment and his desire. "Hanna, forgive me."

Her leg hurt, but it was nothing compared to the ache of sharing his pain. She didn't want him to suffer. She loved him, and she wanted to give him pleasure.

He had been hurt, devastated by the loss of his wife—Eagle Soaring's mother. Perhaps he wasn't ready to love again. Perhaps he never would be. But he desired her—as he had desired no other woman since his wife's death. That was something, wasn't it? she thought.

She would accept what he would give her, because as truth would have it—she wasn't worthy of his love . . . of anyone's love. Her love had failed her mother. Her love had failed to keep the Abbott family happy in a world more primitive than their old one.

So, she would accept that she couldn't be Bear's lifelong mate. She couldn't be his wife, but she could ease White Bear's pain in the only way she knew how . . . by offering him the comfort of her body. And she would take each moment with him as a precious gift to be brought out later and treasured, a glorious memory for the dark days, when he would no longer need her.

He had risen to his feet, perhaps thinking that she hadn't accepted his apology. Her heart melted with love as she stared at his broad, muscled back and remembered how wonderful it had felt to touch him . . . and be touched by him.

"White Bear." She tried to stand and cried out, then sat, clutching her thigh because she couldn't reach the part of her leg that was still sore and tender.

Immediately, White Bear was crouched at her side, rubbing away the soreness. His concern for her was evident in his face and in the gentleness of his soothing hands.

Her eyes filled with tears as she realized just how much she loved him. She would sacrifice all to be with him— her heart included.

Hannah knew then that she would stay . . . for as long as he wanted her.

She reached out and touched his arm. He stilled and tensed beneath her fingers. "White Bear," she beseeched softly, "please look at me."

He raised his head slowly, his face shuttered but for his blue gaze, which glistened with emotion.

Hannah looked at him, conveying her desire for him with her eyes. She shifted slightly and was able to reach his shoulder. She felt him jerk with pleasure as she caressed him, and she smiled, pleased that she had such an effect on him.

She lay back and opened her arms. "Come here," she whispered. "Come here, my Golden Warrior."

An astonished look on his face preceded his expression of gladness. And then White Bear groaned with feeling as he fell into her arms.

Chapter 14

It felt like a homecoming to Hannah. White Bear slipped his arms beneath her, burrowed his face against her neck, and seemed content just to hold her for a while.

A lump of emotion rose to Hannah's throat, while her eyes filled with joyful tears. This was where she wanted to be . . . in White Bear's arms, loving him, cherishing him. If she couldn't have him forever, she would take today.

She hung on to him tightly, her hands clutching the muscles of his back. She closed her eyes, memorizing the moment . . . the soft puffs of his breath against her ear . . . the strength of his embrace . . . the weight of him pressing her to the softly cushioned ground. She stopped breathing to listen, to sense. She didn't want to forget a single thing.

As if he, too, were committing this time to memory, White Bear didn't move except to hold her tighter. Hannah stroked his back and tunneled under his hair to curve her hand about his nape. She felt him shiver as she rubbed his neck and then lovingly combed her fingers through his long, dark golden hair. She enjoyed the wonderful silken texture of his locks, adding the feeling to her memory imprint.

Pleased by White Bear's reaction to her attention, she slid her hand slowly from the crown of his head, down his back, past his waist, to his buttocks. She moved to cup his taut muscles with both hands. Her breath quickened as he moved, and she felt the flex and the hardening of his firm cheeks. Her hands found and enjoyed the same firmness in his thighs.

White Bear, she knew, was not unaffected by her touch. She'd heard the sharp intake of his breath as she rediscovered the smooth hardness of his firm, taut buttocks. When she lifted her hands to bring them back to his neck, he raised himself up and began a journey of discovery of his own. His journey of lips and hands ... and tongue ... made Hannah arch up against him in a silent demand for more of him.

"Han-na ..." he whispered. He nibbled at her ear, sending a shaft of pleasurable sensation down her spine and throughout her limbs. He paused a moment to gaze at her, then he was kissing the long slender column of her throat. She moaned softly, appreciatively, enjoying the moist trail created by his mouth.

He hesitated near her shoulder, touching his lips to the smooth expanse of skin above her full feminine curves. Hannah's breasts swelled in anticipation. Her nipples hardened as if they'd already been kissed. When he seemed in no hurry to continue his journey downward, she became impatient. Capturing his head with her hands, she guided him toward her breasts, her flesh that was ripe with longing for his attention.

He gave it without hesitation. Taking her nipple into his mouth, he played with the tip tenderly, leisurely ... as if he had all the time in the world and he was going to enjoy each and every lasting moment of it. His tongue swirled around the nipple, before his teeth closed gently on the bud. He abraded the tip with loving care, just enough to increase its sensitivity and induce a burst of feeling within Hannah that reached out to re-create itself deep down within her abdomen.

She stiffened, overcome with the spiral of ecstasy that was centered within her womb, a pleasure controlled by White Bear.

"Bear!" she cried out. *"Please."*

He was stroking her where she could feel the most pleasure. Her breath came in short pants; she felt like she was racing . . . toward the magic of flight. But she didn't want to fly alone.

"Dus'hah-wah," she begged. *Give me.* She wanted more of him. It was happening too quickly. She didn't want it to end; she wanted to prolong the joy, to share it with him . . . but she seemed as if she was traveling alone.

"It is all right, my sweet one," he assured softly. "Do not fight it."

"No!" she pleaded. "No, I want you with me!"

His smile was loving. "I will have my time, my Han-na. Together we will soar, but first I want to bring you pleasure. I want you to know how much this man is sorry . . . and that I do not take the gift of this woman lightly."

The pleasure within her was pulsing. White Bear slipped to her side, where he could touch all of her freely, and Hannah alternately gasped and shuddered as he splayed his fingers across her stomach and rubbed and caressed, occasionally bending his head to kiss what his hands had touched. He paid special attention to the silky skin of her smooth belly. He dipped his finger in her navel and seemed to enjoy the way her stomach muscles reacted beneath his hand. He murmured in satisfaction at her response when he placed his tongue in the same hollow . . . when she jerked and her belly went into spasms . . . when she caught her breath before releasing it in a shuddering hiss.

She didn't want to let him go when he moved. Her

hands sought to renew contact with him. She reached out and groaned in frustration when she could touch him in certain places only with her fingertips. She wanted to feel more of him. She wanted to experience the burning heat of his flesh, to touch and kiss his stomach the way he was touching and kissing hers.

White Bear slipped his hand over the moist, secret area that proclaimed her a woman. His caress included the insertion of his finger. Hannah stiffened, then relaxed her legs, moaning with pleasure as she arched in a way that was a female's invitation to her male counterpart. He found her most sensitive area and deliberately, but lovingly, worked to bring her pleasure. He never stopped stroking her, not even after he drew a wild cry from her. He continued past the point when he sent her clear up and over the edge.

Her pleasure was more intense than ever before. As she began slowly to come down from the clouds, shimmering and shivering on her journey home, White Bear sent her spiraling upward again on a whirlwind of boundless ecstasy. But this time, he would go with her; this time it was clear that he had every intention of sharing the joy. His hands were trembling as he touched her breasts and belly. His breath quickened, and his eyes burned with blue fire as he stroked and fondled between her legs, drawing from her the liquid heat that prepared her for him.

When she gasped out his name, White Bear covered her with his length and kissed her passionately, a hot wet mating of open mouths, teeth, and tongues.

Spurred on by her desire for his pleasure, Hannah touched the man she loved everywhere with her hands . . . light gentle finger- caresses trailing over his skin . . . long, pressing strokes that squeezed and fondled and sought to rouse a wild cry from male lips.

Unable to bear their full physical separation any longer,

Hannah opened her legs, and her fingers searched to guide him home.

But White Bear was already ahead of her. He caught her hands before they found their mark and anchored them by her head, not forcefully, but lovingly. He caught her glance, his blues eyes heavy-lidded and slumberous with passion. He widened his gaze, and she saw a flash of desire and a warmth that was something more. That something made Hannah's heart stop and then continue to beat more rapidly with hope.

"Han-na," he said huskily.

"Yes, White Bear." *Yes, I love you.*

He closed his eyes, and when he opened them again, she saw such raw emotion, such love, in his blue gaze that her eyes flooded with tears of gladness.

And then he was pressing himself home. As he filled her with the turgid male heat of his staff, he held her gaze, sending her silent messages of love. When he had buried himself deep within her, he released her hands and tenderly cupped her face. He paused a moment to kiss her lips sweetly. After one more loving kiss, he began a rhythm of joining. He eased himself in and out of her, moving his hips in such a way that would bring her the most pleasure. Hannah was overcome with the act, with the love.

"Han-na," he gasped as he increased the pace, "I love you."

His words came at the exact moment her body flew, sending her into space, freeing her from her inhibitions, fusing her heart, mind, and body with this man.

The shaft of hot pleasure was full and long, the sensation lingering long after she heard White Bear's triumphant shout and felt him stiffen and shudder within her arms.

Hannah became aware of her earthly surrounding once again. She felt the weight of White Bear and heard the sound of his heartbeat and his labored breathing as he struggled to regain his breath. She was conscious of the scent of the man—a clean, masculine fragrance that belonged only to him . . . of the perfume of crushed pine needles and the odor of the woods on a hot summer night.

Their bodies were slick with perspiration, but Hannah didn't care. She had no desire to move. Their lovemaking —his declaration of love—had added an enchantment to the magic of the night.

As White Bear lay over her, pressing her down with his weight, she smiled, glad for once that she was not a small woman. She was a woman made for such a man; their sizes complemented each other. Her body bore his weight easily enough. If she had to use more lung power to take in air, she didn't mind, for she felt wonderful. *He feels wonderful.*

She stroked his head and ran her hand down his hair. A smile curved her lips as she embraced him hard, before she caressed him lovingly again.

White Bear hadn't moved, hadn't said a word, but there was nothing within him that she could sense that said he regretted what had just occurred. What he said, she thought.

That he loved her.

White Bear rolled off Hannah and pulled her against his side. A small smile hovered about his mouth. He loved this woman, and he'd just told her. For the first time since he'd lost his wife, everything about the world seemed warm and beautiful and full of life again.

He felt the brush of her hair against his chest as she snuggled against him. He lifted a hand to stroke her hair and was rewarded with her soft sigh of contentment. She lay curled on her side, her breasts pressed against his flesh, her legs entwined with his, and he was conscious of every silken curve of her against his skin.

He closed his eyes, enjoying the way she felt in his arms. Their joining had been wonderful. Even now his manhood proclaimed that he wanted her again. She had surrendered

herself sweetly. Despite the hurt he'd caused her previously, she'd given him her trust.

Her hand spread across his belly, fondling him with
loving caresses. He raised his head slightly to gaze at her,
just as her fingers trailed down to his groin. Fire shot
through his lower limbs as he felt her fluttering touch on
his left thigh. She looked up suddenly, and his breath
quickened as he caught sight of her twinkling gray eyes
and mischievous smile.

She held his gaze as she continued to stroke him, everywhere but the one part of his body that called out for her
touch.

He narrowed his eyes. "Han-na." His voice held a note
of warning.

Her answering laughter was like music. It was the first
time he'd ever heard such merriment. The sound was
infectious. He had difficulty pretending anger, but he did.
She was the perfect picture of beauty in his mind . . . her
glistening gray eyes . . . her pert little nose . . . her full pink
lips that looked ripe for kissing.

She regarded him warily. "White Bear—" As her face
fell with disappointment, he moved swiftly to flip her onto
her back and pin her hands at her sides.

He chuckled at her surprised expression. When she
arched her lovely eyebrows at him, he knew she had caught
onto the game. He could see her mentally calculating her
next move. The air between them was playful. White Bear
bend his head to kiss her nose and winked at her as he
raised up again.

"You don't play fair," she grumbled good-naturedly.

"Ah-kee'! And what was that you were doing? You touch
this man in every place but the right one."

Her face was picture of innocence. "And what place is
that?" she asked with a sweet smile.

"You, my sweet one, are a flower with hidden thorns,"
he said with a growl. He captured her mouth in a

demanding kiss that stole the smile from her lips and left
her gasping with shock . . . and pleasure.

He studied her as he drew himself up to allow her air.
"Shall I show you what you did?" he asked softly.

"No!" she gasped.

Ignoring her protest, he slid down her length until his
chin was on her stomach. She had lifted herself to watch
him. He studied her raised head between the luscious
mounds that tempted him to taste and touch, and was
struck by her trusting expression . . . and a look anticipated
pleasure.

"You have such smooth skin, my flower," he murmured
a second before he pressed his mouth to the sensitive area
between her hips. He nuzzled her above the dark curly
hair that protected her womanhood.

He looked up, allowing his caressing gaze to feast on
the beauty of her reaction . . . the pleasure in her glistening
gray eyes . . . the slight parting of her pink lips. "One
would never know that you have tiny barbs waiting to entan-
gle." He rubbed his face against her silky skin, while he
moved slowly upward. Their bodies brushed intimately. His
hardness caressed her softness. She moved, her lushness
seeming to cry out for silken steel.

He kissed and nibbled a path that stopped short of her
breasts, and then he paused to observe her response.
Desire had softened her features. Her lips were moist as
if she'd recently used her tongue to dampen them. Her
glorious brown hair lay about her head, a thick silky cloud
against her neck and shoulders.

"What, *O-gä-uh?*" he asked huskily. "Do you want me to
touch your breasts? To kiss them?"

She blinked, then slowly gave a nod.

"But what if I say no?" he teased. "What if I touch
here"—he placed his finger to within an inch below her
right breast—"or kiss here." His voice had sounded
hoarse, full of longing. He shifted to press his mouth

between and just above the soft, white globes with their pouting pink nipples. As he nuzzled and dampened her sweetly scented skin, he sensed Hannah's impatience that he didn't just take the swollen flesh that waited so near for him.

"How does that make you feel?" he asked.

"Like a monster," she said sharply, her tone self-condemning.

Joyous warmth curled in his belly, spreading to make every part of him tingle. "You are not as bad as all that, my little slave," he said. He settled his hand on her breast and smiled as she sighed appreciatively and closed her eyes.

He captured the other breast as well, watching her response as he fondled her with both hands. She shuddered and arched upward. "Oh, Han-na," he murmured. "That's it, little one. You were made to enjoy my touch."

Affection for this woman filled him to overflowing. He smiled, aware that his expression had softened as he gently caressed her ... using his thumb and forefinger to worry her nipples. She opened her eyes, giving him a glimpse of the deep passion within her, and he was humbled by her.

"Han-na." He withdrew his hands. There were things he had to say, before he would take her again, things she deserved to know before he went on to show his love for her.

Shock and then anger lit up her gray eyes. "You bastard!" she cried, believing, it seemed, that he had brought her to such a state only to teach her a lesson.

An answering spark made him frown. "Why do you call me names?"

"Why?" she exclaimed. "You know why!" She looked hurt, and immediately he felt contrite that he hadn't gone on to explain more quickly.

"Han-na," he said quietly. "I have every intention of finishing what I started."

Her eyes widened. "I don't understand."

He gave a twisted smile. "No. No, I think you do not." He changed positions until he was sitting on his haunches beside her. "Han-na, I want to talk . . . need to talk."

"Talk?" Hannah's heart stilled briefly. She was afraid to talk, afraid to learn that their lovemaking hadn't been as emotionally moving to him as it'd been to her. She was afraid to find out that his declaration of love had been a dream. "What about?"

"You. Me. Us."

She pretended ignorance. "What about us? What is there to talk about?"

She felt her pulse jump when he narrowed his gaze at her. "You do not think there should be talk between us?" he asked, his voice low and even.

Hannah swallowed hard. "If you are going to warn me not to expect more from you—"

He captured her arm. His hand was firm and warm; his touch created frissons of sensation from her wrist to her shoulder. His expression held concern. "Han-na, I want more."

She stared at him startled. "You?" She was afraid to hope.

He nodded, his blue eyes filled with love.

"White Bear?" she breathed. "What are you saying?"

"I want us to marry."

Her throat choked up. "You want to marry me?"

"This is so."

"But, White Bear, I'm a slave."

He smiled. "Only until I say differently. I can make you one of the People."

Her stomach fluttered. "You can?"

He inclined his head. "But there is more," he said quietly. "It is our way for the matrons of the *Ho-De'No-Sau-*

Nee to choose a man's mate. We can marry only if they approve."

"Oh . . ." She looked away, so he couldn't see her tears.

"Han-na?" She sensed his frown.

Hannah swung her gaze back to the man she loved. "Why do you want to marry me?" she asked softly.

He looked surprised by her question. "Because I have feelings for you. Feeling of a man for his wife."

She allowed a smile to shine through her tears.

"I don't understand this," he said. "Why are you crying?"

She released a shuddering sigh. "Because I am afraid."

His blue eyes flashed. "Of me?" He looked disturbed, insulted by the idea.

"Oh, no, White Bear," she said with such feeling that he couldn't doubt her sincerity. "Never you."

He caught her shoulders, drawing her up until they were both kneeling and facing each other. "Do you not want Eagle Soaring?"

Hannah's face softened. "I want Eagle Soaring," she said without hesitation.

His features relaxed. "Then what is it?"

"I am afraid to hope that I will be a worthy wife for you."

His lips curved upward; the smile brightened his eyes. Hannah's breath caught with love for this attractive, caring man.

"You care for me, then?" He studied her intently, apparently anxious for her answer.

She touched his cheek, stroking his jaw with soft fingertips. "Oh, I care for you, White Bear." She tilted her head to one side. "What was your English name?" She suddenly wanted to know.

Emotion appeared in his face and was gone. "James. James Rawlins."

Hannah traced his lips with her finger. "Jamie," she

said, smiling. "Yes, I could see you as Jamie." She saw that he appeared startled.

"How did you know—?

She chuckled. "Oh, I didn't know. It seemed right somehow. You—Jamie—as a young boy." Her smile fell as she combed her fingers through his hair, brushing it back from his face. "But you aren't Jamie now. You're White Bear, golden warrior of the *Nun-da-wä'-o-no*—the man I love."

His face was an ever-changing portrait of emotion. It took a moment before he took in her last words. When he did, he lit up like the sun bursting through the clouds after a rain shower.

"Han-na," he breathed, and then he caught her hand and kissed her wrist. He tugged her close and reclaimed her mouth, devouring her completely. Hannah sighed and surrendered herself fully to his kiss. Her spine tingled. Her toes curled with feeling. Her breasts swelled, begging for the touch of his hands.

His breath came harshly as he lifted his head. "I will speak to Woman with Dark Skin," he said.

Hannah nodded and fought the niggling of doubt that threatened to destroy her dreams of loving this man.

He grinned and kissed her. Hannah clung to him fearfully, drawing strength from the warmth of his solid form.

White Bear groaned and deepened the kiss. Fire spread through Hannah's being. She whimpered, pressing herself against him harder. She wanted him, all of him, and sensed the passion within him building even while he obviously fought to control it.

"Han-na—"

"No, White Bear," she begged. "Enough talking. Just hold me. Kiss me."

His eyes flashed with blue fire before he drew her close and obliged without hesitation.

Their lovemaking was hot and fierce, stealing every ounce of passionate energy as they used their bodies to proclaim their love. And when it was over, they lay with limbs entwined, their hearts beating as one, as they held on to the closeness shared only by two people in love.

They left the clearing sometime later, returning to the village and a lodge house shared only by the two of them that night. Eagle Soaring was with his mother's clansmen; he stayed in their longhouse from time to time. If not for his grandmother's understanding of a father's needs, he would be living with and raised by his aunts.

While it concerned Hannah that something seemed to be missing in the relationship between White Bear and his son, she was glad that the boy was not at home this evening. She wanted to treasure this brief moment with White Bear ... She didn't believe, for one moment, that she'd be accepted by the matrons as White Bear's wife. As she lay on her platform with him, snuggled against his side, she thought of Singing Rain and the woman's obvious love for White Bear. Singing Rain was more suitable to be the brave's mate. Hannah knew it; she was sure that the Seneca women would see it, too.

Hannah knew that a man's wishes rarely entered into the matrons' decision of selecting a warrior's wife. Chilled, she moved closer to White Bear, seeking the heat he generated with his body ... and his love. She closed her eyes and felt a sharp stab of pain that she could never marry her golden warrior. Memories attacked her, clearly and insistently. Of Moon Woman when she'd come to escort Hannah to her new master ... and on the day Woman with Dark Skin had returned.

She frowned. Moon Woman had tried to warn her against losing her heart to White Bear.

And what if, by some miracle, the matrons approved of her for White Bear? How could she marry him? How could she—a murderess—become his wife when she still carried the dark secret of her crime?

She couldn't bear it if she allowed herself to love, to

hope, only to have it all end in ruins when he found out the truth . . . that she had killed a man, watched while doing nothing as his blood seeped from his head wound onto her bedchamber floor . . . before she'd run away.

She pressed against him closer, held on to him more tightly, and battled back the tears. She had never dreamed that she would enjoy a glimpse of such happiness. She'd never felt like she deserved it, so she stored up the precious memory.

The happiness wouldn't last. She'd learned that early on. Life often was cruel. Her mother had deserved all the joy this world had to offer her; yet, she'd received only pain and heartache . . . and then death at a young age.

Hannah accepted this gift of her time with White Bear for what it was. A teasing look . . . into a life that would never be hers.

She knew what she was and what future had been ordained by fate for her.

A murderess wasn't deserving of love . . . especially the love of a gentle, caring man.

Chapter 15

Reality, in the form of Jules Boucher, her former master, intruded to disturb Hannah's happy dreams. He arrived at the Seneca village with two other white men as the fourth and final day of the Green Corn Festival was coming to a close.

The people were out in the yard. This day their feast of hominy and succotash would be shared together about the huge cooking fire. The sight of Boucher's bearded face and scruffy appearance as he moved about the circle until he reached He-Who-Comes-In-The-Night set her heart racing with alarm. A hundred reasons for his presence flitted through her mind, all of them boding ill either for her or the *Nun-da-wä'-o-no* people. That he'd chosen to seek out Night first told her more than anything that the men's arrival meant some kind of trouble. It might even have something to do with her.

Although she wanted to jump up and hide, Hannah sat on her woven mat and waited. Had her past finally caught up with her—the murderess? Or was Boucher here for another reason? To trade for beaver pelts or other precious furs?

Hannah's nerves skittered. She silently prayed that Boucher had come only for furs, for she didn't want to leave. She would never willingly go back to him; the Indians treated her better.

Her chest constricted as her gaze sought White Bear and found him watching her from the cluster of men who'd only recently finished playing the peach-stone game. Her fear must have been mirrored in her face, because his expression softened as he met her gaze. His blue eyes seemed to relay the silent message that it would be all right, no one would destroy their new relationship.

Trust me. His look caressed her, implored her with those silent words.

She drew in a calming breath. Hannah tried to believe in their future together, because she wanted so badly to believe. But there were things that White Bear didn't know about her. Would he be so assuring if he'd known? Would he still be regarding her with eyes of warm blue; or would he be avoiding her gaze, his eyes a cold frosty color as he waited for the white men to take her away?

No one knew of their new and wonderful feelings for each other. They were all too startling and fragile yet, even for her. She couldn't imagine facing Moon Woman and the other women with her and White Bear's new discovery of each other.

And what of Woman with Dark Skin? White Bear had said that the matron promised to approve his choice for a wife, but surely that didn't include her as a candidate— a slave . . . and a white woman.

Eagle Soaring sat at her right side. He had become more open and friendly to her since their conversation in the woods. After a day of keeping his distance, the child must have decided that she was worth having as an ally, even if she was only her father's slave.

While she thought of the child, her eyes remained on Jules Boucher. The Frenchman turned and ran his gaze along the gathered circle of people. Hannah's blood turned to ice as his attention brushed over where she sat and then returned, his dark eyes gleaming with sudden, intense interest. The memory of his physical attack on her made her feel violated, dirty. If not for White Bear, she might have continued to believe that men were incapable of kindness toward women. She had been young when her father died, and while her mother had painted a wonderful picture of a caring man, Hannah had only Dorothy's word. Samuel Walpole had certainly been a poor example. John Abbott had treated her kindly, but in the end, hadn't he betrayed her by selling her to Jules Boucher, a man without morals or gentleness?

She forced herself to meet Boucher's gaze; she wouldn't allow him to see her fear. If he was here to take her back, he would leave, she vowed, disappointed. He-Who-Comes-In-The-Night might have traded for her initially, but the brave no longer owned her. She belonged to White Bear.

A seed of hot pleasure took root in Hannah and spread. The memory of her previous night with White Bear filled her thoughts, inspiring confidence and courage.

As her eyes sought to make contact with the golden warrior, she felt her love for him wash over her in a huge, engulfing wave. His gaze was elsewhere, but it didn't matter, for it was her joy just to look at him.

As she studied him, he turned her way. She silently willed him to read her thoughts . . . thoughts filled to overflowing with her love for him.

The brave's eyes darkened as if he'd understood. His gaze caressed her across the distance, each aching moment sending a message of caring . . . of eternity . . . of dreams.

"Han-na."

The Englishwoman pulled away from the lure of her

lover's eyes to smile at his son. "Are you still hungry, Eagle?"

He shook his head.

She studied his solemn face and became concerned. "What is it, child?"

She saw the boy considering Jules Boucher. "I do not like that man," he said with a frown.

"No," she murmured, "I don't either."

"What is he doing here?"

She lifted her hand to smooth away his fierce frown. "I don't know."

Eagle Soaring grabbed her fingers as he studied her. To her amazement, he placed her hand against his cheek, holding it there and stroking the back of her fingers soothingly, as if he sought to calm her fears. He looked so much like his father at that moment that she felt her heart swell with love.

"The white man will not take you away," he said with angry vehemence. "I will not let him." He paused to draw a shuddering breath and focused his gaze on White Bear. "My father will not let him. *You are ours. He cannot have you!*"

There was a wild light in the child's dark, shining eyes when he turned back to her. "That man—he was not kind to you," he said with a sudden maturity that tugged at Hannah's composure.

"No," she whispered, fighting tears.

He grinned then. "Good, then you will be content to stay with us."

She raised her eyebrows. "You want me to stay?"

"Do-gehs'—Truly. You are ours. Where else would you go?"

Hannah cupped her hand over Eagle Soaring's. The warmth of his small fingers comforted her as the sight of a happy infant pleases his mother. "Yes," she murmured, "why would I want to go anywhere? The village is my home now."

She gave him a tender smile, and his answering grin melted the remaining icicles of her fear.

And you are my family . . . the family of my heart, she thought. As she gave the child's fingers an affectionate squeeze, she silently prayed that it would remain so.

She refused to look at the Frenchman again. It felt better to pretend that he wasn't there.

Hannah sighed. If only he would go away . . .

"She is here," Boucher confided to his two cohorts later that evening as they set up outside the village fence. "I have seen her." Satisfaction curled his mouth into a momentary grin. His good humor vanished. "But there is a problem," he said and then paused for effect. "She no longer belongs to the Seneca, Night."

Charles Beakly scowled. "How are we going to get her then?"

"I will approach her new master. The woman is nothing but trouble. I'm sure he will be only too eager to rid himself of her."

"And if he doesn't want to let her go?" Robert Fenwick eyed the Frenchman with a wariness of one who didn't trust.

Jules's eyes suddenly gleamed. "Then we will convince the woman that she is better off escaping." He laughed, well pleased with his alternative plan. "You forget these people are savages. No woman in her right mind would not want to leave here."

"Father," Eagle said while he slipped off his moccasins when readying himself for bed, "why are those white men here?"

It was late. The day had been long and tiring for the inhabitants of White Bear's lodge. White Bear sat on a mat on the dirt floor, making a shaft for a new arrow. At the child's words, he looked up at his son.

"I would suppose they have business with someone."

"Then it isn't to take Hannah?" the boy asked.

White Bear's gaze cut to where Hannah was rearranging the supplies over her sleeping platform. "No one will take Hannah," he said. His hesitancy immediately drew Hannah's attention.

She sent him a look that reassured him of her love and felt his loss of tension as he interpreted it correctly. "No, Eagle," she said softly, turning her smiling gaze to the child, "no one is going to take me away. After all, I belong to your father and you now."

Eagle Soaring sought a reaffirmation from his parent. "She speaks the truth, son. You must not concern yourself with the presence of these white men. If their reasons are not pure, then I will deal with them."

The boy grinned. White Bear's blue gaze glowed hotly as he looked into Hannah's eyes.

Her skin flushed with heat, and she couldn't control the quickening of her pulse. Hannah dragged her gaze from the man she loved and focused it on the son she wanted. "You must rest well tonight, Eagle Soaring. We all must. We've had a busy day, and tomorrow there are still the guests to contend with."

Using his hands, Eagle hopped up onto his platform and sat with his legs hanging over the side. "I like the Green Corn Festival, but I like the Harvest Festival best." He glanced at Hannah and caught her questioning look. "It is a festival much like the Green Corn, only it is when all of our crops are ready. We play lots of games during the Harvest Festival."

He'd spoken slowly and in Iroquoian. Hannah nodded that she understood.

As she watched, the child bade them good night from his bed before pulling the flap down to make a cocoon of his sleeping platform, Hannah wondered why it was that Eagle Soaring never spoke English in front of his father. The child had said that it was his grandfather who was teaching him the English language. Why not White Bear, when it had to be obvious even to the little boy that English had been the language of his earlier life?

Did the boy want to learn it well to surprise his father? Or did he fear his father's reaction to his desire to learn? It was just one puzzle in the relationship of this man and boy. Anyone could see that White Bear and Eagle Soaring loved each other; yet there was some kind of emotional barrier between them that kept them from being fully free and comfortable in each other's presence. Hannah wished there was something she could do to help them. When Eagle had been troubled by Running Brook, he should have sought his father's advice, instead of crying over it in the woods, alone.

She sighed and didn't realize that the sound she'd made was audible enough to attract White Bear's notice.

"Han-na," he said, startling her from her thoughts, "what is it?" He eyed her with concern.

She smiled to assure him that there was nothing seriously the matter. "It *has* been a long day, hasn't it?"

He didn't return her smile. He narrowed his gaze as he continued to study her. "*O-gä-uh*, come here." His tone was quiet.

Looking at him, Hannah felt a jolt of something that momentarily kept her stationary.

His mouth firmed. "Han-na."

She swallowed hard. "Have I done something wrong?" she asked in a voice that quivered.

His features mirrored his surprise, then softened with understanding. "You have done nothing wrong, my love," he said softly. "It is I who've done wrong. I wanted only

to know your thoughts, and I have frightened you instead."
He held out his hand in invitation.

With a cry of gladness, she reached for his fingers and
took courage from his strength. "I'm sorry," she murmured, apologizing for more than he would understand.

He scowled. "You have nothing to be sorry for, Han-
na." He pulled her to his side, encircled her with his arm.

Oh, yes, I do, my love. Yes, I do.

"Are you afraid of the Frenchman?" he asked as he
searched her expression.

"Yes." And it was the truth, but for different reasons
than of which he was aware.

"I will not let him hurt you." He tightened his hold on
her. "I will protect you with everything that's in me."

"You mustn't get hurt on my account." *I killed a man.
I don't deserve your love.*

He grinned, a flash of white teeth in the light from the
fire pit. "I am White Bear. I did not get my name because
I was afraid to get hurt."

He had piqued her curiosity. "How did you get your
Indian name?"

"Some other time, woman. I wish not to waste this hour
on tales of my skills as a warrior." His voice dropped to a
low, husky whisper in her left eat. "I want to kiss your
sweet lips and feel you burn beneath my fingers."

She blushed. "White Bear! What of the boy?"

His lips twitched with amusement. "What of Eagle Soaring? He will not disturb us."

Hannah shook her head. "That's not what I meant—"

"Nor will we bother him," he murmured, tickling her
with his breath. "I plan for us to be very, very quiet." He
snaked his hand under her hair to her nape, and then
cupping her head, he bent to kiss her.

The world, for Hannah, exploded into a tiny, thousand
pinpoints of bright stars. "White Bear . . . Jamie . . ." she

said with a sigh of pleasure when he'd released her lips.
She shifted onto his lap, where she could caress him at
will.

"Yes, my Han-na," he said, his blue eyes glazing over.
"Oh, yes . . ."

Chapter 16

"I will not give her up. She is mine."

Jules Boucher looked at the blond-haired Seneca warrior and fought to stifle his aggravation. "She can be replaced," he said. "All slaves can be replaced."

The Indian eyed him with suspicion. "Then why do you want her?"

"I told you—there is someone who's been looking for her."

"Who is this one?"

The Frenchman scowled, angry at Samuel Walpole for forcing him to promise not to reveal to anyone the real reason for his search for the woman. *She will not want to come.* Walpole had said during their last meeting when the man had upped Jules's reward money for when he brought Hannah back. *Do not tell a soul—you must promise me!* The man had been quite insistent about it. *She will run where she can't be found, and her family will be heartbroken—again!* Jules had thought the whole thing strange, but the money had been too great to pass up.

"I can't tell you," he told the Indian. "All I can say that it is someone who cares for her."

The warrior's lips firmed. "I will not let her go," he insisted.

"Not even if Hannah wants to leave?" Jules asked softly. To his disconcertment, there was nothing in the Indian's expression to give away his thoughts.

"No."

But then the Frenchman saw it—the clenching of the man's fist at his side, a telltale sign that the man cared whether or not the woman stayed. That action was more revealing than any words could have been. The Indian cared for Hannah, a weakness that might ultimately be the man's downfall.

"Very well, monsieur. I will not press you. If, however, you change your mind, I will make the trade well worth your while."

The Indian merely looked at him.

Jules held up a metal-bladed knife. "Steel weapons, White Bear." He dug into the waist of his breeches and pulled out a pistol. "And guns."

"I do not need your white man's guns."

Then, the brave, White Bear, refused to speak with them anymore.

But the Frenchman wasn't discouraged. He had learned something useful, and there was still Hannah herself to convince.

"Well?" Robert Fenwick rose from his position near the campfire with an expression that was hopeful.

Boucher shook his head. "The savage will not give her up."

Charles Beakly cursed loudly and succinctly. "Now what are we gonna do? I've put in over a week for you, Boucher. Now you tell me that the Indian won't part with his slave, you had best convince me that you'll be able to make all this pay for us!"

"Yes, Frenchie," Fenwick said. "I left a hot little woman in a cozy room. You promised big, and you'd better come up with a plan to get our money.

The Frenchman clicked his tongue with impatience. *"Monsieurs, Monsieurs!* Please! You have too little faith in Jules Boucher. We will not lose the woman or our money. We'll not leave here without the prize we came for."

Charles's bugger eyes gleamed. "You've got a plan."

Jules snorted. *"Oui.* Of course, I have a plan. I am no imbecile."

It was Robert's turn to snort. "That remains to be seen, Boucher." He chuckled.

A sharp look from Boucher wiped away the man's merriment. "Do not insult Jules Boucher, Monsieur Fenwick." His face looked dark and dangerous, much different than what the two men had previously seen of the Frenchman.

"What are we going to?" Beakly asked. "Kidnap her?"

A gleam entered Boucher's eyes. "I will try convincing the lady first. If she doesn't come to see her need to escape, then that's exactly what we'll do."

"Christ, Boucher," Fenwick exclaimed. "You're going to take her from these heathens. Are you looking for a slow, torturous way to die?"

"You forget I have an ally within the encampment," Jules said with a smug smile. "He-Who-Comes-In-The-Night. You see he wasn't exactly happy when White Bear paid his wife's price."

"Ah . . ."

"So he'll help us steal the wench?" Fenwick asked, this plan of Boucher's still unclear.

"Not quite," the Frenchman said. "He will simply ensure that we have the opportunity and the time needed to make our escape."

As the two men exclaimed with pleasure, Jules was already mentally calculating his next move. He smiled. "And if the Indian thinks that Hannah wants to leave . . .

all the better." For Jules was as sure of this as he was sure of his own mother, the blond brave cared for his slave more than he should . . . and would not want her to remain if it wasn't her wish. Apparently, White Bear had learned quickly what it had taken him weeks to realize—that Hannah Gibbons was all woman . . . all lush curves and silken smooth skin. She was ripe for a man's attention, and it wouldn't be an Indian who taught her the finer points of physical pleasure.

He experienced a quick flare of anger as he recalled how his last attempts to teach her had been interrupted by the savages. He recalled his first sight of her in the village earlier. She'd worn nothing but a skirt, and memory of her full bare breasts teased and taunted him, making him hard.

So if it took them a little longer to return her to the family who had waited so long for her . . . then so be it! For he had every intention of riding her hard . . . of hearing her scream out with ecstasy as he sucked those luscious tits of hers while he thrust repeatedly between her long white legs.

He found her in the fields, picking beans from bushes planted in between stalks of corn. She'd known he would try to talk with her, but it still unnerved her when the Frenchman cornered her in the middle of a row. The tall corn plants rose up forming a wall before and behind her. There was an opening at the end of each row, but she was some distance from the nearest one when Jules Boucher cut a path through the cornstalks themselves, startling Hannah with his sudden appearance. Her heart started to pound with fear, but she pretended to be unconcerned as he greeted her pleasantly.

"These savages have a great many crops," he said in the way of conversation.

Hannah froze in the act of gathering a handful of bean

pods. "They are not savages," she said tightly. "They are people."

She saw the look of surprise that he masked quickly. Why? she thought. Why was he here and what did he want with her?

"Of course, mademoiselle. *Oui*, you are right."

She tried to ignore him while she continued to work, but the man refused to be dismissed. He grabbed her basket and followed her down the row, holding it up for her to set the bean pods inside.

He was quiet for a time, and she allowed herself to relax slightly, even thanking the man once as he shifted the basket to make it easier for her to reach.

"I have missed you, Hannah."

She stiffened and rose from her crouched position where she'd been checking a single squash plant between the beans and corn. "You miss a cook and animal skinner, Boucher, not me."

His lips twitched. *"Touché,"* he said in such a way that she couldn't stop herself from smiling.

"Still," he continued, "I would be good to you if you came away with me."

"I like it here, Boucher. I don't want to leave."

He made a strangled sound. "You are not a heathen, Hannah. You deserve better than a life with the *Ho-De'No-Sau-Nee.*"

"A life of cooking and physical abuse?" she replied daringly.

She saw his anger, before he looked apologetic. "It was the whiskey, mademoiselle. I no longer indulge in such sorcery."

And I don't believe you, Boucher. she thought with an inner snarl.

His demeanor changed as he became intense, earnest in his plea for her to listen to him. "Hannah, please. I promise to treat you kindly."

"And those two scum-suckers I saw dodging your steps yesterday?"

"They are traveling companions, nothing more." He paused. "I will get rid of them if you will come with me. I can talk to White Bear, trade goods for your indenture."

"No."

He looked horribly upset. "But why? Why will you not trust Jules, your friend?"

"You, friend," she said menacingly, "never cared a horse's arse for anyone but yourself, and it's for reasons of your own that you want me back." She was still as she searched his face. "What reasons, Boucher?"

"Because you were good to Jules. A hard worker I have missed. Because I've been feeling guilty for having sold you to savages."

Hannah thought he made a good player for the stage. She could almost believe him, except that she'd caught the sudden shifting of his eye as he'd pleaded his case. And he'd been tugging on the front of his dirty vest, a sure sign that Boucher was lying. She'd come to recognize several things about him during her month or so with him. He pulled on his beard whenever he was falsely pumping up the worth of an item for trade. And a muscle tic that had appeared when he'd become angry with her in the past . . . just moments before he'd hauled up to hit her with his fist.

"You don't need me, Boucher. And you can stop feeling guilty, because I like it here. I'm happy here. The people have been kind to me."

"You will be sorry that you did not come." He said it pleasantly and with just the right amount of polite disappointment. That fact alone was enough to make her more wary of him.

Hannah raised an eyebrow. "I doubt it." Here was a scruffy, slobbering kind of man, who was suddenly acting the French country gentleman with her. It just didn't make sense.

"Alas, then," he said with a dramatic sigh, further intensifying her fears. "White Bear's gain is my loss. Such is life, I guess. A fitting punishment for my transgressions." He handed her the filled basket with a shy smile. "*Adieu,* Hannah."

She nodded as she murmured some appropriate response. She watched as he left, taking the easier route to disappear, but her relief did not come. Her mistrust of his presence was too complete; their conversation had only made her more uncomfortable.

Jules Boucher had never been one to give up easily. She'd only seen him concede once . . . when he'd traded her to He-Who-Comes-In-The-Night. She couldn't allow herself to believe that he'd concede so easily once again— it was too dangerous to do so.

"Mother."

Woman with Dark Skin saw her late daughter's husband framed in the doorway of her hut. She smiled. "White Bear."

He didn't move. "I would speak with you a moment, if I may."

"Come in, son. Warm your heart at our fire," she said. She was always happy to welcome this warrior, this young man of her heart.

The brave glanced behind him. "Our sachem—" he began, flushing slightly.

Her gaze sharpened with curiosity. "He has gone to the house of the Deer," she said, referring to the longhouse of his clan. "Come in. We will not be disturbed. I sense you have something important to tell me."

White Bear looked grateful as he entered and sat next

to her near the fire. He didn't immediately speak, and Woman with Dark Skin didn't rush him.

"Mother—" he began. She saw him swallow hard. "Two nights past we talked of something."

She nodded and offered an encouraging smile. "That it was past the time for you to marry again."

"Yes."

"And you have thought long and hard on this," she said.

"This is so."

"And what are your thoughts?"

He shifted uncomfortably. The woman knew that this discussion of marriage was a difficult one for him. She sought to ease his burden. "I hope you have decided it is time." Her voice was gentle.

"I have decided this."

"Good." She grinned and was pleased when he smiled back. "You have chosen someone?"

He inclined his head.

"You would marry Hair Face?" she teased, but he didn't laugh as she'd hoped. "Singing Rain?"

He shook his head. "You said that you would respect my choice—help the others to approve."

She frowned. "Who, White Bear?" She felt a stirring of unease when he drew in a sharp breath.

"Han-na."

"Han-na," she murmured. She blinked. "The slave?"

"E-ghe-a," he admitted. *Yes.*

Woman with Dark Skin experienced a rush of mixed feelings. Her daughter's husband wanted to marry his slave! It wasn't something done. She pondered it a moment and then thought, *I was a slave.*

"She is a good woman?" she asked him.

"Oh, yes." His face lit up as he spoke of something he was sure of. "She is wonderful. She works hard, and she is patient with Eagle Soaring."

"She likes Eagle?"

He smiled. "She loves him. And he seems to care for her. At first, it didn't seem so, but I've noticed that he treats her differently now. I'm not sure why, but I believe Eagle had decided that he likes it that Han-na lives with us."

"She will have to become a daughter, for the mothers to accept her."

He nodded. "I know this. But who will agree to adopt her?"

She saw his hope, his fears, and—yes—his love for the slave reflected in his blue gaze. "I will adopt Han-na."

Tears filled his eyes, making them glisten. "You would do this for me?"

A wealth of love for this son poured over her. "I would do this for you and for Han-na." *And Eagle,* she thought.

"Thank you," he whispered.

She acknowledged his thanks with a smile. "You must tell her of this," she said as he rose to leave. "I will need to speak with her."

Suddenly, he looked uncertain again. "I will tell her, and I will send her to you."

The matron frowned. "She would have you as husband?"

"It is my hope."

"And if it is not hers?" she queried softly.

"I cannot think of that."

Because it hurts too much, she decided as she studied him. "I will wait for her to come."

Chapter 17

He was angry with her. She'd never been the object of White Bear's fury, and it hurt her terribly. But she didn't know what to do about it, not without causing him more heartache.

The sun had begun to set over the village; its bright orange glow was reflected on the lake. Hannah stood at the water's edge, gazing over the large glistening expanse with tears in her eyes. She felt a squeezing pain within her chest as she recalled their exchange. White Bear had been so full of excitement, his blue eyes glimmering with happy hope when he'd sought her out in the forest earlier. He had come to tell about his conversation with Woman with Dark Skin and to ask her to marry him again. And she had deflated his happiness by saying no.

She hadn't wanted to. She wanted nothing more than to live the rest of her life with this special man, but she couldn't marry him. But how could she make him see without telling him everything? She was afraid to tell him the truth, to watch his expression change from loving to loathing as she told him about the murder of Samuel Walpole.

She had told him that marriage between them wouldn't work. She was a slave, who would never find acceptance within the village as one worthy of being his wife. It hadn't been difficult to convince him that she felt strongly about this. Hannah did feel unworthy to be his wife, but it wasn't her fear of the Indians' acceptance that concerned her as much as marrying White Bear and then having his love taken away once he learned that she was a murderess.

She honestly believed that their time together was a precious gift that wouldn't last. If she allowed herself to marry him, to believe in a "happily ever after," then her punishment would be even more cruel when White Bear stopped loving her.

"You will not marry me?" The shock on his face had cut her to the bone. "Why, Han-na?" he'd exclaimed. "Why?"

She had torn her gaze from his pained expression to stare at the ground through a haze of tears. "I am a slave, White Bear," she'd whispered. "A white woman. Your people will look at me and see a slave—not a wife. And certainly not a matron!"

She had looked at him then, making no effort to hide her tears. "Please," she'd pleaded, "I love you. I will always love you, but for your good, I cannot marry you."

"You can marry me, but you choose not to!" His words had held anger—so much anger. "If you loved me as you said, you would come to me as my wife. I no longer want—or need—a slave, Han-na! I want a mate to warm my sleeping platform, to love and to hold all night." His blue gaze had sliced through flesh, exposing her bleeding heart. She'd gasped as she felt the lancing chest pain.

His voice softened, wounding her more deeply with the quiet calm of his next words. "I have been alone for eight years. I am weary of being lonely. I have ached for many seasons. It is time I took a wife ... and I had wanted that wife to be you. But ..."

But... He hadn't finished, but the implication had been clear. *But if you choose not to accept my offer, then I will marry another, for I will no longer live my life alone.*

Hannah swallowed against a painful lump. She had known that the happiness would not last, but she had hoped that it would hold just a little while longer. "Couldn't we keep things as they are?"

A strangled sob escaped from her painfully tight throat. "Who will you marry, White Bear? Singing Rain? She will marry you. I have watched her eyes on you, and she wants you perhaps as much as I, but unlike me, she is free to become your wife." *Free of a past like mine, a past that will someday catch up with you, for God frowns down upon cutthroats and murderers ... and I am guilty of taking a man's life.*

"Oh, White Bear, I love you ..." She crumpled to the ground and covered her face with her hands ... and allowed herself to cry for all the joy she'd lost ... that she'd never deserved in the first place.

After a while, she rose to return to the village, her throat tight, her eyes dry. She didn't know how long she had cried her heart out, but it must have been a while, for she suddenly realized that it was very dark.

There was little light along the trail back. Hannah didn't care; she knew the area well and could make it blindfolded. As she continued up the path, she worried about her relationship with the man she loved.

What am I going to do? I should leave, before we both get hurt.

But wasn't it too late? They both were hurting already, and she could see no end to their problem—or their pain.

She couldn't marry him, and she couldn't undo the past.

Preoccupied with White Bear, she failed to hear the footsteps or detect the presence of strangers waiting for her in the forest. It wasn't until she felt someone throw a blanket over her head that Hannah felt alarm.

The blanket was coarse and smelled like Englishmen, not the Indians who bathed regularly. Hannah fought to be free of her fabric prison, struggling to release her arms, kicking out at her captor with her feet.

She heard a grunt of pain as her foot made contact with flesh and bone. Encouraged, she fought harder, even though she was hot and fast losing the ability to breathe.

Her assailant knocked her to the ground. She heard voices as she had the wind knocked out of her as she fell. The realization that there was more than one aggressor came a second before she recognized the French accent. Then one of Boucher's men fell on her and drove the remaining air from her lungs, and her world went black.

"That was too easy," Fenwick said. "Too unbelievably easy!"

Boucher grinned. "Yes, wasn't it? It was quite fortunate that Mademoiselle Gibbons decided to take an evening stroll through the woods on her own."

"She doesn't look too happy about it," Beakly said, looking pleased. "Maybe she wants someone to entertain her."

The Frenchman gazed at the young woman, who sat slumped against the tree in the woods, miles away from the Seneca village from which they'd kidnapped her. He eyed her carefully to assure himself that her bonds still held. After a moment, he glanced back toward his comrades, satisfied that the ropes were adequately secure.

"We'll rest here for only a few hours," Boucher said. His expression hardened when his men groaned. His voice when he explained was cutting. "Do you want White Bear and his friends to catch us? Those savages can run. I want more miles between them and us before nightfall."

"How do you know that White Bear will even bother to come after her?" Beakly asked.

Jules remembered the warrior's vehement refusal to sell Hannah back. "Because we've outsmarted him is how I know," he said. "He'll want her back simply because we dared to take her. Have you forgotten that he turned down my offer to trade for her?"

Robert Fenwick shuddered. He was a young man, who would have been considered attractive but for the marks left on his face by his bout with smallpox. The marks left by the disease had not only marred his face, but they had damaged his ego. Well used to the attention of the opposite sex, the loss of his male beauty had stolen a certain lady's attraction to him. He had become angry and disillusioned, and now he preferred the company of men. Jules Boucher had found him bemoaning the fairer sex while swilling an ale with a group of his cronies. The Frenchman didn't know what it was about Fenwick that made him offer to hire the man on. Perhaps because he understood—even if the man didn't understand himself, Fenwick's quick acceptance of his offer as a way to earn a great deal of money. Money . . . a new lure with which to once again impress the ladies.

As for Charles Beakly—Jules considered the man slime and hired him on in case he needed someone to do something nasty while reaching his goal.

And now they had her. As he went over to stare at his captive, he allowed his delight to surface as he studied the woman's face. She was sleeping, having exhausted herself fighting to get free. He looked at her mouth gag and thought what a pity it had been to confine her sweet lips, but he knew that given the opportunity she would scream out and alert every living soul within miles.

Oh, Hannah, Hannah. Jules stared down at his captive and felt a bright moment of triumph. Not even the possible threat of savages could take away from the satisfaction of having the prize within his possession.

*   *   *

The rain beat against the building, its roar echoing the pounding ache in Hannah's heart. No, Mum. No! *But the terrible truth would not go away. Her mother was dead, having passed on only hours before. The dark hole left by the void seemed to swallow Hannah whole as she stood at her bedchamber window and stared out at the muddy yard below.*

I don't have to stay, she thought. She was free! Free to leave this inn and the horrible man who owned it.

A sound behind her made her spin from the window. To Hannah's disgust, Samuel Walpole stood in the open doorway, swaying on his feet, his brown eyes glazed. He reeked of whiskey. Hannah's alarm senses immediately kicked into alertness.

"*What do you want?*" *she demanded. She saw him scowl and noted how he immediately tried to hid his anger.*

"*Oh, Hannah dear, is that any way to talk to a grieving man?*"

She felt an instant pinprick of guilt. Perhaps he had cared about her mother. But then she remembered the many times he'd hit her, abused her with cruel taunts and vicious language. This was the man who had ultimately caused her mother's death. He—and he alone—was responsible. Hatred burned in her belly, replacing the guilt.

"*Get out,*" *she hissed.* "*Don't speak to me of grief when you know that 'tis you who killed her!*"

Fury hardened the man's features as he stumbled into the room. "*Don't, girl! I did not kill Dorothy! She was a weak and feeble woman. There was never an ounce of strength in her.*" *He came closer as he spoke, his words remarkably without slurring and clear.* "*Not like you, girl. No, never like you. You're the strong one.*"

"*What do you want, Samuel?*" *Hannah's skin tingled as her thoughts screamed a warning. He was dangerous. She had moved from the window and was edging around the room toward the door. To put him off guard, she tried to inject a lightness into her tone. She realized that it was best to disarm him by retreating rather than to brave an attack. Sober, Samuel Walpole posed no real threat to her; but drunk, he became an adversary made dangerous by his instability.*

"You."

She reeled from shock, unsure that she'd interpreted correctly. The gleam in his brown eyes, however, assured her that she had understood his true intent. "I've no desire to wait on customers this late, Samuel," she said, pretending ignorance.

"There are no customers in the common room. They're abed— as you should be."

Her heart tripped and settled into a more rapid rhythm. "Yes, it's late. It's been a difficult night for us both. Go to bed, Samuel." She had managed to make the corner nearest to the door. A chair stood near a small square table. The door was within yards, but Samuel, too, had moved, and was blocking her one avenue of escape.

She didn't like his look. He appeared hard and determined. Still, she thought she could outmaneuver him.

But then suddenly he was upon her, groping her, telling her all the obscene things he'd like to do to her.

And Hannah was fighting for her honor, her life.

She managed to push free from him long enough to grab hold of the chair to raise it to swing. The thud made by the contact of wood hitting Samuel's head should have horrified her, but instead, it gave her immense satisfaction as she watched the man fall. She closed her gaping bodice with her hands and gazed down with loathing at the man who'd made her mother and herself miserable. "Stay away from me, Samuel Walpole! I'm leaving—you hear? There's no reason for me to remain."

And then she saw the blood—his blood pooling on her floor. The crimson puddle stole away her triumph, instilling fear in her . . . and horror, for she hadn't meant to murder the man . . . simply to get away.

Her race to leave was fueled by her combined horror and fear of discovery and the consequences of her crime.

No! No! I didn't mean to kill him. He'd attacked me, I just wanted him to stop!

The thundering at the door downstairs in the common room was louder than the storm that roared and swirled about the inn in fury outside. Fear froze Hannah in place as she heard a thud followed by the splintering sound of wood!

They had come for her, she knew it. Somehow they had found out about the murder, and they were coming to take her away.

Footsteps sounded on the stairs. From the thunderous noise, she knew that there were several of them.

The door to her bedchamber crashed open, and Hannah screamed.

"Christ! How the hell did she manage to get the gag off!" Beakly exclaimed.

"I took it off," Jules said quietly. He hadn't be able to resist his desire to see her pink mouth. His gaze narrowed as he studied the woman against the tree. "The mademoiselle must have had a bad dream."

"That was foolish, Boucher," Fenwick pointed out.

"Perhaps I thought we were far enough to have no cause for worry." He had forgotten that the woman suffered from nightmares. He had been witness to them enough during their first time together. As he scratched his bearded chin, he wondered what it was that haunted Hannah's dreams.

"And are we?" Beakly asked.

Jules blinked and stared at the man. "Are we what?"

Fenwick said something foul and glared at Boucher. "To answer your question, we can never be a far enough distance away when it comes to a savage's hunger for revenge."

Chapter 18

When he'd found out that she was gone, he'd been coldly furious. Her refusal to marry him had come back to taunt him, triggering his anger . . . and his pain. But then he'd learned that the Frenchman was gone, and concern had taken the place of his anger.

As he ran through the forest, stopping and slowing on occasion to check for signs, White Bear couldn't forget the determined look in Jules Boucher's eyes as he'd offered to trade for Hannah. Had Hannah escaped with the aid of the Frenchman, or had the Frenchman, having had his offer refused, taken her?

He stopped, crouched to check the dirt. Black Thunder hunkered down beside him and grunted his confirmation that the earth had been disturbed by human feet. Jules Boucher and his cohorts might have been smart enough to wear moccasins on their white feet, but they weren't that smart to realize that a Seneca could track any animal, whether it be man or beast, through the forest. He knew the woods and the land that well.

Sky Raven was searching the surrounding plant growth. He pointed toward a broken, but barely visible, bush branch, and the three Indians continued in that direction, moving more slowly, more carefully now that they had ventured far from the well-worn Iroquois trail.

White Bear thought of his son's reaction to Hannah's disappearance. While the father had seethed inwardly, Eagle Soaring had been defensive of Hannah, showing only his concern that the bad Frenchman had taken her. He had seen Hannah's fear, he'd told his father. She wouldn't have gone with him willingly. Those men must have taken her! It was up to the People—and his father— to get her back.

And, of course, the boy had wanted to go along. It had taken a lot of patience and not a little convincing that White Bear needed his son to stay in the village . . . in case, Hannah returned.

"Yes, father, I will take care of Han-na if she comes back to us hurt."

White Bear's blood had chilled at the thought, and he'd realized then that he loved her still, that he would go after her whether or not she wanted him to come. He'd recalled how she had given herself so sweetly, surrendering her soul as they'd made love. Or had he been mistaken? What if her heart hadn't been involved at all? She'd been a virgin. Perhaps she'd merely been captivated by the new stirrings of arousal and desire generated by her first sexual experience.

His chest hurt, but it wasn't the pain of lungs overtaxed from running. The burning was fear, fear that she was in trouble, fear that she didn't love him, fear that she did but it was the love that had driven her away.

Han-na. My love. Be safe. If you are in trouble, then hold on. I am coming. I will find you and bring you back . . . and we will live as you wish. As lovers but not as mates, although it will pain me that you will never be completely mine.

Suddenly a soft breeze arose to stir against his skin, to caress White Bear's face, to soothe his churning emotions.

Find her, White Bear. The voice was about him. Or was it in his head? He glanced at his two friends and saw they were unaffected. They hadn't heard anything. And strangely the air about them was still, but yet it rushed by him, comforting him with its cool fingers.

Find her, White Bear. She loves you. You know it. You have seen it in her eyes . . . our son has seen it. but the woman is afraid, a fear that only you can banish . . .

White Bear heard the voice and knew that it belonged to Wind Singer. His late wife. *You are happy?* he asked in his thoughts.

No.

He felt a constriction in his chest. *I am sorry. What can I do?*

You can be happy. Find that woman and love her. Allow her to love you. Understand that I am gone, and you are alive. You must learn to live again.

Warmth curled in his stomach. *I have failed you. Our son.*

You have failed only yourself. A stirring of the breeze. *But it is not too late. You can save yourself—and your Han-na. Redeem yourself by allowing yourself to love . . .*

And if she doesn't want me? White Bear asked silently.

She wants you. You know this, but you were angry when you should have been patient. But it is still not too late. . . .

The breeze stopped as quickly as it had come. He saw Black Thunder eyeing him oddly, but he didn't explain, he just continued on, determined to find Boucher . . . and to rescue the woman he loved.

They came to the Frenchman's camp less than a full day after Hannah and the white men had disappeared. Crouched in the brush, hidden from plain sight, White Bear studied the men, before his gaze searched for Hannah. When he saw her standing alone near the edge of clearing, unencumbered by restraints, the blond Indian felt a burning anger fueled by a feeling of betrayal.

He watched as the Frenchman approached her with an offering of food and saw her polite acceptance.

She had wanted to leave! The realization hurt him, angered him anew, but it didn't banish his desire to take her back. He would have Hannah in his lodge again.

And then Hannah turned, and he could see her ravaged expression . . . and his anger abruptly dispelled itself.

Oh, Han-na . . . I love you . . . and I will make things right.

The Indians slipped away from the edge of the clearing to confer within the woods. They formed a plan of attack and went back to watch and wait until the right time . . .

When it was over, two white men were dead. The Frenchman had escaped, but White Bear had Hannah. As he headed back to the village with his friends and Hannah, the golden warrior vowed to find the Frenchman. Vengeance was a matter of Iroquois honor.

She had all but given up. Her muscles screamed out from the abuse she'd suffered at Boucher's hands. She didn't understand exactly why Boucher had wanted her back so desperately, and the only conclusion she had made frightened her more than anything in her life.

Her kidnapping had started up her nightmares again. For months, she'd feared that someone would come after her. She was sure that once someone had found Samuel's dead body that a manhunt—or in her case womanhunt— would be made to catch the man's killer and make her pay. Boucher wouldn't tell her anything. When she'd asked, taunting him for an answer, the Frenchman had merely smiled. And it was that smile which had terrified her. The man was so pleased with himself. Had the authorities offered a reward?

She rose to her feet and went to the edge of the clearing.

Boucher was so sure that she wouldn't try to escape—or that she would be unsuccessful if she tried. Why? What made him so cocksure?

A wild animal cry rent the still air, making Hannah cry out. Suddenly, White Bear was there, grabbing her, thrusting her into Black Thunder's waiting arms.

"White Bear," she cried out happily.

He looked fierce. "Go, woman!" he said angrily. "Now!"

Hannah paled. "Please!"

"Black Thunder," he said evenly. "Get her out of here!" He drew a steel blade from his leg strap.

One of Boucher's men had pulled his own knife. Hannah watched with mounting horror as he and White Bear began to circle each other as they prepared to strike.

She saw Boucher at White Bear's other side. "No!" she screamed.

White Bear spun to face both attackers. Black Thunder jerked Hannah from the clearing, before she could see the outcome of the fight.

White Bear and Sky Raven met up with Hannah and Black Thunder a short time later. Hannah's joy at finding White Bear alive and unharmed dimmed upon seeing his stone-cold face. In the hours she'd been a captive of Boucher and his men, she'd thought of little else besides the golden warrior. She made herself a solemn vow that if she found her way back to him she would marry him . . . if he asked her again.

Her quick glimpses at the brave did not encourage her as they journeyed along the Iroquois trail on their way back to the Seneca village. White Bear was not unkind to her, but then neither was he openly friendly. But she couldn't forget his anger toward her when he'd rushed into Boucher's camp and shoved her into Black Thunder's waiting arms. And since then, he hadn't paid much attention to her. It was his indifference toward her that worried her. Why had he been so angry? Did he believe that she'd left the village willingly?

Hannah studied him as he called a halt for the night. His gaze brushed over her and then moved on, but she'd seen the accusation in his eyes, the mistrust. She had to make him believe she hadn't wanted to leave him.

What else is he to think when you refused his offer of marriage and disappeared?

Tears stung her eyes as she realized that it might be better this way. She still couldn't marry him; Boucher's abduction had confirmed her worst fears . . . that someone—the British authorities or Samuel's relatives—wanted her caught and punished for the murder of Samuel Walpole. She wanted White Bear to believe in her, but how would it help matters between them to convince him of the truth? And if he didn't believe her about Boucher, how could she even think to confess to a murder?

She watched White Bear search the woods for timber to start a fire, then disappear from view. Dispirited, Hannah sank to the ground and wondered what she should do. Should she go after him and tell the truth about everything from Samuel's murder to Boucher's abduction of her? If she did, would he believe her? Dare she hope that he'd understand and still want her? Or should she wait until he got over his anger, tell him the truth about Boucher and when—if—he proposed to her again, marry him with the dark secret of her past out in the open, gambling that it would never catch up to take away her happiness with the man she loved?

She hung her head, cradling it within her hands.

"Han-na."

With a soft gasp she opened her eyes and found White Bear on the ground beside her, eyeing her with concern.

"Are you all right?" Emotion darkened his blue eyes to deep sapphire.

She recognized love as his features softened, as he

stroked his fingers along her jaw. She nodded. "I'm unhurt." Without conscious thought, she rubbed her wrist where Boucher's rope had burned.

White Bear caught her action and grabbed hold of her hand, turning it gently to examine her sore flesh. He drew in a sharp breath as he saw the proof that she had not gone with the white men willingly.

He raised her hand to her lips and kissed her injured wrist. The gesture brought tears to Hannah's eyes, reminding her again why she loved him.

His mouth soothed her, bringing relief to her stinging flesh, stirring up tendrils of desire. She loved this man. Oh, how she loved him.

"He did this to you," White Bear said quietly, his features suddenly harsh with his anger. "He will not hurt you again."

Hannah shivered. His words had been both a promise and a threat. "Those other men—what happened to them?" She'd been taken from the clearing before learning their fate.

His eyes turned black. "They will not come for you again." His tone forbade any further questioning on the matter.

She felt chilled. The men must be dead. She searched White Bear's face. Gone was the gentle warrior. His expression was implacable, his gaze fierce. She had her answer. Her blood froze to solid ice.

White Bear saw Hannah's horror and fought to banish his anger. "Do not dwell on this, Han-na. A man chooses his own path . . . when he chooses unwisely, then he may stumble . . . or fall down and die."

Her eyes widened before she looked away, and he experienced the overwhelming desire to comfort and protect her.

He cupped her face with his hand and raised it until

her gaze met his. "Han-na, you must not worry. You must forget this. If a man pays for his evil, it is only right."

Her lashes flickered and she looked startled, as if the thought had never occurred to her.

"Hanna . . ." he breathed. He drew her forward and kissed her lips, drawing strength from her sweetness. When she moaned and lifted her arms about his neck, he felt exhilaration. She was where she belonged. Somehow he would prove it to her. He would be patient until she understood that he would always be there for her. In time he'd prove that whatever had hurt her in the past had no power to hurt her now. He felt a jolt as he realized the same could be true for him.

The cry of welcome reached the travelers as they neared the village. Inside the gates, matrons, braves, and children alike came out of their longhouses to greet them. Eagle Soaring, having spotted Hannah, ran forward and flung himself against her, throwing his small arms about her waist.

Hannah felt the sting of happy tears as she hugged the child tightly. Sensing the golden warrior's gaze on her, she looked at him, and her breath quickened at the smile he gave her. She shared the joy of being a family, for at that moment it felt like they were a family—her, White Bear, and Eagle Soaring. She embraced the happiness, holding it as closely to her heart as she held her son. *Her son,* she thought. If only it were so. . . .

The child broke away and his head was raised as he studied her in earnest. "Han-na, you are well?"

She gave him a radiant smile, sharing her joy from within. *"E-ghe-a,"* she said, assuring him that she was. She knelt before him, bringing them to eye level of each other. "You have missed me?" she teased.

To her surprise, his expression was solemn as he nodded his head. "Yes, Han-na, I have missed you." He touched her cheek. "I was worried that the bad Frenchman had hurt you."

She blinked misty eyes, moved by his concern and his affection for her. "Thank you," she said softly.

Eagle looked confused. "Why do you thank me, Hanna? I have done nothing to help you." He flashed his father an accusing glance. "He would not let me come."

She shot White Bear a look of gratitude. "I should say not."

The boy appeared hurt. "You think me not man enough to fight the Frenchman?"

"Of course, you are man enough, Eagle," she said. "But you were needed here. What if I'd come back and both your father and you were gone? Who would have cared for me?"

"That's what my father said," he grumbled.

Hannah smiled. "Your father is a wise man."

To her surprise, the boy snorted. "Not so wise," he said. "He thought you had wanted to go with the Frenchman. I had to tell him that you wouldn't go, because the Frenchman was a bad man who frightened you."

Her spirits plummeted. "I see," she said. "You are wise for a young warrior. I thank you for making your father see." She hid her pain well as she acknowledged the villagers' good wishes and answered their questions. All the while, she was conscious of White Bear doing the same thing.

He thought I went willingly. He believed I would leave him . . . although I confessed my love for him.

Why should she be so surprised? It wasn't as if the thought hadn't occurred to her that he would have thought this.

I wanted him to believe in me. It hurts for me to know that he didn't trust me enough to believe in my love.

It didn't matter that he had good cause to think what he did. She had turned down his marriage proposal. He wouldn't have understood how a woman could love a man and yet refuse to marry him.

It's because I love him that I won't marry him. Perhaps I'd been selfish, but I didn't think I could bear it if we married and then I lost his love.

But she had changed her mind. Her capture at the hands of Boucher's men had convinced her that it was best to grasp what good life had to offer . . . even if it was only temporary . . . even if in the end she suffered more.

Ask me again, White Bear, and I will marry you.

But he didn't ask her. And as a day passed and then a week, Hannah decided with a sinking heart that he must have changed his mind.

Chapter 19

"What do you mean you had her, but she escaped?" Samuel Walpole was livid. His beady eyes burned with brown fire, and the scar on his left cheek was a brighter shade of red than the rest of his face. "How could you have let her slip away?"

Jules Boucher cringed inwardly. "She did not escape, monsieur. She was taken. The savage who held her attacked me and my men."

Walpole stared at him from beneath lowered lids. "Yet, you are unharmed," he said evenly. "What of the fools who went with you?"

The Frenchman couldn't suppress a shudder. "Dead, I think. Both of them."

The other man snorted. "Now you're giving up," Walpole said with a sigh. "And just when I've been granted the authority to raise the reward."

"How much?" He couldn't control the flutter of interest. When he'd escaped from the savages without harm, Jules had made himself a silent vow to forget Hannah

Gibbons and the money she could bring him. He would report to Walpole and tell him that he'd failed and given up the chase. But vows were made to be broken, he thought. Especially if the price was right.

The Englishman named a price, and Jules's eyes gleamed.

"I know where she is. I could find a way to get her . . . only I'll need to find someone willing to go with me into the savages' territory."

"I can find you a man."

"Two men," Boucher decided, wishing he could ask for more, but unwilling to share the profits. *Better yet, I must find me some savages willing to follow my lead. It's best to use Indians to fight Indians.*

Walpole's face contorted into an ugly mask as he frowned thoughtfully. "I will go with you. You bungled the first attempt badly. I'll come along to see that things are done right this time."

Jules scowled. He didn't like it; he didn't like it one bit. But he knew he wasn't in the position to argue with the man who held the ties to the purse strings. "Very well, monsieur. We will leave in two days. Meet me on the back steps of the Wedgwood Ale House. I want to meet the man you find me first. Tomorrow evening at seven, right here at the Jug and Port."

The Englishman nodded, apparently familiar with the other inn. "It will be as you wish, Boucher." His next words were said through teeth clamped tightly. "This is your last chance, Boucher. Make another mistake, and you'll not see a single copper of the money."

Jules only smiled. "Ah, but I won't fail this time, will I? Not when you have graciously consented to assist me in my endeavor."

* * *

"You seem troubled, my son."

White Bear turned from the lake to see Woman with Dark Skin. It was past dusk, that magical time of the day that deceived the eye with shadows and light. A dark shadow against the soft light, Woman with Dark Skin stood a few yards from White Bear. Her eyes glowed without sunshine; the brightness came from within the matron's heart.

"These are troubled times, mother," he said quietly, before focusing his gaze back on the water.

"These days are no different than those that have passed." The matron had moved to stand at his left side. He could sense her study of him, but he couldn't rouse himself to offer her a reassuring smile. For the People, the days were pleasant ones, but for him and Hannah, their time together was strained. They lived as strangers. It was if they'd never shared their bodies or opened their hearts to one another. He'd thought she would come to trust him, that their love would grow if he was patient. But instead they'd grown apart.

The matron placed her hand on his arm. "White Bear—"

He met her gaze. He didn't want her to worry or to cause her pain. She didn't need the burden of his heartache. "Mother, you must not worry about me."

"What is wrong?" Her ebony eyes urged him to tell. Her look was gentle, but her tone commanded.

He sighed, knowing that she wouldn't give up until she'd learned the truth. "It is Han-na. I'm not a patient man. Each day our hearts grow separate. I don't understand this. I believed that she would come to trust me in time, that she would change her mind and take me as husband. But we continue to live as master and slave—nothing more."

"The slave will not marry you?" The matron's eyes widened. "She is not good enough for you then!" she exclaimed angrily. She appeared confused by Hannah's behavior.

Woman with Dark Skin's reaction made White Bear smile. "You must not concern yourself with this, mother," he said. "I believe Han-na cares for me, but there is something troubling her. I wish she would tell me what is hurting her, so that I can help her. I want her to understand that nothing will make me love her any less."

"She loves you then," the matron said, her expression softening.

He shrugged, but his blushing face confirmed the truth. That he believed that Hannah did, in fact, love him.

"Would you like me to speak with her?" she asked gently.

"No. She will come to me when she is ready." *I hope it is soon.*

"I think your Han-na is ready," she said, her voice barely above a whisper.

He looked at her, then followed the direction of the matron's gaze. His heart pounded as he spotted the woman he loved standing several yards away, waiting as if hesitant to approach.

"Come, Han-na," Woman with Dark Skin called out. "I was just leaving."

"Oh, no!" Hannah exclaimed as she started forward. "You mustn't leave because of me. I should be the one to leave. Please—don't let me intrude."

The matron's smile was encouraging. "Come. You are welcome. I must get back, and White Bear has been waiting for you." Her ebony eyes flashed as they settled briefly on the brave. "Is this not so, my son?"

To her surprise, Hannah saw him incline his head.

The Englishwoman heard the roaring in her bloodstream as Woman with Dark Skin swept past her on her return to the village.

Had White Bear and the matron been discussing her? Woman with Dark Skin had seemed sure that White Bear had been waiting for her. The golden warrior himself had just confirmed it.

White Bear remained near the edge of the lake while he waited for her to join him. Hannah's mouth felt dry as she approached, and when she was next to him, they both turned toward the water. The water was calm that evening. Much calmer, Hannah thought, than her own turbulent thoughts.

The strain in her relationship with White Bear since Boucher's kidnapping of her had intensified with each passing day until Hannah had felt like screaming from the pain of it. She had thought long and hard, and decided that she would tell him the truth about her past. They'd been like strangers for too long; having him turn from her completely couldn't hurt any worse than these last few days.

The tension mounted with each moment of silence. Hannah drew a sharp breath as she struggled to find the courage to begin.

"White Bear," she choked out. He turned to her, and she had to swallow to soothe her tight, dry throat. "I—" She shuddered and averted her gaze, afraid to watch his expression change while she confessed what she'd done.

"Han-na," he murmured. "What is it, *O-gä-uh?*"

Tears filled her eyes at his gentle inquiry. She was suddenly thrust into the past, when the time between them had been good . . . She could almost forget that these last tension-fraught days between them had ever existed.

She blinked against tears as she forced herself to meet his gaze. "Were you truly waiting for me?"

He nodded, but then he closed off his expression, as if he were locking his emotions inside. Hannah wanted to know what he was thinking. It might help her confess all her fears . . . and what she held close to her heart.

He is not going to made this easy for me, she thought. She stiffened her spine and made his gaze directly. She had vowed to tell him, and she was going to do so even if she got hurt worse in the end.

Hannah opened her mouth, then shut it abruptly. She took another calming breath, then said, "I killed a man." The even, calm sound of her own voice startled her.

White Bear seemed taken aback by her admission. With a pounding heart, Hannah hurried to explain in a voice filled with emotion.

"I didn't mean to do it! I swear if I could live that night over again, I'd do it differently. I wouldn't have hit him— not with the chair!"

He didn't say a word. His silent censure burned like fire in the pit of Hannah's stomach.

"I'm a murderess, White Bear," she said. "That's why I can't marry you. Because I killed a man!" She spun back to stare at the water again. "He was my mother's husband, a cruel bastard who wasn't above controlling my mum with his fists. It was on the day she died . . ." she said, caught up in the terrible memory. "I hated him. It was his fault that Mum was sick. He worked her until she had no strength . . ."

She shivered and brought her arms up to ward off the chill. "She was dead only hours when he came up to my room," she whispered, uncaring that her tears fell freely. "He—he—cornered me. He'd been drinking. He was always worse when he'd been drinking. He—"

She closed her eyes and swallowed before continuing. "He came at me. I grabbed a chair and struck him with it. I had been slowly making my way to the door, but I hadn't been near enough to escape before he lunged at me. He pawed at me while he told me all the nasty things he was going to do to me."

She knew the exact moment when the man beside her had stiffened in reaction to her words. Her belly churned as she faced him, her vision blurred by tears.

"I couldn't let him touch me." Her soft tone pleaded for his understanding. *"I only wanted him to stop."*

Hannah felt the cold condemning fury emanating from the man who'd once asked her to marry him. She knew that White Bear saw her only as a murderess now. The pain was unbearable; it ripped at her heart and made it bleed. She had trouble drawing breath; the hurt was so terrible. Squeezing shut her eyes, she willed the earth to open and swallow her whole. She wanted to vanish before she was forced to bear his loathing.

"I'm sorry," she whispered. "So sorry . . ."

"So sorry . . ." Her last words finally filtered through to him. White Bear was stunned. He'd known something was troubling Hannah, but he'd had no idea that it was this.

The rage that built within him threatened to erupt. He silently cursed the one who was responsible. If the gods of the People and the Christian God were wise, the husband of Hannah's mother would forever walk in the dark place between death and the Great Spiritual Afterworld.

The sound of Hannah's sobbing drew him from his black, vengeful thoughts. Suddenly, he became aware that she was still apologizing, over and over, as if she were the guilty party rather than that man—the cruel dog who had done this to her.

Again, he had to force down his fury. After breathing deeply to calm himself, he caught Hannah gently by her shoulders. The way she tensed and cried out at his touch made him realize that she was afraid of him, that she believed his anger was at her. It wasn't; his anger was for the man—on her behalf.

"Han-na, *O-gä-uh,*" he said softly, his eyes softening with warmth. He hurt for her and wanted to obliterate her suffering. "You have nothing to be sorry for—do you hear me? Nothing!"

She blinked and looked up, her eyes awash with tears, the gray orbs made more beautiful by the glistening. "I killed a man." She said it again as if she didn't believe that White Bear had heard her the first two times.

He offered her a gentle smile. "You fought to protect yourself. There is no dishonor is that."

"You were angry," she said in a timid voice.

"Not at you," he whispered, stroking her hair back over her ear with fingers that trembled. "Never at my Han-na."

Tears flooded her eyes and overflowed to send tiny, shimmering rivulets down her satin-smooth cheeks. "You are not mad at me?"

"Ah, *O-gä-uh,* you have been worrying about this needlessly," he said. "It matters not that you had to kill this man." He pulled her against him, hugging her tightly. "You must not be ashamed of this. You had no other choice."

Her tears wet his skin. She felt good within his arms. If only he could take away her pain, make her understand that if he had been born a female and been put into the same situation, he—she—would have done much worse than just hitting him with a chair.

"It was an accident," she said, her voice muffled against his chest.

He nodded against her hair. "I know, Han-na," he soothed. "It's all right . . . Do not make yourself sick over it."

She jerked away, suddenly angry. "How can you make light of this?" she asked. "I killed a man. Committed murder! That makes me an animal! Why aren't you not looking at me with hate?"

"If I look at you with hate, Han-na," he said quietly, "then I must hate myself as well, for you are not the only one who has killed."

The admission stirred up his own private hell, for whether he was a Seneca brave or Englishman, it made no difference to him—he'd never been able to accept the killing, even when it had been warranted. It was his guilty feelings, his own struggle to cope, that made him desperately want to help Hannah. She had no reason to feel guilt. He had killed for poorer reasons than hers. He'd been one member of an Iroquois war party. Their purpose had been to conquer for strength. He had not been helpless. His life had not been at stake at the time.

Hannah saw the raw pain in his eyes and felt it, too. "I'm sorry," she whispered. She didn't understand why she'd become mad at him for understanding. It hadn't been her intention to hurt him. She touched his cheek, stroked his jaw, watching with love as he closed his eyes and leaned into her palm. "I hurt you. I didn't want to." And then she understood her feelings. She had wanted him to loathe her as punishment for her crime.

I love you, she thought as she felt him tremble beneath her touch. Suddenly, her guilt, her pain, seemed insignificant in the face of his. *Ask me again, and I'll marry you. Let me help you. Give me a lifetime to help you forget. . . .*

It didn't matter what he'd done in the past. Knowing him, whatever he'd done, whatever killings had taken place, had been necessary at the time. Perhaps the English side of him can't accept or forgive that. But, there was more to him than the English side; there was the Seneca side. Both ways of life had made him into a complex man, torn between what was considered right and wrong by each of his peoples.

Hannah knew and understood the essence of the man. He was kind, gentle, fierce in his loyalties. He wasn't a cruel bastard like Samuel Walpole. He wasn't a greedy scoundrel like Jules Boucher. He was White Bear of the *Nun-da-wä'-o-no*—the Great Hill People—of the *Ho-De'No-Sau-Nee,* the People of the Longhouse.

He was the man she loved with a passion and strength that stole her breath away. . . .

White Bear caught Hannah's hand and raised it to his lips, kissing the palm that had caressed him. As she gazed into his eyes, he was afraid to hope, to believe, that soon she would consent to be his wife.

I love you, he thought, finding comfort and strength in the touch of the woman he'd hoped to comfort and give strength. *I love you and need you like the air I breathe and the water that gives my body life.*

He wouldn't ask her to marry him. They had drifted apart and were coming together again. He didn't want his eagerness for their marriage to overwhelm her and destroy the tiny, fragile threads that had been woven together . . . threads that he hoped would withstand the test of time.

Soon, he thought. Soon, the bond would be strong and resilient enough. Then he could ask her again, and she would answer him. Until he was sure that her answer would be the right one, he would cherish her, hold her, and love her with his body . . . but he would not enjoy the final tie that would bind her to him forever.

The Frenchman returned while Hannah and the matrons were in the fields. She didn't see him at first. It was nearing the time for harvest, and the village women and children were carefully checking each row of crops and picking the vegetables that were ready.

Hannah suffered a jolt when she spied him in the forest. She had hoped she'd never see him again. Given Jules Boucher's determination the last time, she had known that he'd be back for her, but she'd never thought he would come in pure daylight, risking the lives of himself and his men.

She stared at him, and her gaze sharpened as she attempted to count his men. There was one man a few yards away from Boucher . . .

Hannah caught sight of an Indian warrior in the back-ground on Boucher's opposite side. Relief swept over her that there were Seneca braves still about, waiting to see what the Frenchman would do. Many of the Indian warriors had left the village to hunt. White Bear had disappeared early that morning. He hadn't told her of his plans, and she fought the niggling of hurt that he hadn't thought her important or trustworthy enough to tell her of them.

He didn't ask you to marry him again, she thought, as she bent to pick a bright golden squash, forgetting for a quick moment Jules Boucher. *That is why you're upset.*

Still, he must still feel something for her, she decided. Hannah recalled how her golden warrior had comforted her, and then later that same night, how he'd insisted she sleep within his arms.

Where are you, White Bear? She shivered. *Boucher is back, and he'll not leave without me.*

Why did Boucher want her? What could induce him to risk venturing into Iroquois territory after angering White Bear when he'd kidnapped her the last time?

Her blood grew cold with fear. Had word of Walpole's murder somehow reached the Frenchman? Had the authorities perhaps offered a reward for the woman who'd gotten away with murder? Samuel Walpole had had friends in high places back in England. Hannah had always suspected that had been one of the reasons her mother had been afraid to leave him.

Why did Boucher show no fear of being caught?

Icy terror gripped her as she again looked at the Indian and realized that she didn't recognize his face as one of the *Nun-da-wä'-o-no.*

Dear God, he has Indian friends to help him. How could she alert the other women and the children without calling Boucher's attention to her warning?

The Indian brave behind Boucher stepped forward. He was joined by a second, then a third, and Hannah knew she had to shout out a warning now, before it was too late.

"Run!" she cried. "Moon Woman! Singing Rain! Run!

Everyone escape quickly! The enemy is here—by those trees. Don't look—run!''

She couldn't run with them. These men had come for her, and she wouldn't jeopardize the others by racing after Moon Woman and the others. She would wait for the Frenchman to reach her. She cared for the Seneca; she wouldn't allow Boucher's men to hurt them.

As the women and children scattered and started to run, Hannah remained. Several Indian braves shot past her, chasing the others. Hannah yelled out to the Frenchman to stop his men, that she would go with him, if only he would leave the People alone.

''Very wise, mademoiselle.'' Boucher smiled as he gave the order, probably knowing very well that the Indians wouldn't obey him.

The braves didn't listen. Hannah watched in mounting horror as one raced after a young village maiden, who barely eluded his grasp as she ran around a tree and into the forest, screaming.

Many of the women had escaped, but for how long? Hannah wondered. Boucher's Indians would follow them into the village, where there were only a few old men and a couple of young braves left to protect the women and children. If only the women and children could get inside the stockade and lock the gate!

''You've been watching us!'' she exclaimed to the Frenchman. ''You waited until our men left, and then you came when we were the most vulnerable!'' He was a monster, she thought. What kind of man would plan such an assault on women and children, who would bring enemy Indians into a peaceful camp?

Boucher seemed amused by her outburst. *''Our* men?'' he taunted. ''Since when have you become one of them?''

She turned away to watch helplessly as one child climbed a tree to escape his pursuer while another stood in the center of a clearing crying for his mother, who had been carried off by one of the Frenchman's braves.

"You are white, Hannah. I expect you to remember that."

Hannah's eyes burned brightly as she spun back to Boucher. "I'd rather be one of these people than one of you! You make me sick. You're a monster, Jules Boucher. You must be to let your men hurt innocent women and children!"

Boucher's face contorted in anger before he slapped her across the face hard. "Bitch! Think you better than Jules Boucher! You are nothing. I would not bother with you, but for the rich price on your head."

"Price?" Hannah's blood turned to ice.

He nodded. "I'll be only too glad to see the last of you. Just a few more hours and I'll be free from you, free to spend the riches your little hide will have brought me!"

Hannah studied her surroundings, looking for an avenue of escape. There was none that she could see, but she kept looking. She had tried, but had been unable to help her Indian friends.

"What are you waiting for then, Frenchman?" she spat. "Aren't you afraid that our men will return and take you prisoner? Or hasn't it occurred to you what tortures you'll likely suffer when you are caught?"

Boucher blanched; and although he quickly tried to hide his reaction, he was unsuccessful. Hannah smiled, pleased that she'd frightened him. When the man barked out an order for his men to leave, Hannah's satisfaction grew.

The Indians returned to join their leader. Hannah was appalled to see that they had three women and two children with them. Her heart stopped briefly when she saw that one of the children was White Bear's son.

"Eagle," she breathed, hugging herself with her arms. She cursed herself for giving her feelings away when Boucher, after a thoughtful look at her, ordered the men to free everyone but the young boy whom Hannah loved.

"A little insurance that you cooperate," the Frenchman said softly. His brown eyes gleamed with the enjoyment of his power.

"Oh, Eagle," she said to the boy as they were tied up and led away. "Why did you not run with the others?"

His dark eyes, which had been burning with hatred for his captors, warmed with caring as they focused on Hannah. "I would not let them take you! You belong with us in the village. The bad Frenchman has no right to kidnap you. I would not like it! My father will not like it."

"But now your father has two people to worry over," she gently pointed out.

Eagle Soaring's expression fell, and the boy who had worn the bravery of a man was suddenly a young child again.

She would have hugged him if her hands were free. She wanted to hold him in her arms and tell him that they would be all right; his father would return to the village and come to save them from the bad men. Softly, she whispered assurances to him. "Do not worry, Eagle. Your father will find us. And he will make these men pay for what they've done."

"My father has gone on a journey. He will not be back until the sun rises high over our village. We will be far away before he knows we are gone."

Hannah's smile was affectionate. "Your father is a mighty warrior. He will come for you . . . because he loves you." She didn't say "us." Although she knew that White Bear cared for her and desired her in his bed, the fact that he hadn't asked her again to marry him made her doubt the strength of his feelings for her. She wasn't worried about herself; however, it was the child who needed to be reassured.

Surprise had flickered across the little boy's features as

Hannah spoke. She watched as his expression lit up with the joyful radiance of discovering the truth.

"He does love me, doesn't he?" Eagle said as if he'd never fully realized it before.

A lump rose in Hannah's throat. "Never doubt it, Eagle Soaring," she said huskily. "Your father will move heaven and earth to bring you home again."

Chapter 20

"Eagle Soaring," Hannah whispered. "No, don't look at me," she rushed on anxiously. "Listen." She kept a close eye on the Frenchman's guard. "Just answer when I say. All right?"

The child glanced toward the man and nodded.

"Good boy!"

Boucher and his Indians had disappeared. Only one white man remained to watch over them. She watched the man until she knew it was safe to talk. "I want you to scoot closer to the tree. I'm going to work to untie you. If I can get you free, I want you to run back to the village. Do you think you can find the way? Can you make it?"

After a slight pause, he inclined his head.

"Fine!" she praised him softly. "Go ahead and move closer to the tree."

He started to shift, then stopped to eye her. "I don't want to leave you."

The smile she gave him was soft with love. "I know, Eagle, but you must go. I'm depending on you. Run back to the village and tell Man with Eyes of Hawk. He'll know what to do." She didn't really think the Indians would come after her—not once they knew that Eagle Soaring was safely home again.

"My father will come for you," he whispered.

She nodded. *Yes, your father will come if he returns in time . . . if only as a master who seeks the return of his slave.*

She had to convince Eagle that his father would come to rescue her, or the child wouldn't go. She didn't mind the sacrifice to set him free . . . the little boy meant that much to her.

Boucher had been gone for a long while, a fact that made Hannah more nervous with each passing moment. She didn't know where the Frenchman went, but wherever he'd gone, he'd be returning soon.

The rope binding Eagle's wrists was tight. Fortunately, the boy had small hands, and Hannah hoped to loosen the knot—if she couldn't untie it—so that he'd be able to squeeze his hands free. Her own wrists were tied, but she could maneuver her fingers. She had to change positions several times before she could reach Eagle's knot. Her hands scraped bark as she pulled and tugged on the edge of the rope within the knot. Once, she'd been forced to jerk away before the guard saw her, and the ropes burned her wrists. She'd stifled a gasp of pain and smiled at the man.

To his credit, White Bear's son hadn't uttered a word, but he was aware that she hurt herself. She'd heard the tiny sound he'd made when he caught his breath after she'd become injured.

Every half hour or so, the guard would stop whatever he was doing to check on the woman and child, but fortunately he'd leave them alone again a few seconds later.

"Han-na," Eagle Soaring whispered, his dark eyes laced with concern as he studied her. "Are you all right? You don't have to do this! I can stay with you; *I want to stay with you!* My father will come and save us both."

"I'm fine," Hannah said. She managed to hide a grimace as she shifted his way once again.

The process seemed long, and Hannah was about ready to give up when she finally felt the rope give when she pulled it.

Eagle's eyes gleamed as he met her gaze, his smile so like his father's that Hannah felt an instant tug on her emotions. "I can move them, Han-na!"

"Sh-sh, Eagle. That's good, but be careful. Don't let the man see."

Her heart pounded with excitement as Eagle then worked to free himself. The boy's sudden triumphant grin elated Hannah. "Wait now, Eagle," she advised. "Untying your feet without the man seeing you is going to be much harder."

"I can do it," he assured her. "I'll be careful," he promised.

A branch snapped on the other side of the clearing, drawing her gaze and the guard's attention. Hannah's heart tripped, until she realized that it was only a rabbit. She grinned. Fortunately, the guard didn't see the animal yet; he was still searching the woods—and in the wrong direction. With the man's attention elsewhere, Eagle worked quickly to untie his feet.

Once freed, he rose and then bent as if to untie Hannah.

"No, Eagle!" she whispered. "You must go! There's no time to undo me."

The boy's eyes were wild with indecision.

"Go!" she encouraged him. *"Please, Eagle.* Run to the village and get help! You're my only hope."

The guard had discovered the rabbit and was coming back just as Eagle started to run. "Hey, you, wait!" the man cried as he spotted the boy.

"Go, Eagle! Run!" Hannah yelled.

Boucher's man fell full-length into the brush as he raced forward. Eagle Soaring kept running.

Run, Eagle. That's a good boy! Run! Hannah cried silently.

Tears of happiness filled her eyes when the boy disappeared from view long before the guard could pick himself up to follow.

You can make it, Eagle Soaring. You can make it, my little warrior.

"Please, God," she whispered as Boucher's man stood in the clearing and cussed up a blue streak. "Please keep little Eagle safe."

The guard glared at Hannah. She shivered and thought, *Eagle is safe. That's all that matters.*

Oak Point Manor, Pennsylvania

Walt Jennings sat at the desk in his study, poring over his account books. He smiled as he made a notation in the right margin of the left page. His farm—once his Uncle Rodney's—was thriving. He'd worked long, hard hours since he'd inherited the place, time spent much differently than the days he'd worked for Rodney Jennings as his assistant in the man's silver-smithy. Now his farming labors had finally paid off. With the farm profits, as well as the extra money he earned working silver, he was doing quite well for himself.

Walt was pleased.

Oak Point wasn't a large farm, but the crop yield was enough to sustain his small household with a little extra to market at a fair price. He still enjoyed working as a silversmith; he made special-order pieces for customers in the New World. If he'd still been alive, old man Jennings would have approved of the care and the pride Walt took in his work ... he had taken the same care and pride himself. But Uncle Rodney had died in sleep five years before, and Walt himself was a long way from Philadelphia and his uncle's shop, where Rodney had taught both him and Jamie the fine craft of silversmithing.

Thoughts of the old days had Walt reminiscing about his friend. He and Jamie Rawlins had come to the colonies as sixteen-year-olds, yearning for a real taste of life, their eyes wide with excitement, young boys longing to be grown men.

He and Jamie had been friends forever, it seemed. They had known each other for all of their lives. Walt had lived in the English village where Jamie's father had been the resident physician. Near the same age, it was only natural that the two children become friends.

Walt had been with Jamie when Jamie's mother died after a long illness. He watched his friend's father deteriorate with grief after his wife's death. But the hardest thing Walt had witnessed was the change in Jamie after his mother had passed away. The boy had become angry with his father, embittered that the resident physician, who had cured everyone else within miles, had been unable to save his own wife.

Thoughts of the Rawlins family brought on his memories of Jamie's sister Abbey. Walt had once been infatuated with Abbey, with her golden hair, blue eyes, and warm, generous smile. She had been a giving person, always thinking of others. It was Abbey, Walt thought, who'd suffered the most from her mother's death. She and her father had been close; she had often gone doctoring with him, his ever-present assistant who held the patient's hand and readily offered her comforting smile. With the passing of Mrs. Rawlins, Abbey had lost not only her mother, but her father and brother, too. Dr. Rawlins had shut out his children to retreat into his solitary world of grief. Jamie, the young brother, had suddenly become so angry and bitter that he'd felt driven to leave his home in England for a new life in the colonies. Not that Walt had minded that Jamie had come with him to Philadelphia. . . .

Walt leaned back in his chair and closed the ledger, his gaze settling on the cup on the fireplace mantel. The drinking vessel had been Jamie's first handcrafted piece, inscribed with Walt's initials, a gift from one best friend to another. Walt kept it there as tribute to his good friend, the one to whom he owed his life.

Eleven years previously, while they had been delivering a silver tea service to a wealthy family in the Pennsylvania wilds, Walt and Jamie had been taken captive by a band of Iroquois Indians.

He shuddered as he recalled the terror of their capture, the physical discomforts they'd been forced to endure. Jamie had been the stronger one; he had been the one to suffer the most. For some reason, the Indians had singled him out for punishment. Jamie had proven himself to his captors by running the gauntlet without crying out, enduring his pain courageously like a true Indian warrior.

Walt got up from his desk and went to the window. *Jamie was a true warrior,* he thought. His friend had stayed with the Seneca Indians. The young man had fallen in love with the sachem's daughter, and the Indian village had become his new home. It had been Jamie who had arranged for his friend's release . . . Walt didn't know how Jamie had convinced the Seneca to let him go, but his friend had done the impossible.

Walt hadn't seen Jamie in over eight years. He thought of his friend often, wondered if he was happy, and if his new life had treated him well. The last and only time Walt had seen Jamie was when Walt had been making another delivery for his uncle and suddenly out of nowhere came three fierce-looking Indians, their heads bald but for a single scalplock of hair. Walt had been terrified, his mind reliving his previous capture. But his terror became disbelief when one of the braves greeted him, a huge grin on his painted features.

The warrior had been Jamie. Walt had eyed his friend in shock, and then he'd blurted out, "Good God, man, what did you do to your hair?"

Suddenly, the two young men grinned, then laughed. Jamie's Indian friends just stared at the two with disbelief.

Walt turned away from the study window, his mouth curving at the memory. They had spent only an hour together, catching up on their lives, sharing a few memories. Walt had learned that Jamie's Indian name was White Bear and that he'd married his Wind Singer. He and his wife were expecting their first child.

Then, the two friends parted. Walt went back to his uncle's shop in Philadelphia, while Jamie returned to his Indian village. Before they left, they promised to meet again, but eight years had passed since then, and Walt had never seen Jamie—White Bear—again.

Walt frowned as he wondered, not for the first time, if something dreadful had happened to his friend. Eight and a half years was a long time. Was Jamie dead or alive? If he was alive and well, then why hadn't Walt heard from him?

Jamie could have easily found out where to find him. If everything had been all right, wouldn't Jamie have come?

Walt missed his boyhood companion. "Where are you, my friend?"

With a sigh of longing, he went back to his desk. *If you are alive and well, why don't you contact me?*

He had moved; it was true, but he'd left word in several places where White Bear might have gone in the last eight and a half years.

"Mr. Jennings?"

He glanced up to find the young woman who'd been his late uncle's bondservant in the doorway. He had inherited her indenture along with his uncle's farm property. He smiled. "What is it, Sarah?"

The young man frowned when he saw her anxious expression. "What's wrong?"

Sarah glanced nervously toward the back of house. "There's an Indian at the servant's entrance, sir." She bit her lip. "A savage," she whispered fearfully.

"Savage?" Walt echoed blankly. She nodded vehemently as she looked again toward the kitchen.

He came from behind his desk, his heart pumping hard.

Suddenly, the woman gasped and spun out of the way, and the Indian moved into the doorway.

"Hello, Walt." The golden savage smiled.

"Jamie!" Walt stared at his friend as if seeing a ghost, and then he grinned. "Dear Lord, I thought you'd never come." He raised an eyebrow. "Where the hell have you been, and what took you so long?"

"He got away, Boucher," John Daniels said. "I don't know how he got free, but the next thing I know is the boy's running, and I can't catch him."

Jules's brown eyes seemed to snap with anger. "You couldn't catch a little child." The man shook his head. "You're a fool, Daniels. It's a good thing we don't need the savage. He focused his furious gaze on Hannah. "He wasn't the one we needed," he said evenly. *"She's* still here, so it doesn't matter."

Hannah glared back at the man, incensed that he'd called Eagle a savage. "He's a little boy, Boucher."

He arched his eyebrows. "You think I don't know what to do with little boys?" he said, shocking her.

Only two of the Indians had returned with the Frenchman. Boucher had left for several hours; Hannah wondered where he'd gone.

"We'll have to wait here another day," Boucher was

telling his man Daniels. "Something must have come up. He hadn't shown yet."

Hannah frowned as she listened. *Who hasn't shown?* she wondered. Then the Frenchman began to speak rapidly to the two Indians.

Since she was able to make out a few words, Hannah realized that the Indians were Iroquois. There were six Iroquois nations within the League. She wondered which group these men belonged to, and what the Seneca would do if they knew that their Indian brothers had attacked their women and children.

Her hands hurt where she'd scraped and cut them. She leaned against the tree to keep her injuries hidden.

He suspects you freed Eagle, her inner voice said. *What is he going to do when he sees your bleeding wrist?*

I'll tell him that I was trying to free myself. And if he doesn't believe me, I'll look him in the eye and ask him how I managed the amazing feat of undoing Eagle's ropes when I haven't been able to untie my own.

Or maybe she would just gaze at him directly and confess that she had freed the boy and that she was glad he got away.

Oak Point Manor

"I need your help," White Bear told his friend. He wanted to find out whether or not Samuel Walpole, Hannah's stepfather, was still alive. The Indian brave knew that Hannah believed she'd murdered the man, but he wanted to be certain that Walpole was dead. Hannah had never stayed to find out. It was possible that she'd injured him severely, but the man was still alive.

The two men sat in Walt's study, drinking tea like two English gentlemen. Only Walt looked the part—and just barely. The man gazed at his savage-looking friend as he raised the delicate china teacup to his lips, and he grinned.

"What are you smiling at?" White Bear demanded.

"Your hair," Walt said. "It looks a helluva lot better than that blond crown tail you had the last time I saw you."

White Bear scowled. "I am trying to talk to you."

The smile fell from Walt's face. "I'm sorry, Jamie, but I can't help it. Seeing you again—here—I can't believe it. I haven't been able to get you out of my mind lately. I'm just so damned glad you came. It's as if I've created you from my thoughts."

Another grin tugged on the corner of Walt's mouth. "Do you have any idea how ridiculous you look sipping tea?"

It took White Bear a few seconds to respond to Walt's teasing remark. He allowed himself a slight smile. "It's been a long time since I drank real English tea," he admitted. "I am not certain I like it."

His boyhood companion immediately looked contrite. "Would you like to something else?" He sounded anxious to please.

White Bear shook his head. "I would like your help," he said. When he finally had Walt's full attention, the brave explained about Hannah and the young woman's belief that she'd murdered her late mother's husband. Walt's expression changed as he listened to his friend, and White Bear realized that Walt hadn't changed much. The young man was the same: dark hair, dark eyes. A little older perhaps, but he was still a good friend.

"I do not believe this man is dead," White Bear said. He told Walt about the Frenchman's kidnapping of Hannah, omitting some of the details of his own rescue of her.

"Boucher wants her back," he said. "I need to know why. I was there when the man traded her to He-Who-Comes-In-The-Night. The Frenchman couldn't wait to be rid of her."

"Dear God, she belongs to that savage Night?" Walt said.

White Bear smiled darkly. He'd seen the way Walt shivered when he'd mentioned Night's name and didn't take offense to Walt's use of the word savage. He-Who-Comes-In-The-Night *was* a savage.

"She belonged to Night at first, but she doesn't now." White Bear paused. "She belongs to me."

Walt raised an eyebrow. "And how does Wind Singer feel about that?"

"My wife is dead." White Bear was surprised he could say it without as much pain.

His friend drew an audible breath. "I'm sorry, Jamie."

White Bear nodded, his concern with Hannah now.

"This Hannah—she means a great deal to you," Walt said, speculation taking the place of his earlier look of compassion.

"Yes," he admitted. "Hannah means everything to me. Hannah and Eagle Soaring both." He smiled. "Eagle Soaring is my son."

Walt nodded. "I'll do whatever I can to help you," he said.

White Bear looked at his childhood friend with gratitude. "Thank you."

Chapter 21

John Daniels shoved Hannah, and she stumbled and then righted herself as they continued along the trail. Hannah had no idea where they were taking her. It seemed obvious to her that Boucher's men didn't know the Frenchman's plans either.

Jules Boucher himself had been quiet all morning. Except for the occasional glare he sent her, he didn't say a word—not to her or his men. He led the way, but stayed to the well-worn forest path. He looked as if he were silently fuming. Whoever he was supposed to meet hadn't come.

The sun was directly overhead when they stopped to rest. Hannah sighed with relief and sat down on a large boulder about two yards off the trail. Boucher stood, his brow furrowing as he searched his surroundings. Daniels waited nearby; the two Indians began to scout the brush for twigs and branches, picking up whatever they found. When he saw what the Indians were doing, the Frenchman spoke to them rapidly in Iroquoian. Hannah made out the

Indian words for "no" and "leave," and something about a village.

Boucher had no intention of staying at the site long enough for a fire, Hannah realized. She felt a spurt of anger. What was driving the man to such an exhausting pace? What could it hurt to rest for an hour?

Daniels went to the Frenchman's side, and the two men conversed too quietly for Hannah to hear. She sighed and looked around as she waited for them to leave. She lifted a hand to brush back her hair. Fortunately, Boucher had untied her. If he'd noticed her injured wrists, the man hadn't commented. She leaned back using her arms and closed her eyes.

"Mademoiselle." Boucher stood before her. His tone was polite but the man glared at her.

"We will be resting here for a while," he informed her. Hannah's breath caught as she saw that he held some rope. "Give me your hands," he ordered.

"Why?" she taunted. "Afraid I'll crawl away and escape?" She didn't want to be tied up again; her wrists were just starting to feel better.

Boucher cursed and grabbed her arm. "I said, 'Give me your hands.'"

Hannah froze. She'd never seen him this angry before. There was a new air of desperation about him that made him appear unstable. Unwilling to test the strength of his temper, she gave him her wrists.

Jules Boucher tied her up quickly, clumsily, jerking the rope and hurting her, but she didn't complain. He ordered her to slide off the rock and sit on the ground, and she submitted. He bound her ankles as he had her hands. It took all of Hannah's control not to cry out as the jerk of the rope abused her tender flesh.

"Keep silent or I'll use this," he warned. He pulled a filthy rag from a hidden pocket within his breeches.

Hannah grimaced. There was no doubt in her mind that

he would fasten the dirty thing about her mouth—and quite happily—if she didn't obey him. She nodded that she understood. His triumphant smile was evil.

The Frenchman left her alone to speak with his men, then disappeared into the woods, alone.

Hannah sat back against the boulder and grimaced at the rough surface. But she was too tired to sit straight, and she couldn't move far with her wrists and ankles tied.

I'm going to die, she thought.

Or worse.

Hannah closed her eyes and retreated to that place in her mind where she'd stored her precious memories . . . and used the image of White Bear to soothe and comfort herself.

White Bear ran. His heart pounded, and he felt his insides clench up with fear, but he kept the grueling pace. His beloved Hannah was in danger, and every moment counted, for he'd stayed away from the village too long.

He'd been gone from the village two days when he'd returned to hear the news that Boucher had taken Hannah and Eagle Soaring. White Bear had became enraged. The depth of his anger had startled his people; it frightened even himself. Eagle Soaring had escaped and was there when White Bear had arrived, and the brave was grateful. But he was still furious. Hannah was still at the mercy of the Frenchman, and White Bear couldn't rest until he'd brought her safely home. He would stop at nothing to rescue her. He'd found love again—and he wasn't going to lose her. Hannah had given his world new meaning. He loved her desperately enough that he'd sacrifice his own life to see her safe.

His anger turned inward as his feet pounded the forest trail. He ran, heedless of the noise he made. His only thoughts were to find Hannah—and to reach her quickly.

Why did I leave her? he thought with self-reproach. He should have told her where he was going, what he'd planned to do. If she'd demanded she come along, he could have taken her . . . although he hadn't been certain he'd find Walt.

It had been pure luck that he'd gone first to Rodney Jennings's farm. He hadn't known that Uncle Rodney had died or that Walt had inherited his uncle's property. He went there, because it was closer than Philadelphia, which was another half day's journey away . . . and he couldn't go into the city expecting to be welcomed or even tolerated as he was dressed. English-born he might be, but to white people's eyes, he would be an Indian. After all, he looked like one with his long hair and dark skin, without adding his loincloth, moccasins, or silver earrings. And they'd be right to believe him an Indian—he was no longer English or white, he was a warrior of *Nun-da-wä'-o-no*. He'd lived with the *Ho-De'No-Sau-Nee* for eleven years. He had married one and was the father of a Seneca son. In his heart and in the hearts of the People, Jamie Rawlins was dead, but White Bear lived on.

Black Thunder and Sky Raven, his loyal friends, were with him. They kept up with his arduous pace without a word. He had tried to convince them to stay behind, that they shouldn't face the danger that lay in wait for him, but they'd come anyway. There had been no arguments, no discussion. His friends—his people—had known that he was distraught, had understood then how he loved his Hannah; yet, no one had thought it strange or wrong. They'd stood behind him, offering him comfort with their support.

Sky Raven and Black Thunder's presence with him now was a tribute to their friendship with him. Their decision to come was their silent support for what the brave had to do.

And so the three Indian warriors ran through the night

and into the next. They stopped long enough to check for signs and then set off again with the satisfaction of knowing they were on the right path.

Han-na. My flower. I love you. My people love you. Hold on and I will come. It is destined by the spirits that we marry.

White Bear stopped to run his fingers along an area of the ground. After a silent exchange of nods with his friends, he got up and ran again. The litany of his love sought to send reassurance to Hannah over the many miles that might still separate them. It played in his thoughts over and over again.

Hold on, love. Hold on.

"Hannah." That terrible, familiar voice was in her dream again.

Go away! You're dead! Why are you tormenting me? Leave me alone!

She twisted and turned as she napped. She knew she was dreaming, but the voice was too real. It was Samuel's voice that refused to leave her alone. He was there, taunting her with her crime, torturing her with her guilt.

Why wouldn't he go away? she wondered. A cold tremor went through Hannah as she saw his dead body on her bedchamber floor. Suddenly, the body rose and Samuel stood before her, his brown gaze gleaming with hate. The whites of his eyes were bloodred.

"No!" she cried. "Leave me alone. You're dead! You're dead . . ."

He laughed then, a harsh, macabre sound that froze Hannah's blood and drove icy chills down her spine. His laughter continued, growing louder and louder. Hannah clamped her hands over her ears as she tried unsuccessfully to shut out the sound.

The laughter was interrupted by a short burst of silence before it rose again to frighten Hannah. She heard the voice of Jules Boucher, and Hannah tensed. Her eyes flew open as she was dragged from her nightmare.

Blinking, she saw that Boucher had returned. Then, she noted with dawning horror the man behind him.

"Hannah, my sweet," the dark, evil voice that was so familiar said.

She gasped. The laughter—it had been part of her dream, yet it hadn't all been a dream. Neither had she been dreaming about the man who approached her—the man she'd left for dead. The man that stood before her with his mocking smile.

Hannah began to shake; she was unable to control her body's tremors.

Samuel Walpole laughed, and the red, puckered scar down the left side of his face made him appear more sinister than any image of Lucifer that Hannah's imagination had ever conjured.

"I'm been waiting a long time to see you again," her late mother's husband said. "I don't suppose you knew that I was *dying* to see you again."

Hannah shuddered and would have hugged herself if she'd been free. "You're alive!" she breathed.

"Lucky for me." His grin was pure wickedness. He gave a dramatic sigh. "Alas, sweet daughter, I'm afraid your luck has just run out."

Chapter 22

An Onondaga village near a great lake.

She was going to die. It was plain and simple; she knew it as surely as she needed to draw breath to live. Samuel Walpole had been planning to avenge himself for months, since he'd become well enough from his injuries to awaken and think. And she was the target of his revenge.

It was night. Hannah was in an Iroquois hut, much like that which belonged to the Seneca sachem and his wife, Woman with Dark Skin, back in the village of the *Nun-da-wä'-o-no*.

Boucher's two Indian friends had brought them to this place, their village, to spend the night—perhaps several. Hannah didn't know how long they were going to stay; she hadn't been informed of Boucher's plans. The Frenchman and Walpole had disappeared into the village ceremonial house with an elderly man who Hannah suspected was the Onondaga shaman or medicine man. Daniels and the

Indians had disappeared into the forest, while a young maiden had appeared to escort Hannah to the hut.

After untying Hannah's hands, the Indian girl had instructed Hannah to sit on the mat near the fire pit. Hannah's feet had been unbound early in the day so that she could keep up with the others on the journey. The white woman sat and wiggled her toes in an attempt to restore feeling to her aching limbs.

The Onondaga maiden left her alone after murmuring something about food. While she waited for the girl to return, Hannah studied her surroundings and speculated about the reason she might have been brought to the village.

Surely, if the Indians planned to torture and kill her, they wouldn't be planning to feed her first. She released a quivering breath. These Indians were different than the people she'd lived with for months; yet, they seemed the same.

Because they, too, are Iroquois. They were People of the Longhouse, like White Bear and the *Nun-da-wä'-o-no.* How did they justify attacking their own? Or didn't these villages know that several of their Onondaga braves had come into their Seneca sisters' fields and terrorized the sisters and their children. She herself might have been the reason that they'd come, but that had not stopped them from hurting the others ... of kidnapping Eagle Soaring to ensure that she came along with them without incident.

Had Eagle made it back safely? She felt somehow that he had, and it was a good feeling. And White Bear? Had he returned to find her gone? With his son home, did he decide to forget about the white slave who had loved him but refused to marry him?

Hannah stared at the wood bark door. The Indian girl had closed it behind her when she'd left, and Hannah mentally compared the closed door to the shutting of an iron prison gate.

Walpole is alive. She hated the man, but she was glad that he lived. She hadn't killed him; she could go to her resting place free of guilt. There was only one thing that plagued her peace, and that was her regret that she hadn't married White Bear and lived those last days with him as his wife.

She could believe that if she'd married him as he'd wanted, he wouldn't have left the village, that perhaps she'd still be safe in their lodge, enjoying this night within his arms.

But she wasn't so foolish as to think that. Samuel Walpole wanted his revenge. He would have stopped at nothing to find Hannah and get her within his reach again. It might have been a week later, or even a year, but the man was pure evil. He would have found a way, and the outcome would have been the same.

"Samuel is alive," she murmured, "and I'm going to die."

Unless a miracle occurred, and she thought she had long ago lost any belief in miracles.

But that was before she'd met and fallen in love with a golden warrior named White Bear.

The door to the hut swung open, drawing Hannah's attention. She blinked, sure her eyes were deceiving her as a golden-haired Indian woman entered the room. Her blue eyes inspected Hannah and she smiled.

"Welcome, Hannah," the woman said in heavily accented, but flawless, English. "I understand you have come far. My name is Sun Daughter, and you are in my mother's house. She and I will be sharing our meal with you. I hope that you like our food."

Hannah returned the young woman's generous smile. "I love hominy and succotash," she said, guessing at the meal. "And I would be honored to share your meal. *Nee-yah-weh'-ha.*"

Sun Daughter looked pleased that Hannah had thanked her in Iroquoian.

The door opened a second time, and an older woman entered the hut. Her expression was solemn as she brought a cooking bowl to the fire and set it in the coals to heat.

"She is warming the *Oh-no'-kwa,*" the younger woman explained. "It came from my own fire."

The old woman murmured something to Sun Daughter. Sun Daughter frowned and replied in a raised voice— and in Iroquoian, "Hannah understands our language, mother. Please speak so that she can hear you."

The matron shot Hannah a surprised look. "You can speak our way?" she asked.

Hannah nodded. "I have been with the *Nun-da-wä'-o-no* for many months. I learned it from them."

Sun Daughter's mother, Hannah learned, was Spring Rain. The woman's astonishment at her admission of Indian life prompted Hannah to say more.

"I lived by a great lake." She described the village setting and told them about the stockade fence that she was surprised to see missing here. And as she spoke, she had the strangest feeling that these women had been in White Bear's village. Not only had they been there, but from their expressions as she talked, she thought they might know the Seneca of that village well.

Were the two tribes private enemies . . . although they were League brothers?

Hannah needed to find out. "You know Man with Eyes of Hawk and his people?" she asked. *Do you know White Bear?*

I know the place and its people," Sun Daughter said with an odd little smile. "The village is the home of my brother . . . Jamie."

Hannah stared at her and heard the sudden pounding of her own heart. The air about her became too thick for her to breathe. "You are White Bear's sister?" she choked out.

The golden-haired woman nodded. If the Indian woman

was surprised that Hannah knew her brother's Indian name, she didn't show it. Studying her with clear eyes, Hannah realized she should have known—at least have guessed—that this woman was the sister of the man she loved.

How many Indians had golden hair? Only White Bear's was a shade darker than his sister's. But there could be no mistaking the strange coincidence of Sun Daughter's eye color. Her eyes and White Bear's were the exact shade of beautiful blue. As she continued to eye the lovely woman, Hannah began to notice other similarities between brother and sister, things she hadn't noticed earlier because she'd been too worried about her own fate.

"You know my brother," Sun Daughter said, sounding pleased.

Hannah nodded. Unsure, at this time, of White Bear's love, she said, "I know him well. I am—was—White Bear's slave."

"Why are you here? How did you come to be with those men?" Sun Daughter made no secret of her distaste for the white men who had brought her.

Hannah stared at the woman and decided that she could trust her. "I'm here against my will," she admitted. "Those men—Jules Boucher and Samuel Walpole—they kidnapped me from your brother's village. That man with the red scar? He was my mother's husband. I gave that scar to him." She shuddered. "He hates me . . . and he wants me dead."

It was hopeless. He'd never had such difficulty in tracking before, and White Bear was beginning to think that he would never find Hannah, that he was doomed to live his life without the woman he loved.

He'd thought they'd been on the right trail. All the signs had been there—recent signs. They should have reached

Hannah and her kidnappers. Either his judgment was impaired by his concern for Hannah or the Frenchman's Indians Eagle had described were better at covering up their tracks than he was at following them.

The braves had ventured into Onondaga territory and beyond, looking for their quarry. White Bear had the suspicion that the men he pursued had split up and gone two separate ways at some point—and that he, Sky Raven, and Black Thunder had been deceived. Somewhere along the trail, he must have missed the sign that would lead him to Hannah.

Tired and dispirited, White Bear had no intention of giving up. He looked at his friends. "Go home," he urged them. "I can't go back until I find her."

Sky Raven didn't hesitate in answering for the two friends. "We will find her together," he said. Black Thunder agreed.

White Bear gave each brave a smile of gratitude, and the three men looked for the signs they'd missed as they retraced their steps.

"Husband."

Great Arrow looked from his weapon to gaze fondly at his wife. "Sun Daughter," he greeted warmly. Setting his bow in his lap, he raised an arm in invitation to Sun Daughter to sit beside him.

The woman glided toward her husband and sat down. The man slipped his arm around her, kissed her on the forehead, then released her to return to his work on the bow.

Sun Daughter—Abbey Rawlins—wasn't upset with her spouse's behavior. She knew her husband loved her and that he was content just to have her near. Later, within their lodge hut, they would touch and kiss and whisper words of love as they lay together on their sleeping platform. They would continue to hug and kiss until long after they knew their son was fast asleep. Then they would join in love as husband and wife, two persons who shared the belief that they'd been gifted by the spirits with the perfect mate.

Normally, Abbey would have been content to sit by him quietly, but there was something on her mind this night, something disturbing that she needed to discuss with her husband. Great Arrow must have sensed her unease, because suddenly he stopped what he was doing, set his bow aside, and drew her close for a breath-stopping, toe-curling kiss.

He grinned boyishly as he released her. She smiled back, but her concern for Hannah stole away some of her joy.

Great Arrow's brow furrowed as he studied his wife's still smiling face. "What is wrong, *O-ka-o?*"

She touched his cheek. How like her husband to read her so quickly. "You are a wonderful man," she murmured, meaning it. "You know me so well—"

"It is because I love you."

Her eyes beamed. "As I love you." *As Hannah loves my brother. She didn't say it, but I could tell by her face when she talked of him that she does.*

"What is it? Tell me."

"Kwan," she said, "that white woman—I must talk with you about her."

He frowned. "White woman? What woman?"

Abbey raised her eyebrows. "You did not see her?"

Great Arrow shook his head. "I saw no one but that Frenchman and the man with the red scar." His scowl told her he was displeased.

"They brought a woman with them. Twin Moons brought her to the house of my mother." Abbey bit her lip. "I ate with her. Talked with her. Oh, Kwan—she said those men kidnapped her! And not only that—she—Hannah—belongs to my brother!"

The sachem shook his head as if he thought it impossible. "No, *O-ka-o,* White Bear would not take a slave."

"She said he owned her—and I believe her." In her excitement, she leaned toward her husband. "Kwan, she described White Bear's lodge as someone who's lived there." Abbey felt a funny little feeling in her chest as she continued. "And she knows Eagle Soaring! She speaks of the child as if he were her own."

Her husband still couldn't accept that the woman was White Bear's slave. The brother he knew had grieved for his dead wife for eight years. In all that time, White Bear had lived alone . . . except these last years when he'd taken in his son.

Even now, White Bear seemed isolated by his grief. Great Arrow worried that because of the father's sorrow, the relationship between father and son wasn't all that it should be. He noticed on their last hunt that the relationship had begun to change. Could it be that White Bear had learned to get on with life?

"My husband," Abbey said, "Hannah said that she'd once belonged to the Frenchman, but he traded her to He-Who-Comes-In-The-Night. She was a slave to Slow Dancer until White Bear wanted her."

She searched for signs that her husband was beginning to believe. "Didn't you tell me that He-Who-Comes-In-The-Night had bought a woman for Slow Dancer?"

Great Arrow's silver eyes flashed at the memory. He stood abruptly. "Where is this woman now?" he demanded. He didn't sound like Sun Daughter's husband; he spoke as the sachem of the Onondaga tribe.

Abbey rose after he did. "She's in the house of Spring Rain." She was smiling, pleased and confident that her husband would protect Hannah and return the woman safely to Abbey's brother.

Hannah sat quietly in the darkened hut. The only light was from the slowly dying embers in the fire pit. It had been wonderful talking with Sun Daughter. The woman was so like her brother that several times Hannah had stopped and stared, taken aback by some familiar movement Sun Daughter had made or some familiar look in her eyes as she expressed herself.

It was like Sun Daughter was the feminine version of White Bear, Hannah thought. Being with the sister made Hannah feel closer to the brother.

Did Sun Daughter wonder why White Bear hadn't come searching for his slave? Did she believe Hannah when Hannah told her that White Bear was absent when Boucher and his Indians had attacked?

She was silently reliving the conversation when the door to the hut crashed open. Hannah scrambled to her feet and stared at the fiercely scowling Indian in the doorway, her nerves jumping with fear.

"You are Hannah?" he boomed, startling her.

Suddenly, Sun Daughter was behind him, touching his arm. "You're frightening her, Kwan. How can you expect her to answer you when she's afraid to speak?"

To her amazement, Hannah saw the immediate softening of the man's expression as he gazed at Sun Daughter.

Sun Daughter released the man's arm to come forward. Her smile was gentle as she met Hannah's gaze. "Hannah, this is Kwan Kahaiska. He is the sachem of our village and"—she paused to eye him with love—"my husband."

Hannah relaxed. "Oh, I'm pleased to meet you." But she tensed when she noticed how intently the man's silver eyes were studying her.

Sun Daughter looked at Hannah and then her husband. "Kwan!" she scolded.

"She is the one," he said abruptly. "This is the woman who belonged to He-Who-Comes-In-The-Night."

Hannah opened her mouth to tell the man that she no longer belonged to Night, that she belonged to another now, but Sun Daughter's expression stopped her.

There was a glint of satisfaction in the woman's blue eyes as she met Hannah's gaze. "I told you," she said as she turned toward her husband. "I told you she was the one."

Sun Daughter smiled at Hannah again. "We are going to help you."

"Ab-bey!" her husband exclaimed.

She looked at him with raised eyebrows, and it was as if a silent message or memory was shared and understood by only the two of them.

"We will help her," the leader of the Onondaga mumbled.

His wife looked at him with innocence, and the sudden, deep rumble of the man's laughter filled the hut. It was a wonderful thing to hear. The merry sound from the fierce-looking man made Hannah smile and believe in miracles again.

Chapter 23

"We're not staying here!" Walpole exclaimed. "Did you see that savage who brought us here? I don't like the way he was looking at us? Like we'd make good meat for an Indian stew."

"That is ridiculous, monsieur!" Boucher said. "These Indians mean us no harm."

The door to the building opened. Walpole stiffened as a tall, long-haired Indian entered the huge ceremonial house. The two white men had been given the area to sleep in that night. "Don't tell me it's him!" he said. "Tell me it's not White Bear," he urged.

Boucher turned to check the direction of the Englishman's gaze. "It's not White Bear," he confirmed. The Frenchman frowned. "But he's another one like him—a white Indian."

Walpole waited with nervous dread for the savage to approach. "Sir?" He cleared his throat. "Ah, bloody hell, Boucher, what are we supposed to call the man?"

The man in question looked amused by the exchange.

"I am Kwan Kahaiska," he said. "Sachem of this village and all you see here."

The Frenchman eyed the man with interest and surprise. A white man was chief? "You look familiar," he said carefully, wondering where he'd seen him before. He scowled as he searched his memory. "Have we met?"

Kwan Kahaiska gave him a thin-lipped smile. "We have seen each other in another place." He paused to glare at each white man. His hard gaze fastened on the man with the red scar.

"You have a white woman with you," the sachem said. "She does not belong to you." His silver eyes narrowed with warning. "She will be in my care now. I will see that she gets back to the one who will be searching for her."

"No!" Walpole exclaimed without thinking. "You can't have her! I've been searching for her, too, and I'm not about to give her up!"

His hand shot out as the Indian caught the man by the collar. He lifted Walpole high, and the Englishman grabbed at the shirt that choked him as he fought for air.

Kwan locked gazes with the Frenchman while he held the Englishman aloft. "You will leave when the sun rises in the new sky," he commanded, "but you will leave without the woman." His silver eyes flashed with angry fire. "Do you understand this?"

Boucher nodded and felt the closing of his own throat as he watched Walpole bluster and struggle to breathe.

Suddenly, the Indian released Walpole, who fell to the dirt with a grimace. Cursing, Walpole scrambled to his feet. His face was red; his scar burned brightly, a darker shade of crimson. The man looked ready to commit murder.

"Don't try it," Boucher warned him.

Samuel's eyes glinted with hate as he flashed the man a furious glance. Boucher's warning look had him struggling for control of his anger.

"We will leave as you have directed, *Monsieur Kwan.*"

Kwan nodded with satisfaction. "Good. You must rest now."

When he was gone, Walpole turned to glare at the Frenchman. "Damn savage!" he spat. "The bastard's going to pay, Boucher. I haven't come all this way to be outsmarted by an Indian!" His face became flushed as he rubbed his bruised neck.

His eyes gleamed, and a smile curved his mouth, puckering his scar. "Tomorrow we'll leave all right, but we won't be going alone. Hannah will be with us ... and perhaps that the sachem's pretty little wife. What was her name? Ah, yes, Sun Daughter."

"You're insane, Walpole," Boucher said as he stared at the man in disbelief. "You kidnap that man's wife, and he'll hunt you down like an animal. And he'll find you—make no mistake about that. You'll wish you'd died long before then. Your death won't be a pleasant one, monsieur." He shook his head at the man's foolishness. "Take your stepdaughter, if you must, but I'll not play a role in the kidnapping."

"You've got no bullocks, Boucher."

The Frenchman's smile was cruel. "Steal that man's wife, and you'll not only lose your bullocks, Walpole—you'll be eating them as you die."

"Do you honestly think they'll still try to take her?" Sun Daughter asked her husband and her new friend.

"Samuel Walpole is an animal," Hannah confirmed. "He's capable of anything." She gazed at Sun Daughter with concern. "The Frenchman is dangerous. He's more stupid than cruel, but he's not above striking a woman." *Or raping one,* she thought. "It would be in character for him to follow Samuel."

She didn't understand why Samuel had been so deter-

mined to find her that he'd come all this way to the New
World. "I suspect Boucher thinks that he's going to be
paid for bringing me to Samuel. I don't know what Samuel
told the man, but I'm sure that Walpole lied about everything . . . even his real reasons for finding me."

She shuddered as she recalled the night of her mother's
death. "My mother's husband tried to rape me with my
mother dead but a few hours." Hannah grasped Sun
Daughter's arm as she pleaded with her friend. "You, too
could be in danger, Sun Daughter. Don't let him hurt you
because of me!"

"No one is going to hurt either one of you," Kwan said
with quiet determination. "I've seen his kind before. If he
tries to harm either one of you, he'll die."

Oh, but will he? Hannah wondered uneasily. *Or will he get
away?*

White Bear and his friends were exhausted. Forced to
rest for the night, White Bear decided to stop at his sister's
village, where he could confer with Kwan. If anyone knew
how to find Hannah's kidnappers, then Kwan Kahaiska,
his sister's husband, would be the man.

The hour was late when they arrived. White Bear knew
he'd have no difficulty getting in, because Kwan had yet
to built a stockade around his village since he'd last moved
his people to better ground.

There were no wooden fence posts, but there were
guards, White Bear knew. The blond Indian signaled with
the soft call of an owl to alert the guards of their presence.
His signal was returned a second later from somewhere
nearby. White Bear stepped into a clearing within sight of
the Onondaga longhouses and hooted again in greeting.

Two Onondaga warriors suddenly appeared from within
the forest ahead. They were Walking Turtle, followed by

the messenger brave, Crooked Ear. White Bear, having met both men before, recognized them immediately.

The braves eyed White Bear and his two companions, who moved into view behind him.

Crooked Ear grinned. "It is the brother of our Sun," the man exclaimed.

Walking Turtle waved them to come forward. As White Bear reached the brave, he saw that the Indian wore a smile of welcome.

"How is my sister?" White Bear said.

"She is well. She has a new friend."

"My sister has lots of friends," the golden warrior said.

"Yes, but this one is special," Walking Turtle told him. "She is a woman with light skin. She came with two men, but I've heard that she rightfully belongs to you."

White Bear froze in his tracks. "There's a white woman, here, in your village, that says she belongs to me?" His pulse was racing. He felt numb inside; his brain didn't seem to want to function properly. He was afraid to hope, to believe. He was scared that he was dreaming and soon would awaken to find Hannah gone and still out of reach. "Who is this woman?"

"Her name is Han-na," Crooked Ear said.

"Han-na," White Bear breathed with reverence. "Where is she?" His need to see her wouldn't let him wait. He'd searched everywhere, run until he was ready to drop with sheer exhaustion. It seemed impossible that he'd heard correctly ... that Hannah—his beloved Hannah—was here. Adrenaline pumped through his veins, giving him energy.

Crooked Ear and Walking Turtle exchanged glances. Sky Raven and Black Thunder waited patiently behind their good friend.

"It's late, and she sleeps."

"Tell me," he demanded.

Walking Turtle volunteered the answer. "She is with

Spring Rain. She sleeps quietly within the lodge of your sister's mother." He pointed to Spring Rain's lodge.

White Bear didn't wait to hear more. He hurried toward the hut . . . and Hannah.

He burst into the lodge, uncaring that he'd awaken not only Hannah but Spring Rain, his sister's Indian mother. "Han-na!" he cried.

The bundle on the sleeping platform moved. The beaver pelt stirred and was suddenly thrown back to reveal the woman he loved in the glowing embers of a recently tended fire. She looked tousled and inviting. Her golden brown hair was slightly mussed, and the eyes that blinked at him in wonder were a glorious glistening gray. He heard her sudden intake of breath.

"White Bear?" she asked hesitantly.

He rushed forward to climb onto the platform and take her into his arms. "Yes, *O-gä-uh*. It is me." He held on to her tightly with his face buried within her silky hair. "I've been searching for you everywhere, and where do I find you? . . . Here, in my sister's village." His tone had teased her, and she responded with a shy smile.

White Bear released her to frame her face with his hands. "I have missed you, Han-na. I was deathly afraid that Boucher had hurt you."

Her eyes seemed to sparkle as she looked at him. "And Samuel, White Bear. Samuel Walpole, my mother's husband—he's alive. He's the one who had me kidnapped. He hired Boucher. I don't know what he promised the Frenchman. Perhaps the reward was profits from the inn." Hannah frowned. "But I can't see Walpole giving away anything . . . not to a fellow Englishman—and most certainly not to one of the French."

"It does not matter now. You are safe." He frowned as he realized that Spring Rain was absent; Hannah was alone.

"Where is Spring Rain?"

"She's in the longhouse of her clan." She bit the inside of her lip. "Kwan asked her to go there."

White Bear scowled. "Why?" His eyes gleamed. "He expected me to come."

"No," she whispered. Her eyes clouded with worry as she touched his face, caressed his jaw. "White Bear, you must leave here—"

"No!" He grabbed her hand. He was angry. "I'm not leaving you. Not until you promise that we will marry—"

"We'll marry," she said quickly.

"I'm not giving up until you—," he continued without stopping, as if he hadn't heard. "I love you. I've waited my whole life for you—" He stopped and blinked. "What did you say?" he whispered.

She grinned and outlined his mouth with her fingers. "I promised to marry you." Worry replaced the joy in her expression. "Now you must leave here now!"

"No," he said. He felt giddy—and not from lack of sleep. The giddiness came from the pure joy of having Hannah back, in knowing that she was safe and sound.

"You don't understand—"

"No," he said softly, "it is you who doesn't understand. I'm not leaving you. I love you and want to show my love. We're alone, and even if we weren't, I wouldn't go. Anyone who tries to tear us apart this night will be successful only if he kills me."

"You don't know what you're saying," she said, horrified by the picture painted by his words.

"Yes, he does," a male voice said from near the doorway.

White Bear had been so happy, so involved with his love, that he hadn't heard the door open. He silently cursed the man who pointed a pistol at them. The man's red-scarred face identified him to the Indian immediately. Samuel Walpole had been born ugly, White Bear thought. The scar only made him more hideous, but Walpole, he felt, was deserving of the mark.

"Stand up, or I'll have to kill her, too!" Walpole said, waving the gun. "You've stated your desire, and now I'm following your instructions."

The brave started to rise.

"No, White Bear, don't. He's going to kill you!" She drew a shuddering breath. "And then he'll kill me anyway." Her gaze went to her stepfather. "You want me dead, don't you?"

Walpole's smile was her answer. "You gave me this," he said, his expression darkening as his other hand touched the scar. "And there is the matter of the Bird and Barrel." His wicked grin was back. "The inn, my dear. You had no idea that it is yours, did you?"

She shook her head. She didn't care about the inn. She only cared about White Bear and the Indian people she loved.

"Get up!" Walpole ordered White Bear a second time.

"Please!" she pleaded. "You can have the inn!"

"I already have it, daughter," he said. "Your death will only ensure things stay that way."

Hannah was terrified. She studied White Bear, saw him silently gauging the distance to the man's gun. She watched the unfolding drama and realized with horror that she played an important part in this bizarre play.

Where is Great Arrow? she wondered. The sachem had promised to help her. He was supposed to be outside, listening for Walpole or Boucher.

Boucher, Hannah thought. Where was he?

"Jules!" Walpole called loudly, answering Hannah's silent question. "Come in. There's been a change of plans.

Hannah felt her chest tighten as the door opened, and the Frenchman entered. Walpole barely glanced at his partner before returning his attention to the two people before him.

"This is inconvenient, but not a serious problem," Walpole said.

A hand reached over Boucher's shoulder to put a gun to the back of Walpole's head. "An inconvenience, but not a serious problem," Kwan said, keeping the gun against the man's head. "Drop the gun, white man, or I will discharge this gun into your evil brain."

The Englishman cursed as he dropped the pistol.

With a grin in his brother-in-law's direction, Kwan thrust the Frenchman toward the center of the room. "You had the pleasure the last time," he said,

White Bear smiled. Kwan had been referring to the occasion years ago when he and Kwan had rescued Abbey from a certain wicked English colonel—when White Bear had claimed the pleasure of killing the man.

The Onondaga smiled as he and his wife's brother exchanged meaningful glances.

White Bear turned to the woman he loved and opened his arm to her. "Come with me, my love."

She hesitated, looking back as White Bear was escorting her from the hut. "But what about them—"

His blue gaze touched on Kwan's briefly before it settled on the woman he loved. "Kwan will take care of the two men," he said quietly.

Kwan nodded and smiled at his wife's new friend and soon-to-be sister-in-law. "I will see that they do not bother you again, Han-na." Something dark and grim passed through the sachem's gaze and was gone again. "Go with your White Bear, Han-na," he said softly. "The pleasure is mine this time."

Epilogue

September 1748 in the village of the Nun-da-wä'-o-no

The first day of the *Da-yo-nun'-neo-quä-na De-o-ha'-ko* was bright and warm. Golden sunshine spilled across the center square, bathing the villagers with its radiance. The Seneca people were in high spirits, for this occasion was a special one. Today the *Ho-De'-No-Sau-Nee* had gathered for the Harvest Festival, to thank the Great Spirit and all those concerned for their plentiful crop yield. But today was also the day that the white slave Hannah would become an Indian daughter and would marry White Bear, their brave warrior son.

The joy on the faces of the young man and woman, who had waited a long time for this marriage, saw their happiness reflected in the expressions of the People.

The Indians had chosen to hold the ceremonies outside. The morning started with praise and a thanksgiving dance for the Great Spirit, and now it was time for the adoption ceremony that would bring into the village fold a new daughter.

Hannah stood in the center yard, dressed in a fine, highly embroidered, white doeskin tunic. Her golden brown hair hung, unbound, down her back. Her face was lightly dusted with pink powder as was the Indian way. Her lips had been darkened with red berry juice. She wore a beautiful necklace of silver and shell beads with an amulet of beaten silver, jewelry designed and made by her husband-to-be. She wore a beaded armband about her right forearm. On her left hand, she wore a silver finger ring, carefully crafted for White Bear's intended by his English boyhood friend, Walt Jennings, the young man who stood in this Indian village for the first time since his release from captivity eleven years ago. Hannah had met the nice young man only that morning, speaking to him briefly before the festivities had begun. She liked him, could see him and Jamie Rawlins as two young friends.

Hannah was pleased at the man's thoughtfulness in crafting the beautiful ring for her. It was a symbol of both worlds—Indian and English. The engraving of a Christian cross was surrounded by beautiful Indian markings that seemed to cradle the cross protectively, lovingly. The ring was made by Walt but it was a gift from White Bear, signifying all that they were . . . and their love for each other.

"Han-na." Moon Woman's soft voice drew Hannah's attention to the matron who had stood silently by her side. The Indian woman's eyes were thoughtful as they searched Hannah's features. "You are ready to begin?"

"Yes," Hannah said. "Where is my mother?" She searched the compound, smiling as her gaze met Sun Daughter's briefly, because it continued around the gathered circle of Seneca. Sun Daughter had offered to adopt Hannah herself, and although Hannah had been touched and appreciative, she had been given the most unusual choice of selecting a mother from several women who wanted her. Hannah favored one within the *Nun-da-wä'-o-no*. She nodded to assure Moon Woman that it was all right for her to join the villagers who had encircled the yard.

She smiled as she found the woman she'd sought. Hannah left the center of the yard to approach her chosen mother.

Hannah met a startled gaze as she stopped before Woman with Dark Skin. "Mother," she said gently, moved by the matron's reaction to her choice, "you have loved White Bear and you have given your heart to his son. I thank you for them . . . and for your kindness to me . . . and to my people."

She gestured about the circle. "I would ask that you allow me to be your daughter—that I may love and care for you, as you have loved and cared for those I love. I would be honored to call you mother—and have it to be the truth."

Tears had filled the matron's ebony eyes as Hannah spoke to her.

Hannah touched Woman with Dark Skin's cheek. "Will you accept me as your daughter?" she asked. She tensed, worried, for she was White Bear's choice for wife, and this woman had been the mother of Wind Singer.

Woman with Dark Skin smiled warmly, and Hannah beamed back. The matron held out her hand and Hannah accepted it. The shared clasp felt firm and reassuring to Hannah.

"You are a daughter to make a mother proud," Woman with Dark Skin said in a choked voice.

Hannah's eyes misted, moved by the woman's generous love. "Thank you."

As she and her soon-to-be adoptive mother returned to the center of the square, she sought the gaze of the man she loved. From his loving look and gentle nod, Hannah knew that White Bear was deeply moved by her choice of mother. Woman with Dark Skin meant a great deal to him.

Hannah understood, for she too loved the ebony-skinned matron.

The adoption ceremony took only minutes, but it was a time that Hannah would remember with fondness. Woman with Dark Skin stood directly behind Hannah with her hand on the young woman's shoulder as Man with Eyes of Hawk's spoken words transformed the English slave into a beloved Seneca daughter.

Hannah's new Indian name was *Ka-na-a-ge-ne O-we-ha,* a name that was chosen by the People, Man with Eyes of Hawk proclaimed. As the sachem announced the title before the entire village, Hannah felt a deep sense of peace. When he repeated the name, her eyes widened with startled surprise and pleasure. She'd hadn't really heard it the first time; she didn't know what it meant.

"You have been given an honorable name, my daughter," Woman with Dark Skin said in English. "It means Mountain Flower."

"An honorable and beautiful name for a warrior's wife," White Bear said softly as he came up from behind her. The sight of him stole Hannah's breath. His dark blond hair gleamed like spun gold beneath the sun. He wore a kilt with a white linen shirt. His moccasins were new for the occasion, made by Hannah especially for him. As he turned his head slightly, the sun caught fire on a silver earring. He was beautiful, she thought, and he was hers to love.

Woman with Dark Skin smiled and gazed at White Bear and her new daughter with affection. "My children," she said. "Be happy. Be at peace." White Bear and Mountain Flower murmured their thanks, and the matron left to stand with the People.

Taking the matron's original place behind Hannah, White Bear gave his intended's shoulders a loving squeeze before he moved to her side.

It was time for the wedding ceremony that Hannah had

dreamed about, but had never thought would take place. Within moments, White Bear and she would be man and wife. Her throat grew tight with emotion as she looked into her lover's blue eyes and read the depth of his feelings for her.

He loves me, she thought. *He knows everything about me, and he loves me.* She gave him a watery smile and felt her stomach flutter when White Bear tenderly touched her cheek. Tears of joy glistened in his blue eyes.

The past no longer held the power to hurt Hannah— neither did Samuel Walpole and Jules Boucher. She had no idea what Kwan had done with her kidnappers. She'd never asked; she didn't care. White Bear had told her that Kwan had handled matters, just as he'd promised. Both evil men were gone from their lives forever, and Hannah had been content to accept White Bear's assurances without knowing the details. She was free, free to begin her new life as White Bear's wife and Eagle Soaring's mother.

Out of the corner of her eye, within the circumference of the circle, Hannah spied Eagle Soaring. Hannah leaned toward her beloved to whisper something in his ear. White Bear nodded, spoke softly to Man with Eyes of Hawk, and another unusual thing happened when Hannah left her intended's side to reach the little boy.

Hannah hunkered to eye level of the child. "Eagle, will you stand with us?" she asked softly. "We want you with us."

The look of gratitude on Eagle's face was heartwarming. "You want me?"

"Oh, yes, Eagle. I want you," she assured him. "I want you very much." She glanced toward the boy's smiling father. "Look, Eagle Soaring. Look at your father. He loves and wants you." She offered him her hand as she rose to her feet. "Will you come?"

Eagle glanced toward his father for reassurance and found it in the man's loving gaze. The boy placed his hand trustingly within Hannah's, his eyes glowing with love as he met her gaze. "I will come . . . mother." And he smiled with the pure joy of knowing that he was loved. Then he stood near while his father and Hannah knelt and shared the marriage meal. The child was wearing a huge grin as the couple stood as husband and wife.

The bond of love was complete. The carefully woven fragile fibers had strengthened . . . to endure a lifetime . . .

About the Author

Candace McCarthy lives in Delaware with her husband of over twenty-three years and has a son in college. She enjoys writing and feels that a part of her is missing during the times she's not creating stories. "I love romances especially," she says. "Reading or writing a romance novel is reliving those first moments when you first realized you've found love." Candace is the author of nine other published romances, among which are *Irish Linen, Heaven's Fire,* and *Sea Mistress* for Zebra Books. She considers herself fortunate to have a loving family, good friends, and her writing; and she thanks all the wonderful fans who've read her books. Candace loves hearing from her readers. You may write her at: P.O. Box 58, Magnolia, Delaware 19962. She also has a website on the Internet.

DANGEROUS GAMES   (0-7860-0270-0, $4.99)
by Amanda Scott

When Nicholas Barrington, eldest son of the Earl of Ul-
combe, first met Melissa Seacort, the desperation he
sensed beneath her well-bred beauty haunted him. He
didn't realize how desperate Melissa really was . . . until
he found her again at a Newmarket gambling club—being auctioned off by her father to the highest bidder. So,
Nick bought himself a wife. With a villain hot on their
heels, and a fortune and their lives at stake, they would
gamble everything on the most dangerous game of all:
love.

A TOUCH OF PARADISE   (0-7860-0271-9, $4.99)
by Alexa Smart

As a confidence man and scam runner in 1880s America,
Malcolm Northrup has amassed a fortune. Now, posing
as the eminent Sir John Abbot—scholar, and possible
discoverer of the lost continent of Atlantis—he's taking
his act on the road with a lecture tour, seeking funds for
a scientific experiment he has no intention of making.
But scholar Halia Davenport is determined to accompany
Malcolm on his "expedition" . . . even if she must kidnap
him!